SATURDAY

Ian McEwan has written two collections of stories, *First Love, Last Rites* and *In Between the Sheets*, and nine previous novels, *The Cement Garden, The Comfort of Strangers, The Child in Time, The Innocent, Black Dogs, The Daydreamer, Enduring Love, Amsterdam* and *Atonement*. He won the Booker Prize for *Amsterdam* in 1998.

INTERNATIONAL PRAISE FOR *SATURDAY*

'Ian McEwan has triumphantly developed into a writer of outstanding subtlety and substance...Written with superb exactness, complex, suspenseful, reflective and humane, this novel about an expert on the human brain by an expert on the human mind reinforces his status as the supreme novelist of his generation'
Sunday Times

'Ian McEwan's fine new novel belongs to the tradition of *Ulysses* and *Mrs Dalloway* in concentrating its action in a single day and on a single character...In *Saturday* [McEwan] is at his best – thoughtful, eloquent, yet restrained. The novel has all the technical assurance of its predecessors, and suggests as well a newly political sensibility and a seductive, Joycean attention to the textures of normality'
Financial Times

'Ian McEwan may now be the best novelist in Britain – and is certainly operating at the height of his formidable powers...His precise, taut prose cuts clean as a scalpel, and his forensic intelligence addresses steadily the deepest of human horrors...*Saturday* develops into a sinuously plotted drama conforming to the classical unities of time, place and action. It also includes a series of brilliantly vivid tableaux ...Artistically, morally and politically, he excels'
The Times

'Remarkable...McEwan has given us the most observant, responsive, comprehending account of what life in London is like right now...With immense skill, McEwan brings together public and private events, from the tiniest incident in the brain to the biggest street demo of our times, so that they form a troubled unity, as they do in life...*Saturday* is wonderfully involving and affecting on every page. Everybody with any interest in contemporary literature will want to read it at once'
Evening Standard

'The author's mature attention illuminates equally every-thing it falls on. In this regard, McEwan finds in Henry Perowne an ideal alter ego. Exact and erudite, he is a man who leaves nothing in his life unexamined. He palpates experience, looking for vital signs…A profound and urgent novel…never less than surprising'

Observer

'Fiction is not a competitive sport, but for thirty years Ian McEwan has been a contender for the title of best British writer of his generation, and recently he has pulled comfort-ably ahead of his rivals…In *Saturday* he remains at the top of his game – assured, accomplished and ambitious…A detailed portrait of an age, of how we live now…It offers something transcendent, impossible to dissect'

Daily Telegraph

'Mr McEwan has not only produced one of the most pow-erful pieces of post-9/11 fiction yet published, but has also fulfilled that very primal mission of the novel: to show how we – a privileged few of us, anyway – live today'

New York Times

'He is the master clockmaker of novelists, piecing together the cogs and wheels of his plots with unerring meticulous-ness…In *Saturday*, McEwan's new novel, these characteris-tic virtues of structural elegance and coherence are on prominent display…The truest sanctuary we see Perowne find in the course of his 24 hours is…in the human relation-ships. His moments of intimate communion with other people – whether achieved in the transcendent harmonies of music or the "biological hyperspace" of lovemaking or the balletic collaborations of a surgical operation – occasion some of the novel's most elegant and acute prose…Finely wrought and shimmering with intelligence'

New York Times Book Review

'*Saturday* is a tightly wound tour de force of several strands – a Hitchcockian thriller, an allegory of the post-9/11 world, the portrait of a very attractive family, and a meditation on the fragility of life and all that we most value'

Washington Post

'Ian McEwan has been on a roll...*Saturday,* a brilliant, understated coupling of style and substance...is a stunning novel...a whole life compressed into the metaphor of a single day: birth at dawn, midlife at midday and death at night'

Chicago Sun-Times

'This season's most discussed novel...McEwan again and again proves his virtuosity...In McEwan's hands...wars and politicians and terrorists mingle with private satisfactions...McEwan appropriates the subject of personal joy, brings it back into serious literature, and makes it, for the moment at least, his private literary property'

National Post

'*Saturday* showcases McEwan's almost effortless gift for weaving contrapuntal themes into a narrative – the relationship between rationality and creativity, the survival of happiness in the wake of incalculable violence, the necessity for fiction in a world of fact. All shadow the story without intrusion'

Salon

'[A] superb new novel...[The opening scene is] one of the best passages of quiet fiction I've ever read...Such is his skill that we don't notice him, other than a deft hand here or there, doing its work...It's the depth and quality of Perowne himself that may be McEwan's greatest achievement here. His mind is of a kind under-represented in fiction... *Saturday* revives W.H. Auden's definition of great art as "clear thinking about mixed feelings"'

Globe and Mail

Ian McEwan

SATURDAY

VINTAGE

Published by Vintage 2006

4 6 8 10 9 7 5

Copyright © Ian McEwan 2005

First published in Great Britain in 2005 by
Jonathan Cape

Vintage
Random House, 20 Vauxhall Bridge Road, London SW1V 2SA

Random House Australia (Pty) Limited
20 Alfred Street, Milsons Point, Sydney
New South Wales 2061, Australia

Random House New Zealand Limited
18 Poland Road, Glenfield, Auckland 10, New Zealand

Random House (Pty) Limited
Isle of Houghton, Corner of Boundary Road & Carse O'Gowrie,
Houghton 2198, South Africa

The Random House Group Limited Reg. No. 954009
www.randomhouse.co.uk/vintage

A CIP catalogue record for this book
is available from the British Library

ISBN 978 0099 497165 (from Jan 2007)

ISBN 0 099 49716 6

Printed in the UK by CPI Bookmarque, Croydon, CR0 4TD

To Will and Greg McEwan

For instance? Well, for instance, what it means to be a man. In a city. In a century. In transition. In a mass. Transformed by science. Under organised power. Subject to tremendous controls. In a condition caused by mechanization. After the late failure of radical hopes. In a society that was no community and devalued the person. Owing to the multiplied power of numbers which made the self negligible. Which spent military billions against foreign enemies but would not pay for order at home. Which permitted savagery and barbarism in its own great cities. At the same time, the pressure of human millions who have discovered what concerted efforts and thoughts can do. As megatons of water shape organisms on the ocean floor. As tides polish stones. As winds hollow cliffs. The beautiful supermachinery opening a new life for innumerable mankind. Would you deny them the right to exist? Would you ask them to labor and go hungry while you yourself enjoyed old-fashioned Values? You – you yourself are a child of this mass and a brother to all the rest. Or else an ingrate, dilettante, idiot. There, Herzog, thought Herzog, since you ask for the instance, is the way it runs.

Saul Bellow, *Herzog*, 1964

One

Some hours before dawn Henry Perowne, a neurosurgeon, wakes to find himself already in motion, pushing back the covers from a sitting position, and then rising to his feet. It's not clear to him when exactly he became conscious, nor does it seem relevant. He's never done such a thing before, but he isn't alarmed or even faintly surprised, for the movement is easy, and pleasurable in his limbs, and his back and legs feel unusually strong. He stands there, naked by the bed – he always sleeps naked – feeling his full height, aware of his wife's patient breathing and of the wintry bedroom air on his skin. That too is a pleasurable sensation. His bedside clock shows three forty. He has no idea what he's doing out of bed: he has no need to relieve himself, nor is he disturbed by a dream or some element of the day before, or even by the state of the world. It's as if, standing there in the darkness, he's materialised out of nothing, fully formed, unencumbered. He doesn't feel tired, despite the hour or his recent labours, nor is his conscience troubled by any recent case. In fact, he's alert and empty-headed and inexplicably elated. With no decision made, no motivation at all, he begins to move towards the nearest of the three bedroom windows and experiences such ease and lightness in his tread that he suspects at once he's dreaming or sleepwalking. If it is the

3

case, he'll be disappointed. Dreams don't interest him; that this should be real is a richer possibility. And he's entirely himself, he is certain of it, and he knows that sleep is behind him: to know the difference between it and waking, to know the boundaries, is the essence of sanity.

The bedroom is large and uncluttered. As he glides across it with almost comic facility, the prospect of the experience ending saddens him briefly, then the thought is gone. He is by the centre window, pulling back the tall folding wooden shutters with care so as not to wake Rosalind. In this he's selfish as well as solicitous. He doesn't wish to be asked what he's about – what answer could he give, and why relinquish this moment in the attempt? He opens the second shutter, letting it concertina into the casement, and quietly raises the sash window. It is many feet taller than him, but it slides easily upwards, hoisted by its concealed lead counterweight. His skin tightens as the February air pours in around him, but he isn't troubled by the cold. From the second floor he faces the night, the city in its icy white light, the skeletal trees in the square, and thirty feet below, the black arrowhead railings like a row of spears. There's a degree or two of frost and the air is clear. The streetlamp glare hasn't quite obliterated all the stars; above the Regency façade on the other side of the square hang remnants of constellations in the southern sky. That particular façade is a reconstruction, a pastiche – wartime Fitzrovia took some hits from the Luftwaffe – and right behind is the Post Office Tower, municipal and seedy by day, but at night, half-concealed and decently illuminated, a valiant memorial to more optimistic days.

And now, what days are these? Baffled and fearful, he mostly thinks when he takes time from his weekly round to consider. But he doesn't feel that now. He leans forwards, pressing his weight onto his palms against the sill, exulting in the emptiness and clarity of the scene. His vision – always good – seems to have sharpened. He sees the paving stone mica glistening in the pedestrianised square, pigeon excrement hardened by distance and cold into something almost beautiful, like a scattering of snow. He likes the symmetry of black cast-iron posts and their even darker shadows, and the lattice of cobbled gutters. The overfull litter baskets suggest abundance rather than squalor; the vacant benches set around the circular gardens look benignly expectant of their daily traffic – cheerful lunchtime office crowds, the solemn, studious boys from the Indian hostel, lovers in quiet raptures or crisis, the crepuscular drug dealers, the ruined old lady with her wild, haunting calls. Go away! she'll shout for hours at a time, and squawk harshly, sounding like some marsh bird or zoo creature.

Standing here, as immune to the cold as a marble statue, gazing towards Charlotte Street, towards a foreshortened jumble of façades, scaffolding and pitched roofs, Henry thinks the city is a success, a brilliant invention, a biological masterpiece – millions teeming around the accumulated and layered achievements of the centuries, as though around a coral reef, sleeping, working, entertaining themselves, harmonious for the most part, nearly everyone wanting it to work. And the Perownes' own corner, a triumph of congruent proportion; the perfect square laid out by Robert Adam enclosing a perfect circle of garden – an eighteenth-century dream bathed and embraced by modernity, by street light from above, and from below by fibre-optic cables, and cool fresh water coursing down pipes, and sewage borne away in an instant of forgetting.

An habitual observer of his own moods, he wonders about this sustained, distorting euphoria. Perhaps down at the molecular level there's been a chemical accident while he slept – something like a spilled tray of drinks, prompting dopamine-like receptors to initiate a kindly cascade of intracellular events; or it's the prospect of a Saturday, or the paradoxical consequence of extreme tiredness. It's true, he finished the week in a state of unusual depletion. He came home to an empty house, and lay in the bath with a book, content to be talking to no one. It was his literate, too literate daughter Daisy who sent the biography of Darwin which in turn has something to do with a Conrad novel she wants him to read and which he has yet to start – seafaring, however morally fraught, doesn't much interest him. For some years now she's been addressing what she believes is his astounding ignorance, guiding his literary education, scolding him for poor taste and insensitivity. She has a point – straight from school to medical school to the slavish hours of a junior doctor, then the total absorption of neurosurgery training spliced with committed fatherhood – for fifteen years he barely touched a non-medical book at all. On the other hand, he thinks he's seen enough death, fear, courage and suffering to supply half a dozen literatures. Still, he submits to her reading lists – they're his means of remaining in touch as she grows away from her family into unknowable womanhood in a suburb of Paris; tonight she'll be home for the first time in six months – another cause for euphoria.

He was behind with his assignments from Daisy. With one toe occasionally controlling a fresh input of hot water, he blearily read an account of Darwin's dash to complete *The Origin of Species*, and a summary of the concluding pages, amended in later editions. At the same time he was listening to the radio news. The stolid Mr Blix has been addressing the UN again – there's a general impression that he's rather undermined the case for war. Then, certain he'd taken in nothing at all, Perowne switched the radio off, turned back the pages and read again. At times this biography made him comfortably nostalgic for a verdant, horse-drawn, affectionate England; at others he was faintly depressed by the way a whole life could be contained by a few hundred pages – bottled, like homemade chutney. And by how easily an existence, its ambitions, networks of family and friends, all its cherished stuff, solidly possessed, could so entirely vanish. Afterwards, he stretched out on the bed to consider his supper, and remembered nothing more. Rosalind must have drawn the covers over him when she came in from work. She would have kissed him. Forty-eight years old, profoundly asleep at nine thirty on a Friday night – this is modern professional life. He works hard, everyone around him works hard, and this week he's been pushed harder by a flu outbreak among the hospital staff – his operating list has been twice the usual length.

By means of balancing and doubling, he was able to perform major surgery in one theatre, supervise a senior registrar in another, and perform minor procedures in a third. He has two neurosurgical registrars in his firm at present – Sally Madden who is almost qualified and entirely reliable, and a year-two registrar, Rodney Browne from Guyana, gifted, hardworking, but still unsure of himself. Perowne's consultant anaesthetist, Jay Strauss, has his own registrar, Gita Syal. For three days, keeping Rodney at his side, Perowne moved between the three suites – the sound of his own clogs on the corridor's polished floors and the various squeaks and groans of the theatre swing doors sounded like orchestral accompaniments. Friday's list was typical. While Sally closed up a patient Perowne went next door to relieve an elderly lady of her trigeminal neuralgia, her tic douloureux. These minor operations can still give him pleasure – he likes to be fast and accurate. He slipped a gloved forefinger into the back of her mouth to feel the route, then, with barely a glance at the image intensifier, slid a long needle through the outside of her cheek, all the way up to the trigeminal ganglion. Jay came in from next door to watch Gita bringing the lady to brief consciousness. Electrical stimulation of the needle's tip caused a tingling in her face, and once she'd drowsily confirmed the position was correct – Perowne had it right first time – she was put down again while the nerve was 'cooked' by radiofrequency thermocoagulation. The delicate trick was to eliminate her pain while leaving her an awareness of light touch – all done in fifteen minutes; three years' misery, of sharp, stabbing pain, ended.

He clipped the neck of a middle cerebral artery aneurysm – he's something of a master in the art – and performed a biopsy for a tumour in the thalamus, a region where it's not possible to operate. The patient was a 28-year-old professional tennis player, already suffering acute memory loss. As Perowne drew the needle clear from the depths of the brain he could see at a glance that the tissue was abnormal. He held out little hope for radio- or chemotherapy. Confirmation came in a verbal report from the lab, and that afternoon he broke the news to the young man's elderly parents.

The next case was a craniotomy for a meningioma in a 53-year-old woman, a primary school headmistress. The tumour sat above the motor strip and was sharply defined, rolling away neatly before the probing of his Rhoton dissector – an entirely curative process. Sally closed that one up while Perowne went next door to carry out a multi-level lumbar laminectomy on an obese 44-year-old man, a gardener who worked in Hyde Park. He cut through four inches of subcutaneous fat before the vertebrae were exposed, and the man wobbled unhelpfully on the table whenever Perowne exerted downwards pressure to clip away at the bone.

For an old friend, a specialist in Ear, Nose and Throat, Perowne opened up an acoustic in a seventeen-year-old boy – it's odd how these ENT people shy away from making their own difficult routes in. Perowne made a large, rectangular bone flap behind the ear, which took well over an hour, irritating Jay Strauss who was wanting to get on with the firm's own list. Finally the tumour lay exposed to the operating microscope – a small vestibular schwannoma lying barely three millimetres from the cochlea. Leaving his specialist friend to perform the excision, Perowne hurried out to a second minor procedure which in turn caused him some irritation – a loud young woman with an habitually aggrieved manner wanted her spinal stimulator moved from back to front. Only the month before he had shifted it round after she complained that it was uncomfortable to sit down. Now she was saying the stimulator made it impossible to lie in bed. He made a long incision across her abdomen and wasted valuable time, up to his elbows inside her, searching for the battery wire. He was sure she'd be back before long.

For lunch he had a factory-wrapped tuna and cucumber sandwich with a bottle of mineral water. In the cramped coffee room whose toast and microwaved pasta always remind him of the odours of major surgery, he sat next to Heather, the much-loved Cockney lady who helps clean the theatres between procedures. She gave him an account of her son-in-law's arrest for armed robbery after being mistakenly picked out of a police line-up. But his alibi was perfect – at the time of the crime he was at the dentist's having a wisdom tooth removed. Elsewhere in the room, the talk was of the flu epidemic – one of the scrub nurses and a trainee Operating Department Practitioner working for Jay Strauss were sent home that morning. After fifteen minutes Perowne took his firm back to work. While Sally was next door drilling a hole in the skull of an old man, a retired traffic warden, to relieve the pressure of his internal bleeding – a chronic subdural haematoma – Perowne used the theatre's latest piece of equipment, a computerised image-guidance system, to help him with a craniotomy for a resection of a right posterior frontal glioma. Then he let Rodney take the lead in another burr hole for a chronic subdural.

The culmination of today's list was the removal of a pilocytic astrocytoma from a fourteen-year-old Nigerian girl who lives in Brixton with her aunt and uncle, a Church of England vicar. The tumour was best reached through the back of the head, by an infratentorial supracerebellar route, with the anaesthetised patient in a sitting position. This in turn created special problems for Jay Strauss, for there was a possibility of air entering a vein and causing an embolism. Andrea Chapman was a problem patient, a problem niece. She arrived in England at the age of twelve – the dismayed vicar and his wife showed Perowne the photograph – a scrubbed girl in a frock and tight ribbons with a shy smile. Something in her that village life in rural north Nigeria kept buttoned down was released once she started at her local Brixton comprehensive. She took to the music, the clothes, the talk, the values – the street. She had attitude, the vicar confided while his wife was trying to settle Andrea on the ward. His niece took drugs, got drunk, shoplifted, bunked off school, hated authority, and 'swore like a merchant seaman'. Could it be the tumour was pressing down on some part of her brain?

Perowne could offer no such comfort. The tumour was remote from the frontal lobes. It was deep in the superior cerebellar vermis. She'd already suffered early-morning headaches, blind spots and ataxia – unsteadiness. These symptoms failed to dispel her suspicion that her condition was part of a plot – the hospital, in league with her guardians, the school, the police – to curb her nights in the clubs. Within hours of being admitted she was in conflict with the nurses, the ward sister and an elderly patient who said she wouldn't tolerate the obscene language. Perowne had his own diffi-culties talking her through the ordeals that lay ahead. Even when Andrea wasn't aroused, she affected to talk like a rapper on MTV, swaying her upper body as she sat up in bed, making circular movements with her palms downwards, soothing the air in front of her, in preparation for one of her own storms. But he admired her spirit, and the fierce dark eyes, the perfect teeth, and the clean pink tongue lashing itself round the words it formed. She smiled joyously, even when she was shouting in apparent fury, as though she was tickled by just how much she could get away with. It took Jay Strauss, an American with the warmth and directness that no one else in this English hospital could muster, to bring her into line.

Andrea's operation lasted five hours and went well. She was placed in a sitting position, with her head-clamp bolted to a frame in front of her. Opening up the back of the head needed great care because of the vessels running close under the bone. Rodney leaned in at Perowne's side to irrigate the drilling and cauterise the bleeding with the bipolar. Finally it lay exposed, the tentorium – the tent – a pale delicate structure of beauty, like the little whirl of a veiled dancer, where the dura is gathered and parted again. Below it lay the cerebellum. By cutting away carefully, Perowne allowed gravity itself to draw the cerebellum down – no need for retractors – and it was possible to see deep into the region where the pineal lay, with the tumour extending in a vast red mass right in front of it. The astrocytoma was well defined and had only partially infiltrated surrounding tissue. Perowne was able to excise almost all of it without damaging any eloquent region.

He allowed Rodney several minutes with the microscope and the sucker, and let him do the closing up. Perowne did the head dressing himself, and when he finally came away from the theatres, he wasn't feeling tired at all. Operating never wearies him – once busy within the enclosed world of his firm, the theatre and its ordered procedures, and absorbed by the vivid foreshortening of the operating microscope as he follows a corridor to a desired site, he experiences a superhuman capacity, more like a craving, for work.

As for the rest of the week, the two morning clinics made no more demand than usual. He's too experienced to be touched by the varieties of distress he encounters – his obligation is to be useful. Nor did the ward rounds or the various weekly committees tire him. It was the paperwork on Friday afternoon that brought him down, the backlog of referrals, and responses to referrals, abstracts for two conferences, letters to colleagues and editors, an unfinished peer review, contributions to management initiatives, and government changes to the structure of the Trust, and yet more revisions to teaching practices. There's to be a new look – there's always a new look – at the hospital's Emergency Plan. Simple train crashes are no longer all that are envisaged, and words like 'catastrophe' and 'mass fatalities', 'chemical and biological warfare' and 'major attack' have recently become bland through repetition. In the past year he's become aware of new committees and subcommittees spawning, and lines of command that stretch up and out of the hospital, beyond the medical hierarchies, up through the distant reaches of the Civil Service to the Home Secretary's office.

Perowne dictated monotonously, and long after his secretary went home he typed in his overheated box of an office on the hospital's third floor. What dragged him back was an unfamiliar lack of fluency. He prides himself on speed and a sleek, wry style. It never needs much forethought – typing and composing are one. Now he was stumbling. And though the professional jargon didn't desert him – it's second nature – his prose accumulated awkwardly. Individual words brought to mind unwieldy objects – bicycles, deckchairs, coat hangers – strewn across his path. He composed a sentence in his head, then lost it on the page, or typed himself into a grammatical cul-de-sac and had to sweat his way out. Whether this debility was the cause or the consequence of fatigue he didn't pause to consider. He was stubborn and he pushed himself to the end. At eight in the evening he concluded the last in a series of e-mails, and stood up from his desk where he had been hunched since four. On his way out he looked in at his patients in the ICU. There were no problems, and Andrea was doing fine – she was sleeping and all her signs were good. Less than half an hour later he was back home, in his bath, and soon after, he too was asleep.

Two figures in dark overcoats are crossing the square diagonally, walking away from him towards Cleveland Street, their high heels ticking in awkward counterpoint – nurses surely, heading home, though this is a strange time to be coming off shift. They aren't speaking, and though their steps don't match, they walk close, shoulders almost touching in an intimate, sisterly way. They pass right beneath him, and make a quarter-circular route around the gardens before striking off. There's something touching about the way their breath rises behind them in single clouds of vapour as they go, as though they're playing a children's game, imitating steam trains. They cross towards the far corner of the square, and with his advantage of height and in his curious mood, he not only watches them, but watches over them, supervising their progress with the remote possessiveness of a god. In the lifeless cold, they pass through the night, hot little biological engines with bipedal skills suited to any terrain, endowed with innumerable branching neural networks sunk deep in a knob of bone casing, buried fibres, warm filaments with their invisible glow of consciousness – these engines devise their own tracks.

He's been at the window several minutes, the elation is passing, and he's beginning to shiver. In the gardens, which are enclosed within a circle of high railings, a light frost lies on the landscaped hollows and rises of the lawn beyond the border of plane trees. He watches an ambulance, siren off, blue lights flashing, turn into Charlotte Street and accelerate hard southwards, heading perhaps for Soho. He turns from the window to reach behind him for a thick woollen dressing gown where it lies draped over a chair. Even as he turns, he's aware of some new element outside, in the square or in the trees, bright but colourless, smeared across his peripheral vision by the movement of his head. But he doesn't look back immediately. He's cold and he wants the dressing gown. He picks it up, threads one arm through a sleeve, and only steps back towards the window as he's finding the second sleeve and looping the belt around his waist.

He doesn't immediately understand what he sees, though he thinks he does. In this first moment, in his eagerness and curiosity, he assumes proportions on a planetary scale: it's a meteor burning out in the London sky, traversing left to right, low on the horizon, though well clear of the taller buildings. But surely meteors have a darting, needle-like quality. You see them in a flash before their heat consumes them. This is moving slowly, majestically even. In an instant, he revises his perspective outward to the scale of the solar system: this object is not hundreds but millions of miles distant, far out in space swinging in timeless orbit around the sun. It's a comet, tinged with yellow, with the familiar bright core trailing its fiery envelope. He watched Hale-Bopp with Rosalind and the children from a grassy hillock in the Lake District and he feels again the same leap of gratitude for a glimpse, beyond the earthly frame, of the truly impersonal. And this is better, brighter, faster, all the more impressive for being unexpected. They must have missed the media coverage. Working too hard. He's about to wake Rosalind – he knows she'll be thrilled by the sight – but he wonders if she'd get to the window before the comet disappears. Then he'll miss it too. But it's too extraordinary not to share.

He's moving towards the bed when he hears a low rumbling sound, gentle thunder gathering in volume, and stops to listen. It tells him everything. He looks back over his shoulder to the window for confirmation. Of course, a comet is so distant it's bound to appear stationary. Horrified, he returns to his position by the window. The sound holds at a steady volume while he revises the scale again, zooming inwards this time, from solar dust and ice back to the local. Only three or four seconds have passed since he saw this fire in the sky and changed his mind about it twice. It's travelling along a route that he himself has taken many times in his life, and along which he's gone through the routines, adjusting his seat-back and his watch, putting away his papers, always curious to see if he can locate his own house down among the immense almost beautiful orange-grey sprawl; east to west, along the southern banks of the Thames, two thousand feet up, in the final approaches to Heathrow.

It's directly south of him now, barely a mile away, soon to pass into the topmost lattice of the bare plane trees, and then behind the Post Office Tower, at the level of the lowest microwave dishes. Despite the city lights, the contours of the plane aren't visible in the early-morning darkness. The fire must be on the nearside wing where it joins the fuselage, or perhaps in one of the engines slung below. The leading edge of the fire is a flattened white sphere which trails away in a cone of yellow and red, less like a meteor or comet than an artist's lurid impression of one. As though in a pretence of normality, the landing lights are flashing. But the engine note gives it all away. Above the usual deep and airy roar, is a straining, choking, banshee sound growing in volume – both a scream and a sustained shout, an impure, dirty noise that suggests unsustainable mechanical effort beyond the capacity of hardened steel, spiralling upwards to an end point, irresponsibly rising and rising like the accompaniment to a terrible fairground ride. Something is about to give.

He no longer thinks of waking Rosalind. Why wake her into this nightmare? In fact, the spectacle has the familiarity of a recurrent dream. Like most passengers, outwardly subdued by the monotony of air travel, he often lets his thoughts range across the possibilities while sitting, strapped down and docile, in front of a packaged meal. Outside, beyond a wall of thin steel and cheerful creaking plastic, it's minus sixty degrees and forty thousand feet to the ground. Flung across the Atlantic at five hundred feet a second, you submit to the folly because everyone else does. Your fellow passengers are reassured because you and the others around you appear calm. Looked at a certain way – deaths per passenger mile – the statistics are consoling. And how else attend a conference in Southern California? Air travel is a stock market, a trick of mirrored perceptions, a fragile alliance of pooled belief; so long as nerves hold steady and no bombs or wreckers are on board, everybody prospers. When there's failure, there will be no half measures. Seen another way – deaths per journey – the figures aren't so good. The market could plunge.

Plastic fork in hand, he often wonders how it might go –

the screaming in the cabin partly muffled by that deadening acoustic, the fumbling in bags for phones and last words, the airline staff in their terror clinging to remembered fragments of procedure, the levelling smell of shit. But the scene construed from the outside, from afar like this, is also familiar. It's already almost eighteen months since half the planet watched, and watched again the unseen captives driven through the sky to the slaughter, at which time there gathered round the innocent silhouette of any jet plane a novel association. Everyone agrees, airliners look different in the sky these days, predatory or doomed.

Henry knows it's a trick of vision that makes him think he can see an outline now, a deeper black shape against the dark. The howl of the burning engine continues to rise in pitch. It wouldn't surprise him to see lights coming on across the city, or the square fill with residents in dressing gowns. Behind him Rosalind, well practised at excluding the city's night troubles from her sleep, turns on her side. The noise is probably no more intrusive than a passing siren on the Euston Road. The fiery white core and its coloured tail have grown larger – no passengers sitting in that central section of the plane could survive. That is the other familiar element – the horror of what he can't see. Catastrophe observed from a safe distance. Watching death on a large scale, but seeing no one die. No blood, no screams, no human figures at all, and into this emptiness, the obliging imagination set free. The fight to the death in the cockpit, a posse of brave passengers assembling before a last-hope charge against the fanatics. To escape the heat of that fire which part of the plane might you run to? The pilot's end might seem less lonely somehow. Is it pathetic folly to reach into the overhead locker for your bag, or necessary optimism? Will the thickly made-up lady who politely served you croissant and jam now be trying to stop you?

The plane is passing behind the tops of the trees. Briefly, the fire twinkles festively among the branches and twigs. It occurs to Perowne that there's something he should be doing. By the time the emergency services have noted and passed on his call, whatever is to happen will be in the past. If he's alive, the pilot will have radioed ahead. Perhaps they're already covering the runway in foam. Pointless at this stage to go down and make himself available to the hospital. Heathrow isn't in its area under the Emergency Plan. Elsewhere, further west, in darkened bedrooms, medics will be pulling on their clothes with no idea of what they face. Still fifteen miles of descent. If the fuel tanks explode there will be nothing for them to do.

The plane emerges from the trees, crosses a gap and disappears behind the Post Office Tower. If Perowne were inclined to religious feeling, to supernatural explanations, he could play with the idea that he's been summoned; that having woken in an unusual state of mind, and gone to the window for no reason, he should acknowledge a hidden order, an external intelligence which wants to show or tell him something of significance. But a city of its nature cultivates insomniacs; it is itself a sleepless entity whose wires never stop singing; among so many millions there are bound to be people staring out of windows when normally they would be asleep. And not the same people every night. That it should be him and not someone else is an arbitrary matter. A simple anthropic principle is involved. The primitive thinking of the supernaturally inclined amounts to what his psychiatric colleagues call a problem, or an idea, of reference. An excess of the subjective, the ordering of the world in line with your needs, an inability to contemplate your own unimportance. In Henry's view such reasoning belongs on a spectrum at whose far end, rearing like an abandoned temple, lies psychosis.

And such reasoning may have caused the fire on the plane. A man of sound faith with a bomb in the heel of his shoe. Among the terrified passengers many might be praying – another problem of reference – to their own god

17

for intercession. And if there are to be deaths, the very god who ordained them will soon be funereally petitioned for comfort. Perowne regards this as a matter for wonder, a human complication beyond the reach of morals. From it there spring, alongside the unreason and slaughter, decent people and good deeds, beautiful cathedrals, mosques, cantatas, poetry. Even the denial of God, he was once amazed and indignant to hear a priest argue, is a spiritual exercise, a form of prayer: it's not easy to escape from the clutches of the believers. The best hope for the plane is that it's suffered simple, secular mechanical failure.

It passes beyond the Tower and begins to recede across an open patch of western sky, angling a little towards the north. The fire appears to diminish with the slowly changing perspective. His view now is mostly of the tail and its flashing light. The noise of the engine's distress is fading. Is the undercarriage down? As he wonders, he also wishes it, or wills it. A kind of praying? He's asking no one any favours. Even when the landing lights have shrunk to nothing, he continues to watch the sky in the west, fearing the sight of an explosion, unable to look away. Still cold, despite the dressing gown, he wipes the pane clear of the condensation from his breath, and thinks how remote it now seems, that unprompted, exalted mood that brought him from his bed. Finally he straightens and quietly unfolds the shutters to mask the sky.

As he comes away, he remembers the famous thought experiment he learned about long ago on a physics course. A cat, Schrödinger's Cat, hidden from view in a covered box, is either still alive, or has just been killed by a randomly activated hammer hitting a vial of poison. Until the observer lifts the cover from the box, both possibilities, alive cat and dead cat, exist side by side, in parallel universes, equally real. At the point at which the lid is lifted from the box and the cat is examined, a quantum wave of probability collapses. None of this has ever made any sense to him at all. No human sense. Surely another example of a problem of reference. He's heard that even the physicists are abandoning it. To Henry it seems beyond the requirements of proof: a result, a consequence, exists separately in the world, independent of himself, known to others, awaiting his discovery. What then collapses will be his own ignorance. Whatever the score, it is already chalked up. And whatever the passengers' destination, whether they are frightened and safe, or dead, they will have arrived by now.

Most people at their first consultation take a furtive look at the surgeon's hands in the hope of reassurance. Prospective patients look for delicacy, sensitivity, steadiness, perhaps unblemished pallor. On this basis, Henry Perowne loses a number of cases each year. Generally, he knows it's about to happen before the patient does: the downward glance repeated, the prepared questions beginning to falter, the overemphatic thanks during the retreat to the door. Other patients don't like what they see but are ignorant of their right to go elsewhere; some note the hands, but are placated by the reputation, or don't give a damn; and there are still others who notice nothing, or feel nothing, or are unable to communicate due to the cognitive impairment that has brought them in the first place.

Perowne himself is not concerned. Let the defectors go along the corridor or across town. Others will take their place. The sea of neural misery is wide and deep. These hands are steady enough, but they are large. Had he been a proper pianist – he's dabbled inexpertly – his ten-note span might be of use. They are knobbly hands, bulging with bone and sinew at the knuckles, with a thatch of gingerish hair at the base of each finger – the tips of which are flat and broad, like the suckers on a salamander. There's an immodest length to the thumbs which curve back, banana-style, and even at rest have a double-jointed look, more suited to the circus ring, among the clowns and trapezists. And the hands, like much of the rest of Perowne, are gaily freckled in a motley

19

of orange and brown melanin extending right up to his highest knuckles. To a certain kind of patient this looks alien, even unwholesome: you might not want such hands, even gloved, tinkering with your brain.

They are the hands of a tall, sinewy man on whom recent years have added a little weight and poise. In his twenties, his tweed jacket hung on him as though on narrow poles. When he exerts himself to straighten his back, he stands at six foot two. His slight stoop gives him an apologetic look which many patients take as part of his charm. They're also put at their ease by the unassertive manner and the mild green eyes with deep smile-wrinkles at their corners. Until his early forties, the boyish freckles on his face and forehead had the same unintimidating effect, but recently they've begun to fade, as though a senior position has at last obliged him to abandon a frivolous display. Patients would be less happy to know that he's not always listening to them. He's a dreamer sometimes. Like a car-radio traffic alert, a shadowy mental narrative can break in, urgent and unbidden, even during a consultation. He's adept at covering his tracks, continuing to nod or frown or firmly close his mouth around a half-smile. When he comes to, seconds later, he never seems to have missed much.

To a degree, the stoop is deceptive. Perowne has always had physical ambitions and he's reluctant to let them go. On his rounds he hits the corridors with an impatient stride his retinue struggles to match. He's healthy, more or less. If he takes time after a shower to scrutinise himself in the full-length bathroom mirror, he notes around his waist a first thickening, an almost sensual swelling below the ribs. It vanishes when he holds himself erect or raises his arms. Otherwise, the muscles – the pecs, the abs – though modest, keep a reasonable definition, especially when the overhead lamp is off and light falls from the side. He is not done yet. His head hair, though thinning, is still reddish brown. Only on his pubes are the first scattered coils of silver.

Most weeks he still runs in Regent's Park, through William Nesfield's restored gardens, past the Lion Tazza to Primrose Hill and back. And he still beats some of the younger medics at squash, centring his long reach on the 'T' at the centre of the court, from where he flaunts the lob shots which are his special pride. Almost half the time he beats the consultant anaesthetist in their Saturday games. But if an opponent is good enough to know how to shift him from the centre of the court and make him run, then Henry is done for in twenty minutes. Leaning against the back wall, he might unobtrusively check his own pulse and ask himself whether his 48-year-old frame can really sustain a rate of one hundred and ninety? On a rare day off he was two games up against Jay Strauss when they were called – it was the Paddington rail crash, everyone was called – and they worked twelve hours at a stretch in their trainers and shorts under their greens. Perowne runs a half-marathon for charity every year, and it's said, wrongly, that all those under him wanting advancement must run it too. His time last year – one hour forty-one – was eleven minutes slower than his best.

The unassertiveness is misleading, more style than character – it's not possible to be an unassertive brain surgeon. Naturally, students and junior staff see less of his charm than the patients. The student who, referring to a CT scan in Perowne's presence, used the words 'low down on the left side', provoked a moment's rage and was banished in shame to relearn his directional terms. In the operating theatre Perowne is said by his firm to be at the inexpressive end of the scale: no stream of obscenities ascending as the difficulties and risks increase, no hissed threats to throw an incompetent from the room, none of those tough guy asides – *Uhuh, there go the violin lessons* – that are supposed to relieve tension. On the contrary, in Perowne's view, when things are difficult, tension is best maintained. His taste then is for terse murmurs or silence. If a registrar fumbles with the positioning of a retractor, or the scrub nurse places a pituitary forceps in his hand at an awkward angle, Perowne might on a bad day utter a single staccato 'fuck', more troubling for its rarity and lack of emphasis, and the silence in the room will tighten. Otherwise, he likes music in the theatre when he's working, mostly piano works by Bach – the 'Goldberg' Variations, the *Well-Tempered Klavier*, the Partitas. He favours Angela Hewitt, Martha Argerich, sometimes Gustav Leonhardt. In a really good mood he'll go for the looser interpretations of Glenn Gould. In committee he likes precision, all items addressed and disposed of within the set time, and to this end he's an effective chairman. Exploratory musings and anecdotes by senior colleagues, tolerated by most as an occupational hazard, make him impatient; fantasising should be a solitary pursuit. Decisions are all.

So despite the apologetic posture, the mild manner and an inclination to occasional daydreaming, it's unlike Perowne to dither as he does now – he's standing at the foot of the bed – unable to decide whether to wake Rosalind. It makes no sense at all. There's nothing to see. It's an entirely selfish impulse. Her alarm is due to go off at six thirty, and once he's told her the story, she'll have no hope of going back to sleep. She'll hear it all anyway. She has a difficult day ahead. Now that the shutters are closed and he's in darkness again, he understands the extent of his turmoil. His thoughts have a reeling, tenuous quality – he can't hold an idea long enough to force sense out of it. He feels culpable somehow, but help-less too. These are contradictory terms, but not quite, and it's the degree of their overlap, their manner of expressing the same thing from different angles, which he needs to com-prehend. Culpable in his helplessness. Helplessly culpable. He loses his way, and thinks again of the phone. By daylight, will it seem negligent not to have called the emergency ser-vices? Will it be obvious that there was nothing to be done, that there wasn't time? His crime was to stand in the safety of his bedroom, wrapped in a woollen dressing gown, without moving or making a sound, half dreaming as he watched people die. Yes, he should have phoned, if only to talk, to measure his voice and feelings against a stranger's.

And that is why he wants to wake her, not simply to give her the news, but because he's somewhat deranged, he keeps floating away from the line of his thoughts. He wants to tether himself to the precise details of what he's seen, arrange them before her worldly, legal mind and steady gaze. He'd like the touch of her hands – they are small and smooth, always cooler than his own. It's five days since they made love, Monday morning, before the six o'clock news, during a rainstorm, with only the dimmed light from the bathroom, twenty minutes snatched – so they often joke – from the jaws of work. Well, in ambitious middle life it sometimes seems there is only work. He can be at the hospital until ten, then it can pull him from his bed at 3 a.m., and he can be back there again at eight. Rosalind's work proceeds by a series of slow crescendos and abrupt terminations as she tries to steer her newspaper away from the courts. For certain days, even weeks on end, work can shape every hour; it's the tide, the lunar cycle they set their lives by, and without it, it can seem, there's nothing, Henry and Rosalind Perowne are nothing.

Henry can't resist the urgency of his cases, or deny the egotistical joy in his own skills, or the pleasure he still takes in the relief of the relatives when he comes down from the operating room like a god, an angel with the glad tidings – life, not death. Rosalind's best moments are outside court, when a powerful litigant backs down in the face of superior argument; or, rarer, when a judgment goes her way and establishes a point of principle in law. Once a week, usually on a Sunday evening, they line up their personal organisers side by side, like little mating creatures, so that their appointments can be transferred into each other's diary along an infrared beam. When they steal time for love they always leave the phone connected. By some perverse synchronism, it often rings just as they're getting started. It'll be for Rosalind as often as for him. If he's the one who is obliged to get

dressed and hurry from the room – perhaps returning with
a curse for keys or loose change – he does so with a longing
backward glance, and sets off from his house to the hospital
– ten minutes at a brisk pace – with his burden, his fading
thoughts of love. But once he's through the double swing
doors, and crossing the worn chessboard linoleum tiles by
Accident and Emergency, once he's ridden the lift to the
third-floor operating suite and is in the scrub room, soap in
hand, listening to his registrar's difficulties, the last touches
of desire leave him and he doesn't even notice them go. No
regrets. He's renowned for his speed, his success rate and
his list – he takes over three hundred cases a year. Some fail,
a handful endure with their lights a little fogged, but most
thrive, and many return to work in some form; work – the
ultimate badge of health.

And work is why he cannot wake her. She's due in the
High Court at ten for an emergency hearing. Her paper has
been prevented from reporting the details of a gagging order
on another newspaper. The powerful party who obtained the
original order successfully argued before a duty judge that
even the fact of the gagging cannot be divulged. A point of
press freedom is at issue, and it's Rosalind's quest to have
the second order overturned by the end of the day. Before
the hearing, briefings in chambers, then – so she hopes – an
exploratory chat in the corridors with the other side. Later
she'll lay out the options to the editor and management.
She'd have come in late last night from meetings, long after
Henry dozed off without his supper. Probably she drank tea
at the kitchen table and read through her papers. She may
have had difficulty falling asleep.

Feeling unhinged and unreasonable and still in need of
talking to her, he remains at the foot of the bed, staring
towards her shape under the duvet. She sleeps like a child,
with her knees drawn up. In the near-total darkness, how
small she seems in the hugeness of the bed. He listens to her
breathing, which is almost inaudible on the intake, quietly

emphatic on the exhalation. She makes a sound with her tongue, a wet click against the roof of her mouth. Many years ago he fell in love with her in a hospital ward, at a time of terror. She was barely aware of him. A white coat coming to her bedside to remove the stitches from the inside of her upper lip. Then it was another three months before he kissed those lips. But he knew more of her, or at least had seen more of her, than any prospective lover could expect.

He approaches now and leans over her and kisses the warm back of her head. Then he comes away, closing the bedroom door quietly, and goes down to the kitchen to turn on the radio.

It's a commonplace of parenting and modern genetics that parents have little or no influence on the characters of their children. You never know who you are going to get. Opportunities, health, prospects, accent, table manners – these might lie within your power to shape. But what really determines the sort of person who's coming to live with you is which sperm finds which egg, how the cards in two packs are chosen, then how they are shuffled, halved and spliced at the moment of recombination. Cheerful or neurotic, kind or greedy, curious or dull, expansive or shy and anywhere in between; it can be quite an affront to parental self-regard, just how much of the work has already been done. On the other hand, it can let you off the hook. The point is made for you as soon as you have more than one child; two entirely different people emerge from their roughly similar chances in life. Here in the cavernous basement kitchen at 3.55 a.m., in a single pool of light, as though on stage, is Theo Perowne, eighteen years old, his formal education already long behind him, reclining on a tilted-back kitchen chair, his legs in tight black jeans, his feet in boots of soft black leather (paid for with his own money) crossed on the edge of the table. As unlike his sister Daisy as randomness will allow. He's drinking from a large tumbler of water. In the other hand he holds the folded-back music magazine he's reading. A studded leather jacket lies in a heap on the floor. Propped against a cupboard is his guitar in its case. It's already acquired a few steamer trunk labels – Trieste, Oakland, Hamburg, Val d'Isère. There's space for more. From a compact stereo player on a shelf above a library of cookery books comes the sound, like soft drizzle, of an all-night pop station.

Perowne sometimes wonders if, in his youth, he could ever have guessed that he would one day father a blues musician. He himself was simply processed, without question or complaint, in a polished continuum from school, through medical school, to the dogged acquisition of clinical experience, in London, Southend-on-Sea, Newcastle, Bellevue Emergency Department in New York and London again. How have he and Rosalind, such dutiful, conventional types, given rise to such a free spirit? One who dresses, with a certain irony, in the style of the bohemian fifties, who won't read books or let himself be persuaded to stay on at school, who's rarely out of bed before lunchtime, whose passion is for mastery in all the nuances of the tradition, Delta, Chicago, Mississippi, for certain licks that contain for him the key to all mysteries, and for the success of his band, New Blue Rider. He has an enlarged version of his mother's face and soft eyes, not green though, but dark brown – the proverbial almonds, with a faint and exotic slant. He has his mother's wide open good-willed look – and a stronger more compact variant on his father's big-boned lankiness. Usefully for his line of work, he's also got the hands. In the confined, gossipy world of British blues, Theo is spoken of as a man of promise, already mature in his grasp of the idiom, who might even one day walk with the gods, the British gods that is – Alexis Korner, John Mayall, Eric Clapton. Someone has written somewhere that Theo Perowne plays like an angel.

Naturally, his father agrees, despite his doubts about the limits of the form. He likes the blues well enough – in fact, he was the one who showed the nine-year-old Theo how it worked. After that, grandfather took over. But is there a lifetime's satisfaction in twelve bars of three obvious chords? Perhaps it's one of those cases of a microcosm giving you the whole world. Like a Spode dinner plate. Or a single cell. Or, as Daisy says, like a Jane Austen novel. When player and listener together know the route so well, the pleasure is in the deviation, the unexpected turn against the grain. To see a world in a grain of sand. So it is, Perowne tries to convince himself, with clipping an aneurysm: absorbing variation on an unchanging theme.

And there's something in the loping authority of Theo's playing that revives for Henry the inexplicable lure of that simple progression. Theo is the sort of guitarist who plays in an open-eyed trance, without moving his body or ever glancing down at his hands. He concedes only an occasional thoughtful nod. Now and then, during a set he might tilt back his head to indicate to the others that he is 'going round' again. He carries himself on stage as he does in conversation, quietly, formally, protecting his privacy within a shell of friendly politeness. If he happens to spot his parents at the back of a crowd, he'll lift his left hand from the fret in a shy and private salute. Henry and Rosalind remember then the cardboard crib in the school gymnasium, the solemn five-year-old Joseph, tea towel bound to his head by a crown of rubber bands, holding the hand of a stricken Mary, making the same furtive, affectionate gesture as he located at last his parents in the second row.

This restraint, this cool, suits the blues, or Theo's version of it. When he breaks on a medium-paced standard like 'Sweet Home Chicago', with its slouching dotted rhythm – he's said he's beginning to tire of these evergreen blues – he'll set off in the lower register with an easy muscular stride, like some sleek predatory creature, shuffling off tiredness, devouring miles of open savannah. Then he moves on up the fret and the diffidence begins to carry a hint of danger.

A little syncopated stab on the turnaround, the sudden chop of an augmented chord, a note held against the tide of harmony, a judiciously flattened fifth, a seventh bent in sensuous microtones. Then a passing soulful dissonance. He has the rhythmic gift of upending expectation, a way of playing off triplets against two- or four-note clusters. His runs have the tilt and accent of bebop. It's a form of hypnosis, of effortless seduction. Henry has told no one, not even Rosalind, that there are moments, listening from the back of a West End bar, when the music thrills him, and in a state of exaltation he feels his pride in his son – inseparable from his pleasure in the music – as a constricting sensation in his chest, close to pain. It's difficult to breathe. At the heart of the blues is not melancholy, but a strange and worldly joy.

Theo's guitar pierces him because it also carries a reprimand, a reminder of buried dissatisfaction in his own life, of the missing element. This feeling can grow when a set is over, when the consultant neurosurgeon makes his affectionate farewells to Theo and his friends and, emerging onto the pavement, decides to go home on foot and reflect. There's nothing in his own life that contains this inventiveness, this style of being free. The music speaks to unexpressed longing or frustration, a sense that he's denied himself an open road, the life of the heart celebrated in the songs. There has to be more to life than merely saving lives. The discipline and responsibility of a medical career, compounded by starting a family in his mid-twenties – and over much of it, a veil of fatigue; he's still young enough to yearn for the unpredictable and unrestrained, and old enough to know the chances are narrowing. Is he about to become that man, that modern fool of a certain age, who finds himself pausing by shop windows to stare in at the saxophones or the motorbikes, or driven to find himself a mistress of his daughter's age? He's already bought himself an expensive car. Theo's playing carries this burden of regret into his father's heart. It is, after all, the blues.

By way of greeting, Theo lets his chair tip forward onto four legs and raises a hand. It's not his style to show surprise.

'Early start?'

'I've just seen a plane on fire, heading into Heathrow.'

'You're kidding.'

Henry is going towards the hi-fi, intending to retune it, but Theo picks up the remote from the kitchen table and turns on the small TV they keep near the stove for moments like this, breaking stories. They wait for the grandiose preamble to the four o' clock news to finish – pulsing synthetic music, spiralling, radiating computer graphics, combined in a *son et lumière* of Wagnerian scale to suggest urgency, technology, global coverage. Then the usual square-jawed anchor of about Perowne's age begins to list the main stories of the hour. Straight away it's obvious that the burning plane has yet to enter the planetary matrix. It remains an unreliable subjective event. Still, they listen to some of the list.

'Hans Blix – a case for war?' the anchor intones over the sound of tom-toms, and pictures of the French Foreign Minister, M. de Villepin, being applauded in the UN debating chamber. 'Yes, say US and Britain. No, say the majority.' Then, preparations for anti-war demonstrations later today in London and countless cities around the world; a tennis championship in Florida disrupted by woman with a bread-knife . . .

He turns the set off and says, 'How about some coffee?' and while Theo gets up to oblige, Henry gives him the story, his main story of the hour. It shouldn't surprise him how little there is to tell – the plane and its point of light traversing his field of view, left to right, behind the trees, behind the Post Office Tower, then receding to the west. But he feels he's been through so much more.

'But uh, so what were you doing at the window?'

'I told you. I couldn't sleep.'

'Some coincidence.'

'Exactly that.'

Their eyes meet – a moment of potential challenge – then Theo looks away and shrugs. His sister, on the other hand, likes adversarial argument – Daisy and Henry share an inspired love – a pathetic addiction, Rosalind and Theo would say – for a furious set-to. In the ripe teenage mulch of his bedroom, among the guitar magazines, discarded shirts and socks and smoothie bottles, are barely touched books on UFOs, a term these days interchangeable with spacecraft, alien-owned and driven. As Henry understands it, Theo's world-view accommodates a hunch that somehow everything is connected, interestingly connected, and that certain authorities, notably the US government, with privileged access to extra-terrestrial intelligence, is excluding the rest of the world from such wondrous knowledge as contemporary science, dull and strait-laced, cannot begin to comprehend. This knowledge is divulged in other paperbacks, also barely touched by Theo. His curiosity, mild as it is, has been hijacked by peddlers of fakery. But does it matter, when he can play the guitar like an angel ringing a bell, when he's at least keeping faith with forms of wondrous knowledge, when there's so much time ahead to change his mind, if indeed he has made it up?

He's a gentle boy – those big lashes, those dark velvety eyes with their faint oriental pitch; he isn't the sort to enter easily into disputes. Their eyes meet, and he looks away with his own thoughts intact. The universe might be showing his father a connection, a sign which he chooses not to read. What can anyone do about that?

Assuming a daydreaming episode like one of his own, Henry says, to bring him down to ground, 'So it crashes minutes after I saw it disappear. How long do you think it would take to feed through the news channels?'

Theo, who's at the counter filtering the coffee, looks back over his shoulder and fingers his lower lip, a full dark red lip, presumably not much kissed of late. He dismissed his last girlfriend in that way he has with girls, of saying nothing much and letting them fade, without drama. Saying little, minimalism in the matter of salutations, introductions, farewells, even thanks, is contemporary etiquette. On the phone, however, the young unbutton. Theo often hunkers down for three hours at a stretch.

He speaks soothingly, as to a fussing child, with the authority of a citizen, an official even, of the electronic age. 'It'll be on the next news, Dad. Half four.'

Fair enough. Naked under his dressing gown – itself a uniform of the old and sick – with thinning hair tousled from lack of sleep, his voice, the consultant's even baritone, now lightened by turmoil – Henry's a candidate for soothing. Here's how it starts, the long process by which you become your children's child. Until one day you might hear them say, Dad, if you start crying again we're taking you home.

Theo sits down and slides the coffee cup across the table, within his father's reach. He has made none for himself. Instead, he snaps the lid off another half-litre bottle of mineral water. The purity of the young. Or he is warding off a hangover? The point has long been passed when Henry feels he can ask, or express a view.

Theo says, 'You reckon it's terrorists?'

'It's a possibility.'

The September attacks were Theo's induction into international affairs, the moment he accepted that events beyond friends, home and the music scene had bearing on his existence. At sixteen, which was what he was at the time, this seemed rather late. Perowne, born the year before the Suez Crisis, too young for the Cuban missiles, or the construction of the Berlin Wall, or Kennedy's assassination, remembers being tearful over Aberfan in 'sixty-six – one hundred and sixteen schoolchildren just like himself, fresh from prayers in school assembly, the day before half-term, buried

under a river of mud. This was when he first suspected that
the kindly child-loving God extolled by his headmistress
might not exist. As it turned out, most major world events
suggested the same. But for Theo's sincerely godless generation, the question hasn't come up. No one in his bright,
plate-glass, forward-looking school ever asked him to pray,
or sing an impenetrable cheery hymn. There's no entity for
him to doubt. His initiation, in front of the TV, before the
dissolving towers, was intense but he adapted quickly. These
days he scans the papers for fresh developments the way
he might a listings magazine. As long as there's nothing
new, his mind is free. International terror, security cordons,
preparations for war – these represent the steady state, the
weather. Emerging into adult consciousness, this is the
world he finds.

It can't trouble him the way it does his father, who reads
the same papers with morbid fixation. Despite the troops
mustering in the Gulf, or the tanks out at Heathrow on
Thursday, the storming of the Finsbury Park mosque, the
reports of terror cells around the country, and Bin Laden's
promise on tape of 'martyrdom attacks' on London, Perowne
held for a while to the idea that it was all an aberration,
that the world would surely calm down and soon be otherwise, that solutions were possible, that reason, being a
powerful tool, was irresistible, the only way out; or that like
any other crisis, this one would fade soon, and make way
for the next, going the way of the Falklands and Bosnia,
Biafra and Chernobyl. But lately, this is looking optimistic.
Against his own inclination, he's adapting, the way patients
eventually do to their sudden loss of sight or use of their
limbs. No going back. The nineties are looking like an innocent decade, and who would have thought that at the time?
Now we breathe a different air. He bought Fred Halliday's
book and read in the opening pages what looked like a conclusion and a curse: the New York attacks precipitated a
global crisis that would, if we were lucky, take a hundred

years to resolve. *If we were lucky.* Henry's lifetime, and all of Theo's and Daisy's. And their children's lifetime too. A Hundred Years' War.

Inexpertly, Theo has made the coffee at triple strength. But fatherly to the last, Henry drinks it down. Now he is surely committed to the day.

Theo says, 'You didn't see what airline it was?'

'No. Too far away, too dark.'

'Just that Chas is due in from New York this morning.'

He is New Blue Rider's sax player, a gleaming giant of a lad from St Kitts, in New York for a week's master class, nominally supervised by Branford Marsalis. These kids have the instincts, the sense of entitlement proper to an elite. Ry Cooder heard Theo play slide guitar in Oakland. Taped to a mirror in Theo's bedroom is a beer coaster with a friendly salute from the maestro. If you put your face up close you can make out in loopy blue biro, under a beer stain, a signature and, Keep it going Kid!

'I wouldn't worry. The red-eyes don't start coming in until half five.'

'Yeah, I suppose.' He swigs on the water bottle. 'You think it's jihadists . . . ?'

Perowne is feeling dizzy, pleasantly so. Everything he looks at, including his son's face, is receding from him without growing smaller. He hasn't heard Theo use this word before. Is it the right word? It sounds harmless, even quaint, rendered in his light tenor. This deepening of the boyish treble is an advance Henry still can't entirely take for granted, even though it's five years old. On Theo's lips – he takes the trouble to do something fancy with the 'j' – the Arabic word sounds as innocuous as some stringed Moroccan instrument the band might take up and electrify. In the ideal Islamic state, under strict Shari'a law, there'll be room for surgeons. Blues guitarists will be found other employment. But perhaps no one is demanding such a state. Nothing is demanded. Only hatred is registered, the purity of nihilism. As a

Londoner, you could grow nostalgic for the IRA. Even as your legs left your body, you might care to remember the cause was a united Ireland. Now that's coming anyway, according to the Reverend Ian Paisley, through the power of the perambulator. Another crisis fading into the scrapbooks, after a mere thirty years. But that's not quite right. Radical Islamists aren't really nihilists – they want the perfect society on earth, which is Islam. They belong in a doomed tradition about which Perowne takes the conventional view – the pursuit of utopia ends up licensing every form of excess, all ruthless means of its realisation. If everyone is sure to end up happy for ever, what crime can it be to slaughter a million or two now?

'I don't know what I think,' Henry says. 'It's too late to think. Let's wait for the news.'

Theo looks relieved. In his obliging way, he's prepared to debate the issues with his father, if that's what is required. But at four twenty in the morning he's happier saying little. So they wait in unstrained silence for several minutes. In the past months they have sat across this table and touched on all the issues. They've never talked so much before. Where's the adolescent rage, the door-slamming, the muted fury that's supposed to be Theo's rite of passage? Is all that feeling sunk in the blues? They discussed Iraq of course, America and power, European distrust, Islam – its suffering and self-pity, Israel and Palestine, dictators, democracy – and then the boys' stuff: weapons of mass destruction, nuclear fuel rods, satellite photography, lasers, nanotechnology. At the kitchen table, this is the early-twenty-first-century menu, the specials of the day. On a recent Sunday evening Theo came up with an aphorism: the bigger you think, the crappier it looks. Asked to explain he said, 'When we go on about the big things, the political situation, global warming, world poverty, it all looks really terrible, with nothing getting better, nothing to look forward to. But when I think small, closer in – you know, a girl I've just met, or this song we're going to do with Chas, or snowboarding next month, then it looks great. So this is going to be my motto – think small.'

Remembering this now, with still some minutes to go before the news, Henry says, 'How was the gig?'

'We did this set of really basic, headbanging stuff, nearly all Jimmy Reed numbers. You know, like this . . .' He sings with parodic emphasis a little boogie bass figure, his left hand clenching and unclenching, unconsciously shaping the chords. 'They went wild for it. Wouldn't let us do anything else. Bit depressing really, because it's not what we're about at all.' But he's smiling broadly at the memory.

It's time for the news. Once again, the radio pulses, the synthesised bleeps, the sleepless anchor and his dependable jaw. And there it is, made real at last, the plane, askew on the runway, apparently intact, surrounded by firefighters still spraying foam, soldiers, police, flashing lights, and ambulances backed up and ready. Before the story, irrelevant praise for the rapid response times of the emergency services. Only then is it explained. It's a cargo plane, a Russian Tupolev on a run from Riga to Birmingham. As it passed well to the east of London a fire broke out in one of the engines. The crew radioed for permission to land, and tried to shut down the fuel supply to the burning engine. They turned west along the Thames and were guided into Heathrow and made a decent landing. Neither of the two-man crew is hurt. The cargo is not specified, but a part of it, thought to be mostly mail, is destroyed. Then, still in second place, the anti-war protests only hours away. Hans Blix, yesterday's man, is third.

Schrödinger's dead cat is alive after all.

Theo picks up his jacket from the floor and stands. His manner is wry.

'So, not an attack on our whole way of life then.'

'A good result,' Henry agrees.

He would like to embrace his son, not only out of relief, but because it occurs to him that Theo has become such a likeable adult. Leaving school did the trick after all – boldly stepping where his parents didn't dare, out of formal education, taking charge of his life. But these days he and Theo have to be apart for at least a week before they allow themselves to embrace. He was always a physical child – even at thirteen he sometimes took his father's hand in the street. No way back to that. Only Daisy holds out the chance of a bedtime kiss when she's home.

As Theo crosses the kitchen, his father says, 'So you'll be on the march today?'

'Sort of. In spirit. I've got to get this song ready.'

'Sleep well then,' Henry says.

'Yeah. And you.'

On his way out the door Theo says, 'Night then,' and seconds later, when he's a little way up the stairs he calls back, 'See you in the morning,' and from the top of the stairs, tentatively, on a rising question note, 'Night?' To each call Henry responds, and waits for the next. These are Theo's characteristic slow fades, the three or four or even five goes he has at making his farewells, the superstition that he should have the last word. The held hand slowly slipping away.

Perowne has a theory that coffee can have a paradoxical effect, and it seems so now as he moves heavily about the kitchen turning off the lights; not only his broken night, but the whole week, and the weeks before bearing down on him. He feels feeble in his knees, in the quadriceps, as he goes up the stairs, making use of the handrail. This is how it will be in his seventies. He crosses the hallway, soothed by the cool touch of the smooth stone flags under his bare feet. On his way to the main stairs, he pauses by the double front doors. They give straight on to the pavement, on to the street that leads into the square, and in his exhaustion they suddenly loom before him strangely with their accretions – three stout Banham locks, two black iron bolts as old as the house, two tempered steel security chains, a spyhole with a brass cover, the box of electronics that works the Entryphone system, the red panic button, the alarm pad with its softly gleaming digits. Such defences, such mundane embattlement: beware of the city's poor, the drug-addicted, the downright bad.

In darkness again, standing by his side of the bed, he lets the dressing gown drop around his feet and blindly feels his way between the cold covers towards his wife. She's lying on her left side, facing away from him, with her knees still drawn up. He settles himself around her familiar shape, puts his arm about her waist and draws closer to her. As he kisses the nape of her neck she speaks from the recesses of sleep – the tone is welcoming, gratified, but her single indistinct word, like a weight too heavy to lift, doesn't move from her tongue. He feels her body warmth through the silk of her pyjamas spread across his chest and groin. Walking up three flights of stairs has revived him, his eyes are wide open in the dark; the exertion, his minimally raised blood pressure, is causing local excitement on his retina, so that ghostly swarms of purple and iridescent green are migrating across his view of a boundless steppe, then rolling in on themselves to become bolts of cloth, swathes of swagged velvet, drawing back like theatre curtains on new scenes, new thoughts. He doesn't want any thoughts at all, but now he's alert. His workless day lies ahead of him, a track across the steppe; after his squash game, which insomnia is already losing for him, he must visit his mother. Her face as it is now eludes him. He sees instead the county champion swimmer of forty years ago – he's remembering from photographs – that floral rubber cap that gave her the appearance of an eager seal. He was proud of her even as she tormented his childhood, dragging him on winter evenings to loud municipal pools on whose concrete changing-room floors discarded sticking plasters with their pink and purplish stains stewed in lukewarm puddles. She made him follow her into sinister green lakes and the grey North Sea before season. It was another element, she used to say, as if it were an explanation or an enticement. Another element was precisely what he objected to lowering his skinny freckled frame into. It was the division between the elements that hurt most, the unfriendly surface, rising in a bitter cutting edge up his sunken goosefleshed belly as he advanced on tiptoe, to please her, into the unclear waters of the Essex coast in early June. He could never throw himself in, the way she did, the way she wanted him to. Submersion in another element, every day, making every day special, was what she wanted and thought he should have. Well, he was fine with that now, as long as the other element wasn't cold water.

The bedroom air is fresh in his nostrils, he's half-aroused sexually as he moves closer to Rosalind. He can hear the first stirring of steady traffic on the Euston Road, like a breeze moving through a forest of firs. People who have to be at work by six on a Saturday. The thought of them doesn't make him feel sleepy, as it often does. He thinks of sex. If the world was configured precisely to his needs, he would be making love to Rosalind now, without preliminaries, to a very willing Rosalind, and afterwards falling in a clear-headed swoon towards sleep. But even despotic kings, even the ancient gods, couldn't always dream the world to their convenience. It's only children, in fact, only infants who feel a wish and its fulfilment as one; perhaps this is what gives tyrants their childish air. They reach back for what they can't have. When they meet frustration, the man-slaying tantrum is never far away. Saddam, for example, doesn't simply look like a heavy-jowled brute. He gives the impression of an overgrown, disappointed boy with a pudgy hangdog look, and dark eyes a little baffled by all that he still can't ordain. Absolute power and its pleasures are just beyond reach and keep receding. He knows that another fawning general dispatched to the torture rooms, another bullet in the head of a relative won't deliver the satisfaction it once did.

Perowne shifts position and nuzzles the back of Rosalind's head, inhaling the faint tang of perfumed soap mingled with the scent of warm skin and shampooed hair. What a stroke of luck, that the woman he loves is also his wife. But how quickly he's drifted from the erotic to Saddam – who belongs in a mess, a stew of many ingredients, of foreboding and pre-occupation. Sleepless in the early hours, you make a nest out of your own fears – there must have been survival advantage in dreaming up bad outcomes and scheming to avoid them. This trick of dark imagining is one legacy of natural selection in a dangerous world. This past hour he's been in a state of wild unreason, in a folly of overinterpretation. It doesn't console him that anyone in these times, standing at the window in his place, might have leaped to the same conclusions. Misunderstanding is general all over the world. How can we trust ourselves? He sees now the details he half-ignored in order to nourish his fears: that the plane was not being driven into a public building, that it was making a reg-ular, controlled descent, that it was on a well-used flight path – none of this fitted the general unease. He told himself there were two possible outcomes – the cat dead or alive. But he'd already voted for the dead, when he should have sensed it straight away – a simple accident in the making. Not an attack on our whole way of life then.

Half aware of him, Rosalind shifts position, fidgeting with a feeble turn of her shoulders so that her back is snug against his chest. She slides her foot along his shin and rests the arch of her foot on his toes. Aroused further, he feels his erection trapped against the small of her back and reaches down to free himself. Her breathing resumes its steady rhythm. Henry lies still, waiting for sleep. By contemporary standards, by any standards, it's perverse that he's never tired of making love to Rosalind, never been seriously tempted by the opportunities that have drifted his way through the generous logic of medical hierarchy. When he thinks of sex, he thinks of her. These eyes, these breasts, this tongue, this welcome. Who else could love him so know-ingly, with such warmth and teasing humour, or accumu-late so rich a past with him? In one lifetime it wouldn't be possible to find another woman with whom he can learn to be so free, whom he can please with such abandon and expertise. By some accident of character, it's familiarity that excites him more than sexual novelty. He suspects there's something numbed or deficient or timid in himself. Plenty of male friends sidle into adventures with younger women; now and then a solid marriage explodes in a firefight of recrimination. Perowne watches on with unease, fearing he lacks an element of the masculine life force, and a bold and healthy appetite for experience. Where's his curiosity? What's wrong with him? But there's nothing he can do about himself. He meets the occasional questioning glance of an attractive woman with a bland and level smile. This fidelity might look like virtue or doggedness, but it's neither of these because he exercises no real choice. This is what he has to have: possession, belonging, repetition.

It was a calamity – certainly an attack on *her* whole way of life – that brought Rosalind into his life. His first sight of her was from behind as he walked down the women's neurology ward one late afternoon in August. It was striking, this abundance of reddish-brown hair – almost to the waist – on such a small frame. For a moment he thought she was a large child. She was sitting on the edge of her bed, still fully dressed, talking to the registrar in a voice that strained to contain her terror. Perowne caught some of the history as he stopped by, and learned the rest later from her notes. Her health was generally fine, but she'd suffered headaches on and off during the past year. She touched her head to show them where. Her hands, he noticed, were very small. The face was a perfect oval, with large eyes of pale green. She had missed periods now and then, and sometimes a substance oozed from her breasts. Early that afternoon, while she was working in the law department library at University College, reading up on torts – she was specific on this point – her vision had started, as she said, to go wonky. Within minutes she could no longer see the numbers on her wristwatch. She left her books, grabbed her bag and went downstairs holding the banisters tightly. She was groping her way along the street to the casualty department when the day started to darken. She thought that there was an eclipse, and was surprised that no one was looking at the sky. Casualty had sent her straight here, and now she could barely see the stripes on the registrar's shirt. When he held up his fingers she could not count them.

'I don't want to go blind,' she said in a small, shocked voice. 'Please don't let me go blind.'

How was it possible that such large clear eyes could lose their sight? When Henry was sent off to find the consultant, who couldn't be raised on his pager, he felt an unprofessional pang of exclusion, a feeling that he could not afford to leave the registrar – a smooth predatory type – alone with such a rare creature. He, Perowne, wanted to do everything himself to save her, even though he had only a rudimentary sense of what her problem might be.

The consultant, Mr Whaley, was in an important meeting. He was a grand, shambling figure in three-piece pinstripe suit with a fob watch and a purple silk handkerchief poking from his top pocket. Perowne had often seen from a distance the distinctive pate gleaming in the sombre corridors. Whaley's booming theatrical voice was much parodied by the juniors. Perowne asked the secretary to go in and interrupt him. While he waited, he mentally rehearsed, keen to impress the great man with a succinct presentation. Whaley came out and listened with a scowl as Perowne started to tell him of a nineteen-year-old female's headache, her sudden onset of acute visual field impairment, and a history of amenorrhea and galactorrhea.

'For God's sake, lad. Irregular menstruation, nipple discharge!' He proclaimed this in his clipped, wartime news announcer's voice, but he was also moving down the corridor at speed with his jacket under his arm.

A chair was brought so that he could sit facing his patient. As he examined her eyes, his breathing appeared to slow.

Perowne watched the beautiful pale intelligent face tilted up at the consultant. He would have given much for her to be listening that way to him. Deprived of visual clues, she had to rely on every shifting nuance in Whaley's voice. The diagnosis was swift.

'Well, well, young lady. It seems you have a tumour on your pituitary gland, which is an organ the size of a pea in the centre of your brain. There's a haemorrhage around the tumour pressing on your optic nerves.'

There was a tall window behind the consultant's head, and Rosalind must have been able to discern his outline, for her eyes seemed to scan his face. She was silent for several seconds. Then she said wonderingly, 'I really could go blind.'

'Not if we get to work on you straight away.'

She nodded her assent. Whaley told the registrar to order a confirmatory CT scan for Rosalind on her way to the theatre. Then leaning forward and speaking to her softly, almost tenderly, he explained how the tumour was making prolactin, a hormone associated with pregnancy that caused periods to stop and breasts to make milk. He reassured her that her tumour would be benign and that he expected her to make a complete recovery. Everything depended on speed. After a cursory look at her breasts to confirm the diagnosis – Henry's view was obstructed – Mr Whaley stood and assumed a loud, public voice as he issued instructions. Then he strode away to reschedule his afternoon.

Henry escorted her from the radiology department to the operating suite. She lay on the trolley in anguish. He was a Senior House Officer of four months who couldn't even pretend to know much about the procedure that lay ahead. He waited with her in the corridor for the anaesthetist to arrive. Making small talk, he discovered she was a law student and had no immediate family nearby. Her father was in France, and her mother was dead. An adored aunt lived in Scotland, in the Western Isles. Rosalind was tearful, struggling against powerful emotions. She got control of her voice and, gesturing towards a fire extinguisher, told him that since this might be her last experience of the colour red, she wanted to remember it. Would he move her closer? Even now she could barely see. He said there was no question, the operation would be a success. But of course, he knew nothing, and his mouth was dry and his knees weak as he moved the trolley nearer to the wall. He had yet to learn clinical detachment. This may have been the time, rather than later in the ward, when he began to fall in love. The swing doors opened and they entered the theatre together, he walking at the side of the trolley while the porter pushed, and she worrying the tissue in her hand, gazing at the ceiling, as though hungry for last details.

The deterioration in her vision had come on suddenly, in the library, and now she was alone, facing momentous change. She steadied herself with deep, slow breaths. She was intent on the anaesthetist's face as he slipped a cannula into the back of her hand, and administered thiopentone. Then she was gone, and Perowne was hurrying away to the scrub room. He had been told to observe closely this radical procedure. Transsphenoidal hypophysectomy. One day he would perform it himself. Yes, even now, so many years later, it calmed him to think how brave she had been. And how benignly their lives had been shaped by this catastrophe.

What else did the young Henry Perowne do to help this beautiful woman suffering a pituitary apoplexy regain her sight? He helped slide her anaesthetised body from the trolley onto the operating table. Obeying the instructions of the registrar, he slipped the sterile covers into place on the handles of the operating lights. He watched as the three steel points of the head-clamp were fixed tightly onto her head. Again guided by the registrar, while Whaley was briefly out of the room, Henry scrubbed Rosalind's mouth with antiseptic soap, and noted the perfection of her teeth. Later, after Mr Whaley had made an incision in her upper gum, rolled her face away from the opening of the nasal passages, stripping the nasal

mucosa from the septum, Henry helped manoeuvre into position the massive operating microscope. There was no screen
to watch – video technology was new in those days, and had
yet to be installed in this theatre. But throughout the operation he was allowed frequent glimpses through the registrar's eyepiece. Henry watched as Whaley moved in on the
sphenoid sinus, passing through it after removing its front
wall. Then he skilfully chipped and drilled away at the bony
base of the pituitary fossa and revealed, in less than forty-
five minutes, the tightly swollen purplish gland within.

Perowne studied closely the decisive jab of the surgical
blade and saw the surge of dark clot and ochre tumour the
consistency of porridge disappearing into the tip of Whaley's
sucker. At the sudden appearance of clear liquid – cerebral
spinal fluid – the surgeon decided to take an abdominal fat
graft to seal the leak. He made a small transverse incision
in Rosalind's lower abdomen, and with a pair of surgical
scissors removed a piece of subcutaneous fat which he
dropped into a kidney dish. With great delicacy, the graft
was passed through the nose and set into the remains of
the sphenoid sinus, and held in place with nasal packs.

The elegance of the whole procedure seemed to embody
a brilliant contradiction: the remedy was as simple as
plumbing, as elemental as a blocked drain – the optic nerves
were decompressed and the threat to Rosalind's vision vanished. And yet the making of a safe route into this remote
and buried place in the head was a feat of technical mastery and concentration. To go in right through the face,
remove the tumour through the nose, to deliver the patient
back into her life, without pain or infection, with her vision
restored was a miracle of human ingenuity. Almost a century of failure and partial success lay behind this one procedure, of other routes tried and rejected, and decades of
fresh invention to make it possible, including this microscope and the fibre optic lighting. The procedure was
humane and daring – the spirit of benevolence enlivened

by the boldness of a high-wire circus act. Until then, Perowne's intention to become a neurosurgeon had always been a little theoretical. He'd chosen brains because they were more interesting than bladders or knee joints. Now his ambition became a matter of deep desire. As the closing up began and the face, this particular, beautiful face, was reassembled without a single disfiguring mark, he felt excitement about the future and impatient to acquire the skills. He was falling in love with a life. He was also, of course, falling in love. The two were inseparable. In his elation he even had some love left over for the maestro himself, Mr Whaley, as he bent his massive form over his minute and exacting tasks, breathing noisily through his nostrils behind his mask. When he was sure that he had removed all the tumour and clot he strode off to see another patient. It was left to the predatory registrar to put together again Rosalind's beautiful features.

Was it improper of Henry, to try and position himself in the recovery room so that he would be the first person she saw as she came round? Did he really think that with her perceptions and mood cradled in a gentle swell of morphine, she would notice him and become enraptured? As it turned out, the busy anaesthetist and his team swept Perowne aside. He was told to go and make himself useful elsewhere. But he lingered, and was standing several feet behind her head as she began to stir. At least he saw her eyes open, and her face remain immobile as she struggled to remember her place in the story of her existence, and her wary, painful smile as she began to understand that her sight was returning. Not yet perfect, but in a matter of hours it would be.

Some days later he was genuinely useful, removing the stitches from inside her upper lip, and helping in the removal of the nasal packing. He stayed on after shifts to talk to her. She appeared an isolated figure, pale from the ordeal, propped up on her pillows, surrounded by fat law manuals, her hair in two heavy schoolgirlish braids. Her only visitors were the two studious girls she shared a flat with. Because it hurt to talk, she sipped water between sentences. She told him that three years ago, when she was sixteen, her mother died in a car accident, and that her father was the famous poet John Grammaticus, who lived in seclusion in a chateau near the Pyrenees. To jog Henry's memory, Rosalind helpfully mentioned 'Mount Fuji', the poem anthologised in all the school editions. But she didn't seem to mind so much that he'd never heard of it or the author. Nor did she care that Henry's background was less exotic – an unchanging suburban street in Perivale, an only child, with a father he didn't remember.

After their love affair finally began months later, past midnight, in the cabin of a ferry on a wintry crossing to Bilbao, she teased him about his 'long and brilliant campaign of seduction'. A masterpiece of stealth, she also called it. But pace and manner were set by her. Early on, he sensed how easy it would be to scare her away. Her isolation was not confined to the neurology ward. It was always there, a wariness curbing spontaneity, lowering the excitement levels. She kept the lid on her youth. She could be unsettled by a sudden proposal of a picnic in the country, the unannounced arrival of an old friend, some free tickets for the theatre that night. She might end up saying yes to all three, but the first response was always a turning away, a hidden frown. She felt safer in those days with her law books, in the knowable long-closed matter of Donoghue versus Stevenson. Such distrust of life was bound to extend to himself if he made an unusual move. There were two women to consider, and to earn the trust of the daughter he would have to know and like everything about the mother. This ghost would have to be courted too.

Marianne Grammaticus was not so much grieved for as continually addressed. She was a constant restraining presence, watching over her daughter, and watching with her. This was the secret of Rosalind's inwardness and caution.

The death was too senseless to be believed – a late-night drunk jumping traffic lights near Victoria Station – and three years on, at some level, Rosalind didn't accept it. She remained in silent contact with an imaginary intimate. She referred everything back to her mother whom she'd always first-named, even as a little girl. She also talked about her freely to Henry, mentioning her often in passing and fantasising about her reactions. Marianne would have loved that, Rosalind might say of a movie they had just seen and liked. Or: Marianne showed me how to make this onion soup, but I can never get it to taste as good as hers. Or referring to the Falklands invasion: the funny thing is, she wouldn't have been against this war. She simply hated Galtieri. Many weeks into their friendship – affectionate, physically restrained, it was really no more than that – Henry dared ask Rosalind what her mother would have made of him. She answered without hesitation, 'She would have adored you.' He took this to be significant, and later that night kissed her with unusual freedom. She was responsive enough, though hardly abandoned, and for almost a week found herself too busy in the evenings to see him. Solitude and work were less threatening to her inner world than kisses. He began to understand that he was in a competition. In the nature of things he was bound to win, but only if he moved at the old-fashioned pace of a slow loris.

In the ferry's swaying cabin, on a narrow bunk, the matter was finally settled. It was not easy for Rosalind. To love him she had to begin to relinquish her constant friend, her mother. In the morning, when she woke and remembered the line she had crossed, she cried – for joy as much as for sorrow, she kept trying unconvincingly to tell him. Happiness seemed like a betrayal of principle, but happiness was unavoidable.

They went on deck to watch the dawn over the port. It was a harsh and alien world. Squalls of rain came flying over low concrete customs buildings and were driven against the grey derricks by a bitter wind which moaned among the steel cables. On the dock, where vast puddles had formed, was the solitary figure of an elderly man manoeuvring a heavy rope onto a bollard. He wore a leather jacket over an open-necked shirt. In his mouth was an extinguished cigar. When he was finished, he walked slowly towards the customs shed, immune to the weather. They retreated from the cold and went back down the many stairways into the clammy depths of the ship and made love again in their narrow space, and afterwards lay still, listening to the ship's PA announce that foot passengers were to disembark immediately. Again, she was tearful, and told him that lately she could no longer quite hear the special quality of her mother's voice. It was to be a long goodbye. Many fine moments like this were to have their shadow. Even then, as they lay entwined, listening to the thumps and muffled calls of passengers filing by in the corridors, he understood the seriousness of what was beginning. Coming between Rosalind and her ghost he must assume responsibilities. They had entered into an unspoken contract. Starkly put, to make love to Rosalind was to marry her. In his place a reasonable man might have panicked with dignity, but the simplicity of the arrangement gave Henry Perowne nothing but delight.

Here she is, almost a quarter of a century later, beginning to stir in his arms, in sleep somehow aware that her alarm is about to sound. Sunrise – generally a rural event, in cities a mere abstraction – is still an hour and a half away. The city's appetite for Saturday work is robust. At six o'clock, the Euston Road is in full throat. Now occasional motorbikes soar above the ensemble, whining like busy wood saws. Also about this time come the first chorus of police sirens, rising and falling in Doppler shifts: it's no longer too early for bad deeds. Finally she rolls over to face him. This side of the human form exhales a communicative warmth. As they kiss he imagines the green eyes seeking out his own. This commonplace cycle of falling asleep and waking, in darkness, under private cover, with another creature, a pale soft tender mammal, putting faces together in a ritual of affection, briefly settled in the eternal necessities of warmth, comfort, safety, crossing limbs to draw nearer – a simple daily consolation, almost too obvious, easy to forget by daylight. Has a poet ever written it up? Not the single occasion, but its repetition through the years. He'll ask his daughter.

Rosalind says, 'I had the feeling you were up all night. In and out of bed.'

'I went downstairs at four and sat around with Theo.'

'Is he all right?'

'Hmm.'

This is not the time to tell her about the plane, especially now that its significance has faded. As for his episode of euphoria, he doesn't possess at this moment the inventiveness to portray it. Later. He'll do it later. She's waking just as he's sinking. And still his erection proceeds, as though by a series of inhalations, endlessly tightening. No breathing out. It may be exhaustion that's sensitising him. Or five days' neglect. All the same, there's something familiarly taut in the way she shrugs herself closer, toasting him with an excess of body heat. He himself is in no shape to take initiatives, preferring to count on his luck, on her needs. If it doesn't happen, so be it. Nothing will stop him from falling asleep.

She kisses his nose. 'I'll try and pick up my dad straight from work. Daisy's getting in from Paris at seven. Will you be here?'

'Mm.'

Sensuous, intellectual Daisy, small-boned, pale and correct. What other postgraduate aspiring poet wears short-skirted business suits and fresh white blouses, and rarely drinks and does her best work before 9 a.m.? His little girl, slipping away from him into efficient Parisian womanhood, is expecting her first volume of poems to be published in May. And not by some hand-cranked press, but a venerable

49

institution in Queen Square, right across from the hospital where he clipped his first aneurysm. Even her cantankerous grandfather, grandly intolerant of contemporary writing, sent from his chateau a barely legible letter that on deciphering turned out to be rapturous. Perowne, no judge of such things, and pleased for her, of course, has been pained by the love lyrics, by her knowing so much, or dreaming so vividly about the bodies of men he's never met. Who is this creep whose tumescence resembles an 'excited watering can' approaching a 'peculiar rose'? Or the other one who sings in the shower 'like Caruso' as he shampoos 'both beards'? He has to check this indignation – hardly a literary response. He's been trying to shrug off the fatherly possessiveness and see the poems in their own terms. He already likes the less charged, but still sinister line in another poem that notes 'how each/ rose grew on a shark-infested stem'. The pale young girl with the roses hasn't been home for a long while. Her arrival is an oasis at the far end of the day.

'I love you.'

This isn't merely an affectionate token, for Rosalind reaches down and takes firm hold of him, and without letting go, turns and reaches behind her to disable the alarm clock, an awkward stretch that sends muscle tremors through the mattress.

'I'm glad you do.'

They kiss and she says, 'I've been half awake for a while, feeling you getting harder against my back.'

'And how was that?'

She whispers, 'It made me want you. But I don't have much time. I daren't be late.'

Such effortless seduction! His wish come true, not a finger lifted, the envy of gods and despots, Henry is raised from his stupor to take her in his arms and kiss her deeply. Yes, she's ready. And so his night ends, and this is where he begins his day, at 6 a.m., wondering whether all the essences of marital compromise have been flung carelessly into one moment: in darkness, in the missionary position, in a hurry, without preamble. But these are the externals. Now he is freed from thought, from memory, from the passing seconds and from the state of the world. Sex is a different medium, refracting time and sense, a biological hyperspace as remote from conscious existence as dreams, or as water is from air. As his mother used to say, another element; the day is changed, Henry, when you take a swim. And that day is bound to be marked out from all the rest.

Two

There is grandeur in this view of life. He wakes, or he thinks he does, to the sound of her hairdryer and a murmuring voice repeating a phrase, and later, after he's sunk again, he hears the solid clunk of her wardrobe door opening, the vast built-in wardrobe, one of a pair, with automatic lights and intricate interior of lacquered veneer and deep, scented recesses; later still, as she crosses and re-crosses the bedroom in her bare feet, the silky whisper of her petticoat, surely the black one with the raised tulip pattern he bought in Milan; then the business-like tap of her boot heels on the bathroom's marble floor as she goes about her final preparations in front of the mirror, applying perfume, brushing out her hair; and all the while, the plastic radio in the form of a leaping blue dolphin, attached by suckers to the mosaic wall in the shower, plays that same phrase, until he begins to sense a religious content as its significance swells – *there is grandeur in this view of life*, it says, over and again.

There is grandeur in this view of life. When he wakes properly two hours later she's gone and the room is silent. There's a narrow column of light where a shutter stands ajar. The day looks fiercely white. He pushes the covers aside and lies on his back in her part of the bed, naked in the warmth of the central heating, waiting to place the phrase. Darwin of course, from last night's read in the bath, in the final paragraph of his great work Perowne has never actually read. Kindly, driven, infirm Charles in all his humility, bringing on the earthworms and planetary cycles to assist him with a farewell bow. To soften the message, he also summoned up a Creator in later editions, but his heart was never really in it. Those five hundred pages deserved only one conclusion: endless and beautiful forms of life, such as you see in a common hedgerow, including exalted beings like ourselves, arose from physical laws, from war of nature, famine and death. This is the grandeur. And a bracing kind of consolation in the brief privilege of consciousness.

Once, on a walk by a river – Eskdale in low reddish sunlight, with a dusting of snow – his daughter quoted to him an opening verse by her favourite poet. Apparently, not many young women loved Philip Larkin the way she did. 'If I were called in/ To construct a religion/ I should make use of water.' She said she liked that laconic 'called in' – as if he would be, as if anyone ever is. They stopped to drink coffee from a flask, and Perowne, tracing a line of lichen with a finger, said that if he ever got the call, he'd make use of evolution. What better creation myth? An unimaginable sweep of time, numberless generations spawning by infinitesimal steps complex living beauty out of inert matter, driven on by the blind furies of random mutation, natural selection and environmental change, with the tragedy of forms continually dying, and lately the wonder of minds emerging and with them morality, love, art, cities – and the unprecedented bonus of this story happening to be demonstrably true.

At the end of this not entirely facetious recitation – they were standing on a stone bridge at the junction of two streams – Daisy laughed and put down her cup to applaud. 'Now that's genuine old-time religion, when you say it happens to be demonstrably true.'

He's missed her these past months and soon she'll be here. Amazingly for a Saturday, Theo has promised to stick around this evening, at least until eleven. Perowne's plan is to cook a fish stew. A visit to the fishmonger's is one of the simpler tasks ahead: monkfish, clams, mussels, unpeeled prawns. It's this practical daylight list, these salty items, that make him leave the bed at last and walk into the bathroom. There's a view that it's shameful for a man to sit to urinate because that's what women do. Relax! He sits, feeling the last scraps of sleep dissolve as his stream plays against the bowl. He's trying to locate a quite different source of shame, or guilt, or of something far milder, like the memory of some embarrassment or foolishness. It passed through his thoughts only minutes ago, and now what remains is the feeling without its rationale. A sense of having behaved or spoken laughably. Of having been a fool. Without the memory of it, he can't talk himself out of it. But who cares? These diaphanous films of sleep are still slowing him down – he imagines them resembling the arachnoid, that gossamer covering of the brain through which he routinely cuts. The grandeur. He must have hallucinated the phrase out of the hairdryer's drone, and confused it with the radio news. The luxury of being half asleep, exploring the fringes of psychosis in safety. But when he trod the air to the window last night he was fully awake. He's even more certain of that now.

He rises and flushes his waste. At least one molecule of it will fall on him one day as rain, according to a ridiculous article in a magazine lying around in the operating suite coffee room. The numbers say so, but statistical probabilities aren't the same as truths. *We'll meet again, don't know where, don't know when.* Humming this wartime tune, he crosses the wide green-and-white marble floor to his basin to shave. He feels incomplete without this morning rite, even on a day off. He ought to learn from Theo how to let go. But Henry likes the wooden bowl, the badger brush, the extravagantly disposable triple-bladed razor, with cleverly arched and ridged jungle-green handle – drawing this industrial gem over familiar flesh sharpens his thoughts. He should look out what William James wrote on forgetting a word or name; a tantalising, empty shape remains, almost but not quite defining the idea it once contained. Even as you struggle against the numbness of poor recall, you know precisely what the forgotten thing is not. James had the knack of fixing on the surprising commonplace – and in Perowne's humble view, wrote a better-honed prose than the fussy brother who would rather run round a thing a dozen different ways than call it by its name. Daisy, the arbiter of his literary education, would never agree. She wrote a long undergraduate essay on Henry James's late novels and can quote a passage from *The Golden Bowl*. She also knows dozens of poems by heart which she learned in her early teens, a means of earning pocket money from her grandfather. Her training was so different from her father's. No wonder they like their disputes. What Daisy knows! At her prompting, he tried the one about the little girl suffering from her parents' vile divorce. A promising subject, but poor Maisie soon vanished behind a cloud of words, and at page forty-eight Perowne, who can be on his feet seven hours for a difficult procedure, who has his name down for the London Marathon, fell away, exhausted. Even the tale of his daughter's namesake baffled him. What's an adult to conclude or feel about Daisy Miller's predictable decline? That the world can be unkind? It's not enough. He stoops to the tap to rinse his face. Perhaps he's becoming, in this one respect at least, like Darwin in later years who found Shakespeare dull to the point of nausea. Perowne is counting on Daisy to refine his sensibilities.

Fully awake at last, he returns to the bedroom, suddenly impatient to be dressed and free of the various entanglements of the room, of sleep and insomnia and overheated thinking, and even of sex. The rumpled bed with its ruined, porno-graphic look embodies all these elements. It's clarifying to be without desire. Still naked, he makes a quick pass at smoothing out the covers, picks up some pillows from the floor and tosses them towards the headboard, and goes to the dressing room, to the corner where he stores his sports gear. These are the small pleasures at the start of a Saturday morning – the promise of coffee, and this faded squash kit. Daisy, a neat dresser, fondly calls it his scarecrow outfit. The blue shorts are bleached by patches of sweat that won't wash out. Over a grey T-shirt he puts on an old cashmere jumper with moth-holes across the chest. Over the shorts, a track-suit bottom, fastened with chandler's cord at the waist. The white socks of prickly stretch towelling with yellow and pink bands at the top have something of the nursery about them. Unboxing them releases a homely aroma of the laundry. The squash shoes have a sharp smell, blending the synthetic with the animal, that reminds him of the court, the clean white walls and red lines, the unarguable rules of gladiatorial combat, and the score.

It's pointless pretending not to care about the score. He lost last week's game against Jay Strauss, but as he crosses the room with cushioned, springy stride Henry feels he'll win today. He's reminded of how he glided across this same stretch of floor in the night, and as he opens the same shutters the half-remembered foolishness almost comes back to him. But it's instantly dispersed by the flood of low winter sunlight, and by the sudden interest of what's happening in the square.

At first sight they look like two girls in their late teens, slight and with pale delicate faces, and underdressed for February. They could be sisters, standing by the railings of the central gardens, oblivious to passers-by, lost to a family drama of their own. Then Perowne decides that the figure facing him is a boy. It's difficult to tell because he wears a cycle helmet from under which thick brown hair curls. Perowne is persuaded by the posture, the way the feet are planted well apart, the thickness of the wrist as he places a hand on the girl's shoulder. She shrugs him off. She's agitated and crying, and undecided in her movements – she raises her hands to cover her face, but when the boy moves closer to draw her towards him, she lands ineffectual blows on his chest, like an old-fashioned Hollywood heroine. She turns from him, but doesn't walk away. Perowne thinks he sees in her face a reminder of his daughter's delicate oval, the little nose and elfin chin. That connection made, he watches more closely. She wants the boy, she hates him. His look is feral, sharpened by hunger. Is it for her? He's not letting her go and all the time he's talking, coaxing, wheedling, attempting to persuade or mollify her. Repeatedly, her left hand wanders behind her back, to dig under her T-shirt and scratch hard. She does this compulsively, even as she's crying and half-heartedly shoving the boy away. Amphetamine-driven formication – the phantom ants crawling through her arteries and veins, the itch that can never be reached. Or an exogenous opioid-induced histamine reaction, common among new users. The pallor and emotional extravagance are telling. These are addicts, surely. A missed score rather than a family matter is behind her distress and the boy's futile comforting.

People often drift into the square to act out their dramas. Clearly, a street won't do. Passions need room, the attentive spaciousness of a theatre. On another scale, Perowne considers, drawn now by sunlight and a fresh day into his usual preoccupation, this could be the attraction of the Iraqi desert – the flat and supposedly empty landscape approximating a strategist's map on which fury of industrial proportions can be let loose. A desert, it is said, is a military planner's dream. A city square is the private equivalent. Last Sunday there was a boy striding up and down the square for two hours, shouting into his phone, his voice fading each time he marched off south, and swelling in the afternoon gloom as he returned. Next morning, on his way to work, Perowne saw a woman snatch her husband's phone and shatter it on the pavement. In the same month there was a fellow in a dark suit on his knees, umbrella at his side, apparently with his head stuck between the garden railings. In fact he was clinging to the bars and sobbing. The old lady with the whisky would never get away with her shouts and squawks in the narrowness of a street, not for three hours at a stretch. The square's public aspect grants privacy to these intimate dramas. Couples come to talk or cry quietly on the benches. Emerging from small rooms in council flats or terraced houses, and from cramped side streets, into a wider view of generous sky and a tall stand of plane trees on the green, of space and growth, people remember their essential needs and how they're not being met.

But there's no shortage of happiness either. Perowne can see it now, on the far side, by the Indian hostel, as he goes to open the other shutters and the bedroom fills with light. There is real excitement in that part of the square. Two Asian lads in tracksuits – he recognises them from the newsagent's in Warren Street – are unloading a van onto a handcart on the pavement. Placards are already piled high, and folded banners and cards of lapel buttons and whistles, football rattles and trumpets, funny hats and rubber masks of politicians – Bush and Blair in wobbling stacks, the topmost faces gazing blankly skywards, ghastly white in the sunshine. Gower Street a few blocks away to the east is one of the starting points of the march, and some of the overspill has reached back here. A small crowd round the cart wants to buy stuff before the vendors are ready. The general cheerfulness Perowne finds baffling. There are whole families, one with four children in various sizes of bright red coats, clearly under instruction to hold hands; and students, and a coachful of greying ladies in quilted anoraks and stout shoes. The Women's Institute perhaps. One of the tracksuited men holds up his hands in mock surrender, his friend standing on the back of the van makes his first sale. Displaced by the commotion, the square's pigeons take off and wheel and dip in formation. Waiting for them below on a bench by a litter bin is a trembling red-faced man wrapped in a grey blanket with a sliced loaf ready on his lap. Among the Perowne children, 'pigeon feeder' is a term synonymous with mentally deficient. Behind the throng round the cart is a bunch of kids in leather jackets and cropped hair, looking on with tolerant smiles. They have already unfurled their banner which proclaims simply, Peace not Slogans!!

The scene has an air of innocence and English dottiness. Perowne, dressed for combat on court, imagines himself as Saddam, surveying the crowd with satisfaction from some Baghdad ministry balcony: the good-hearted electorates of the Western democracies will never allow their governments to attack his country. But he's wrong. The one thing Perowne thinks he knows about this war is that it's going to happen. With or without the UN. The troops are in place, they'll have to fight. Ever since he treated an Iraqi professor of ancient history for an aneurysm, saw his torture scars and listened to his stories, Perowne has had ambivalent or confused and shifting ideas about this coming invasion. Miri Taleb is in his late sixties, a man of slight, almost girlish build, with a nervous laugh, a whinnying giggle that could have something to do with his time in prison. He did his Ph.D. at University College London and speaks excellent English. His field is Sumerian civilisation, and for more than twenty years he taught at the university in Baghdad and was involved in various archaeological surveys in the Euphrates area. His arrest came one winter's afternoon in 1994, outside a lecture room where he was about to teach. His students were waiting for him inside and did not see what happened. Three men showed their security accreditation, and asked him to go with them to their car. There they handcuffed him, and it was at that point that his torture began. The cuffs were so tight that for sixteen hours, until they were removed, he could think of nothing else but the pain. Permanent damage was done to both shoulders. For the following ten months he was moved around central Iraq between various jails. He had no idea what these moves meant, and no means of letting his wife know he was still alive. Even on the day of his release, he didn't discover what the charges were against him.

Perowne listened in his office to the professor, and later talked to him in the ward after his operation – fortunately, a complete success. For a man approaching his seventieth birthday, Taleb has an unusual appearance – a childlike smooth skin and long eyelashes, and a carefully groomed black moustache – surely dyed. In Iraq he had no involvement or interest in politics, and declined to join the Ba'ath Party. That may have been the cause of his problems. Equally, it could have been the fact that one of his wife's cousins, long dead, was once a member of the Communist Party, or that another cousin had received a letter from Iran from a friend exiled because of his supposed Iranian descent; or that the husband of a niece had refused to return from a teaching job in Canada. Another possible reason was that the professor himself had travelled to Turkey to advise on archaeological digs. He was not particularly surprised by his arrest, and nor would his wife have been. They both knew, everyone knew, someone who'd been taken in, held for a while, tortured perhaps, and then released. People suddenly turned up at work again, and did not speak about their experiences, and no one dared ask – there were too many informers around, and inappropriate curiosity could get you arrested. Some came back in sealed coffins – it was strictly forbidden to open them. It was common to hear of friends and acquaintances making the rounds of the hospitals, police stations and government offices hoping for news of their relatives.

Miri spent his time in stinking, unventilated cells – six feet by ten with twenty-five men crammed inside. And who were these men? The professor giggled mirthlessly. Not the expected combination of common criminals mixed in with intellectuals. They were mostly very ordinary people, held for not showing a car licence plate, or because they got into an argument with a man who turned out to be a Party official, or because their children were coaxed at school into reporting their parents' unappreciative remarks at the dinner table about Saddam. Or because they refused to join the Party during one of the many recruitment drives. Another common crime was to have a family member accused of deserting from the army.

Also in the cells were security officers and policemen. The various security services existed in a state of nervous competition with each other, and agents had to work harder and harder to show how diligent they were. Whole branches of security could come under suspicion. The torture was routine – Miri and his companions heard the screaming from their cells, and waited to be called. Beatings, electrocution, anal rape, near-drowning, thrashing the soles of the feet. Everyone, from top officials to street sweepers, lived in a state of anxiety, constant fear. Henry saw the scars on Taleb's buttocks and thighs where he was beaten with what he thought was a branch of some kind of thorn bush. The men who beat him did so without hatred, only routine vigour – they were scared of their supervisor. And that man was frightened for his position, or his future liberty, because of an escape the year before.

'Everyone hates it,' Taleb told Perowne. 'You see, it's only terror that holds the nation together, the whole system runs on fear, and no one knows how to stop it. Now the Americans are coming, perhaps for bad reasons. But Saddam and the Ba'athists will go. And then, my doctor friend, I will buy you a meal in a good Iraqi restaurant in London.'

The teenage couple head off across the square. Resigned to, or eager for, whatever she's walking towards, she lets the boy put his arm around her shoulder and her head lolls against him. She's still digging away with a free hand, along her waistband and into the small of her back. That girl should be wearing a coat. Even from here he can see the pink trails made by her scratching. A tyrannical fashion compels her to bare her umbilicus, her midriff, to the February chill. The pruritus suggests that her tolerance of heroin is not yet well developed. She's new on the job. What she needs is an opioid antagonist like naloxone to reverse the effect. Henry has left the bedroom and has paused at the head of the stairs, facing the nineteenth-century French chandelier that hangs from the high ceiling, and wonders about going after her with a prescription; he is, after all, dressed for running. But she also needs a boyfriend who isn't a pusher. And a new life. He starts down the stairs, while above him the chandelier's glass pendants tinkle and chime to the vibrations of the Victoria line tube train far beneath the house slowing into Warren Street station. It troubles him to consider the powerful currents and fine-tuning that alter fates, the close and distant influences, the accidents of character and circumstance that cause one young woman in Paris to be packing her weekend bag with the bound proof of her first volume of poems before catching the train to a welcoming home in London, and another young woman of the same age to be led away by a wheedling boy to a moment's chemical bliss that will bind her as tightly to her misery as an opiate to its mu receptors.

The quality of silence in the house is thickened, Perowne can't help unscientifically thinking, by the fact of Theo deeply asleep on the third floor, face-down under the duvet of his double bed. Some oblivious hours lie ahead of him yet. When he wakes he'll listen to music fed through his hi-fi via the Internet, he'll shower, and talk on the phone. Hunger won't drive him from his room until the early afternoon when he'll come down to the kitchen and make it his own, placing more calls, playing CDs, drinking a pint or two of juice and messily concocting a salad or a bowl of yoghurt, dates, honey, fruit and chopped nuts. This fare seems to Henry to be at odds with the blues.

Arriving on the first floor, he pauses outside the library, the most imposing room in the house, momentarily drawn by the way sunshine, filtering through the tall gauzy oatmeal drapes, washes the room in a serious, brown and bookish light. The collection was put together by Marianne. Henry never imagined he would end up living in the sort of house that had a library. It's an ambition of his to spend whole weekends in there, stretched out on one of the Knole sofas, pot of coffee at his side, reading some world-rank masterpiece or other, perhaps in translation. He has no particular book in mind. He thinks it would be no bad thing to understand what's meant, what Daisy means, by literary genius. He's not sure he's ever experienced it at first hand, despite various attempts. He even half doubts its existence. But his free time is always fragmented, not only by errands and family obligations and sports, but by the restlessness that comes with these weekly islands of freedom. He doesn't want to spend his days off lying, or even sitting, down. Nor does he really want to be a spectator of other lives, of imaginary lives – even though these past hours he's put in an unusual number of minutes gazing from the bedroom window. And it interests him less to have the world reinvented; he wants it explained. The times are strange enough. Why make things up? He doesn't seem to have the dedication to read many books all the way through. Only at work is he single-minded; at leisure, he's too impatient. He's surprised by what people say they achieve in their spare time, putting in four or five hours a day in front of the TV to keep the national averages up. During a lull in a procedure last week – the micro-doppler failed and a replacement had to come from another theatre – Jay Strauss stood up from the monitors and dials of his anaesthetic machine and, stretching his arms and yawning, said he was awake in the small hours, finishing an eight-hundred-page novel by some new American prodigy. Perowne was impressed, and bothered – did he himself simply lack seriousness?

In fact, under Daisy's direction, Henry has read the whole of *Anna Karenina* and *Madame Bovary*, two acknowledged masterpieces. At the cost of slowing his mental processes and many hours of his valuable time, he committed himself to the shifting intricacies of these sophisticated fairy stories. What did he grasp, after all? That adultery is understandable but wrong, that nineteenth-century women had a hard time of it, that Moscow and the Russian countryside and provincial France were once just so. If, as Daisy said, the genius was in the detail, then he was unmoved. The details were apt and convincing enough, but surely not so very difficult to marshal if you were halfway observant and had the patience to write them all down. These books were the products of steady, workmanlike accumulation.

They had the virtue, at least, of representing a recognisable physical reality, which could not be said for the so-called magical realists she opted to study in her final year. What were these authors of reputation doing – grown men and women of the twentieth century – granting supernatural powers to their characters? He never made it all the way through a single one of those irksome confections. And written for adults, not children. In more than one, heroes and heroines were born with or sprouted wings – a symbol, in Daisy's term, of their liminality; naturally, learning to fly became a metaphor for bold aspiration. Others were granted a magical sense of smell, or tumbled unharmed out of high-flying aircraft. One visionary saw through a pub window his parents as they had been some weeks after his conception, discussing the possibility of aborting him.

A man who attempts to ease the miseries of failing minds by repairing brains is bound to respect the material world, its limits, and what it can sustain – consciousness, no less. It isn't an article of faith with him, he knows it for a quotidian fact, the mind is what the brain, mere matter, performs. If that's worthy of awe, it also deserves curiosity; the actual, not the magical, should be the challenge. This reading list persuaded Perowne that the supernatural was the recourse of an insufficient imagination, a dereliction of duty, a childish evasion of the difficulties and wonders of the real, of the demanding re-enactment of the plausible.

'No more magic midget drummers,' he pleaded with her by post, after setting out his tirade. 'Please, no more ghosts, angels, satans or metamorphoses. When anything can happen, nothing much matters. It's all kitsch to me.'

'You ninny,' she reproved him on a postcard, 'you Gradgrind. It's literature, not physics!'

They had never conducted one of their frequent arguments by post before. He wrote back: 'Tell that to your Flaubert and Tolstoy. Not a single winged human between them!'

She replied by return of post, 'Look at your Mme Bovary again' – there followed a set of page references. 'He was warning the world against people *just like you*,' – last three words heavily underscored.

So far, Daisy's reading lists have persuaded him that fiction is too humanly flawed, too sprawling and hit-and-miss to inspire uncomplicated wonder at the magnificence of human ingenuity, of the impossible dazzlingly achieved. Perhaps only music has such purity. Above all others he admires Bach, especially the keyboard music; yesterday he listened to two Partitas in the theatre while working on Andrea's astrocytoma. And then there are the usual suspects – Mozart, Beethoven, Schubert. His jazz idols, Evans, Davis, Coltrane. Cézanne, among various painters, certain cathedrals Henry has visited on holidays. Beyond the arts, his list of sublime achievement would include Einstein's General Theory, whose mathematics he briefly grasped in his early twenties. He should make that list, he decides as he descends the broad stone stairs to the ground floor, though he knows he never will. Work that you cannot begin to imagine achieving yourself, that displays a ruthless, nearly inhuman element of self-enclosed perfection – this is his idea of genius. This notion of Daisy's, that people can't 'live' without stories, is simply not true. He is living proof.

By the front door he picks up the post and the newspapers.

Walking down to the kitchen he reads the headlines. Blix telling the UN the Iraqis are beginning to cooperate. In response, the Prime Minister is expected to emphasise in a speech in Glasgow today the humanitarian reasons for war. In Perowne's view, the only case worth making. But the PM's late switch looks cynical. Henry is hoping that his own story, breaking at four thirty, might just have made the late editions in London. But there's nothing.

No one's been in the kitchen since he left it. On the table are his cup, Theo's empty mineral water bottle and, beside it, the remote control. It's still faintly surprising, this rigid fidelity of objects, sometimes reassuring, sometimes sinister. He takes the remote, turns the set on and pushes the mute button – the nine o'clock bulletin is several minutes away yet – and fills the kettle. What simple accretions have brought the humble kettle to this peak of refinement: jug-shaped for efficiency, plastic for safety, wide spout for ease of filling, and clunky little platform to pick up the power. He never complained about the old style – the sticking tin lid, the thick black feminine socket waiting to electrocute wet hands seemed in the nature of things. But someone had thought about this carefully, and now there's no going back. The world should take note: not everything is getting worse.

The news comes on while he's grinding the beans. The new anchor is an attractive dark-skinned woman whose plucked, widely arched eyebrows express surprise at the challenge of yet another new morning. First, pictures from a motorway bridge of scores of coaches bringing marchers into the city for what is expected to be the biggest display of public protest ever seen. Then a reporter down among an early gathering of demonstrators by the Embankment. All this happiness on display is suspect. Everyone is thrilled to be together out on the streets – people are hugging themselves, it seems, as well as each other. If they think – and they could be right – that continued torture and summary executions, ethnic cleansing and occasional genocide are preferable to an invasion, they should be sombre in their view. The airplane, Henry's airplane, is now second item. The same pictures, and only a few more details: an electrical fault is suspected to be the cause of the fire. Standing with some policemen, the two Russians – the pilot, a shrivelled fellow with oily hair, and his co-pilot, plump and oddly merry. They look suntanned, or perhaps they're from one of the southern republics. The fading life-chances of a disappointing news story – no villains, no deaths, no suspended outcome – are revived by a dose of manufactured controversy: an aviation expert has been found who's prepared to say that it was reckless to bring a burning plane in over a densely populated area when there were other options. A representative of the airport authority says there was no threat to Londoners. The government is yet to comment.

He turns the TV off, pulls up a stool and sets himself up with his coffee and the phone. Before his Saturday can begin, there's a follow-up call to make to the hospital. He's put through to intensive care and asks to speak to the nurse in charge. While someone fetches her he listens to the familiar background murmur, a porter's voice he recognises, a book or folder slapped down on a table.

Then he hears the expressionless tone of a busy woman say, 'ICU.'

'Deirdre? I thought Charles was on this weekend.'

'He's away with the flu, Mr Perowne.'

'How's Andrea?'

'GCS is fifteen, good oxygenation, not confused.'

'EVD?'

'Still draining at around five centimetres. I'm thinking of sending her back to the ward.'

'That's fine then,' Perowne said. 'Can you let the anaesthetist know that I'm happy for her to go.' He's about to hang up when he adds, 'Is she giving you any trouble?'

'Too overwhelmed by it all, Mr Perowne. We love her like this.'

He takes his keys and phone and garage remote control from a silver dish by the recipe books. His wallet is in an overcoat hanging in a room behind the kitchen, outside the wine vaults. His squash racket is upstairs on the ground floor, in a cupboard in the laundry. He puts on an old hiking fleece, and is about to set the burglar alarm when he remembers Theo inside. As he steps outside and turns from closing the door, he hears the squeal of seagulls come inland for the city's good pickings. The sun is low and only one half of the square – his half – is in full sunlight. He walks away from the square along blinding moist pavement, surprised by the freshness of the day. The air tastes almost clean. He has an impression of striding along a natural surface, along some coastal wilderness, on a smooth slab of basalt causeway he vaguely recalls from a childhood holiday. It must be the cry of the gulls bringing it back. He can remember the taste of spray off a turbulent blue-green sea, and as he reaches Warren Street he reminds himself that he mustn't forget the fishmonger's. Lifted by the coffee, and by movement at last, as well as the prospect of the game and the comfortable fit of the sheathed racket in his hand, he increases his pace.

The streets round here are usually empty at weekends, but up ahead, along the Euston Road, a big crowd is making its way east towards Gower Street, and in the road itself, crawling in the eastbound lanes, are the same nose-to-tail coaches he saw on the news. The passengers are pressed against the glass, longing to be out there with the rest. They've hung their banners from the windows, along with football scarves and the names of towns from the heart of England – Stratford, Gloucester, Evesham. From the impatient pavement crowds, some dry runs with the noisemakers – a trombone, a squeeze-ball car horn, a lambeg drum. There are ragged practice chants which at first he can't make out. Tumty

tumty tum. Don't attack Iraq. Placards not yet on duty are held at a slope, at rakish angles over shoulders. Not in My Name goes past a dozen times. Its cloying self-regard suggests a bright new world of protest, with the fussy consumers of shampoos and soft drinks demanding to feel good, or nice. Henry prefers the languid, Down With this Sort of Thing. A placard of one of the organising groups goes by – the British Association of Muslims. Henry remembers that outfit well. It explained recently in its newspaper that apostasy from Islam was an offence punishable by death. Behind comes a banner proclaiming the Swaffham Women's Choir, and then, Jews Against the War.

On Warren Street he turns right. Now his view is east, towards the Tottenham Court Road. Here's an even bigger crowd, swelled by hundreds disgorging from the tube station. Backlit by the low sun, silhouetted figures break away and merge into a darker mass, but it's still possible to see a makeshift bookstall and a hot-dog stand, cheekily set up right outside McDonald's on the corner. It's a surprise, the number of children there are, and babies in pushchairs. Despite his scepticism, Perowne in white-soled trainers, gripping his racket tighter, feels the seduction and excitement peculiar to such events; a crowd possessing the streets, tens of thousands of strangers converging with a single purpose conveying an intimation of revolutionary joy.

He might have been with them, in spirit at least, for nothing now will keep him from his game, if Professor Taleb hadn't needed an aneurysm clipped on his middle cerebral artery. In the months after those conversations, Perowne drifted into some compulsive reading up on the regime. He read about the inspirational example of Stalin, and the network of family and tribal loyalties that sustained Saddam, and the palaces handed out as rewards. Henry became acquainted with the sickly details of genocides in the north and south of the country, the ethnic cleansing, the vast system of informers, the bizarre tortures, and Saddam's taste for getting personally involved, and the strange punishments passed into law – the brandings and amputations. Naturally, Henry followed closely the accounts of measures taken against surgeons who refused to carry out these mutilations. He concluded that viciousness had rarely been more inventive or systematic or widespread. Miri was right, it really was a republic of fear. Henry read Makiya's famous book too. It seemed clear, Saddam's organising principle was terror.

Perowne knows that when a powerful imperium – Assyrian, Roman, American – makes war and claims just cause, history will not be impressed. He also worries that the invasion or the occupation will be a mess. The marchers could be right. And he acknowledges the accidental nature of opinions; if he hadn't met and admired the professor, he might have thought differently, less ambivalently, about the coming war. Opinions are a roll of the dice; by definition, none of the people now milling around Warren Street tube station happens to have been tortured by the regime, or knows and loves people who have, or even knows much about the place at all. It's likely most of them barely registered the massacres in Kurdish Iraq, or in the Shi'ite south, and now they find they care with a passion for Iraqi lives. They have good reasons for their views, among which are concerns for their own safety. Al-Qaeda, it's said, which loathes both godless Saddam and the Shi'ite opposition, will be provoked by an attack on Iraq into revenge on the soft cities of the West. Self-interest is a decent enough cause, but Perowne can't feel, as the marchers themselves probably can, that they have an exclusive hold on moral discernment.

The sandwich bars along the street are closed up for the weekend. Only the flute shop and newsagent are open. Outside the Rive Gauche *traiteur*, the owner is using a zinc bucket to sluice down the pavement, Parisian-style. Coming towards Perowne, his back to the crowds, is a pink-faced man of about his own age, in a baseball cap and yellow Day-Glo jacket, with a handcart, sweeping the gutter for the council. He seems oddly intent on making a good job, jabbing the corner of his broom hard into the angles of the kerb, chasing out the scraps. His vigour and thoroughness are uncomfortable to watch, a quiet indictment on a Saturday morning. What could be more futile than this underpaid urban scale housework when behind him, at the far end of the street, cartons and paper cups are spreading thickly under the feet of demonstrators gathered outside McDonald's on the corner. And beyond them, across the metropolis, a daily blizzard of litter. As the two men pass, their eyes meet briefly, neutrally. The whites of the sweeper's eyes are fringed with egg-yellow shading to red along the lids. For a vertiginous moment Henry feels himself bound to the other man, as though on a seesaw with him, pinned to an axis that could tip them into each other's life.

Perowne looks away and slows before turning into the mews where his car is garaged. How restful it must once have been, in another age, to be prosperous and believe that an all-knowing supernatural force had allotted people to their stations in life. And not see how the belief served your own prosperity – a form of anosognosia, a useful psychiatric term for a lack of awareness of one's own condition. Now we think we do see, how do things stand? After the ruinous experiments of the lately deceased century, after so much vile behaviour, so many deaths, a queasy agnosticism has settled around these matters of justice and redistributed wealth. No more big ideas. The world must improve, if at all, by tiny steps. People mostly take an existential view – having to sweep the streets for a living looks like simple bad luck. It's not a visionary age. The streets need to be clean. Let the unlucky enlist.

He walks down a faint incline of greasy cobbles to where the owners of houses like his own once kept their horses. Now, those who can afford it cosset their cars here with off-street parking. Attached to his key ring is an infrared button which he presses to raise a clattering steel shutter. It's revealed in mechanical jerks, the long nose and shining eyes at the stable door, chafing to be free. A silver Mercedes S500 with cream upholstery – and he's no longer embarrassed by it. He doesn't even love it – it's simply a sensual part of what he regards as his overgenerous share of the world's goods. If he didn't own it, he tries to tell himself, someone else would. He hasn't driven it in a week, but in the gloom of the dry dustless garage the machine breathes an animal warmth of its own. He opens the door and sits in. He likes driving it wearing his threadbare sports clothes. On the front passenger seat is an old copy of the *Journal of Neurosurgery* which carries a report of his on a convention in Rome. He tosses his squash racket on top of it. It's Theo who disapproves most, saying it's a doctor's car, as if this were the final word in condemnation. Daisy, on the other hand, said she thought that Harold Pinter owned something like it, which made it all fine with her. Rosalind encouraged him to buy it. She thinks his life is too guiltily austere, and never buying clothes or good wine or a single painting is a touch pretentious. Still living like a postgraduate student. It was time for him to fill out.

For months he drove it apologetically, rarely at speed, reluctant to overtake, waving on right-turning traffic, punctilious in permitting cheaper cars their road space. He was cured at last by a fishing trip to north-west Scotland with Jay Strauss. Seduced by the open road and Jay's exultant celebration of 'Lutheran genius', Henry finally accepted himself as the owner, the master, of his vehicle. In fact, he's always quietly considered himself a good driver: as in the theatre, firm, precise, defensive to the correct degree. He and Jay fished the streams and lochans around Torridon for brown trout. One wet afternoon, glancing over his shoulder while casting, Henry saw his car a hundred yards away, parked at an angle on a rise of the track, picked out in soft light against a backdrop of birch, flowering heather and thunderous black sky – the realisation of an ad man's vision – and felt for the first time a gentle, swooning joy of possession. It is, of course, possible, permissible, to love an inanimate object. But this moment was the peak of the affair; since then his feelings have settled into mild, occasional pleasure. The car gives him vague satisfaction when he's driving it; the rest of the time it rarely crosses his mind. As its makers intended and promised, it's become part of him.

But certain small things still stir him particularly, like the way the car idles without vibration; the rev counter alone confirms the engine is turning. He switches on the radio, which is playing sustained, respectful applause as he eases out of the garage, lets the steel shutter drop behind him, and goes slowly up the mews and turns left, back into Warren Street. His squash club is in Huntley Street in a converted nurses' home – no distance at all, but he's driving because he has errands to do afterwards. Shamelessly, he always enjoys the city from inside his car where the air is filtered and hi-fi music confers pathos on the humblest details – a Schubert trio is dignifying the narrow street he's slipping down now. He's heading a couple of blocks south in order to loop eastwards across the Tottenham Court Road. Cleveland Street used to be known for garment sweatshops and prostitutes. Now it has Greek, Turkish and Italian restaurants – the local sort that never get mentioned in the guides – with terraces where people eat out in summer. There's a man who repairs old computers, a fabric shop, a cobbler's, and further down, a wig emporium, much visited by transvestites. This is the fair embodiment of an inner city byway – diverse, self-confident, obscure. And it's at this point he remembers the source of his vague sense of shame or embarrassment: his readiness to be persuaded that the world has changed beyond recall, that harmless streets like this and the tolerant life they embody can be destroyed by the new enemy – well-organised, tentacular, full of hatred and focused zeal. How foolishly apocalyptic those apprehensions seem by daylight, when the self-evident fact of the streets and the people on them are their own justification, their own insurance. The world has not fundamentally changed. Talk of a hundred-year crisis is indulgence. There are always crises, and Islamic terrorism will settle into place, alongside recent wars, climate change, the politics of international trade, land and fresh water shortages, hunger, poverty and the rest.

He listens to the Schubert sweetly fade and swell. The street is fine, and the city, grand achievement of the living and all the dead who've ever lived here, is fine too, and robust. It won't easily allow itself to be destroyed. It's too good to let go. Life in it has steadily improved over the centuries for most people, despite the junkies and beggars now. The air is better, and salmon are leaping in the Thames, and otters are returning. At every level, material, medical, intellectual, sensual, for most people it has improved. The teachers who educated Daisy at university thought the idea of progress old-fashioned and ridiculous. In indignation, Perowne grips the wheel tighter in his right hand. He remembers some lines by Medawar, a man he admires: 'To deride the hopes of progress is the ultimate fatuity, the last word in poverty of spirit and meanness of mind.' Yes, he's a fool to be taken in by that hundred-year claim. In Daisy's final term he went to an open day at her college. The young lecturers there like to dramatise modern life as a sequence of calamities. It's their style, their way of being clever. It wouldn't be cool or professional to count the eradication of smallpox as part of the modern condition. Or the recent spread of democracies. In the evening one of them gave a lecture on the prospects for our consumerist and technological civilisation: not good. But if the present dispensation is wiped out now, the future will look back on us as gods, certainly in this city, lucky gods blessed by supermarket cornucopias, torrents of accessible information, warm clothes that weigh nothing, extended lifespans, wondrous machines. This is an age of wondrous machines. Portable telephones barely bigger than your ear.

Whole music libraries held in an object the size of a child's hand. Cameras that can beam their snapshots around the world. Effortlessly, he ordered up the contraption he's riding in now through a device on his desk via the Internet. The computer-guided stereotactic array he used yesterday has transformed the way he does biopsies. Digitalised entertainment binds that Chinese couple walking hand in hand, listening through a Y-socket to their personal stereo. And she's almost skipping, that stringy girl in a shell suit behind a three-wheel all-terrain pushchair. In fact, everyone he's passing now along this pleasantly down-at-heel street looks happy enough, at least as content as he is. But for the professors in the academy, for the humanities generally, misery is more amenable to analysis: happiness is a harder nut to crack.

In a spirit of aggressive celebration of the times, Perowne swings the Mercedes east into Maple Street. His wellbeing appears to need spectral entities to oppose it, figures of his own invention whom he can defeat. He's sometimes like this before a game. He doesn't particularly like himself in this frame, but the second-by-second wash of his thoughts is only partially his to control – the drift, the white noise of solitary thought is driven by his emotional state. Perhaps he isn't really happy at all, he's psyching himself up. He's passing by the building at the foot of the Post Office Tower – less ugly these days with its aluminium entrance, blue cladding and geometric masses of windows and ventilation grilles looking like a Mondrian. But further along, where Fitzroy becomes Charlotte Street, the neighbourhood is packed with penny-pinching office blocks and student accommodation – ill-fitting windows, low ambition, not lasting well. In the rain, and in the right temper, you can imagine yourself back in Communist Warsaw. Only when enough of them have been torn down, will it be possible to start loving them.

Henry is now parallel to and two blocks south of Warren

Street. He's still bothered by his peculiar state of mind, this happiness cut with aggression. As he approaches the Tottenham Court Road, he begins a familiar routine, listing the recent events that may have shaped his mood. That he and Rosalind made love, that it's Saturday morning, that this is his car, that no one died in the plane and there's a game ahead and the Chapman girl and his other patients from yesterday are stable, that Daisy is coming – all this is to the good. And on the other hand? On the other hand, he's touching the brake. There's a motorbike policeman in a yellow jacket, in the middle of the Tottenham Court Road with his machine on its stand, holding out an arm to stop him. Of course, the road is closed for the march. He should have known. But still Perowne keeps coming, slowing all the while, as if by pretending not to know, he can be exempted – after all, he only wants to cross this road, not drive down it; or at least, he'll receive his due: a little drama of exchange between a firm but apologetic policeman and the solemnly tolerant citizen.

He stops at the junction of the two roads. And indeed, the cop is coming towards him, with a glance up the street at the marchers and a pursed tolerant smile that suggests he himself would have bombed Iraq long ago, and many other countries besides. Perowne, relaxed at the wheel, would have responded with a collegiate closed-mouth smile of his own, but two things happen, almost at the same time. Behind the patrolman, on the far side of the road, three men, two tall, one thickset and short and wearing a black suit, are hurrying out of a lap-dancing club, the Spearmint Rhino, almost stumbling in their efforts not to run. When they turn the corner, into the street Perowne is wanting to enter, they're no longer so restrained. With the shorter man lagging behind, they run towards a car parked on the nearside.

The second thing to happen is that the cop meanwhile, unaware of the men, suddenly stops on his way to Perowne and raises a hand to his left ear. He nods and speaks into a microphone fixed in front of his mouth and turns towards his bike. Then, remembering what he was about, he glances back. Perowne meets his eye, and with a self-deprecating, interrogative look, points across the road at University Street. The cop shrugs, and then nods, and makes a gesture with his hand to say, Do it quickly then. What the hell. The marchers are still mostly up the other end, and he's had fresh instructions.

Perowne isn't late for his game, nor is he impatient to be across the road. He likes his car, but he's never been interested in the details of its performance, its acceleration from a standing start. He assumes it's impressive, but he's never put it to the test. He's far too old to be leaving rubber at the traffic lights. As he rolls forward, he looks diligently in both directions, even though it's a one-way flow northwards; he knows that pedestrians could be coming from either direction. If he moves briskly across the four-lane width of the road, it's out of consideration for the policeman who's already starting up his bike. Perowne doesn't want the man in trouble with his superiors. And something about the hand gesture has communicated the need to be quick. By the time the Mercedes has travelled the sixty or seventy feet to the entrance of University Street, which is where he changes into second, he may be doing twenty miles an hour. Twenty-five perhaps. Thirty at a stretch. And almost immediately, he's easing off, looking out for the right turn before Gower Street, which is also closed off.

And the forward motion is a prompt, it instantly returns him to his list, the proximal and distal causes of his emotional state. A second can be a long time in introspection. Long enough for Henry to make a start on the negative features, certainly enough time for him to think, or sense, without unwrapping the thought into syntax and words, that it is in fact the state of the world that troubles him most, and the marchers are there to remind him of it. The world probably has changed fundamentally and the matter is being clumsily handled, particularly by the Americans. There are people around the planet, well-connected and organised, who would like to kill him and his family and friends to make a point. The scale of death contemplated is no longer at issue; there'll be more deaths on a similar scale, probably in this city. Is he so frightened that he can't face the fact? The assertions and the questions don't spell themselves out. He experiences them more as a mental shrug followed by an interrogative pulse. This is the pre-verbal language that linguists call mentalese. Hardly a language, more a matrix of shifting patterns, consolidating and compressing meaning in fractions of a second, and blending it inseparably with its distinctive emotional hue, which itself is rather like a colour. A sickly yellow. Even with a poet's gift of compression, it could take hundreds of words and many minutes to describe. So that when a flash of red streaks in across his left peripheral vision, like a shape on his retina in a bout of insomnia, it already has the quality of an idea, a new idea, unexpected and dangerous, but entirely his, and not of the world beyond himself.

He's driving with unconscious expertise into the narrow column of space framed on the right by a kerb-flanked cycle path, and on the left by a line of parked cars. It's from this line that the thought springs, and with it, the snap of a wing mirror cleanly sheared and the whine of sheet-steel surfaces sliding under pressure as two cars pour into a gap wide enough for one. Perowne's instant decision at the moment of impact is to accelerate as he swerves right. There are other sounds – the staccato rattle of the red car on his left side raking a half-dozen stationary vehicles, and the thwack of concrete against rubber, like an amplified single handclap as the Mercedes mounts the cycle-path kerb. His back wheel hits the kerb too. Then he's ahead of the intruder and braking. The slewed cars stop thirty yards apart, engines cut, and for a moment there's silence, and no one gets out.

*   *   *

By the standards of contemporary road traffic accidents –
Henry has done a total of five years in Accident and
Emergency – this is a trivial matter. No one can possibly be
hurt, and he won't be in the role of doctor at the scene. He's
done it twice in the past five years, both for heart attacks,
once on a flight to New York, another time in an airless
London theatre during a June heatwave, both occasions
unsatisfactory and complicated. He's not in shock, he's not
weirdly calm or elated or numbed, his vision isn't unusually sharp, he isn't trembling. He listens to the click of hot
metal contracting. What he feels is rising irritation struggling against worldly caution. He doesn't have to look –
one side of his car is wrecked. He already sees ahead into
the weeks, the months of paperwork, insurance claims and
counterclaims, phone calls, delays at the garage. Something
original and pristine has been stolen from his car, and can
never be restored, however good the repair. There's also the
impact on the front axle, on the bearings, on those mysterious parts which conjure the essence of prolonged torture – *rack and pinion*. His car will never be the same again.
It's ruinously altered, and so is his Saturday. He'll never
make his game.

Above all, there swells in him a peculiarly modern emo-
tion – the motorist's rectitude, spot-welding a passion for
justice to the thrill of hatred, in the service of which various worn phrases tumble through his thoughts, revitalised,
cleansed of cliché: just pulled out, no signal, stupid bastard,
didn't even look, what's his mirror for, fucking *bastard*. The
only person in the world he hates is sitting in the car behind,
and Henry is going to have to talk to him, confront him,
exchange insurance details with him – all this when he
could be playing squash. He feels he's been left behind. And
he seems to see it: receding obliviously down a side street
is the other, most likely version of himself, like a vanishing
rich uncle, introspective and happy, motoring carefree
through his Saturday, leaving him alone and wretched, in

his new, improbable, inescapable fate. This is real. Telling himself it is so betrays how little he believes it yet. He picks his racket off the car floor and puts it back on top of the *Journal*. His right hand is on the door catch. But he doesn't move yet. He's looking in the mirror. There are reasons to be cautious.

There are, as he expected, three heads in the car behind. He knows he's subject to unexamined assumptions, and he tries to examine them now. As far as he's aware, lap-dancing is a lawful pursuit. But if he'd seen the three men hurrying, even furtively, from the Wellcome Trust or the British Library he might already have stepped from his car. That they were running makes it possible they'll be even more irritated than him by delay. The car is a series five BMW, a vehicle he associates for no good reason with criminality, drug-dealing. And there are three men, not one. The shortest is in the front passenger's seat, and the door on that side is opening as he watches, followed immediately by the driver's, and then the rear offside door. Perowne, who does not intend to be trapped into talking from a sitting position, gets out of his car. The half-minute's pause has given the situation a game-like quality in which calculations have already been made. The three men have their own reasons for holding back and discussing their next move. It's important, Perowne thinks as he goes round to the front of his car, to remember that he's in the right, and that he's angry. He also has to be careful. But these contradictory notions aren't helpful, and he decides he'll be better off feeling his way into the confrontation, rather than troubling himself with ground rules. His impulse then is to ignore the men, walk away from them, round the front of the Mercedes to get a view of the damaged side. But even as he stands, with hands on hips, in a pose of proprietorial outrage, he keeps the men, now advancing as a group, on the edge of vision.

At a glance, there seems to be no damage at all. The wing mirror is intact, there are no dents in the panels; amazingly, the metallic silver paintwork is clean. He leans forward to catch the light at a different angle. With fingers splayed, he runs a hand lightly over the bodywork, as if he really knew what he's about. There is nothing. Not a blemish. In immediate, tactical terms, this seems to leave him at a disadvantage. He has nothing to show for his anger. If there's any damage at all, it is out of sight, between the front wheels.

The men have stopped to look at something in the road. The short fellow in the black suit touches with the tip of his shoe the BMW's shorn-off wing mirror, turning it over the way one might a dead animal. One of the others, a tall young man with the long mournful face of a horse, picks it up, cradling it in both hands. They stare down at it together and then, at a remark from the short man, they turn their faces towards Perowne simultaneously, with abrupt curiosity, like deer disturbed in a forest. For the first time, it occurs to him that he might be in some kind of danger. Officially closed off at both ends, the street is completely deserted. Behind the men, on the Tottenham Court Road, a broken file of protesters is making its way south to join the main body. Perowne glances over his shoulder. There, behind him on Gower Street, the march proper has begun. Thousands packed in a single dense column are making for Piccadilly, their banners angled forwards heroically, as in a revolutionary poster. From their faces, hands and clothes they emanate the rich colour, almost like warmth, peculiar to compacted humanity. For dramatic effect, they're walking in silence to the funereal beat of marching drums.

The three men resume their approach. As before, the short man – five foot five or six perhaps – is out in front. His gait is distinctive, with a little jazzy twist and dip of his trunk, as though he's punting along a gentle stretch of river. The punter from the Spearmint Rhino. Perhaps he's listening to his personal stereo. Some people go nowhere, even into disputes, without a soundtrack. The other two have the manner of subordinates, sidekicks. They're wearing trainers, tracksuits and hooded tops – the currency of the street, so general as to be no style at all. Theo sometimes dresses this way in order, so he says, not to make decisions about how he looks. The horse-faced fellow is still holding the wing mirror in two hands, presumably to make a point. The unrelenting throb of drums is not helpful to the situation, and the fact that so many people are close by, unaware of him, makes Henry feel all the more isolated. It's best to go on looking busy. He drops down closer by the car, noting a squashed Coke can under his front tyre. There is, he sees now, with both relief and irritation, an irregular area on the rear door where the sheen is diminished, as though rubbed with a fine emery cloth. Surely the contact point, confined to a two-foot patch. How right he was, swerving away before he hit the brake. He feels steadier now, straightening up to face the men as they stop in front of him.

Unlike some of his colleagues – the surgical psychopaths – Henry doesn't actually relish personal confrontation. He isn't the machete-wielding type. But clinical experience is, among all else, an abrasive, toughening process, bound to wear away at his sensitivities. Patients, juniors, the recently bereaved, management of course – inevitably in two decades, the moments have come around when he's been required to fight his corner, or explain, or placate in the face of a furious emotional upsurge. There's usually a lot at stake – for colleagues, questions of hierarchy and professional pride or wasted hospital resources, for patients a loss of function, for their relatives, a suddenly dead spouse or child – weightier affairs than a scratched car. Especially when they involve patients, these moments have a purity and innocence about them; everything is stripped down to the essentials of being – memory, vision, the ability to recognise faces, chronic pain, motor function, even a sense of self. What lie in the background, glowing faintly, are the issues of medical science, the wonders it performs, the faith it inspires, and against that, its slowly diminishing but still vast ignorance of the brain, and the mind, and the relation between the two. Regularly penetrating the skull with some modest success is a relatively recent adventure. There's bound to be disappointment sometimes, and when it comes, the showdown with the relatives in his office, no one needs to calculate how to behave or what to say, no one feels watched. It pours out.

Among Perowne's acquaintance are those medics who deal not with the brain, but only with the mind, with the diseases of consciousness; these colleagues embrace a tradition, a set of prejudices only rarely voiced nowadays, that the neurosurgeons are blundering arrogant fools with blunt instruments, bone-setters let loose upon the most complex object in the known universe. When an operation fails, the patient or the relatives tend to come round to this view. But too late. What is said then is tragic and sincere. However appalling these heartfelt engagements, however much he knows himself to be maligned by a patient's poor or self-serving recollection of how the risks have been outlined, whatever his certainty that he's performed in the theatre as well as current knowledge and techniques allow, Perowne comes away not only chastened – he has manifestly failed to lower expectations – but obscurely purified: he's had a fundamental human exchange, as elemental in its way as love.

But here on University Street it's impossible not to feel that play-acting is about to begin. Dressed as a scarecrow, in mangy fleece, his sweater with its row of holes, his paint-stained trousers supported by a knotted cord, he stands by his powerful machine. He is cast in a role, and there's no way out. This, as people like to say, is urban drama. A century of movies and half a century of television have rendered the matter insincere. It is pure artifice. Here are the cars, and here are the owners. Here are the guys, the strangers, whose self-respect is on the line. Someone is going to have to impose his will and win, and the other is going to give way. Popular culture has worn this matter smooth with reiteration, this ancient genetic patrimony that also oils the machinations of bullfrogs and cockerels and stags. And despite the varied and casual dress code, there are rules as elaborate as the *politesse* of the Versailles court that no set of genes can express. For a start, it is not permitted as they stand there to acknowledge the self-consciousness of the event, or its overbearing irony: from just up the street, they can hear the tramping and tribal drums of the peace mongers. Furthermore, nothing can be predicted, but everything, as soon as it happens, will seem to fit.

'Cigarette?'

Exactly so. This is how it's bound to start.

In an old-fashioned gesture, the other driver offers the pack with a snap of the wrist, arranging the untipped cigarettes like organ pipes. The gripped hand extending towards Perowne is large, given the man's height, and papery pale, with black hair coiled on the back, and extending to the distal interphalangeal joints. The persistent tremor also draws Perowne's professional attention. Perhaps there's reassurance to be had in the unsteadiness of the grip.

'I won't, thanks.'

He lights one for himself and blows the smoke past Henry who is already one point down – not man enough to smoke, or more essentially, to offer gifts. It's important not to be passive. It has to be his move. He puts out his own hand.

'Henry Perowne.'

'Baxter.'

'Mr Baxter?'

'Baxter.'

Baxter's hand is large, Henry's fractionally larger, but neither man attempts a show of strength. Their handshake is light and brief. Baxter is one of those smokers whose pores exude a perfume, an oily essence of his habit. Garlic affects certain people the same way. Possibly the kidneys are implicated. He's a fidgety, small-faced young man with thick eyebrows and dark brown hair razored close to the skull. The mouth is set bulbously, with the smoothly shaved shadow of a strong beard adding to the effect of a muzzle. The general simian air is compounded by sloping shoulders, and the built-up trapezoids suggest time in the gym, compensating for his height perhaps. The sixties-style suit – tight cut, high lapels, flat-fronted trousers worn from the hip – is taking some strain around the jacket's single fastened button. There's also tightness in the fabric round the biceps. He half-turns and dips away from Perowne, then bobs back. He gives an impression of fretful impatience, of destructive energy waiting to be released. He may be about to lash out. Perowne is familiar with some of the current literature on violence. It's not always a pathology; self-interested social organisms find it rational to be violent sometimes. Among the game theorists and radical criminologists, the stock of Thomas Hobbes keeps on rising. Holding the unruly, the thugs, in check is the famous 'common power' to keep all men in awe – a governing body, an arm of the state, freely granted a monopoly on the legitimate use of violence. But drug dealers and pimps, among others who live beyond the law, are not inclined to dial nine-nine-nine for Leviathan; they settle their quarrels in their own way.

Perowne, almost a foot taller than Baxter, considers that if it comes to a scrap he'll be wise to protect his testicles. But it's a ridiculous thought; he hasn't been in a hand-to-hand fight since he was eight. Three against one. He simply won't let it happen.

As soon as they've shaken hands, Baxter says, 'I expect you're all ready to tell me how sincerely sorry you are.' He looks back, past the Mercedes to his own car where it's parked at a diagonal across the road. Behind it is an irregular line, three feet from the ground, scraped along the sides of half a dozen parked cars by the BMW's door handle. The appearance on the street now of just one outraged owner will be enough to set off a cascade of insurance claims. Henry, knowing a good deal about paperwork, can already sense the prolonged trauma of it. Far better to be one of many victims than the original sinner.

He says, 'I am indeed sorry that you pulled out without looking.'

He surprises himself. This fussy, faintly archaic 'indeed' is not generally part of his lexicon. Deploying it entails decisions; he isn't going to pretend to the language of the street. He's standing on professional dignity.

Baxter lays his left hand on his right, as though to calm it. He says patiently, 'I didn't need to be looking, did I? The Tottenham Court Road's closed. You aren't supposed to be there.'

Perowne says, 'The rules of the road aren't suspended. Anyway, a policeman waved me across.'

'Police man?' Baxter dividing and leaning on the construction makes it sound childish. He turns to his friends. 'You seen a police man?' And then back to Perowne, with mocking politeness, 'This is Nark, and this is Nigel.'

Until now, the two have stood off to one side, just behind Baxter, listening without expression. Nigel is the horse-faced man. His companion may be a police informer, or addicted to narcotics or, given his comatose look, presenting with narcolepsy.

'No policemen round here,' Nigel explains. 'They all busy with the marching scum.'

Perowne pretends to ignore both men. His business is with Baxter. 'This is the moment we swap insurance details.' All three chuckle at this, but he continues, 'If we can't agree on what happened, we'll phone the police.' He looks at his watch. Jay Strauss will be on court, warming up the ball. It's not too late to settle the matter and get on his way. Baxter hasn't reacted to the mention of a phone call. Instead, he takes the wing mirror from Nigel and displays it to Perowne. The spider web fissures in the glass show the sky in mosaics of white and ragged blue which shimmer with the agitation in Baxter's hand. His tone is genial.

'Fortunately for you, I got a mate does bodywork, on the cheap. But he does a nice job. Seven fifty I reckon he'd sort me out.'

Nark rouses himself. 'There's a cashpoint on the corner.'

And Nigel, as though pleasantly surprised by the idea, says, 'Yeah. We could walk down there with you.'

These two have shifted their position so they're almost, but not quite, flanking Henry. Baxter meanwhile steps back. The manoeuvrings are clumsily deliberate, like an ill-rehearsed children's ballet. Perowne's attention, his professional regard, settles once again on Baxter's right hand. It isn't simply a tremor, it's a fidgety restlessness implicating practically every muscle. Speculating about it soothes him, even as he feels the shoulders of both men pressing lightly through his fleece. Perversely, he no longer believes himself to be in any great danger. It's hard to take the trio seriously; the cash idea has a boyish, make-believe quality. Everything said seems like a quotation from something they've all seen a dozen times before and half-forgotten.

At the sound of a trumpet expertly played, the four men turn to watch the march. It's a series of intricate staccato runs which end on a high tapering note. It might be a passage from a Bach cantata, because Henry immediately imagines a soprano and a sweetly melancholic air, and in the background, a supportive cello squarely sawing away. On Gower Street the concept of a reproachful funeral march no longer holds. It was difficult to sustain with thousands in a column stretching over hundreds of yards. Now the chants and clapping rise and fall in volume as different sections of the crowd move past the junction with University Street. Baxter's fixed regard is on it as it passes, his features faintly distorted, strained by pity. A textbook phrase comes to Henry in much the same way as the cantata melody – a modest rise in his adrenaline level is making him unusually associative. Or the pressures of the past week won't release him from the habits, the intellectual game of diagnosis. The phrase is, *a false sense of superiority*. Yes, it can be down to a slight alteration in character, preceding the first tremors, somewhat short of, a little less disabling than, those other neurological conditions – grandiosity, delusions of grandeur. But he may be misremembering. Neurology is not his field. As Baxter stares at the marchers, he makes tiny movements with his head, little nods and shakes. Watching him unobserved for a few seconds, Perowne suddenly understands – Baxter is unable to initiate or make saccades – those flickering changes of eye position from one fixation to another. To scan the crowd, he is having to move his head.

As though in confirmation, he turns his whole body towards Perowne and says genially, 'Horrible rabble. Sponging off the country they hate.'

Perowne thinks he understands enough about Baxter to know he should get clear. Shrugging off Nigel and Nark at his side, he turns towards his car. 'I'm not giving you cash,' he says dismissively. 'I'm giving you my details. If you don't want to give me yours, that's fine. Your registration number will do. I'll be on my way.' He then adds, barely truthfully, 'I'm late for an important meeting.'

But most of this sentence is obliterated by a single sound, a shout of rage.

Even as he turns back towards Baxter in surprise, and even as he sees, or senses, what's coming towards him at such speed, there remains in a portion of his thoughts a droning, pedestrian diagnostician who notes poor self-control, emotional lability, explosive temper, suggestive of reduced levels of GABA among the appropriate binding sites on striatal neurons. There is much in human affairs that can be accounted for at the level of the complex molecule. Who could ever reckon up the damage done to love and friendship and all hopes of happiness by a surfeit or depletion of this or that neurotransmitter? And who will ever find a morality, an ethics down among the enzymes and amino acids when the general taste is for looking in the other direction? In her second year at Oxford, dazzled by some handsome fool of a teacher, Daisy tried to convince her father that madness was a social construct, a wheeze by means of which the rich – he may have got this wrong – squeezed the poor. Father and daughter engaged in one of their energetic arguments which ended with Henry, in a rhetorical coup, offering her a tour of a closed psychiatric wing. Resolutely, she accepted, and then the matter was forgotten.

Despite Baxter's impaired ocular fixation, and his chorea, those quick, jerky movements, the blow that's aimed at Perowne's heart and that he dodges only fractionally, lands on his sternum with colossal force, so that it seems to him, and perhaps it really is the case, that there surges throughout his body a sharp ridge, a shock wave, of high blood pressure, a concussive thrill that carries with it not so much pain as an electric jolt of stupefaction and a brief deathly chill that has a visual component of blinding, snowy whiteness.

'All right,' he hears Baxter say, which is an instruction to his companions.

They grab Henry by his elbows and forearms, and as his vision clears he sees that he's being propelled through a gap between two parked cars. Together they cross the pavement at speed. They turn him and slam his back against a chain-locked double door in a recess. He sees on the wall to his left a polished brass plaque which says Fire Exit, Spearmint Rhino. Just up the street is a pub, the Jeremy Bentham. But if it's open this early, the drinkers are all inside in the warmth. Perowne has two immediate priorities whose importance holds as his full consciousness returns. The first is to keep the promise to himself not to fight back. The punch has already told him how much expertise he lacks. The second is to stay on his feet. He's seen a fair number of brain injuries among those unlucky enough to fall to the ground before their attackers. The foot, like some roughneck hick town, is a remote province of the brain, liberated by distance from responsibility. A kick is less intimate, less involving, than a punch, and one kick never quite seems enough. Back in the epic days of organised football violence when he was a registrar, he learned a good deal about subdural haematomas from steel-tipped Doc Martens.

He stands facing them in a little whitewashed brick cave of a recess, well out of sight of the march. The structure amplifies the rasp of their breathing. Nigel takes a fistful of Perowne's fleece and with the other hand seeks out the bulge of his wallet which is in an inside zipped pocket.

'Nah,' Baxter says. 'We don't want his money.'

By this Perowne understands that honour is to be satisfied by a thorough beating. As with the insurance claims, he sees the dreary future ahead. Weeks of painful convalescence. Perhaps that's optimistic. Baxter's gaze is on him, a gaze that can't be shifted unless he moves the whole of his heavy shaven head. His face is alive with small tremors that never quite form into an expression. It is a muscular restlessness that will one day – this is Perowne's considered opinion – become athetoid, plagued by involuntary, uncontrollable movements.

There's a sense among the trio of a pause for breath, a steadying before the business. Nark is already bunching his right fist. Perowne notes three rings on the index, middle and ring fingers, bands of gold as broad as sawn-off plumbing. He has, he reckons, a few seconds left. Baxter is in his mid-twenties. This isn't the moment to be asking for a family history. If a parent has it, you have a fifty-fifty chance of going down too. Chromosome four. The misfortune lies within a single gene, in an excessive repeat of a single sequence – CAG. Here's biological determinism in its purest form. More than forty repeats of that one little codon, and you're doomed. Your future is fixed and easily foretold. The longer the repeat, the earlier and more severe the onset. Between ten and twenty years to complete the course, from the first small alterations of character, tremors in the hands and face, emotional disturbance, including – most notably – sudden, uncontrollable alterations of mood, to the helpless jerky dance-like movements, intellectual dilapidation, memory failure, agnosia, apraxia, dementia, total loss of muscular control, rigidity sometimes, nightmarish hallucinations and a meaningless end. This is how the brilliant machinery of being is undone by the tiniest of faulty cogs, the insidious whisper of ruin, a single bad idea lodged in every cell, on every chromosome four.

Nark is drawing back his right arm to strike. Nigel seems content to let him go first. Henry has heard that early onset tends to indict the paternal gene. But that may not be right. There's nothing to lose by making a guess. He speaks into the blaze of Baxter's regard.

'Your father had it. Now you've got it too.'

He has the impression of himself as a witch doctor delivering a curse. Baxter's expression is hard to judge. He makes a vague, febrile movement with his left hand to restrain his companions. There's silence as he swallows and strains forward, frowning, as if about to clear an obstruction from his throat. Perowne has expressed himself ambiguously. His 'had' could easily have been taken for a 'has'. And Baxter's father, alive or dead, might not even be known to his son. But Perowne is counting on Baxter knowing about his condition. If he does, he won't have told Nigel or Nark or any of his friends. This is his secret shame. He may be in denial, knowing and not knowing; knowing and preferring not to think about it.

When Baxter speaks at last, his voice is different, cautious perhaps. 'You knew my father?'

'I'm a doctor.'

'Like fuck you are, dressed like that.'

'I'm a doctor. Has someone explained to you what's going to happen? Do you want me to tell you what I think your problem might be?'

It works, the shameless blackmail works. Baxter flares suddenly. 'What problem?'

And before Perowne can reply, he adds ferociously, 'And you'll shut the fuck up.' Then, as quickly, he subsides, and turns away. They are together, he and Perowne, in a world not of the medical, but of the magical. When you're diseased it is unwise to abuse the shaman.

Nigel says, 'What's going on? What did your dad have?'

'Shut up.'

The moment of the thrashing is passing and Perowne senses the power passing to him. This fire escape recess is his consulting room. Its mean volume reflects back to him a voice regaining the full timbre of its authority. He says, 'Are you seeing someone about it?'

'What's he on about, Baxter?'

Baxter shoves the broken wing mirror into Nark's hands. 'Go and wait in the car.'

'You're kidding.'

'I mean it. Both of you. Go and wait in the fucking car.'

It is pitifully evident, Baxter's desperation to separate his friends from the sharer of his secret. The two young men exchange a look and shrug. Then, without a glance at Perowne, they set off back up the road. Hard to imagine they don't think something is wrong with Baxter. But these are the early stages of the disease, and its advance is slow. They might not have known him long. And a jazzy walk, an interesting tremor, the occasional lordly flash of temper or mood swing might in their milieu mark out a man of character. When they reach the BMW Nark opens a rear door and tosses the wing mirror in. Side by side, they lean on the front of the car watching Baxter and Perowne, arms folded like movie hoods.

Perowne persists gently. 'When did your father die?'

'Leave it.'

Baxter is not looking at him. He stands fidgeting with shoulder turned, like a sulky child waiting to be coaxed, unable to make the first move. Here is the signature of so many neurodegenerative diseases – the swift transition from one mood to another, without awareness or memory, or understanding of how it seems to others.

'Is your mother still alive?'

'Not as far as I'm concerned.'

'Are you married?'

'No.'

'Is your real name Baxter?'

'That's my business.'

'All right. Where are you from?'

'I grew up in Folkestone.'

'And where do you live now?'

'My dad's old flat. Kentish Town.'

'Any occupation, training, college?'

'I didn't get on with school. What's that to do with you?'

'And what's your doctor said about your condition?'

Baxter shrugs. But he's accepted Perowne's right to interrogate. They've slipped into their roles and Perowne keeps going.

'Has anyone mentioned Huntington's Disease to you?'

A feeble dry rattling sound, like that of stones shaken in a tin, reaches them from the march. Baxter is looking at the ground. Perowne takes his silence as confirmation.

'Do you want to tell me who your doctor is?'

'Why would I do that?'

'We could get you referred to a colleague of mine. He's good. He could make things easier for you.'

At this Baxter turns and angles his head in his attempt to settle the taller man's image on his fovea, that small depression on the retina where vision is most acute. There's nothing anyone can do about a damaged saccadic system. And generally, there's nothing on offer at all for this condition, beyond managing the descent. But Henry sees now in Baxter's agitated features a sudden avidity, a hunger for information, or hope. Or simply a need to talk.

'What sort of thing?'

'Exercises. Certain drugs.'

'Exercise ...' He snorts on the word. He is right to pick up on the fatuity, the feebleness of the idea. Perowne presses on.

'What has your doctor told you?'

'He said there's nothing, didn't he.'

He says this as a challenge, or a calling in of a debt; Perowne's been reprieved, and in return he has to come up with a reason for optimism, if not a cure. Baxter wants his doctor proved wrong.

But Perowne says, 'I think he's right. There was some work with stem-cell implantation in the late nineties but ...'

'It was shit.'

'Yes, it was disappointing. Best hope now apparently is RNA interference.'

'Yeah. Gene silencing. One day perhaps. After I'm dead.'

'You're well up on this then.'

'Oh thank you, doctor. But what's this about certain drugs?'

Perowne is familiar with this impulse in patients, this pursuit of the slenderest leads. If there's a drug, Baxter or his doctor will know about it. But it's necessary for Baxter to check. And check again. Someone might know something he doesn't. A week passes and there could be a new development. And when the line runs out in this field, the charlatans lie in wait for the fearful, offering the apricot-stone diet, the aura massage, the power of prayer. Over Baxter's shoulder Perowne can see Nigel and Nark. They're no longer leaning against the car, but walking up and down in front of it, talking animatedly, gesturing up the road.

Perowne says, 'I'm talking about pain relief, help with loss of balance, tremors, depression.'

Baxter moves his head from side to side. The muscles in his cheeks are independently alive. Henry senses an approaching shift of mood. 'Oh fuck,' Baxter keeps murmuring to himself. 'Oh fuck.' In this transitional phase of perplexity or sorrow, the vaguely ape-like features are softened, even attractive. He's an intelligent man, and gives the impression that, illness apart, he's missed his chances, made some big mistakes and ended up in the wrong company. Probably dropped out of school long ago and regrets it. No parents around. And now, what worse situation than this could he find himself in? There's no way out for him. No one can help. But Perowne knows himself to be incapable of pity. Clinical experience wrung that from him long ago. And a part of him never ceases to calculate how soon he can safely end this encounter. Besides, the matter is beyond pity. There are so many ways a brain can let you down. Like an expensive car, it's intricate, but mass-produced nevertheless, with more than six billion in circulation.

Rightly, Baxter believes he's been cheated of a little violence and the exercise of a little power, and the more he considers it, the angrier he becomes. Another rapid change in mental weather, a new mood front is approaching, and it's turbulent. He ceases his murmuring and moves in close enough for Perowne to smell a metallic flavour on his breath.

'You streak of piss,' Baxter says quickly as he pushes him in the chest. 'You're trying to fuck with me. In front of those two. You think I care? Well fuck you. I'm calling them back.'

From his position, with his back to the fire exit, Perowne can already see that a bad moment awaits Baxter. He turns away from Perowne and steps out into the centre of the pavement in time to see Nigel and Nark walking away from the BMW, back towards the Tottenham Court Road.

Baxter makes a short run in their direction and shouts, 'Oi!'

They glance back, and Nark, uncharacteristically energetic, gives him the finger. As they walk on, Nigel makes a limp-wristed dismissive gesture. The general has been indecisive, the troops are deserting, the humiliation is complete. Perowne too sees his opportunity to withdraw. He crosses the pavement, steps into the road and around his car. His keys are in the ignition. As he starts the engine he sees Baxter in his rear-view mirror, dithering between the departing factions, shouting at both. Perowne eases forwards – for pride's sake, he does not want to appear hurried. The insurance is an irrelevance, and it amazes him now that he ever thought it important. He sees his racket on the front seat beside him. This is surely the moment to slip away, while the possibility remains that he can still rescue his game.

After he's parked, and before getting out of the car, he phones Rosalind at work – his long fingers still trembling, fumbling with the miniature keys. On this important day for her he doesn't intend to distract her with the story of his near-thrashing. And he doesn't need sympathy. What he wants is more fundamental – the sound of her voice in an everyday exchange, the resumption of normal existence. What can be more reassuringly plain than husband and wife discussing the details of tonight's dinner? He speaks to a temp, what they call in Rosalind's office a hot-desker, and learns that her meeting with the editor has started late and is running on. He leaves no message, and says he'll try later.

It's unusual to see the glass-fronted squash courts deserted on a Saturday. He walks along the row, on stained blue carpet, past the giant Coke and energy bar dispensers, and finds the consultant anaesthetist at the far end, in number five, smacking the ball in fast repeated strokes low along the back-hand wall, giving the appearance of a man working off a bad temper. But, it turns out, he's been waiting only ten minutes. He lives across the river in Wandsworth; the march forced him to abandon his car by the Festival Hall. Furious with himself for being late, he jogged across Waterloo Bridge and saw below him tens of thousands pouring along the Embankment towards Parliament Square. Too young for the Vietnam war protests, he's never in his life seen so many people in one place. Despite his own views, he was some-what moved. This, he told himself, is the democratic process, however inconvenient. He watched for five minutes, then jogged up Kingsway, against the flow of bodies. He describes all this while Perowne sits on the bench removing his sweater and tracksuit bottom, and making a heap of his wallet, keys and phone to store at one of the corners by the front wall – he and Strauss are never serious enough to insist on a completely cleared court.

'They dislike your Prime Minister, but boy do they fucking loathe my President.'

Jay is the only American medic Perowne knows to have taken a huge cut in salary and amenities to work in England. He says he loves the health system. He also loved an Englishwoman, had three children by her, divorced her, married another similar-looking English rose twelve years younger and had another two children – still toddlers, and a third is on its way. But his respect for socialised medicine or his love of children do not make him an ally of the peace cause. The proposed war, Perowne finds, generally doesn't divide people predictably; a known package of opinions is not a reliable guide. According to Jay, the matter is stark: how open societies deal with the new world situation will determine how open they remain. He's a man of untroubled certainties, impatient of talk of diplomacy, weapons of mass destruction, inspection teams, proofs of links with Al-Qaeda and so on. Iraq is a rotten state, a natural ally of terrorists, bound to cause mischief at some point and may as well be taken out now while the US military is feeling perky after Afghanistan. And by taken out, he insists he means liberated and democratised. The USA has to atone for its previous disastrous policies – at the very least it owes this to the Iraqi people. Whenever he talks to Jay, Henry finds himself tending towards the anti-war camp.

Strauss is a powerful, earthbound, stocky man, physically affectionate, energetic, direct in manner – to some of his English colleagues, tiresomely so. He's been completely bald since he was thirty. He works out for more than an hour each day, and looks like a wrestler. When he busies himself around his patients in the anaesthetic room, readying them for oblivion, they are reassured by the sight of the sculpted muscles on his forearms, the dense bulk of his neck and shoulders, and by the way he speaks to them – matter-of-fact, cheerful, without condescension. Anxious patients can believe this squat American will lay down his life to spare them pain.

They have worked together six years. As far as Henry is concerned, Jay is the key to the success of his firm. When things go wrong, Strauss becomes calm. If, for example, Perowne is obliged to cut off a major blood vessel to make a repair, Jay keeps time in a soothing way, ending with a murmured, 'You've got one minute, Boss, then you're out of there.' On the rare occasions when things go really badly, when there's no way back, Strauss will find him out afterwards, alone in a quiet stretch of corridor, and put his hands on his shoulders, squeeze tightly and say, 'OK Henry. Let's talk it through now. Before you start crucifying yourself.' This isn't the way an anaesthetist, even a consultant, usually speaks to a surgeon. Consequently, Strauss has an above average array of enemies. On certain committees, Perowne has protected his friend's broad back from various collegiate daggers. Now and then he finds himself saying to Jay something like, 'I don't care what you think. Be nice to him. Remember our funding next year.'

While Henry does his stretching exercises, Jay goes back on court to keep the ball warm, driving it down the right-hand wall. There appears to be an extra punch today in his low shots, and the sequence of fast volleys is surely planned to intimidate an opponent. It works. Perowne feels the echoing rifle-shot crack of the ball as an oppression; there's an unusual stiffness in his neck as he goes through his routine, pushing with his left hand against his right elbow. Through the open glass door, he raises his voice to explain why he's late, but it's a truncated account, centred mostly on the scrape itself, the way the red car pulled out, and how he swerved, how the damage to the paintwork was surprisingly light. He skips the rest, saying only that it took a while to sort out. He doesn't want to hear himself describe Baxter and his friends. They'll interest Strauss too much, and prompt questions he doesn't feel like answering yet. He's already feeling a rising unease about the encounter, a disquiet he can't yet define, though guilt is certainly an element.

He feels his left knee creak as he stretches his hamstrings. When will it be time to give up this game? His fiftieth birthday? Or sooner. Get out before he rips an anterior cruciate ligament, or crashes to the parquet with his first coronary. He's working on the tendons of his other leg, Strauss is still performing his rapid-fire volleys. Perowne suddenly feels his own life as fragile and precious. His limbs appear to him as neglected old friends, absurdly long and breakable. Is he in mild shock? His heart will be all the more vulnerable after that punch. His chest still aches. He has a duty to others to survive, and he mustn't endanger his own life for a mere game, smacking a ball against a wall. And there's no such thing as a gentle game of squash, especially with Jay. Especially with himself. They both hate to lose. Once they get going, they fight points like madmen. He should make excuses and pull out now, and risk irritating his friend. A negligible price. As he straightens up, it occurs to Perowne that what he really wants is to go home and lie down in the bedroom and think it through, the dispute in University Street, and decide how he should have handled it, and what it was he got wrong.

But even as he's thinking this, he's pulling on his goggles and stepping onto the court and closing the door behind him. He kneels to settle his valuables in a front-wall corner. There's a momentum to the everyday, a Saturday morning game of squash with a good friend and colleague, that he doesn't have the strength of will to interrupt. He stands on the backhand side of the court, Strauss sends a brisk, friendly ball down the centre, automatically Perowne returns it, back along its path. And so they are launched into the familiar routines of a warm-up. The third ball he mishits, slapping it loudly into the tin. A couple of strokes later he stops to retie his laces. He can't settle. He feels slow and encumbered and his grip feels misaligned, too open, too closed, he doesn't know. He fiddles with his racket between strokes. Four minutes pass and they've yet to have a decent exchange. There's none of that easy rhythm that usually works them into their game. He notices that Jay is slowing his pace, offering easier angles to keep the ball in play. At last, Perowne feels obliged to say he's ready. Since he lost last week's game – this is their arrangement – he is to serve.

He takes up his position in the right-hand service box. From behind him on the other side of the court, he hears Jay mutter, 'OK.' The silence is complete, of that hissing variety rarely heard in a city; no other players, no street sounds, not even from the march. For two or three seconds Perowne stares at the dense black ball in his left hand, willing himself to narrow the range of his thoughts. He serves a high lob, well placed in so far as it arcs too high for a volley, and slides off the side wall onto the back. But even as it leaves him, he knows he's hit it too hard. It comes off the back wall with some residual speed, leaving Jay plenty of space to drive a straight return down the side wall to a good length. The ball dies in the corner, dribbling off the back wall as Perowne reaches it.

With barely a pause, Jay snatches up the ball to serve from the right box. Perowne, gauging his opponent's mood, is expecting an overarm smash and is crouched forwards, prepared to take a volley before the ball nicks the side wall. But Strauss has made his own calculations about mood. He serves a soft bodyline, angled straight into Perowne's right shoulder. It's the perfect shot to play at an indecisive opponent. He steps back, but too late and not far enough and, at some point in his confusion, loses sight of the ball. His return drops into the front of the court and Strauss drives it hard

into the right-hand corner. They've been playing less than
a minute, Perowne has lost his serve, is one point down and
knows already that he's lost control. And so it goes on,
relentlessly for the next five points, with Jay in possession
of the centre of the court, and Perowne, dazed and defensive, initiating nothing.

At six-love, Strauss finally makes an unforced error.
Perowne serves the same high lob, but this time it falls nicely
off the back wall. Strauss does well to hook it out, but the
ball sits up on the short line and Perowne amazes himself
with a perfect dying-length drive. With that little swoon of
euphoria comes the ability to concentrate. He takes the next
three points without trouble, and on the last of these, clinched
by a volley drop, he hears Jay swearing at himself as he walks
to the back of the court. Now, the magical authority, and all
the initiatives are Henry's. He has possession of the centre
of the court and is sending his opponent running from front
to back. Soon he's ahead at seven-six and is certain he'll take
the next two points. Even as he thinks this, he makes a careless cross-court shot which Strauss pounces on and, with a
neat slice, drops into the corner. Perowne manages to resist
the lure of self-hatred as he walks to the left-hand court to
receive the serve. But as the ball floats off the front wall
towards him, unwanted thoughts are shaking at his concentration. He sees the pathetic figure of Baxter in the rear-view
mirror. This is precisely the moment he should have stepped
forwards for a backhand volley – he could reach it at a stretch
– but he hesitates. The ball hits the nick – the join between
the wall and the floor – and rolls insultingly over his foot.
It's a lucky shot, and in his irritation he longs to say so. Seven-
all. But there's no fight to the end. Perowne feels himself
moving through a mental fog, and Jay takes the last two
points in quick succession.

Neither man has any illusions about his game. They are
halfway decent club players, both approaching fifty. Their
arrangement is that between games – they play the best of

five – they pause to let their pulse rates settle. Sometimes they even sit on the floor. Today, the first game hasn't been strenuous, so they walk slowly up and down the court. The anaesthetist wants to know about the Chapman girl. He's gone out of his way to make friends with her. The girl's street manner didn't withstand the pep talk that Perowne, passing in the corridor, overheard Strauss deliver. The anaesthetist had gone up to the ward to introduce himself. He found a Filipino nurse in tears over some abuse she'd received. Strauss sat on the bed and put his face close to the girl's.

'Listen honey. You want us to fix that sorry head of yours, you've got to help us. You hear? You don't want us to fix it, take your attitude home. We got plenty of other patients waiting to get in your bed. Look, here's your stuff in the locker. You want me to start putting it in your bag? OK. Here we go. Toothbrush. Discman. Hairbrush . . . No? So which is it to be? Fine. OK, look, I'm taking them out again. No, look, I really am. You help us, we help you. We got a deal? Let's shake hands.'

Perowne reports on her good progress this morning.

'I like that kid,' Jay says. 'She reminds me of myself at that age. A pain in the ass in every direction. She might go down in flames, she might do something with herself.'

'Well, she'll pull through this one,' Perowne says as he takes up his position to receive. 'At least it'll be her own decision to crash. Let's go.'

He's spoken too soon. Jay's serve is on him, but his own word 'crash', trailing memories of the night as well as the morning, fragments into a dozen associations. Everything that's happened to him recently occurs to him at once. He's no longer in the present. The deserted icy square, the plane and its pinprick of fire, his son in the kitchen, his wife in bed, his daughter on her way from Paris, the three men in the street – he occupies the wrong time coordinates, or he's in them all at once. The ball surprises him – it's as if he left the court for a moment. He takes the ball late, scooping it from the floor. At once Strauss springs out from the 'T' for the kill shot. And so the second game begins as the first. But this time Henry has to run hard to lose. Jay's prepared to let the rallies go on while he hogs centre court and lobs to the back, drops to the front, and finds his angle shots. Perowne scampers around his opponent like a circus pony. He twists back to lift balls out of the rear corners, then dashes forwards at a stretch to connect with the drop shots. The constant change of direction tires him as much as his gathering self-hatred. Why has he volunteered for, even anticipated with pleasure, this humiliation, this torture? It's at moments like these in a game that the essentials of his character are exposed: narrow, ineffectual, stupid – and morally so. The game becomes an extended metaphor of character defect. Every error he makes is so profoundly, so irritatingly typical of himself, instantly familiar, like a signature, like a tissue scar or some deformation in a private place. As intimate and self-evident as the feel of his tongue in his mouth. Only he can go wrong in quite this way, and only he deserves to lose in just this manner. As the points fall he draws his remaining energy from a darkening pool of fury.

He says nothing, to himself or his opponent. He won't let Jay hear him curse. But the silence is another kind of affliction. They're at eight-three. Jay plays a cross-court drive – probably a mistake, because the ball is left loose, ready for interception. Perowne sees his chance. If he can get to it, Jay will be caught out of position. Aware of this, Jay moves out from his stroke towards centre court, blocking Perowne's path. Immediately Perowne calls for a let. They stop and Strauss turns to express surprise.

'Are you kidding?'

'For fuck's sake,' Perowne says through his furious breathing, and pointing his racket in the direction he was heading. 'You stepped right into me.'

The language startles them both. Strauss immediately concedes. 'OK, OK. It's a let.'

As he goes to the service box and tries to calm himself, Perowne can't help considering that at eight-three, and already a game up, it's ungenerous of Jay to query such an obvious call. Ungenerous is generous. The judgment doesn't help him deliver the service he needs, for this is his last chance to get back in the game. The ball goes so wide of the wall that Jay is able to step to his left and reach for an easy forehand smash. He takes the service back, and the game is over in half a minute.

The prospect of making small talk on court for a few minutes is now unendurable. Henry puts his racket down, pulls off his goggles and mutters something about needing water. He leaves the court and goes to the changing room and drinks from the fountain there. The place is deserted except for an unseen figure in the showers. A TV high on the wall is showing a news channel. He splashes his face at a basin, and rests his head on his forearms. He hears his pulse knocking in his ears, sweat is dribbling down his spine, his face and feet are burning. There's only one thing in life he wants. Everything else has dropped away. He has to beat Strauss. He needs to win three games in a row to take the set. Unbelievably difficult, but for the moment he desires and can think of nothing else. In this minute or two alone, he must think carefully about his game, cut to the fundamentals, decide what he's doing wrong and fix it. He's beaten Strauss many times before. He has to stop being angry with himself and think about his game.

When he raises his head, he sees in the washroom mirror, beyond his reddened face, a reflection of the silent TV behind him showing the same old footage of the cargo plane on the runway. But then, briefly, enticingly, two men with coats over their heads – surely the two pilots – in handcuffs being led towards a police van. They've been arrested. Something's happened. A reporter outside a police station is talking to the camera. Then the anchor is talking to the reporter. Perowne shifts position so the screen is no longer in view. Isn't it possible to enjoy an hour's recreation without this invasion, this infection from the public domain? He begins to see the matter resolving in simple terms: winning his game will be an assertion of his privacy. He has a right now and then – everyone has it – not to be disturbed by world events, or even street events. Cooling down in the locker room, it seems to Perowne that to forget, to obliterate a whole universe of public phenomena in order to concentrate is a fundamental liberty. Freedom of thought. He'll emancipate himself by beating Strauss. Stirred, he walks up and down between the changing-room benches, averting his eyes from a ripplingly obese teenager, more seal than human, who's emerged from the shower without a towel. There isn't much time. He has to arrange his game around simple tactics, play on his opponent's weakness. Strauss is only five foot eight, with no great reach and not a brilliant volleyer. Perowne decides on high lobs to the rear corners. As simple as that. Keep lobbing to the back.

When he arrives back on court, the consultant anaesthetist comes straight over to him. 'You all right Henry? You pissed off?'

'Yeah. With myself. But having to argue that let didn't help.'

'You were right, I was wrong. I'm sorry. Are you ready?'

Perowne stands in the receiving position, intent on the rhythm of his breathing, prepared to perform a simple move, virtually a standard procedure: he'll volley the serve before it touches the side wall, and after he's hit it he'll cross to the 'T' at the centre of the court and lob. Simple. It's time to dislodge Strauss.

'Ready.'

Strauss hits a fast serve, and once again it's a bodyline, aimed straight for the shoulder. Perowne manages to push his racket through the ball, and the volley goes more or less as he hoped, and now he's in position, on the 'T'. Strauss flicks the ball out of the corner, and it comes back along the same side wall. Perowne goes forward and volleys again. Half a dozen times the ball travels up and down the left-hand wall, until Perowne finds the space on his backhand to lift it high into the right-hand corner. They play that wall in hard straight drives, dancing in and out of each other's path, then they're chasing shots all over the court, with the advantage passing between them.

They've had this kind of rally before – desperate, mad, but also hilarious, as if the real contest is to see who will break down laughing first. But this is different. It's humourless, and longer, and attritional, for hearts this age can't race at above one hundred and eighty beats per minute for long, and soon someone will tire and fumble. And in this unwitnessed, somewhat inept, merely social game, both men have acquired an urgent sense of the point's importance. Despite the apology, the disputed let hangs between them. Strauss will have guessed that Perowne has given himself a good talking-to in the changing room. If his fightback can be resisted now, he'll be demoralised in no time and Strauss will take the match in three straight sets. As for Perowne, it's down to the rules of the game; until he's won the serve, he can't begin to score points.

It's possible in a long rally to become a virtually unconscious being, inhabiting the narrowest slice of the present, merely reacting, taking one shot at a time, existing only to keep going. Perowne is already at that state, digging in deep, when he remembers he's supposed to have a game plan. As it happens, just then the ball falls short and he's able to get under it to lob high into the rear left corner. Strauss raises his racket to volley, then changes his mind and runs back. He boasts the ball out, and Perowne lobs to the other side. Running from corner to corner to grub the ball out when you're tired is hard work. Each time he hits the ball, Strauss grunts a little louder, and Perowne is encouraged. He resists the kill shot because he thinks he'll mishit. Instead, he goes on lobbing, five times in a row, wearing his man down. The point ends on the fifth when Strauss's powerless ball falls feebly against the tin.

Love-all. They put down their rackets, and stand bent over, breathless, hands on knees, staring blindly into the floor, or press their palms and faces into the cool white walls, or wander aimlessly about the court mopping their brows with their untucked T-shirts and groaning. At other times they'd have a post-mortem on a point like that, but neither man speaks. Keen to force the pace, Perowne is ready first, and waits in the service box bouncing the ball against the floor. He serves right over Strauss's head and the ball, cooler and softer now, dies in the corner. One-love, and no effort wasted. This, rather than the point before, might be the important one. Perowne has his height and length now. The next point goes his way, and the next. Strauss is becoming exasperated by a series of identical serves, and because the rallies are brief or non-existent, the ball remains cold and inert, like putty, difficult to fish out of a tight space. And as he becomes more annoyed, Jay becomes even less competent. He can't reach the ball in the air, he can't get under it once it falls. A couple of serves he simply walks away from, and goes to the box to wait for the next. It's the repetition, the same angle, the same impossible height, the same dead ball that's getting to him. Soon he's lost six points.

Perowne wants to laugh wildly – an impulse he disguises as a cough. He isn't gloating, or triumphant – it's far too early for that. This is the delight of recognition, sympathetic laughter. He's amused because he knows exactly how Strauss is feeling: Henry is too well acquainted with the downward spiral of irritation and ineptitude, the little ecstasies of self-loathing. It's hilarious to recognise how completely another person resembles your imperfect self. And he knows how annoying his serve is. He wouldn't be able to return it himself. But Strauss was merciless when he was on top, and

Perowne needs the points. So he keeps on and on, floating the ball over his opponent's head and cruising right through to take the game, no effort at all, nine-love.

'I need a piss,' Jay says tersely, and leaves the court, still wearing his goggles and holding his racket.

Perowne doesn't believe him. Though he sees that it's a sensible move, the only way to interrupt the haemorrhaging of points, and even though he did the same thing less than ten minutes before, he still feels cheated. He could have taken the next set too with his infuriating serve. Now Strauss will be dousing his head under the tap and rethinking his game.

Henry resists the temptation to sit down. Instead he steps out to take a look at the other games – he's always hoping to learn something from the classier players. But the place is still deserted. The club members are either massing against the war, or unable to find a way through central London. As he comes back along the courts, he lifts his T-shirt and examines his chest. There's a dense black bruise to the left of his sternum. It hurts when he extends his left arm. Staring at the discoloured skin helps focus his troubled feelings about Baxter. Did he, Henry Perowne, act unprofessionally, using his medical knowledge to undermine a man suffering from a neurodegenerative disorder? Yes. Did the threat of a beating excuse him? Yes, no, not entirely. But this haematoma, the colour of an aubergine, the diameter of a plum – just a taste of what might have come his way – says yes, he's absolved. Only a fool would stand there and take a kicking when there was a way out. So what's troubling him? Strangely, for all the violence, he almost liked Baxter. That's to put it too strongly. He was intrigued by him, by his hopeless situation, and his refusal to give up. And there was a real intelligence there, and dismay that he was living the wrong life. And he, Henry, was obliged, or forced, to abuse his own power – but he allowed himself to be placed in that position. His attitude was wrong from the start, insufficiently defensive; his manner may have seemed pompous, or disdainful. Provocative perhaps. He could have been friendlier, even made himself accept a cigarette; he should have relaxed, from a position of strength, instead of which he was indignant and combative. On the other hand, there were three of them, they wanted his cash, they were eager for violence, they were planning it before they got out of their car. The loss of a wing mirror was cover for a mugging.

He arrives back outside the court, his unease intact, just as Strauss appears. His thick shoulders are drenched from his session at the washbasin, and his good humour is restored.

'OK,' he says as Perowne goes to the service box. 'No more Mister Nice Guy.'

Perowne finds it disabling, to have been left alone with his thoughts; just before he serves, he remembers his game plan. But the fourth game falls into no obvious pattern. He takes two points, then Strauss gets into the game and pulls ahead, three-two. There are long, scrappy rallies, with a run of unforced errors on both sides which bring the score to seven-all, Perowne to serve. He takes the last two points without trouble. Two games each.

They take a quick break to gather themselves for the final battle. Perowne isn't tired – winning games has been less physically demanding than losing them. But he feels drained of that fierce desire to beat Jay and would be happy to call it a draw and get on with his day. All morning he's been in some form of combat. But there's no chance of backing out. Strauss is enjoying the moment, playing it up, and saying as he goes to his position, 'Fight to the death,' and 'No pasaran!'

So, with a suppressed sigh, Perowne serves and, because he's run out of ideas, falls back on the same old lob. In fact, the moment he hits the ball, he knows it's near-perfect, curving high, set to drop sharply into the corner. But Strauss is in a peculiar, elated mood and he does an extraordinary thing. With a short running jump, he springs two, perhaps three feet into the air, and with racket fully extended, his thick, muscular back gracefully arched, his teeth bared, his head flung back and his left arm raised for balance, he catches the ball just before the peak of its trajectory with a whip-like backhand smash that shoots the ball down to hit the front wall barely an inch above the tin – a beautiful, inspired, unre-turnable shot. Perowne, who's barely moved from his spot, instantly says so. A fabulous shot. And suddenly, with the serve now in his opponent's hands, all over again, he wants to win.

Both men raise their games. Every point is now a drama, a playlet of sudden reversals, and all the seriousness and fury of the third game's long rally is resumed. Oblivious to their protesting hearts, they hurl themselves into every corner of the court. There are no unforced errors, every point is wrested, bludgeoned from the other. The server gasps out the score, but otherwise they don't speak. And as the score rises, neither man moves more than one point ahead. There's nothing at stake – they're not on the club's squash ladder. There's only the irreducible urge to win, as biological as thirst. And it's pure, because no one's watching, no one cares, not their friends, their wives, their children. It isn't even enjoy-able. It might become so in retrospect – and only to the winner. If a passer-by were to pause by the glass back wall to watch, she'd surely think these elderly players were once rated, and even now still have a little fire. She might also wonder if this is a grudge match, there's such straining desperation in the play.

What feels like half an hour is in fact twelve minutes. At seven-all Perowne serves from the left box and wins the point. He crosses the court to serve for the match. His con-centration is good, his confidence is up and so he plays a forceful backhand serve, at a narrow angle, close to the wall. Strauss slices it with his backhand, almost a tennis stroke, so that it drops to the front of the court. It's a good shot, but Perowne is in position and nips forward for the kill. He catches the ball on the rise and smashes it on his forehand, into the left rear corner. End of game, and victory. The instant he makes his stroke, he steps back – and collides with Strauss. It's a savage jolt, and both men reel and for a moment neither can talk.

Then Strauss, speaking quietly through heavy breathing, says, 'It's my point, Henry.'

And Perowne says, 'Jay, it's over. Three games to two.'

They pause again to take the measure of this calamitous difference.

Perowne says, 'What were you doing at the front wall?'

Jay walks away from him, to the box where, if they play the point again, he'll receive the serve. He's wanting to move things on – his way. He says, 'I thought you'd play a drop shot to your right.'

Henry tries to smile. His mouth is dry, his lips won't easily slide over his teeth. 'So I fooled you. You were out of position. You couldn't have returned it.'

The anaesthetist shakes his head with the earthbound calm his patients find so reassuring. But his chest is heaving. 'It came off the back wall. Plenty of bounce. Henry, you were right in my path.'

This deployment of each other's first name is tipped with poison. Henry can't resist it again himself. He speaks as though reminding Strauss of a long-forgotten fact. 'But Jay. You couldn't've reached that ball.'

Strauss holds Perowne's gaze and says quietly, 'Henry, I could.'

The injustice of the claim is so flagrant that Perowne can only repeat himself. 'You were way out of position.'

Strauss says, 'That's not against the rules.' Then he adds, 'Come on Henry. I gave you the benefit of the doubt last time.'

So he thinks he's calling in a debt. Perowne's tone of reasonableness becomes even harder to sustain. He says quickly, 'There was no doubt.'

'Sure there was.'

'Look, Jay. This isn't some kind of equal-opportunity forum. We take the case on its merits.'

'I agree. No need to give a lecture.'

Perowne's falling pulse rises briefly at the reproof – a moment's sudden anger is like an extra heartbeat, an unhelpful stab of arrhythmia. He has things to do. He needs to drive to the fishmonger's, go home and shower, and head out again, come back, cook a meal, open wine, greet his daughter, his father-in-law, reconcile them. But more than that, he needs what's already his; he fought back from two games down, and believes he's proved to himself something essential in his own nature, something familiar that he's forgotten lately. Now his opponent wants to steal it, or deny it. He leans his racket in the corner by his valuables to demonstrate that the game is over. Likewise, Strauss stands resolutely in the service box. They've never had anything like this before. Is it possibly about something else? Jay is looking at him with a sympathetic half-smile through pursed lips – an entirely concocted expression designed to further his claim. Henry can see himself – his pulse rate spikes again at the thought – crossing the parquet in four steps to give that complacent expression a brisk backhand slap. Or he could shrug and leave the court. But his victory is meaningless without consent. Fantasy apart, how can they possibly resolve this, with no referee, no common power?

Neither man has spoken for half a minute. Perowne spreads his hands and says, in a tone as artificial as Strauss's smile, 'I don't know what to do, Jay. I just know I hit a winner.'

But Strauss knows exactly what to do. He raises the stakes. 'Henry, you were facing the front. You didn't see the ball come off the back wall. I did because I was going towards it. So the question is this. Are you calling me a liar?'

This is how it ends.

'Fuck you, Strauss,' Perowne says and picks up his racket and goes to the service box.

And so they play the let, and Perowne serves the point again, and as he suspected might happen, he loses it, then he loses the next three points and before he knows it, it's all over, he's lost, and he's back in the corner picking up his wallet, phone, keys and watch. Outside the court, he pulls on his trousers and ties them with the chandler's cord, straps on his watch and puts on his sweater and fleece. He minds, but less than he did two minutes ago. He turns to Strauss who is just coming off the court.

'You were bloody good. I'm sorry about the dispute.'

'Fuck that. It could've been anyone's game. One of our best.'

They zip their rackets into their cases and sling them over their shoulders. Freed from red lines and the glaring white walls and the rules of the game, they walk along the courts to the Coke machine. Strauss buys a can for himself. Perowne doesn't want one. You have to be an American to want, as an adult, anything quite so sweet.

As they leave the building Strauss, pausing to drink deep, says, 'They're all going down with the flu and I'm on call tonight.'

Perowne says, 'Have you seen next week's list? Another heavy one.'

'Yeah. That old lady and her astrocytoma. She's not going to make it, is she?'

They are standing on the steps above the pavement on Huntley Street. There's more cloud now, and the air is cold and damp. It could well rain on the demonstration. The lady's name is Viola, her tumour is in the pineal region. She's seventy-eight, and it turns out that in her working life she was an astronomer, something of a force at Jodrell Bank in the sixties. On the ward, while the other patients watch TV, she reads books on mathematics and string theory. Aware of the lowering light, a winter's late-morning dusk, and not wanting to part on a bad note, a malediction, Perowne says, 'I think we can help her.'

Understanding him, Strauss grimaces, raises a hand in farewell, and the two men go their separate ways.

Three

Back in the padded privacy of his damaged car, its engine idling inaudibly in deserted Huntley Street, he tries Rosalind again. Her meeting has ended, and she's gone straight in to see the editor and is still with him, after forty-five minutes. The temporary secretary asks him to hold while she goes to find out more. While he waits, Perowne leans against the headrest and closes his eyes. He feels the itch of dried sweat on his face where he shaved. His toes, which he wiggles experimentally, seem encased in liquid, rapidly cooling. The importance of the game has faded to nothing, and in its place is a craving for sleep. Just ten minutes. It's been a tough week, a disturbed night, a hard game. Without looking, he finds the button that secures the car. The door locks are activated in rapid sequence, little resonating clunks, four semiquavers that lull him further. An ancient evolutionary dilemma: the need to sleep, the fear of being eaten. Resolved at last, by central locking.

Through the tiny receiver he holds to his left ear he hears the murmur of the open-plan office, the soft rattle of computer keys, and nearby a man's plaintive voice saying to someone out of earshot, 'He's not denying it . . . but he doesn't deny it . . . Yes, I know. Yes, that's our problem. He won't deny a thing.'

With eyes closed he sees the newspaper offices, the curled-edged coffee-stained carpet tiles, the ferocious heating system that bleeds boiling rusty water, the receding phalanxes of fluorescent lights illuminating the chaotic corners, the piles of paper that no one touches, for no one cares to know what they contain, what they are for, and the overinhabited desks pushed too close together. It's the spirit of the school art room. Everyone too hard-pressed to start sorting through the old dust heaps. The hospital is the same. Rooms full of junk, cupboards and filing cabinets that no one dares open. Ancient equipment in cream tin-plate housing, too heavy, too mysterious to eject. Sick buildings, in use for too long, that only demolition can cure. Cities and states beyond repair. The whole world resembling Theo's bedroom. A race of extraterrestrial grown-ups is needed to set right the general disorder, then put everyone to bed for an early night. God was once supposed to be a grown-up, but in disputes He childishly took sides. Then sending us an actual child, one of His own – the last thing we needed. A spinning rock already swarming with orphans . . .

'Mr Perowne?'

'What? Yes?'

'Your wife will phone you as soon as she's free, in about half an hour.'

Revived, he puts on his seatbelt, makes a three-point turn and heads towards Marylebone. The marchers are still in packed ranks on Gower Street, but the Tottenham Court Road is now open, with attack-waves of traffic surging northwards. He joins one briefly, then turns west and then north again and soon he's where Goodge and Charlotte Streets meet – a spot he's always liked, where the affairs of utility and pleasure condense to make colour and space brighter: mirrors, flowers, soaps, newspapers, electrical plugs, house paints, key cutting urbanely interleaved with expensive restaurants, wine and tapas bars, hotels. Who was the American novelist who said a man could be happy living on

Charlotte Street? Daisy will have to remind him again. So much commerce in a narrow space makes regular hillocks of bagged garbage on the pavements. A stray dog is worrying the sacks – gnawing filth whitens the teeth. Before turning west again, he sees way down the end of the street, his square, and on its far side, his house framed by bare trees. The blinds on the third floor are drawn – Theo is still asleep. Henry can still remember it, the exquisite tumbling late-morning doze of adolescence, and he never questions his son's claim to those hours. They won't last.

He crosses sombre Great Portland Street – it's the stone façades that make it seem always dusk here – and on Portland Place passes a Falun Gong couple keeping vigil across the road from the Chinese embassy. Belief in a miniaturised universe ceaselessly rotating nine times forwards, nine times backwards in the practitioner's lower abdomen is threatening the totalitarian order. Certainly, it's a non-material view. The state's response is beatings, torture, disappearances and murder, but the followers now outnumber the Chinese Communist Party. China is simply too populous, Perowne often thinks whenever he comes this way and sees the protest, to maintain itself in paranoia for much longer. Its economy's growing too fast, the modern world's too connected for the Party to keep control. Now you see mainland Chinese in Harrods, soaking up the luxury goods. Soon it will be ideas, and something will have to give. And here's the Chinese state meanwhile, giving philosophical materialism a bad name.

Then the embassy with its sinister array of roof aerials is behind him and he's passing through the orderly grid of medical streets west of Portland Place – private clinics and chintzy waiting rooms with bow-legged reproduction furniture and *Country Life* magazines. It is faith, as powerful as any religion, that brings people to Harley Street. Over the years his hospital has taken in and treated – free of charge, of course – scores of cases botched by some of the elderly overpaid incompetents around here. Waiting at red lights he watches three figures in black burkhas emerge from a taxi on Devonshire Place. They huddle together on the pavement comparing the number on a door with a card one of them holds. The one in the middle, the likely invalid, whose form is somewhat bent, totters as she clings to the forearms of her companions. The three black columns, stark against the canyon of creamy stucco and brick, heads bobbing, clearly arguing about the address, have a farcical appearance, like kids larking about at Halloween. Or like Theo's school pro-duction of *Macbeth* when the hollowed trees of Birnam Wood waited in the wings to clump across the stage to Dunsinane. They are sisters perhaps, bringing their mother to her last chance. The lights remain stubbornly red. Perowne pushes the gear shift into 'park'. What's he doing, pushing down so hard on the brake, tensing up his tender quadriceps? He can't help his distaste, it's visceral. How dismal, that anyone should be obliged to walk around so entirely obliterated. At least these ladies don't have the leather beaks. They really turn his stomach. And what would the relativists say, the cheerful pessimists from Daisy's college? That it's sacred, traditional, a stand against the fripperies of Western con-sumerism? But the men, the husbands – Perowne has had dealings with various Saudis in his office – wear suits, or trainers and tracksuits, or baggy shorts and Rolexes, and are entirely charming and worldly and thoroughly educated in both traditions. Would they care to carry the folkloric torch, and stumble about in the dark at midday?

The changed lights at last, the shift of scene – new porti-coes, different waiting rooms – and the mild demands of traffic on his concentration edge him out of these constricting thoughts. He's caught himself in a nascent rant. Let Islamic dress codes be! What should he care about burkhas? Veils for his irritation. No, irritation is too narrow a word. They and the Chinese Republic serve the gently tilting negative pitch of his mood. Saturdays he's accustomed to being thoughtlessly content, and here he is for the second time this morning sifting the elements of a darker mood. What's giving him the shivers? Not the lost game, or the scrape with Baxter, or even the broken night, though they all must have some effect. Perhaps it's merely the prospect of the afternoon when he'll head out towards the immensity of suburbs around Perivale. While there was a squash game posed between himself and his visit, he felt protected. Now there's only the purchase of fish. His mother no longer possesses the faculties to anticipate his arrival, recognise him when he's with her, or remember him after he's left. An empty visit. She doesn't expect him and she wouldn't be disappointed if he failed to show up. It's like taking flowers to a graveside – the true business is with the past. But she can raise a cup of tea to her mouth, and though she can't put a name to his face, or conjure any association, she's content with him sitting there, listening to her ramble. She's content with anyone. He hates going to see her, he despises himself if he stays away too long.

It's only while he's parking off Marylebone High Street that he remembers to turn on the midday news. The police are saying that two hundred and fifty thousand have gathered in central London. Someone for the rally is insisting on two million by the middle of the afternoon. Both sources agree that people are still pouring in. An elated marcher, who turns out to be a famous actress, raises her voice above the din of chanting and cheers to say that never in the history of the British Isles has there been such a huge assembly. Those who stay in their beds this Saturday morning will curse themselves they are not here. The earnest reporter reminds listeners that this is a reference to Shakespeare's St Crispin's Day speech, Henry the Fifth before the battle of Agincourt. The allusion is lost on Perowne as he reverses into a tight space between two four-wheel-drive jeeps. He doubts that Theo will be cursing himself. And why should a peace demonstrator want to quote a warrior king? The bulletin continues while Perowne sits with engine stilled, staring at a point of blue-green light among the radio buttons. Across Europe, and all around the world, people are gathering to express their preference for peace and torture. That's what the professor would say – Henry can hear his insistent, high-tenor voice. The story Henry regards as his own comes next. Pilot and co-pilot are being held for questioning at separate locations in west London. The police are saying nothing else. Why's that? Through the windscreen the prosperous street of red brick, the receding geometry of pavement cracks and small bare trees, look provisional, like an image projected onto a sheet of thin ice. Now an airport official is conceding that one of the men is of Chechen origin, but denying a rumour about a Koran found in the cockpit. And even if it were true, he adds, it would mean nothing. It is, after all, hardly an offence.

Quite so. Henry snaps open his door. The secular authority, indifferent to the babel of various gods, will guarantee religious freedoms. They should flourish. It's time to go shopping. Despite the muscle pain in his thighs, he strides briskly away from his car, locking it with the remote without looking back. Sudden winter sunlight clarifies his path along the High Street. The largest gathering of humanity in the history of the islands, less than two miles away, is not disturbing Marylebone's contentment, and Perowne himself is soothed as he dodges around the oncoming crowds and all the pushchairs with their serenely bundled infants. Such prosperity, whole emporia dedicated to cheeses, ribbons, Shaker furniture, is protection of a sort. This commercial wellbeing is robust and will defend itself to the last. It isn't rationalism that will overcome the religious zealots, but ordinary shopping and all that it entails – jobs for a start, and peace, and some commitment to realisable pleasures, the promise of appetites sated in this world, not the next. Rather shop than pray.

He turns the corner into Paddington Street and stoops in front of the open-air display of fish on a steeply raked slab of white marble. He sees at a glance that everything he needs is here. Such abundance from the emptying seas. On the tiled floor by the open doorway, piled in two wooden crates like rusting industrial rejects, are the crabs and lobsters, and in the tangle of warlike body parts there is discernible movement. On their pincers they're wearing funereal black bands. It's fortunate for the fishmonger and his customers that sea creatures are not adapted to make use of sound waves and have no voice. Otherwise there'd be howling from those crates. Even the silence among the softly stirring crowd is troubling. He turns his gaze away, towards the bloodless white flesh, and eviscerated silver forms with their unaccusing stare, and the deep-sea fish arranged in handy overlapping steaks of innocent pink, like cardboard pages of a baby's first book. Naturally, Perowne the fly-fisherman has seen the recent literature: scores of polymodal nociceptor sites just like ours in the head and neck of rainbow trout. It was once convenient to think biblically, to believe we're surrounded for our benefit by edible automata on land and sea. Now it turns out that even fish feel pain. This is the growing complication of the modern condition, the expanding circle of moral sympathy. Not only distant peoples are our brothers and sisters, but foxes too, and laboratory mice, and now the fish. Perowne goes on catching and eating them, and though he'd never drop a live lobster into boiling water, he's prepared to order one in a restaurant. The trick, as always, the key to human success and domination, is to be selective in your mercies. For all the discerning talk, it's the close at hand, the visible that exerts the overpowering force. And what you don't see . . . That's why in gentle Marylebone the world seems so entirely at peace.

Crab and lobsters are not on tonight's menu. If the clams and mussels he buys are alive, they are inert and decently closed up. He buys prawns already cooked in their shells, and three monkfish tails that cost a little more than his first car. Admittedly, a pile of junk. He asks for the bones and

heads of two skates to boil up for stock. The fishmonger is
a polite, studious man who treats his customers as members
of an exclusive branch of the landed gentry. He wraps each
species of fish in several pages of a newspaper. This is the
kind of question Henry liked to put to himself when he was
a schoolboy: what are the chances of this particular fish, from
that shoal, off that continental shelf ending up in the pages,
no, on this page of this copy of the *Daily Mirror*? Something
just short of infinity to one. Similarly, the grains of sand on
a beach, arranged just so. The random ordering of the world,
the unimaginable odds against any particular condition, still
please him. Even as a child, and especially after Aberfan, he
never believed in fate or providence, or the future being
made by someone in the sky. Instead, at every instant, a trillion trillion possible futures; the pickiness of pure chance and
physical laws seemed like freedom from the scheming of a
gloomy god.

The white plastic bag that holds the family dinner is heavy,
dense with flesh and sodden paper, and the handles bite into
his palm as he walks back to his car. Because of the pain in
his chest, he isn't able to transfer the load to his left hand.
Coming away from the dank seaweed odours of the fishmonger's, he thinks he can taste sweetness in the air, like
warm hay drying in the fields in August. The smell – surely
an illusion generated by contrast – persists, even with the
traffic and the February chill. All those family summers at
his father-in-law's place in the Ariège, in a south-west corner
of France where the land begins to ripple and swell before
the Pyrenees. The Chateau St Felix of warm, faintly pink
stone, and two rounded towers and the fragment of a moat
was where John Grammaticus retreated when his wife died,
and where he mourned her with the famous sad-sweet love
songs collected up in the volume called *No Exequies*. Not
famous to Henry Perowne, who read no poetry in adult life
even after he acquired a poet father-in-law. Of course, he

began as soon as he discovered he'd fathered a poet himself. But it cost him an effort of an unaccustomed sort. Even a first line can produce a tightness behind his eyes. Novels and movies, being restlessly modern, propel you forwards or backwards through time, through days, years or even generations. But to do its noticing and judging, poetry balances itself on the pinprick of the moment. Slowing down, stopping yourself completely, to read and understand a poem is like trying to acquire an old-fashioned skill like drystone walling or trout tickling.

When Grammaticus came out of mourning, more than twenty years ago, he began a series of love affairs that still continues. The pattern is well established. A younger woman, usually English, sometimes French, is taken on as secretary and housekeeper, and by degrees becomes a kind of wife. After two or three years she'll walk out, unable to bear any more, and it will be her replacement who greets the Perowne family in late July. Rosalind is scathing at each turnaround, always preferring the last to the next, then, over time, developing a fondness. After all, it's hardly the new arrival's fault. The children, entirely without judgment, even as teenagers, are immediately kind to her. Perowne, constitutionally bound to love one woman all his life, has been quietly impressed, especially as the old man advances into his seventies. Perhaps he's slowing down at last, for Teresa, a jolly forty-year-old librarian from Brighton, has been with him almost four years.

The dinners outside in the interminable dusk, the scented wheels of hay in the small steep fields that surround the gardens, and the fainter smell of swimming-pool chlorine on the children's skin, and warm red wine from Cahors or Cabrières, – it should be paradise. It almost is, which is why they continue to visit. But John can be a childish, domineering man, the sort of artist who grants himself the licence of a full-spectrum mood swing. He can migrate in the space of a bottle of red wine from twinkly anecdotes to sudden eruption, then a huffy retreat to his study – that tall stooping back receding across the lawn in the gloom towards the lighted house, with Betty or Jane or Francine, and now Teresa following him in to smooth things out. He's never quite got the trick of conversation, tending to hear in dissenting views, however mild, a kind of affront, an invitation to mortal combat. The years and the drink are not softening him. And naturally, as he ages and writes less, he's become unhappier. His exile in France has been a prolonged sulk, darkened over two decades by various slights from the home country. There was a bad four-year patch when his *Collected Poems* was out of print and another publisher had to be found. John minded when Spender and not he was knighted, when Raine not Grammaticus got the editorship at Faber, when he lost the Oxford Professorship of Poetry to Fenton, when Hughes and later Motion were preferred as Poets Laureate, and above all when it was Heaney who got the Nobel. These names mean nothing to Perowne. But he understands how eminent poets, like senior consultants, live in a watchful, jealous world in which reputations are edgily tended and a man can be brought low by status anxiety. Poets, or at least this poet, are as earthbound as the rest.

For a couple of summers when the children were babies the Perownes went elsewhere, but they found nothing in southern Europe as beautiful as St Felix. It was where Rosalind spent her childhood holidays. The chateau was enormous and it was easy to keep out of John's way – he liked to spend several hours a day alone. There were rarely more than two or three bad moments in a week, and with time they've mattered less. And as the pattern of his love life became established, Rosalind has had her own delicate reasons to keep close contact with her father. The chateau belonged to her maternal grandparents and was the love of her mother's life. She was the one who modernised and restored the place. The worry is that if age and illness wear John down into finally marrying one of his secretaries, the chateau could pass out of the family into the hands of a newcomer. French inheritance laws might have prevented that, but there's a document, an old tontine, to show that St Felix has been exempted and that English law prevails. In his irritable way, John has assured his daughter he'll never remarry and that the chateau will be hers, but he refuses to put anything in writing.

That background anxiety will probably be resolved. Another more forceful reason why they've kept up their summer visits to the chateau is because Daisy and Theo used to insist – those were the old days, before John and Daisy fell out. They loved their grandfather and considered his silly moods proof of his difference, his greatness – a view he rather shared himself. He doted on them, never raised his voice against them, and hid from them his worst outbursts. From the beginning, he considered himself – rightly as it's turned out – a figure in their intellectual development. Once it became clear that Theo was never going to take more than a polite interest in books, John encouraged him at the piano and taught him a simple boogie in C. Then he bought him an acoustic guitar and lugged up from the cellars cardboard boxes of blues recordings on heavy old 78s as well as LPs, and made tapes which arrived in London in regular packages. On Theo's fourteenth birthday, his grandfather drove him to Toulouse to hear John Lee Hooker in one of his last appearances. One summer evening after dinner, Grammaticus and Theo performed 'St James' Infirmary' under a brilliant sky of stars, the old man tipping back his head and warbling in a husky American accent that made Rosalind tearful. Theo, still only fourteen, improvised a sweet and melancholy solo. Perowne, sitting apart with his wine by the pool, bare feet in the water, was touched too and blamed himself for not taking his son's talent seriously enough.

That autumn Theo began travelling to east London for lessons with various elderly figures of the British blues scene, contacted through a friend of Rosalind's at her paper. According to Theo, Jack Bruce was the most impressive because he had formal training in music, played several instruments, revolutionised bass playing, knew everything about theory and recorded with everyone during the heroic period of the British blues, in the early sixties, the long-ago days of Blues Incorporated. He was also, Theo said, more patient with him than the others, and very kind. Perowne was surprised how an elevated figure like Bruce could be troubled to spend time instructing a mere boy. Disarmingly, Theo saw nothing unusual in it at all.

Through Bruce, Theo met some of the legendary figures. He was allowed to sit in on a Clapton masterclass. Long John Baldry came over from Canada for a reunion. Theo liked hearing about Cyril Davies and Alexis Korner, and the Graham Bond Organisation, and Cream's first concert. By some accident Theo jammed for several minutes with Ronnie Wood and met his older brother, Art. A year on, Art asked Theo to join a jamming session at the Eel Pie Club in the Cabbage Patch pub in Twickenham. In less than five years he seems to have possessed the whole tradition. Now, whenever he's at the chateau he plays for his grandfather and shows him his latest tricks. He seems to need John's approval, and the old man obliges. Perowne has to hand it to him, he opened up something in Theo that he, Perowne, might never have known about. It's true that on a body-surfing holiday in Pembrokeshire when Theo was nine, Henry showed him three simple chords on someone's guitar and how the blues worked in E. That was just one thing along with the frisbee throwing, grass skiing, quad biking, paintballing, stone skipping and in-line skating. He worked seriously on his children's fun back then. He even broke an arm keeping up on the skates. But he never could have guessed those three chords would become the basis of his son's professional life.

John Grammaticus has also been a force in Daisy's life, at least, until something went wrong between them. When she was thirteen, about the time he was teaching her brother the boogie in C, he asked her to tell him about the books she enjoyed. He heard her out and announced she was under-stretched – he was contemptuous of the 'young adult' fiction she was reading. He persuaded her to try *Jane Eyre*, and read the first chapters aloud to her, and mapped out for her the pleasures to come. She persisted, but only to please him. The language was unfamiliar, the sentences long, the pictures in her head, she kept saying, wouldn't come clear. Perowne tried the book and had much the same experience. But John kept his granddaughter at it, and finally, a hundred pages in, she fell for Jane and would hardly stop for meals. When the family went for a walk across the fields one afternoon, they left her with forty-one pages to go. When they returned they found her under a tree by the dovecote weeping, not for the story but because she had reached the end and emerged from a dream to grasp that it was all the creation of a woman she would never meet. She cried, she said, out of admiration, out of joy that such things could be made up. What sort of things, Grammaticus wanted to know. Oh Grandad, when the orphanage children die and yet the weather is so beautiful, and that bit when Rochester pretends to be a gypsy, and when Jane meets Bertha for the first time and she's like a wild animal . . .

He gave her Kafka's 'Metamorphosis', which he said was ideal for a thirteen-year-old girl. She raced through this domestic fairy story and demanded her parents read it too. She came into their bedroom in the chateau far too early one morning and sat on the bed to lament: that poor Gregor Samsa, his family are so *horrid* to him. How lucky he was to have a sister to clean out his room and find him the foods he liked. Rosalind took it in at a gulp, as though it were a legal brief. Perowne, by nature ill-disposed towards a tale of impossible transformation, conceded that by the end he was intrigued – he wouldn't have put it higher than that. He liked the unthinking cruelty of that sister on the final page, riding the tram with her parents to the last stop, stretching her young limbs, ready to begin a sensual life. A transformation he could believe in. This was the first book Daisy recommended to him, and marked the beginning of his literary education at her hands. Though he's been diligent over the years and tries to read almost everything she puts his way, he knows she thinks he's a coarse, unredeemable materialist. She thinks he lacks an imagination. Perhaps it's so, but she hasn't quite given up on him yet. The books are piled at his bedside, and she'll be arriving with more tonight. He hasn't even finished the Darwin biography, or started the Conrad.

From the summer of Brontë and Kafka onwards, Grammaticus took charge of Daisy's reading. He had firm, old-fashioned views of the fundamentals, not all of which he thought should be too pleasurable. He believed in children learning by rote, and he was prepared to pay up. Shakespeare, Milton and the King James Bible – five pounds for every twenty lines memorised from the passages he marked. These three were the sources of all good English verse and prose; he instructed her to roll the syllables around her tongue and feel their rhythmic power. The summer of her sixteenth birthday, Daisy earned a teenage fortune at the chateau, chanting, even singing, parts of *Paradise Lost*, and Genesis and various gloomy musings of Hamlet. She recited Browning, Clough, Chesterton and Masefield. In one good week she earned forty-five pounds. Even now, six years on, at the age of twenty-three, she claims to be able to spout – her word – non-stop for more than two hours. By the time she was eighteen and leaving school she'd read a decent fraction of what her grandfather called the obvious stuff. He wouldn't hear of her going anywhere to study English Literature other than his own Oxford college. Though Henry and Rosalind begged him not to, he probably put in a good word for her. Dismissively, he told them that these days the system was incorruptible and he couldn't help even if he wanted to. Familiarity with their own professions told them this could never be strictly true. But it soothed their consciences, the handwritten note to Daisy's headmaster from a tutor which said she'd given a dazzling interview, backing every insight with a quotation.

A year later she may have had a little too much success for her grandfather's taste. She arrived at St Felix two days after the rest of the family, and brought with her the poem that had won her that year's Newdigate Prize. Henry and Rosalind had never heard of the Newdigate, but were automatically pleased. But it meant more, perhaps too much, to Daisy's grandfather who had won it himself back in the late fifties. He took her pages into his study – her parents were only allowed to see them later. The poem described at length the tender meditations of a young woman at the end of another affair. Once more she has stripped the sheets from her bed and taken them to the launderette where she watches through the 'misted monocle' of the washing machine, 'all stains of us turning to be purged'. These affairs also turned, like the seasons, too quickly, 'running green to brown' with 'windfalls sweetly rotting to oblivion'. The stains are not really sins but 'watermarks of ecstasy' or later 'milky palimpsests', and therefore not so easily removed after all. Vaguely religious, mellifluously erotic, the poem suggested to a troubled Perowne that his daughter's first year at university had been more crowded than he could ever have guessed. Not just a boyfriend, or a lover, but a whole succession, to the point of serenity. This may have been why Grammaticus took against the poem – his protégée had struck out and found other men. Or it may have been one more pitiful attack of status anxiety – in forming Daisy's literary education he hadn't intended to produce yet another rival poet. This Newdigate after all had also been won by Fenton and Motion.

Teresa made a simple supper of salade niçoise with fresh tuna from the market in Pamiers. The dining table was set right outside the kitchen, on the edge of a wide expanse of lawn. It was another unexceptionally beautiful evening, with purplish shadows of trees and shrubs advancing across the dried grass, and crickets beginning to take up where the afternoon cicadas left off. Grammaticus was last to appear, and Perowne's guess, as his father-in-law lowered himself into the chair next to Daisy's, was that he'd already sunk a bottle of wine or more on his own. This was confirmed when he laid his hand on his granddaughter's wrist, and with that hectoring frankness that drunks mistake for intimacy, told her that her poem was ill-advised and not the sort of thing that generally won the Newdigate. It wasn't good at all, he told her, as though she must know it already and was bound to agree. He was, as a psychiatrist might have said, disinhibited.

As early as her final year at school, just eighteen, head girl and academic star of the sixth form, Daisy had developed her precise and self-contained manner. She's a light-boned young woman, trim and compact, with a small elfin face, short black hair and straight back. Her composure looks impregnable. At dinner that night, only her parents and brother knew how fragile that controlled appearance was. But she was cool as she unhurriedly withdrew her hand and looked at her grandfather, waiting for him to say more. He took a long pull on his wine, as though it were a pint pot of lukewarm beer, and advanced into her silence. He said the rhythms were loose and clumsy, the stanzas were of irregular length. Henry looked at Rosalind, willing her to intervene. If she didn't, he would have to, and the matter would assume too much importance. To his shame, he was not absolutely certain what a stanza was until he looked in a dictionary later that night. Rosalind held back – breaking into her father's flow too early could cause an explosion. Managing him was a delicate art. On her side of the table, Teresa was already suffering. In her time, and on many occasions in the years before her time, there had been scenes like this, though never one that involved the children. She knew it could not end well. Theo rested his jaw in his palm and stared at his plate.

Encouraged by his granddaughter's silence, John went on a roll, warming to his own authority, stupidly affectionate in his manner. He was confusing the young woman in front of him with the sixteen-year-old whom he had coached in the Elizabethan poets of the silver age. If he'd ever known, he had forgotten what one good year at a university could do. He could only imagine she felt as he did, and he was only telling her the obvious: the poem was too long, it tried too hard to shock, there was a simile they both knew was convoluted. He paused to drink deeply again, and still she said nothing.

Then he told her her poem was not original, and finally got a reaction. She cocked her neat head and raised an eyebrow. Not original? Perowne, seeing a telltale tremble in the dainty chin, thought the cool manner wouldn't hold. Rosalind spoke up at last, but her father talked over her. Yes, a little-known but gifted poet, Pat Jourdan, a woman of the Liverpool school, had written up a similar idea in the sixties – the end of the affair, the spinning sheets at the launderette displayed before the thoughtful poet. Was it possible that Grammaticus knew how idiotic his behaviour was but could not pull back? In the old man's weak eyes there was a dog-like cringing look, as if he was scaring himself and was pleading for someone to restrain him. His voice cracked as he strained for affability, and he talked on and on, making himself more ridiculous. The silence around the table that had enabled him was now his punishment, his affliction. Theo was gazing at him in amazement, shaking his head. Of course, John was saying, he wasn't accusing Daisy of plagiarism, she may have read the poem and forgotten about it, or simply reinvented it for herself. After all, it wasn't such an exceptional or unusual idea, but either way . . .

At last he wound down, unable to make his situation worse. Perowne was pleased to see that his daughter wasn't crushed. She was furious. He could see the pulse in her neck throbbing beneath the skin. But she was not going to relieve her grandfather with any sort of outburst. Suddenly, unable to bear the silence, he started up again, talking hurriedly, trying to soften his judgment without actually altering it. Daisy cut in and said she thought they should talk about something else, at which Grammaticus muttered a simple 'Oh fuck!', stood up and went indoors. They watched him go – a familiar sight, that receding form, but upsetting too, for it was the first time that summer.

Daisy stayed on another three days, long enough for her grandfather to have thought of ways of resuming relations. But the next day he was brisk and cheerfully self-absorbed and seemed to have forgotten. Or he was simply pretending – like many drinkers, he liked to think each new day drew a line under the day before. When Daisy left for Barcelona – it was an arrangement that had long been in place – she brought herself to kiss him goodbye on both cheeks and he gripped her arm, and afterwards was able to persuade himself that a reconciliation had taken place. When Rosalind and then Henry tried to convince him that he still had work to do on Daisy, he told them they were making trouble. He must have wondered then why she didn't appear at St Felix the following two summers. She found good reasons to travel with friends in China and Brazil. He should have written to her when she got her first, but by then he had fallen into a sulk about the matter. So it was a risky move when Rosalind sent him a proof copy of Daisy's poems. Wasn't he bound to dislike them? Especially when her publisher was the one who let his *Collected* go out of print.

If his enthusiasm for *My Saucy Bark* was tactical, he concealed it brilliantly. His long letter to her opened by conceding he had been 'a disgraceful boor' about the launderette poem. It wasn't included in the book, and Henry wondered, though never aloud, whether she thought her grandfather was right about it all along. She had found a conversational tone, he told her in his letter, that was nevertheless rich with meaning and association. Every now and then that everyday, level voice was interrupted by lines of sudden emotional intensity and 'secular transcendence'. In this respect, he found everywhere in her poems the spirit of his beloved Larkin, but 'invigorated by a young woman's sensuality', and darker humour. In his near-illegible longhand he praised the 'intellectual muscle', the 'courage of hard and independent thinking' that informed the scheme of her poems. He loved the 'slatternly wit' of her 'Six Short Songs'. He said he 'laughed like an idiot' at 'The Ballad of the Brain on my Shoe' – a poem that resulted from Daisy's visit to the operating theatre one morning to watch her father at work. It's the one, of course, that Henry likes least. His daughter was present for a straightforward MCA aneurysm. No grey or white matter was lost. He thought he caught in the poem art's essential but – he had to suppose – forgivable dishonesty. Daisy sent her grandfather an affectionate postcard. She told him how much she missed him and how much she owed to him. She said his remarks thrilled her and she was reading them over and again and was giddy with his praise.

Now the old man and Daisy are converging from Toulouse and Paris. A TV company wanting to make a programme about his life is putting Grammaticus up in style at Claridge's. At dinner tonight the reconciliation will be sealed – this is the idea, but Perowne, lugging his bag of fish, moving with the crowds back down the High Street, has shared too many meals with his father-in-law to be optimistic; and matters have moved on in the past three years. These days Grammaticus starts his evenings or late afternoons the way he used to, with a few serious jolts of gin before the wine – a habit he managed to kick for a while in his sixties. Another development is the tumblers of Scotch to round out the day, before he visits the pre-bedtime 'cleansing' beer. If he appears on the doorstep in a cheerful or excited state, he'll feel that unexamined compulsion of his to dominate in his daughter's house which makes him drink faster. Becoming drunk is a journey that generally elates him in the early stages – he's good company, expansive, mischievous and fun, the famous old poet, almost as happy listening as talking. But once the destination is met, once established up there on that unsunny plateau, a fully qualified drunk, the nastier muses, the goblins of aggression, paranoia, self-pity take control. The expectation now is that an evening with John will go bad somehow, unless everyone around is prepared to toil at humouring and flattering and hours of frozen-faced listening. No one will be.

Perowne reaches his car and stows his odorous bag in the boot, in among the family's hiking boots and backpacks and last summer's tennis balls. The unprofessional thought sometimes occurs to him that the kindest touch for everyone, including the old man himself, would be to slip him a minor tranquilliser while he's still on the cheerful rising track, some short-acting benzodiazepine derivative dissolved into a strong red wine like Rioja, and as his yawns multiply, guide him up the stairs to his room, or towards his taxi – the famous old poet in bed half an hour before midnight, tired and happy, and no harm done.

He's driven a couple of hundred yards through Marylebone in slow-moving traffic when he notices in his rear-view mirror, two cars back, a red BMW. All he can actually see is a corner of its offside wing and he can't tell whether the wing mirror is missing. A white van interposes itself at a junction, and he can barely see the red car at all. It's not impossible that it's Baxter, but he feels no particular anxiety about seeing him again. In fact, he wouldn't mind talking to him. His case is interesting, and the offer of help was sincere. What concerns him more is that the Saturday-morning traffic is no longer moving – there's an obstruction ahead. When he looks again, the red car has gone. And then he forgets about it; his attention is caught by a television shop to his left.

In its window display are angled banks of identical images on various kinds of screen – cathode ray, plasma, handheld, home cinema. What's showing on every device is the Prime Minister giving a studio interview. The close-up of a face is steadily becoming a close-up of a mouth, until the lips fill half the screen. He has suggested in the past that if we knew as much as he did, we too would want to go to war. Perhaps in this slow zoom the director is consciously responding to a calculation a watching population is bound to want to make: is this politician telling the truth? But can anyone really know the sign, the tell of an honest man? There's been some good work on this very question. Perowne has read Paul Ekman on the subject. In the smile of a self-conscious liar certain muscle groups in the face are not activated. They only come to life as the expression of genuine feeling. The smile of a deceiver is flawed, insufficient. But can we see these muscles resting there inert when there's so much local variation in faces, pads of fat, odd concavities, differences of bone structure? Especially difficult when the first and best unconscious move of a dedicated liar is to persuade himself he's sincere. And once he's sincere, all deception vanishes.

For all the difficulties, the instinctive countermeasures, we go on watching closely, trying to read a face, trying to measure intentions. Friend or foe? It's an ancient preoccupation. And even if, down through the generations, we are only right slightly more than half the time, it's still worth doing. More than ever now, on the edge of war, when the country still imagines it can call back this deed before it's too late. Does this man sincerely believe that going to war will make us safer? Does Saddam possess weapons of terrifying potential? Simply, the Prime Minister might be sincere and wrong. Some of his bitterest opponents don't doubt his good faith. He could be on the verge of a monstrous miscalculation. Or perhaps it will work out – the dictator vanquished without hundreds of thousands of deaths, and after a year or two, a democracy at last, secular or Islamic, nestling among the weary tyrannies of the Middle East. Wedged in traffic alongside the multiple faces, Henry experiences his own ambivalence as a form of vertigo, of dizzy indecision. In neurosurgery he chose a safe and simple profession.

He knows of patients who can't even recognise, let alone read, the faces of their closest family or friends. In most cases the right middle fusiform gyrus has been compromised, usually by a stroke. Nothing a neurosurgeon can do about that. And it must have been a moment of deficient face recognition – transient prosopagnosia – that was involved in his one meeting with Tony Blair. It was back in May 2000, a time now acquiring a polish, a fake gleam of innocence. Before the current preoccupations, there was a public project widely accounted a success. No one seemed to deny, something went right. A disused power station on the south bank of the Thames was discovered to be useful as a museum for contemporary art. The conversion was bold and brilliant. At the opening party for the Tate Modern there were four thousand guests – celebrities, politicians, the great and good – and hundreds of young men and women distributing champagne and canapés, and a general euphoria untainted by cynicism – unusual at such events. Henry was there as a member of the Royal College of Surgeons. Rosalind was invited through her newspaper. Theo and Daisy came along too, and vanished into the crowd as soon as they arrived. Their parents didn't see them until the following morning. The guests gathered in the industrial vastness of the old turbine hall where the din of thousands of excited voices seemed to bear aloft a giant spider hovering below iron girders. After an hour, Henry and Rosalind broke away from their friends and wandered with their drinks among the exhibits through the relatively deserted galleries.

Such was their wellbeing that even the sullen orthodoxies of conceptual art seemed part of the fun, like earnest displays of pupils' work at a school open day. Perowne liked Cornelia Parker's 'Exploding Shed' – a humorous construction, like a brilliant idea bursting out of a mind. They came into a room of Rothkos and for several minutes remained pleasantly becalmed among the giant slabs of dusky purple and orange. Then they went through a wide portal into the gallery next door and came across what at first seemed like another installation. Part of it, a low pile of bricks, really was an exhibit. Standing beyond it, at the far end of the large room, was the Prime Minister and at his side the gallery director. Twenty feet away, on the nearside of the bricks, nominally restrained by a velvet rope, was the press corps – thirty photographers or more, and reporters – and what looked like gallery officials and Downing Street staff. The Perownes had come in on an oddly silent moment. Blair and the director smiled and posed for the cameras, whose pictures would also include the famous bricks. The flashes twinkled randomly, but none of the photographers was calling out in the usual way. The calmness of the scene seemed an extension of the Rothko gallery next door.

Then the director, perhaps looking for an excuse to bring the session to an end, raised a hand in greeting to Rosalind. They knew each other through some legal matter that had ended amicably. The director guided Blair around the bricks and crossed the gallery towards the Perownes, and behind them wheeled the retinue, the photographers with their cameras up and ready, the diarists with their notebooks in case something interesting should happen at last. Helplessly, the Perownes watched them all approach. In a sudden press of bodies they were introduced to the Prime Minister. He took Rosalind's hand first, then Henry's. The grip was firm and manly, and to Perowne's surprise, Blair was looking at him with recognition and interest. The gaze was intelligent and intense, and unexpectedly youthful. So much had yet to happen.

He said, 'I really admire the work you're doing.'

Perowne said automatically, 'Thank you.' But he was impressed. It was just conceivable, he supposed, that Blair with his good memory and reputation for absorbing the details of his ministers' briefs, would have heard of the hospital's excellent report last month – all targets met – and even of the special mention of the neurosurgery department's exceptional results. Procedures twenty-three per cent up on last year. Later Henry realised what an absurd notion that was.

The Prime Minister, who still had hold of his hand, added, 'In fact, we've got two of your paintings hanging in Downing Street. Cherie and I adore them.'

'No, no,' Perowne said.

'Yes, yes,' the Prime Minister insisted, pumping his hand. He was in no mood for artistic modesty.

'No, I think you – '

'Honestly. They're in the dining room.'

'You're making a mistake,' Perowne said, and on that word there passed through the Prime Minister's features for the briefest instant a look of sudden alarm, of fleeting self-doubt. No one else saw his expression freeze and his eyes bulge minimally. A hairline fracture had appeared in the assurance of power. Then he continued as before, no doubt making the rapid calculation that given all the people pushing in around them trying to listen, there could be no turning back. Not without a derisive press tomorrow.

'Anyway. They truly are marvellous. Congratulations.'

One of the aides, a woman in a black trouser suit, cut in and said, 'Prime Minister, we have three and a half minutes. We have to move.'

Blair let go of Perowne's hand and without a farewell beyond a nod and a curt pursing of the lips, turned and let himself be led away. And the crew, the press, the flunkeys, the bodyguards, the gallery underlings and their director surged behind him, and within seconds the Perownes were standing in the empty gallery with the bricks as if nothing had happened at all.

Watching from his car the multiple images cutting between interviewer and guest, Perowne wonders if such moments, stabs of cold panicky doubt, are an increasing part of the Prime Minister's days, or nights. There might not be a second UN resolution. The next weapons inspectors' report could also be inconclusive. The Iraqis might use biological weapons against the invasion force. Or, as one former inspector keeps insisting, there might no longer be any weapons of mass destruction at all. There's talk of famine and three million refugees, and they're already preparing the reception camps in Syria and Iran. The UN is predicting hundreds of thousands of Iraqi deaths. There could be revenge attacks on London. And still the Americans remain vague about their post-war plans. Perhaps they have none. In all, Saddam could be overthrown at too high a cost. It's a future no one can read. Government ministers speak up loyally, various newspapers back the war, there's a fair degree of anxious support in the country along with the dissent, but no one really doubts that in Britain one man alone is driving the matter forward. Night sweats, hideous dreams, the wild, lurching fantasies of sleeplessness? Or simple loneliness? Whenever he sees him now on screen, Henry looks out for an awareness of the abyss, for that hairline crack, the moment of facial immobility, the brief faltering he privately witnessed. But all he sees is certainty, or at worst a straining earnestness.

He finds a vacant residents' parking space across the road from his front door. As he takes the shopping from the boot of his car, he sees in the square, lounging by the bench nearest his house, the same young men who are often there in the early evening, and then again late at night. There are two West Indians and two, sometimes three Middle Easterners who might be Turks. All of them look genial and prosperous, and frequently lean on each other's shoulders and laugh loudly. At the kerb is a Mercedes, same model as Perowne's, but black, and a figure always at the wheel. Now and then a stranger will come by and stop to talk to the group. One of them will cross to the car, consult with the driver and return, there'll be another huddle, and then the stranger will walk on. They are entirely self-contained and unthreatening, and Perowne assumed for a long time they were dealers, running a pavement café in cocaine perhaps, or ecstasy and marijuana. Their customers do not look haunted or degenerate enough to be heroin or crack users. It was Theo who put his father right. The group sells tickets for various fringe rap gigs around the city. They also sell bootleg CDs and can arrange cheap long-distance flights as well as fix up cut-rate premises and DJs for parties, limos for weddings and airports and cut-rate health and travel insurance; for a commission they can introduce asylum seekers and illegal aliens to solicitors. The group pays no taxes or office overheads and is highly competitive. Whenever Perowne sees these people he vaguely feels, as he does now, crossing the road to his door, that he owes them an apology. One day he'll buy something from them.

Theo is down in the kitchen, probably preparing one of his fruit and yoghurt breakfasts. Henry leaves the fish at the top of the stairs, calls down a greeting and goes up to the second floor. The bedroom feels overheated and confined, and depleted by daylight. It looks and feels a better, kinder place lit by dimmed lamps, with the day's work done and the promise of sleep; being here in the early afternoon reminds him of a bad spell of flu. He pulls off his trainers, peels away his damp socks and drops them in the laundry basket, and goes to the central window to open it. And there it is again, or another one, directly below him, slowly rounding the corner of the house where the street meets the square. His view is mostly of its roof, and his sightline to the off-side wing mirror is entirely obscured, even though he pushes the window up and leans right out. Nor can he see the driver, or any passengers. He watches it cruise along the northern side of the square and turn right into Conway Street and disappear. This time he doesn't feel quite so detached. But what is he then? Interested, or even faintly troubled? It's a common enough make, and until two or three years ago, red was a common choice. On the other hand, why reason away the possibility of it being Baxter? His predicament is terrible and fascinating – the tough-guy street existence must have masked

a longing for a better kind of life even before the degenera-
tive disease showed its first signs. Perowne comes away from
the window and goes towards the bathroom. Baxter would
hardly need to tail him. The Mercedes is distinctive enough,
and it's parked right outside the house. Yes, he'd like to see
Baxter again, in office hours, and hear more and give him
some useful contacts. But Henry doesn't want him hanging
around the square.

As he finishes undressing, his mobile rings from within
the heap of clothes he's let fall at his feet. He fumbles and
finds it.

'Darling?' she says.

Rosalind at last. What better moment? He takes the phone
through to the bedroom and sprawls naked on his back on
the half-made bed where hours before they made love. From
the radiators he feels on his bare skin waves of heat like a
desert breeze. The thermostat is set too high. He has a half,
or perhaps really a quarter of an erection. If she hadn't been
working today, if there were no weekend crisis on the paper,
if her mild-mannered editor wasn't such a bruiser when it
comes to the small print of press freedom, she and Henry
might be here together now. It's how they sometimes pass
an hour or two on a winter's Saturday afternoon. The sexi-
ness of a four o'clock dusk.

The bathroom mirror, with the help of kindly illumination
and a correct angle, allows Henry an occasional reminder of
his youth. But Rosalind, by some trick of inner light or his
own loving folly, still appears to resemble strongly, constantly,
the woman he first knew all those years ago. The older sister
of that young Rosalind, but not yet her mother. How long
can this last? In their essentials, the individual elements
remain unchanged: the near luminous pallor of her skin –
her mother, Marianne, was of Celtic descent; the scant, delicate eyebrows – almost non-existent; that level, soft green
regard; and her teeth, white as ever, (his own are going grey)
the upper set perfectly shaped, the lower, faintly awry – a

girlish imperfection he's never wanted her to remedy; the way the unfeigned breadth of the smile proceeds from a shy start; on her lips, an orange-rose gleam that is all her own; the hair, cut short now, still reddish-brown. In repose she has an air of merry intelligence, an undiminished taste for fun. It remains a beautiful face. Like everyone in their forties, she has her moments of dismay, weary before the mirror at bedtime, and he's recognised in himself that look, almost a snarl, of savage appraisal. We're all travelling in the same direction. Reasonably, she's not entirely convinced when he tells her that the soft swelling at her hips is rather to his taste, as is the heaviness in her breasts. But it's true. Yes, he would be happy lying down with her now.

He guesses that her state of mind will be remote from his own – in her black office clothes, hurrying in and out of meetings – so he pulls himself up into a sitting position on the bed to talk sensibly.

'How's it going?'

'Our judge is stuck in a traffic jam south of Blackfriars Bridge. It's the demonstration. But I think he's going to give us what we want.'

'Lift the injunction?'

'Yup. Monday morning. ' She sounds speedy and pleased.

'You're a genius,' Henry says. 'What about your dad?'

'I can't collect him from his hotel. It's the demonstration. The traffic's hell. He's going to make his own way in a taxi.' She pauses and says at a slightly slower pace, 'And how are you?' The downward inflection and extension of the final word is tender, a clear reference to this morning. He was wrong about her mood. He's about to tell her that he's naked on the bed, wanting her, then he changes his mind. This isn't the time for telephone foreplay, when he has to get out of the house and she has her own business to conclude. And there are more important things he's yet to tell her which will have to wait until after tonight's dinner, or tomorrow morning.

He says, 'I'm heading off to Perivale as soon as I've had a shower.' And because that isn't the answer to her question, he adds, 'I'm all right, but I'm looking forward to some time with you.' That isn't enough either, so he says, 'Various things've happened I need to talk to you about.'

'What sort of things?'

'Nothing terrible. I'd rather tell you when I see you.'

'OK. But give me a clue.'

'Last night when I couldn't sleep I was at the window. I saw that Russian cargo plane.'

'Darling. That must have been scary. What else?'

He hesitates, and his hand, by its own volition, caresses the area around the bruise on his chest. What would be the heading, as she sometimes puts it? Road-rage showdown. Attempted mugging. A neural disease. The wing mirror. The rear-view mirror.

'I lost at squash. I'm getting too old for this game.'

She laughs. 'I don't believe that's what it is.' But she sounds reassured. She says, 'There's something you may have forgotten. Theo's got a big rehearsal this afternoon. A few days ago I heard you promising to be there.'

'Damn. What time?' He has no memory of such a promise.

'At five in that place in Ladbroke Grove.'

'I better move.'

He rises from the bed and takes the phone into the bathroom for the farewells.

'I love you.'

'I love you,' she answers, and rings off.

He steps under the shower, a forceful cascade pumped down from the third floor. When this civilisation falls, when the Romans, whoever they are this time round, have finally left and the new dark ages begin, this will be one of the first luxuries to go. The old folk crouching by their peat fires will tell their disbelieving grandchildren of standing naked mid-winter under jet streams of hot clean water, of lozenges of scented soaps and of viscous amber and vermilion liquids

they rubbed into their hair to make it glossy and more vol-
uminous than it really was, and of thick white towels as big
as togas, waiting on warming racks.

He wears a suit and tie five days a week. Today he's
wearing jeans, sweater and scuffed brown boots, and who's
to know that he himself is not the great guitarist of his generation? As he bends to tie his laces, he feels a sharp pain in
his knees. It's pointless holding out until he's fifty. He'll give
himself six more months of squash and one last London
Marathon. Will he be able to bear it, having these pastimes
only in his past? At the mirror he's lavish with his aftershave
– in winter especially, there's sometimes a scent in the air at
the old people's home that he prefers to counteract.

He steps out of the bedroom and then, sideways on, skips
down the first run of stairs two at a time, without holding
the banister for safety. It's a trick he learned in adolescence,
and he can do it better than ever. But a skidding boot heel,
a shattered coccyx, six months on his back in bed, a year
rebuilding his wasted muscles – the premonitory fantasy fills
less than half a second, and it works. He takes the next flight
in the ordinary way.

In the basement kitchen Theo has already taken the fish
and stowed it in the fridge. The tiny TV is on with muted
sound, and shows a helicopter's view of Hyde Park. The
massed crowds appear as a smear of brown, like lichen on
a rock. Theo has constructed his breakfast in a large salad
bowl which contains close to a kilo of oatmeal, bran, nuts,
blueberries, loganberries, raisins, milk, yoghurt, chopped
dates, apple and bananas.

Theo nods at it. 'Want some?'

'I'll eat leftovers.'

Henry takes a plate of chicken and boiled potatoes from the
fridge and eats standing up. His son sits on a high stool at the
centre island, hunched over his giant bowl. Beyond the debris
of crumbs, wrappers and fruit skins are pages of music
manuscript with chords written out in pencil. His shoulders

are broad, and the bunched muscle stretches the fabric of his clean white T-shirt. The hair, the skin of his bare arms, the thick dark brown eyebrows still have the same rich, smooth new-made quality Perowne used to admire when Theo was four.

Perowne gestures towards the TV. 'Still not tempted?'

'I've been watching. Two million people. Truly amazing.'

Naturally, Theo is against the war in Iraq. His attitude is as strong and pure as his bones and skin. So strong he doesn't feel much need to go tramping through the streets to make his point.

'What's the latest on that plane? I heard about the arrests.'

'No one's saying anything.' Theo tips more milk into his salad bowl. 'But there are rumours on the Internet.'

'About the Koran.'

'The pilots are radical Islamists. One's a Chechen, the other's Algerian.'

Perowne pulls up a stool and as he sits feels his appetite fading. He pushes his plate aside.

'So how does it work? They set fire to their own plane in the cause of jihad, then land safely at Heathrow.'

'They bottled out.'

'So their idea was to sort of join in today's demonstration.'

'Yeah. They'd be making a point. Make war on an Arab nation and this is the kind of thing that's going to happen.'

It doesn't sound plausible. But in general, the human disposition is to believe. And when proved wrong, shift ground. Or have faith, and go on believing. Over time, down through the generations, this may have been the most efficient: just in case, believe. All day, Perowne himself has suspected the story was not all it seemed, and now Theo is feeding this longing his father has to hear the worst. On the other hand, if the rumours about the plane come from the Internet, the chances of their inaccuracy are increased.

Henry gives a condensed account of his scrape with Baxter and his friends and of the symptoms of Huntington's and the lucky escape.

Theo says, 'You humiliated him. You should watch that.'

'Meaning what?'

'These street guys can be proud. Also, Dad, I can't believe we've lived here all this time and you and Mum have never been mugged.'

Perowne looks at his watch and stands. 'Mum and I just don't have the time. I'll see you in Notting Hill around five.'

'You're coming. Excellent!'

It is part of Theo's charm, not to have pressed him. And if his father hadn't shown up, he wouldn't have mentioned it.

'Start without me. You know what it's like, getting from Granny's.'

'We'll be doing the new song. Chas'll be there. We'll keep it till you arrive.'

Chas is his favourite among Theo's friends, and the most educated too, dropping out of an English degree in his third year at Leeds to play in a band. A wonder that life so far – suicidal mother, absent father, two brothers, members of a strict Baptist sect – hasn't crushed all that relaxed good nature out of him. Something about the name of St Kitts – saints, kids, kittens – has produced a profusion of kindness in one giant lad. Since meeting him, Perowne has developed a vague ambition to visit the island.

From a corner of the room he picks up a potted plant wrapped in tissue, an expensive orchid he bought a few days ago in the florist's by Heal's. He stops at the doorway and raises a hand in farewell. 'I'm cooking tonight. Don't forget to straighten out the kitchen.'

'Yeah.' Then Theo adds without irony, 'Remember me to Granny. Give her my love.'

Clean and scented, with a dull, near-pleasurable ache in his limbs, driving west in light traffic, Perowne finds he's feeling better about seeing his mother. He knows the routine well enough. Once they're established together, face to face, with their cups of dark brown tea, the tragedy of her situation will be obscured behind the banality of detail, of managing the suffocating minutes, of inattentive listening. Being with her isn't so difficult. The hard part is when he comes away, before this visit merges in memory with all the rest, when the woman she once was haunts him as he stands by the front door and leans down to kiss her goodbye. That's when he feels he's betraying her, leaving her behind in her shrunken life, sneaking away to the riches, the secret hoard of his own existence. Despite the guilt, he can't deny the little lift he feels, the lightness in his step when he turns his back and walks away from the old people's place and takes his car keys from his pocket and embraces the freedoms that can't be hers. Everything she has now fits into her tiny room. And she hardly possesses the room because she's incapable of finding it unaided, or even of knowing that she has one. And when she is in it, she doesn't recognise her things. It's no longer possible to bring her to the Square to stay, or take her on excursions; a small journey disorients or even terrifies her. She has to remain behind, and naturally she doesn't understand that either.

But the thought of the leave-taking ahead doesn't trouble him now. He's at last suffused by the mild euphoria that follows exercise. That blessed self-made opiate, beta-endorphin, smothering every kind of pain. There's a merry Scarlatti harpsichord on the radio tinkling through a progression of chords that never quite resolves, and seems to lead him on towards a playfully receding destination. In the rear-view mirror, no red BMW. Along this stretch, where the Euston becomes the Marylebone Road, the traffic signals are phased, Manhattan-style, and he's wafted forwards on a leading edge of green lights, a surfer on a perfect wave of simple information: *go!* Or even, *yes!* The long line of tourists – teenagers mostly – outside Madame Tussaud's seems less futile than usual; a generation raised on thunderous Hollywood effects still longs to stand and gawp at waxworks, like eighteenth-century peasants at a country fair. The reviled Westway, rearing on stained concrete piles and on which he rises swiftly to second-floor level, offers up a sudden horizon of tumbling cloud above a tumult of rooftops. It's one of those moments when to be a car owner in a city, the owner of this car, is sweet. The seven-speed automatic shifts smoothly up. A sign on a gantry above the traffic lanes proclaims The West, The North, as though there lies, spread beyond the suburbs, a whole continent, and the promise of a six-day journey.

The traffic must be stalled somewhere else by the march. For almost half a mile he alone possesses this stretch of elevated road. For seconds on end he thinks he grasps the vision of its creators – a purer world that favours machines rather than people. A rectilinear curve sweeps him past recent office buildings of glass and steel where the lights are already on in the February early afternoon. He glimpses people as neat as architectural models, at their desks, before their screens, even on a Saturday. This is the tidy future of his childhood science fiction comics, of men and women with tight-fitting collarless jumpsuits – no pockets, trailing laces or untucked shirts – living a life beyond litter and confusion, free of clutter to fight evil.

But from a vantage point on the White City flyover, just before the road comes down to earth among rows of red-brick housing, he sees the tail lights massing ahead and begins to brake. His mother never minded traffic lights and long delays. Only a year ago she was still well enough – forgetful, vague, but not terrified – to enjoy being driven around the streets of west London. The lights gave her an opportunity to examine other drivers and their passengers. 'Look at him. He's got a spotty face.' Or simply to say companionably, 'Red again!'

She was a woman who gave her life to housework, to the kind of daily routines of polishing, dusting, vacuuming and tidying that were once common, and these days are only undertaken by patients with obsessive compulsive disorders. Every day, while Henry was at school, she spring-cleaned her house. She drew her deepest satisfactions from a tray of well-roasted beef, the sheen on a nest of tables, a pile of ironed candy-striped sheets folded in smooth slabs, a larder of neat provisions; or from one more knitted matineé jacket for one more baby in the remoter reaches of the family. The invisible sides, the obverse, the underneath and the insides of everything were clean. The oven and its racks were scrubbed after every use. Order and cleanliness were the outward expression of an unspoken ideal of love. A book he was reading would be back on the hallway shelf upstairs as soon as he put it aside. The morning paper could be in the dustbin by lunchtime. The empty milk bottles she put out for collection were as clean as her cutlery. To every item its drawer or shelf or hook, including her various aprons, and her yellow rubber gloves held by a clothes peg, hanging near the egg-shaped egg-timer.

Surely it was because of her that Henry feels at home in an operating theatre. She too would have liked the waxed black floor, the instruments of surgical steel arrayed in parallel rows on a sterile tray, and the scrub room with its devotional routines – she would have admired the niceties, the clean headwear, the short fingernails. He should have had her in while she was still capable. It never crossed his mind. It never occurred to him that his work, his fifteen years' training, had anything to do with what she did.

Nor did it occur to her. He barely knew it at the time, but he grew up thinking her intelligence was limited. He used to think she was without curiosity. But that wasn't right. She liked a good exploratory heart-to-heart with her neighbours. The eight-year-old Henry liked to flop on the floor behind the furniture and listen in. Illness and operations were important subjects, especially those associated with childbirth. That was when he first heard the phrase 'under the knife' as well as 'under the doctor'. 'What the doctor said' was a powerful invocation. This eavesdropping may have set Henry on his career. Then there were running accounts of infidelities, or rumours of them, and ungrateful children, and the unreasonableness of the old, and what someone's parent left in a will, and how a certain nice girl couldn't find a decent husband. Good people had to be sifted from the bad, and it wasn't always easy to tell at first which was which. Indifferently, illness struck the good as well as the bad. Later, when he made his dutiful attempts on Daisy's undergraduate course in the nineteenth-century novel, he recognised all his mother's themes. There was nothing small-minded about her interests. Jane Austen and George Eliot shared them too. Lilian Perowne wasn't stupid or trivial, her life wasn't unfortunate, and he had no business as a young man being condescending towards her. But it's too late for apologies now. Unlike in Daisy's novels, moments of precise reckoning are rare in real life; questions of misinterpretation are not often resolved. Nor do they remain pressingly unresolved. They simply fade. People don't remember clearly, or they die, or the questions die and new ones take their place.

Besides, Lily had another life that no one could have predicted, or could remotely guess at now. She was a swimmer. On Sunday morning, September the third 1939, while Chamberlain was announcing in his radio broadcast from Downing Street that the country was at war with Germany, the fourteen-year-old Lily was at a municipal pool near Wembley, having her first lesson with a sixty-year-old international athlete who had swum for Britain in the Stockholm Olympics in 1912 – the first ever women's swimming event. She had spotted Lily in the pool and offered to give her lessons for free, and coached her in the crawl, a most unladylike stroke. Lily went in for local matches in the late forties. In 1954 she swam for Middlesex in the county championships. She came second, and her tiny silver medal, set on a wooden shield made of oak, always stood on the mantelpiece while Henry was growing up. It's on a shelf in her room now. That silver was as far, or as high, as she got, but she always swam beautifully, fast enough to push out in front of her a deep and sinuous bow wave.

She taught Henry, of course, but his treasured memory of her swimming was of when he was ten, on a school visit one morning to the local pool. He and his friends were changed and ready, had been through the shower and footbath, and had to wait on the tiles for the adult session to end. Two teachers stood by, shushing and fussing, trying to contain the children's excitement. Soon there was only one figure remaining in the pool, one in a white rubber cap with a frieze of petals he should have recognised earlier. His whole class was admiring her speed as she surged up the lane, the furrow in the water she left behind, just at the small of her back, and the way she turned her head to breathe without breaking her line in the water. When he knew it was her, he convinced himself he'd known from the beginning. To add to his exultation, he didn't even have to claim her out loud. Someone called out, 'That's Mrs Perowne!' In silence they watched as she reached the end of her lane right at their feet and performed a flashy underwater turn that was novel at the time. This was no mere duster of sideboards. He'd seen her swim often enough, but this was entirely different; all his friends were there to witness her superhuman nature, in which he shared. Surely she knew, and put on in the last half-length a show of demonic speed just for him. Her feet churned, her slender white arms rose and chopped at the water, her bow wave swelled, the furrow deepened. Her body shaped itself round her own wave in a shallow undulating S. You would have had to sprint along the pool to keep up with her. She stopped at the far end and stood, and put her hands on the edge and flipped herself out of the water. She would have been about forty then. She sat there, feet still immersed, pulled off her cap and, tilting her head, smiled shyly in their direction. One of the teachers led the kids into solemn applause. Though it was 1966 – the boys' hair was growing thickly over

their ears, the girls wore jeans to class – a degree of fifties for-
mality still prevailed. Henry clapped with the rest, but when
his friends gathered round, he was too choked with pride,
too exhilarated to answer their questions, and was relieved
to get in the pool where he could conceal his feelings.

In the twenties and thirties, great tracts of agricultural land to
the west of London disappeared before an onslaught of high-
speed housing development, and even now the streets of
frowning, respectable two-storey houses haven't quite shaken
off their air of suddenness. Each near-identical house has an
uneasy, provisional look, as if it knows how readily the land
would revert to cereal crops and grazing. Lily now lives only
a few minutes away from the old Perivale family home. Henry
likes to think that in the misty landscape of her dementia, a
sense of familiarity breaks through occasionally and reassures
her. By the standards of old people's homes, Suffolk Place is
minute – three houses have been knocked through to make
one, and an annexe has been added. Out front, privet hedges
still mark the old garden boundaries and two laburnum trees
survive. One of the three front gardens has been cemented
over to make parking space for two cars. The oversized dust-
bins behind a lattice fence are the only institutional clues.

Perowne parks and takes the potted plant from the back
seat. He pauses a moment before ringing the bell – there's a
taste in the air, sweet and vaguely antiseptic, that reminds
him of his teenage years in these streets, and of a general
state of longing, a hunger for life to begin that from this distance seems like happiness. As usual, Jenny opens the door.
She's a large, cheerful Irish girl in a blue gingham tabard
who's due to start nurse's training in September. Henry
receives special consideration on account of his medical connection – an extra three tea bags in the brew she'll bring soon
to his mother's room, and perhaps a plate of chocolate fingers. Without knowing much at all about each other, they've
settled on teasing forms of address.

'If it isn't the good doctor!'

'How's my fair colleen?'

Off the narrow space of the suburban hallway, tinted yellow by the front door's leaded glass, is a kitchen of fluorescent light and stainless steel. From there comes a clammy aroma of the lunch the residents ate two hours earlier. After a lifetime's exposure, Perowne has a mild fondness, or at least a complete lack of disgust, for institutional food. On the other side of the entrance hall is a narrower door that leads through into the three interconnecting sitting rooms of three houses. He can hear the bottled sound of televisions in other rooms.

'She's waiting for you,' Jenny says. They both know this to be a neurological impossibility. Even boredom is beyond his mother's reach.

He pushes the door open and goes through. She is right in front of him, sitting on a wooden chair at a round table covered with a chenille cloth. There's a window at her back, and beyond it, a window of the house next door, ten feet away. There are other women ranged around the edges of the room sitting in high-backed chairs with curved wooden arms. Some are watching, or looking in the direction of, the television mounted on the wall, out of reach. Others are staring at the floor. They stir or seem to sway as he enters, as if gently buffeted by the air the door displaces. There's a general, cheery response to his 'Good afternoon, ladies' and they watch him with interest. At this stage they can't be sure he isn't one of their own close relatives. To his right, in the farthest of the connecting sitting rooms, is Annie, a woman with wild grey hair which radiates from her head in fluffy spokes. She's shuffling unsupported towards him at speed. When she reaches the end of the third sitting room she'll turn back, and keep moving back and forwards all day until she's guided towards a meal, or bed.

His mother is watching him closely, pleased and anxious all at once. She thinks she knows his face – he might be the doctor, or the odd-job man. She's waiting for a cue. He kneels by her chair and takes her hand, which is smooth and dry and very light.

'Hello Mum, Lily. It's Henry, your son Henry.'

'Hello darling. Where are you going?'

'I've come to see you. We'll go and sit in your room.'

'I'm sorry dear. I don't have a room. I'm waiting to go home. I'm getting the bus.'

It pains him whenever she says that, even though he knows she's referring to her childhood home where she thinks her mother is waiting for her. He kisses her cheek and helps her out of her chair, feeling the tremors of effort or nervousness in her arms. As always, in the first dismaying moments of seeing her again, his eyes prick.

She protests feebly. 'I don't know where we can go.'

He dislikes speaking with the forced cheerfulness nurses use on the wards, even on adult patients with no mental impairment. *Just pop this in your mouth for me.* But he does it anyway, partly to disguise his feelings. 'You've got a lovely little room. As soon as you see it, you'll remember. This way now.'

Arm in arm, they walk slowly through the other sitting rooms, standing aside to let Annie pass. It's reassuring that Lily is decently dressed. The helpers knew he was coming. She wears a deep red skirt with a matching brushed-cotton blouse, black tights and black leather shoes. She always dressed well. Hers must have been the last generation to care as a matter of course about hats. There used to be dark rows of them, almost identical, on the top shelf of her wardrobe, cocooned in a whiff of mothball.

When they step out into a corridor, she turns away to her left and he has to put his hand on her narrow shoulder to guide her back. 'Here it is. Do you recognise your door?'

'I've never been out this way before.'

He opens her door and hands her in. The room is about eight feet by ten, with a glazed door giving on to a small back garden. The single bed is covered by a floral eiderdown and various soft toys that were part of her life long before her illness. Some of her remaining ornaments – a robin on a log, two comically exaggerated glass squirrels – are in a glazed corner cupboard. Others are ranged about a sideboard close to the door. On the wall near the handbasin is a framed photograph of Lily and Jack, Henry's father, standing on a lawn. Just in shot is the handle of a pram, presumably in which lies the oblivious Henry. She's pretty in a white summer dress and has her head cocked in that shy, quizzical way he remembers well. The young man is smoking a cigarette and wears a blazer and open-necked white shirt. He's tall, with a stoop, and has big hands like his son. His grin is wide and untroubled. It's always useful to have solid proof that the old have had their go at being young. But there is also an element of derision in photography. The couple appear vulnerable, easily mocked for appearing not to know that their youth is merely an episode, or that the tasty smouldering item in Jack's right hand will contribute – Henry's theory – later that same year to his sudden death.

Having failed to remember its existence, Lily isn't surprised to find herself in her room. She instantly forgets that she didn't know about it. However, she dithers, uncertain of where she should sit. Henry shows her into her high-backed chair by the French window, and sits facing her on the edge of the bed. It's ferociously hot, even hotter than his own bedroom. Perhaps his blood is still stirred by the game, and the hot shower and the warmth of the car. He'd be content to stretch out on the oversprung bed and start to think about the day, and perhaps doze a little. How interesting his life suddenly appears from the confines of this room. At that moment, with the eiderdown beneath him, and the heat, he feels a heaviness in his eyes and can't stop them closing. And his visit has hardly begun. To revive himself, he pulls off his sweater, then he shows Lily the plant he has brought.

'Look,' he says. 'It's an orchid for your room.'

As he holds it out towards her, and the frail white flower bobs between them, she recoils.

'Why have you got that?'

'It's yours. It'll keep flowering through the winter. Isn't it pretty? It's for you.'

'It's not mine,' Lily says firmly. 'I've never seen it before.'

He had the same baffling conversation last time. The disease proceeds by tiny unnoticed strokes in small blood vessels in the brain. Cumulatively, the infarcts cause cognitive decline by disrupting the neural nets. She unravels in little steps. Now she's lost her grasp of the concept of a gift, and with it, the pleasure. Adopting again the tone of the cheerful nurse, he says, 'I'll put it up here where you can see it.'

She's about to protest, but her attention wanders. She has seen some decorative china pieces on a display shelf above her bed, right behind her son. Her mood is suddenly conciliatory.

'I've got plenty of them cups and saucers. So I can always go out with one of them. But the thing is, the space between people is so tiny' – she brings up two wavering hands to show him a gap – 'that there's hardly enough space to squeeze through. There's too much binding.'

'I agree,' Henry says as he settles back on the bed. 'There's far too much binding.'

Damage from the small-vessel clotting tends to accumulate in the white matter and destroy the mind's connectivity. Along the way, well before the process is complete, Lily is able to deliver her rambling treatises, her nonsense monologues with touching seriousness. She doesn't doubt herself at all. Nor does she think that he's unable to follow her. The structure of her sentences is intact, and the moods which inflect her various descriptions make sense. It pleases her if he nods and smiles, and chimes in from time to time.

She isn't looking at him as she gathers her thoughts, but past him, concentrating on an elusive matter, staring as though through a window at an unbounded view. She goes to speak, but remains silent. Her pale green eyes, sunk deep in bowls of finely folded light brown skin, have a flat, dulled quality, like dusty stones under glass. They give an accurate impression of understanding nothing. He can't bring her news of the family – the mention of strange names, any names, can alarm her. So although she won't understand, he often talks to her about work. What she warms to is the sound, the emotional tone of a friendly conversation.

He is about to describe to her the Chapman girl, and how well she's come through, when Lily suddenly speaks up. Her mood is anxious, even a little querulous. 'And you know that this . . . you know, Aunty, what people put on their shoes to make them . . . you know?'

'Shoe polish?' He never understands why she calls him Aunty, or which of her many aunts is haunting her.

'No, no. They put it all over their shoes and rub it with a cloth. Well, anyway, it's a bit like shoe polish. It's that sort of thing. We had side plates and God knows what, all along the street. We had everything but the right thing because we were in the wrong place.'

Then she suddenly laughs. It's become clearer to her.

'If you turn the picture round and take the back off like I did you get such a lot of pleasure out of it. It's all what it meant. And the laugh we had out of it!'

And she laughs gaily, just like she used to, and he laughs too. It's all what it meant. Now she's away, describing what might be a disintegrated memory of a street party, and a little watercolour she once bought in a jumble sale.

Some time later, when Jenny arrives with the refreshments, Lily stares at her without recognition. Perowne stands and clears space on a low table. He notices the suspicion Lily is showing towards what she takes to be a complete stranger, and so, as soon as Jenny leaves, and before Lily can speak, he says, 'What a lovely girl she is. Always helpful.'

'She's marvellous,' Lily agrees.

The memory of whoever was in the room is already fading.

His emotional cue is irresistible and she immediately smiles and begins to elaborate while he spoons all six tea bags out of the metal pot.

'She always comes running, even if it's narrow all the way down. She wants to come on one of them long things but she doesn't have the fare. I sent her the money, but she doesn't have it in her hand. She wants some music, and I said you might as well make up a little band and play it yourself. I worry about her though. I said to her, why do you put all the slices in one bowl when no one's standing up? You can't do it yourself.'

He knows who she's talking about, and waits for more. Then he says, 'You should go and see her.'

It's a long time since he last tried to explain to her that her mother died in 1970. It is easier now to support the delusion and keep the conversation moving along. Everything belongs in the present. His immediate concern is to prevent her eating a tea bag, the way she almost did last time. He piles them onto a saucer which he places on the floor by his foot. He puts a half-filled cup within her reach and offers her a biscuit and a napkin. She spreads it over her lap and carefully places the biscuit in its centre. She raises the cup to her lips and drinks. At moments like these, when she's skilful in the long-established routines, and looks demure in her colour-matched clothes, a perfectly well-looking 77-year-old with amazing legs for her age, athlete's legs, he can imagine that it's all been a mistake, a bad dream, and that she'll leave her tiny room and come away with him into the heart of the city and eat fish stew with her daughter-in-law and grandchildren and stay a while.

Lily says, 'I was there last week, Aunty, on the bus and my mum was in the garden. I said to her, You can walk down there, see what you're going to get, and the next thing is the balancing of everything you've got. She's not well. Her feet. I'll go there in a minute and I can't help losing her a jersey.'

How strange it would have been for Lily's mother, an

aloof, unmaternal woman, to have known that the little girl at her skirts would one day, in a remote future, a science fiction date in the next century, talk of her all the time and long to be home with her. Would that have softened her?

Now Lily is set, she'll talk on for as long as he sits there. It's hard to tell if she's actually happy. Sometimes she laughs, at others she describes shadowy disputes and grievances, and her voice becomes indignant. In many of the situations she conjures, she's remonstrating with a man who won't see sense.

'I told him anything that's going for a liberty and he said, I don't care. You can give it away, and I said don't let it waste in the fire. And all the new stuff that's going to be picked up.'

If she becomes too agitated by the story she's telling, Henry will cut in and laugh loudly and say, 'Mum, that's really very funny!' Being suggestible, she'll laugh too and her mood will shift, and the story she tells then will be happier. For now, she's in neutral mode – there's a clock, and a jersey again, and again, a space too narrow to pass through – and Henry, sipping the thick brown tea, half listening, half asleep in the small room's airless warmth, thinks how in thirty-five years or less it could be him, stripped of everything he does and owns, a shrivelled figure meandering in front of Theo or Daisy, while they wait to leave and return to a life of which he'll have no comprehension. High blood pressure is one good predictor of strokes. A hundred and twenty-two over sixty-five last time. The systolic could be lower. Total cholesterol, five point two. Not good enough. Elevated levels of lipoprotein-a are said to have a robust association with multi-infarct dementia. He'll eat no more eggs, and have only semi-skimmed milk in his coffee, and coffee too will have to go one day. He isn't ready to die, and nor is he ready to half die. He wants his prodigiously connected myelin-rich white matter intact, like an unsullied snowfield. No cheese then. He'll be ruthless with himself in his pursuit of boundless health to avoid his mother's fate. Mental death.

'I put sap in the clock,' she's telling him, 'to make it moist.'

An hour passes, and then he forces himself fully awake and stands up, too quickly perhaps, because he feels a sudden dizziness. Not a good sign. He extends both hands towards her, feeling immense and unstable as he looms over her tiny form.

'Come on now, Mum,' he says gently. 'It's time for me to go. And I'd like you to see me to the door.'

Childlike in her obedience, she takes his hands and he helps her from her chair. He piles up the tray and puts it outside the room, then remembers the tea bags, half concealed under the bed, and puts them out too. She might have feasted on them. He guides her into the corridor, reassuring her all the while, aware that she's stepping into an alien world. She has no idea which way to turn as they leave her room. She doesn't comment on the unfamiliar surroundings, but she grips his hand tighter. In the first of the sitting rooms two women, one with snowy hair in braids, the other completely bald, are watching television with the sound off. Approaching from the middle room is Cyril, as always in cravat and sports jacket, and today carrying a cane and wearing a deerstalker. He's the home's resident gent, sweet-mannered, marooned in one particular, well-defined fantasy: he believes he owns a large estate and is obliged to go around visiting his tenants and be scrupulously polite. Perowne has never seen him unhappy.

Cyril raises his hat at Lily and calls, 'Good morning, my dear. Everything well? Any complaints?'

Her face tightens and she looks away. On the screen above her head Perowne sees the march – Hyde Park still, a vast crowd before a temporary stage, and in the far distance a tiny figure at a microphone, then the aerial shot of the same, and then the marchers in columns with their banners, still arriving through the park gates. He and Lily stop to let Cyril pass. There's a shot of the newsreader at her space-age desk, then the plane as he saw it in the early hours, the blackened fuselage vivid in a lake of foam, like a tasteless ornament on an iced cake. Now, Paddington police station – said to be secure against terrorist attack. A reporter is standing outside, speaking into a microphone. There's a development. Are the Russian pilots really radical Muslims? Perowne is reaching up for the volume control, but Lily is suddenly agitated and trying to tell him something important.

'If it gets too dry it will curl up again. I told him, and I told him you have to water it, but he wouldn't put it down.'

'It's all right,' he tells her. 'He will put it down. I'll tell him to. I promise you.'

He decides against the television and they come away. He needs to concentrate on his leavetaking, for he knows that she'll think she's coming with him. He'll be standing once more at the front door, with his meaningless explanation that he'll return soon. Jenny or one of the other girls will have to distract her as he steps outside.

Together they walk back through the first sitting room. Tea and crustless sandwiches are being served to the ladies at the round table with the chenille cloth. He calls a greeting to them, but they seem too distracted to reply. Lily is happier now, and leans her head against his arm. As they come into the hall they see Jenny Lavin by the door, already raising her hand to the high double security lock and smiling in their direction. Just then his mother pats his hand with a feathery touch and says, 'Out here it only looks like a garden, Aunty, but it's the countryside really and you can go for miles. When you walk here you feel lifted up, right high across the counter. I can't manage all them plates without a brush, but God will take care of you and see what you're going to get because it's a swimming race. You'll squeeze through somehow.'

It is a slow haul back into central London – more than an hour to reach Westbourne Grove from Perivale. Dense traffic is heading into the city for Saturday night pleasures just as the first wave of coaches is bringing the marchers out. During the long crawl towards the lights at Gypsy Corner, he lowers his window to taste the scene in full – the bovine patience of a jam, the abrasive tang of icy fumes, the thunderous idling machinery in six lanes east and west, the yellow street light bleaching colour from the bodywork, the jaunty thud of entertainment systems, and red tail lights stretching way ahead into the city, white headlights pouring out of it. He tries to see it, or feel it, in historical terms, this moment in the last decades of the petroleum age, when a nineteenth-century device is brought to final perfection in the early years of the twenty-first; when the unprecedented wealth of masses at serious play in the unforgiving modern city makes for a sight that no previous age can have imagined. Ordinary people! Rivers of light! He wants to make himself see it as Newton might, or his contemporaries, Boyle, Hooke, Wren, Willis – those clever, curious men of the English Enlightenment who for a few years held in their minds nearly all the world's science. Surely, they would be awed. Mentally, he shows it off to them: this is what we've done, this is commonplace in our time. All this teeming illumination would be wondrous if he could only see it through their eyes. But he can't quite trick himself into it. He can't feel his way past the iron weight of the actual to see beyond the boredom of a traffic tailback, or the delay to which he himself is contributing, or the drab commercial hopes of a parade of shops he's been stuck beside for fifteen minutes. He doesn't have the lyric gift to see beyond it – he's a realist, and can never escape. But then, perhaps two poets in the family are enough.

Beyond Acton the traffic eases. In the late-afternoon dusk a single slab of red in the western sky, almost rectangular, an emblem of the natural world, of wilderness somewhere out of sight, fades slowly as it pursues him in his rear-view mirror. Even if the westbound lanes out of the city were free, he's glad not to be heading that way. He wants to get home and collect himself before he starts cooking. He needs to check that there's champagne in the fridge, and bring some red wine into the kitchen to warm. The cheese too needs to be softened in the centrally-heated air. He needs to lie down for ten minutes. He's certainly in no mood for Theo's amplified blues.

But this is parenthood, as fixed as destiny, and at last he's parking in a street off Westbourne Grove, a couple of hundred yards from the old music hall theatre. He's forty-five minutes late. When he reaches it, the building is silent and in darkness and the doors are closed. But they open easily when he pushes against them, so that he stumbles as he enters the foyer. He waits to let his eyes adjust to the low light, straining to hear sounds, aware of the familiar smell of dusty carpeting. Is he too late? It would almost be a relief. He moves deeper into the lobby, past what he thinks must be the ticket office, until he comes to another set of double doors. He gropes for a metal bar, pushes down and enters.

A hundred feet away, the stage is in soft bluish light, broken by pinpricks of red on the amplifier racks. By the drums, the high hat catches the light and projects an elongated purple disc across the floor of the theatre which is without seats. There's no other light apart from an orange exit sign beyond the stage. People are moving and crouching by the equipment, and stirring beside the gleam of a keyboard. Just discernible above the low fuzzy hum of the speaker banks is a murmur of voices. A silhouetted figure stands at the front of the stage adjusting the heights of two microphones.

Perowne moves to his right, and in total darkness follows the wall with his hand until he's facing the centre of the stage. A second person appears by the microphones carrying a saxophone whose intricate outline is sharply defined against the blue. In response to a call, the keyboard sounds a single note, and a bass guitar tunes its top string to it. Another guitar plays a broken open chord – all in tune, then a third does the same. The drummer sits in and moves his cymbals closer and fiddles with the pedal on a bass drum. The murmur of voices ceases, and the roadies disappear into the wings.

Theo and Chas are at the front of the stage by the microphones looking out across the auditorium.

It's only at this point that Perowne realises they've seen him come in and that they've been waiting. Theo's guitar starts out alone with a languorous two-bar turnaround, a simple descending line from the fifth fret, tumbling into a thick chord which oozes into a second and remains hanging there, an unresolved fading seventh; then, with a sharp kick and roll on the tom, and five stealthy, rising notes from the bass, the blues begins. It's a downbeat 'Stormy Monday' kind of song, but the chords are dense and owe more to jazz. The stage light is shifting to white. Theo, motionless in his usual trance, goes three times round the twelve bars. It's a smooth, rounded tone, plenty of feedback to mould the notes into their wailing lament, with a little sting in the attack on the shorter runs. The piano and rhythm guitar lay down their thick jazzy chords. Henry feels the bassline thump into his sternum and puts his hand to the sore spot there. It's building into a big sound, and he's uncomfortable, and resists it. In his present state, he'd prefer to be at home with a Mozart trio on the hi-fi, and a glass of icy white wine.

But he doesn't hold out for long. Something is swelling, or lightening in him as Theo's notes rise, and on the second turnaround lift into a higher register and begin to soar. This is what the boys have been working on, and they want him to hear it, and he's touched. He's catching on to the idea, to the momentum of their exuberance and expertise. At the same time he discovers that the song is not in the usual pattern of a twelve-bar blues. There's a middle section with an unworldly melody that rises and falls in semitones. Chas leans into his microphone to sing with Theo in a close, strange harmony.

> *Baby, you can choose despair,*
> *Or you can be happy if you dare.*
> *So let me take you there,*
> *My city square, city square.*

Then Chas, with all his fresh tricks from New York, turns aside, lifts his sax and comes in on a wild and ragged high note, like a voice cracking with joy that holds and holds, then tapers and drops away in a downward spiral, echoing Theo's intro, and delivers the band back into the twelve-bar round. Chas too goes three times round. The sax is edgy, with choppy rhythms and notes held against the chord changes, then released in savage runs. Theo and the bass guitarist are playing in octaves a tricksy repeated figure that shifts in unexpected ways and never quite returns to its starting point. This is a blues at walking speed, but a driving rhythm is building up. On Chas's third turnaround, the two boys come back to the mikes, back to the lilting refrain whose harmonies are so close they're discords. Is Theo paying tribute to his teacher, to Jack Bruce of Cream?

> *So let me take you there*
> *City square, city square.*

Then it's the keyboard's break, and the others join in the difficult, circular riff.

No longer tired, Henry comes away from the wall where he's been leaning, and walks into the middle of the dark auditorium, towards the great engine of sound. He lets it engulf him. There are these rare moments when musicians together touch something sweeter than they've ever found before in rehearsals or performance, beyond the merely collaborative or technically proficient, when their expression becomes as easy and graceful as friendship or love. This is when they give us a glimpse of what we might be, of our best selves, and of an impossible world in which you give everything you have to others, but lose nothing of yourself. Out in the real world there exist detailed plans, visionary projects for peaceable realms, all conflicts resolved, happiness for everyone, for ever – mirages for which people are prepared to die and kill. Christ's kingdom on earth, the workers' paradise, the ideal Islamic state. But only in music, and only on rare occasions, does the curtain actually lift on this dream of community, and it's tantalisingly conjured, before fading away with the last notes.

Naturally, no one can ever agree when it's happening. Henry last heard it for himself at the Wigmore Hall, a utopian community briefly realised in the Schubert Octet, when the wind players with little leaning, shrugging movements of their bodies, wafted their notes across the stage at the string section who sent them back sweetened. He also heard it long ago at Daisy and Theo's school, when a discordantly wailing school orchestra, with a staff and pupil choir, attempted Purcell, and made with cracked notes an innocent and blissful concord of adults and children. And here it is now, a coherent world, everything fitting at last. He stands swaying in the dark, staring up at the stage, his right hand in his pocket gripping his keys. Theo and Chas drift back to centre stage to sing their unearthly chorus. *Or you can be happy if you dare.* He knows what his mother meant. He can go for miles, he feels lifted up, right high across the counter. He doesn't want the song to end.

Four

He doesn't bother to park in the mews. Instead, he pulls up right outside his front door – it's legal at this time of evening to be on a yellow line and he's impatient to be indoors. But he takes a few seconds to examine the damage to the passenger door – barely a mark. As he looks up from the car, he notices that the house is in darkness. Naturally, Theo is still at rehearsal, Rosalind will be picking her way through the last fine points of her court application. A few widely separated flakes of snow picked out by street light show up vividly against the windows' glossy black. His father-in-law and daughter are due and he's pressed for time. As he opens the door he's trying to remember the exact phrasing of a remark Theo made earlier in the day that didn't trouble him at the time. It nags at him briefly now, but the half-hearted effort of recall itself fades as he steps into the warmth of the hall and turns on the lights; a mere light bulb can explode a thought. He goes straight down to the wine racks and takes out four bottles. His kind of fish stew needs a robust country wine – red, not white. Grammaticus introduced him to a Tautavel, Côtes du Roussillon Villages and Henry has made it his house wine – delicious, and less than fifty pounds a case. Uncorking wines hours before they're drunk is a form of magical thinking; the surface area exposed to the air is minute and can't possibly make a detectable difference. However, he does want the bottles warmer, and he carries them into the kitchen and puts them by the stove.

Three bottles of champagne are already in the fridge. He takes a step towards the CD player, then changes his mind for he's feeling the pull, like gravity, of the approaching TV news. It's a condition of the times, this compulsion to hear how it stands with the world, and be joined to the generality, to a community of anxiety. The habit's grown stronger these past two years; a different scale of news value has been set by monstrous and spectacular scenes. The possibility of their recurrence is one thread that binds the days. The government's counsel – that an attack in a European or American city is an inevitability – isn't only a disclaimer of responsibility, it's a heady promise. Everyone fears it, but there's also a darker longing in the collective mind, a sickening for self-punishment and a blasphemous curiosity. Just as the hospitals have their crisis plans, so the television networks stand ready to deliver, and their audiences wait. Bigger, grosser next time. Please don't let it happen. But let me see it all the same, as it's happening and from every angle, and let me be among the first to know. Also, Henry needs to hear about the pilots in custody.

With the idea of the news, inseparable from it, at least at weekends, is the lustrous prospect of a glass of red wine. He empties the last of a Côtes du Rhône into a glass, puts the TV on mute and sets about stripping and chopping three onions. Impatient of the papery outer layers, he makes a deep incision, forcing his thumb in four layers deep and ripping them away, wasting a third of the flesh. He chops the remainder rapidly and tips it into a casserole with a lot of olive oil. What he likes about cooking is its relative imprecision and lack of discipline – a release from the demands of the theatre. In the kitchen, the consequences of failure are mild: disappointment, a wisp of disgrace, rarely voiced. No one actually dies. He strips and chops eight fat cloves of garlic and adds them to the onions. From recipes he draws only the broadest principles. The cookery writers he admires speak of 'handfuls' and 'a sprinkling', of 'chucking in' this or that. They list alternative ingredients and encourage experimentation. Henry accepts that he'll never make a decent cook, that he belongs to what Rosalind calls the hearty school. Into his palm he empties several dried red chillies from a pot and crushes them between his hands and lets the flakes fall with their seeds into the onions and garlic. The TV news comes up but he doesn't touch the mute. It's the same helicopter shot from before it got dark, the same crowds still filing into the park, the same general celebration. Onto the softened onions and garlic – pinches of saffron, some bay leaves, orange-peel gratings, oregano, five anchovy fillets, two tins of peeled tomatoes. On the big Hyde Park stage, sound-bite extracts of speeches by a venerable politician of the left, a pop star, a playwright, a trade unionist. Into a stockpot he eases the skeletons of three skates. Their heads are intact, their lips girlishly full. Their eyes go cloudy on contact with the boiling water. A senior police officer is answering questions about the march. By his tight smile and the tilt of his head he appears satisfied with the day. From the green string bag of mussels Henry takes a dozen or so and drops them in with the skate. If they're alive and in pain, he isn't to know. Now that same earnest reporter, silently mouthing all there is to know about the unprecedented gathering. The juice of the tomatoes is simmering with the onions and the rest, and turning reddish-orange with the saffron.

Perowne, his hearing not yet fully recovered from the rehearsal, his feelings dimmed, even numbed, by his visit to his mother, decides he needs to be listening to something punchy, to Steve Earle, the thinking man's Bruce Springsteen, according to Theo. But the record he wants, *El Corazón*, is upstairs, so he drinks the wine instead, and keeps glancing towards the set, waiting for his story. The Prime Minister is giving his Glasgow speech. Perowne touches the control in time to hear him say that the number of marchers today has been exceeded by the number of deaths caused by Saddam. A clever point, the only case to make, but it should have been made from the start. Too late now. After Blix it looks tactical. Henry turns the sound off. It occurs to him how content he is to be cooking – even self-consciousness doesn't diminish the feeling. Into the biggest colander he pours the rest of the mussels and scrubs them with a vegetable brush at the sink under running water. The pale greenish clams on the other hand look dainty and pure, and he merely rinses them. One of the skates has arched its spine, as if to escape the boiling. As he pushes it back down with a wooden spatula, the vertebral column breaks, right below T3. Last summer he operated on a teenage girl who broke her back at C5 and T2 falling out of a tree at a pop festival, trying to get a better view of Radiohead. She'd just finished school and wanted to study Russian at Leeds. Now, after eight months' rehab she's doing fine. But he dismisses the memory. He isn't thinking about work, he wants to cook. From the fridge he takes a quarter-full bottle of white wine, a Sancerre, and tips it over the tomato mix.

On a broader, thicker chopping block, Perowne arranges the monkfish tails and cuts them into chunks and tips them into a big white bowl. Then he washes the ice off the tiger prawns and puts them in too. In a second bowl, he puts the clams and mussels. Both bowls go into the fridge, with dinner plates as lids. An establishing shot shows the United Nations building in New York, and next, Colin Powell getting into a black limousine. It's demotion for Henry's story, but he doesn't mind. He's cleaning up the kitchen, wiping his mess from the central island into a large bin, and scrubbing the chopping boards under running water. Then it's time to tip the boiling juice off the skates and mussels into the casserole. When that's done he has now, he reckons, about two and a half litres of bright orange stock which he'll cook for another five minutes. Just before dinner, he'll reheat it, and simmer the clams, monkfish, mussels and prawns in it for ten minutes. They'll eat the stew with brown bread, salad and red wine. After New York, there's the Kuwait–Iraq border, and military trucks moving in convoy along a desert road, and our lads kipping down by the tracks of their tanks, then eating bangers next morning from their mess-tins. He takes two bags of mâche from the bottom of the fridge and empties them into a salad tosser. He runs the cold tap over the leaves. An officer, barely in his twenties, is standing outside his tent pointing with a stick at a map on an easel. Perowne isn't tempted to disable the mute – these items from the front have a cheerful, censored air that lowers his spirits. He spins the salad and tips it into a bowl. Oil, lemon, pepper and salt he'll throw on later. There's cheese and fruit for pudding. Theo and Daisy can set the table.

His preparations are done, just as the burning plane story comes up, fourth item. With a confused sense that he's about to learn something significant about himself, he turns on the sound and stands facing the tiny set, drying his hands on a towel. Placed fourth could mean no developments, or sinister silence from the authorities; but in fact the story has collapsed – you can almost hear in the introduction the presenter's regretful tone. There they are, the pilot, the wizened fellow with slicked-back hair and his tubby co-pilot standing outside a hotel near Heathrow. They are not, the pilot explains through a translator, Chechens or Algerians, they are not Muslims, they are Christians, though only in name, for they never attend church and own neither a Koran nor a Bible. Above all, they are Russians and proud of the fact. They are certainly not responsible for the American child pornography found half-destroyed in the burned-out cargo. They work for a good company, registered in Holland, and their only responsibilities are to their plane. And yes, of course, child pornography is an abomination, but it's not part of their duties to inspect every package listed on the manifest. They've been released without charge, and when the Civil Aviation Authority tells them it's appropriate, they'll return to Riga. Also dead is the controversy about the plane's route into the airport; the correct procedures were followed. Both men insist they've been treated with courtesy by the Metropolitan Police. The plump co-pilot says he wants a bath and a long drink.

Good news, but as he walks out of the kitchen in the direction of the larder, Henry feels no particular pleasure, not even relief. Have his anxieties been making a fool of him? It's part of the new order, this narrowing of mental freedom, of his right to roam. Not so long ago his thoughts ranged more unpredictably, over a longer list of subjects. He suspects he's becoming a dupe, the willing, febrile consumer of news fodder, opinion, speculation and of all the crumbs the authorities let fall. He's a docile citizen, watching Leviathan grow stronger while he creeps under its shadow for protection. This Russian plane flew right into his insomnia, and he's been only too happy to let the story and every little nervous shift of the daily news process colour his emotional state. It's an illusion, to believe himself active in the story. Does he think he's contributing something, watching news programmes, or lying on his back on the sofa on Sunday afternoons, reading more opinion columns of ungrounded certainties, more long articles about what really lies behind this or that development, or about what is most surely going to happen next, predictions forgotten as soon as they are read, well before events disprove them? For or against the war on terror, or the war in Iraq; for the termination of an odious tyrant and his crime family, for the ultimate weapons inspection, the opening of the torture prisons, locating the mass graves, the chance of liberty and prosperity, and a warning to other despots; or against the bombing of civilians, the inevitable refugees and famine, illegal international action, the wrath of Arab nations and the swelling of Al-Qaeda's ranks. Either way, it amounts to a consensus of a kind, an orthodoxy of attention, a mild subjugation in itself. Does he think that his ambivalence – if that's what it really is – excuses him from the general conformity? He's deeper in than most. His nerves, like tautened strings, vibrate obediently with each news 'release'. He's lost the habits of scepticism, he's becoming dim with contradictory opinion, he isn't thinking clearly, and just as bad, he senses he isn't thinking independently.

The Russian pilots are shown walking into the hotel, and that's the last he'll ever see of them. He fetches a few bottles of tonic from the larder, checks on the ice-cube maker and the gin – three quarters of a litre is surely enough for one man – and turns off the heat under his stock. Upstairs, on the ground floor, he draws the curtains in the L-shaped living room, and turns on the lamps, and lights the gas in the mock-coal fires. These heavy curtains, closed by pulling on a cord weighted with a fat brass knob, have a way of cleanly eliminating the square and the wintry world beyond it. The tall-ceilinged room in creams and browns is silent, soothing, its only bright colour is in the blues and rubies of the rugs and an abstract slash of orange and yellow against green in a Howard Hodgkin on one of the chimney breasts. The three people in the world he, Henry Perowne, most loves, and who most love him, are about to come home. So what's wrong with him? Nothing, nothing at all. He's fine, everything is fine. He pauses at the foot of the stairs, wondering what it is he was intending to do next. He goes up to his study on the first floor, and remains standing as he looks at his screen to remind himself of the week ahead. There are four names on Monday's list, five for Tuesday's. The old astronomer, Viola, will be first, at eight thirty. Jay is right, she may not make it. All the names conjure a history he knows well from the past weeks or months. In each case he knows exactly what he intends to do, and he feels plea-sure in the prospect of the work. How different for the nine individuals, some already on the wards, some at home, others travelling into London tomorrow or Monday, with their dread of the approaching moment, the anaesthetic oblivion, and their reasonable suspicion that when they come round they will never be quite the same.

From downstairs he hears the front-door lock turning, and by the sound of the door opening and closing – a style of entering a place with economy, and of easing the door shut behind her – he knows it's Daisy. What luck, that she should arrive before her grandfather. As he hurries down the stairs towards her, she does a little jig of delight.

'You're in!'

As they embrace, he makes a low, sighing, growling noise, the way he used to greet her when she was five. And it is the child's body he feels as he almost lifts her clear off the floor, the smoothness of muscle under the clothes, the springi-ness he can feel in her joints, the sexless kisses. Even her breath is like a child's. She doesn't smoke, she rarely drinks, and she's about to become a published poet. His own breath smells richly of red wine. What abstemious children he's fathered.

'So. Let me have a look at you.'

Six months is the longest she's ever been away from her family. The Perownes, though permissive to a high degree, are also possessive parents. Holding her at arm's length, he hopes she doesn't notice the glistening in his eyes or the little struggle in his throat. His moment of pathos rises and falls in a single smooth wave, and is gone. He's still only in rehearsal as an old fool, a mere beginner. Despite his fan-tasies, this is no child. She's an independent young woman, gazing back at him with head cocked – so like her grand-mother in that tilted look – lips smiling but unparted, her intelligence like warmth in her face. This is the pain-pleasure of having newly adult children; they're innocent and ruthless in forgetting their sweet old dependence. But perhaps she's been reminding him – during their embrace she half rubbed, half patted his back, a familiar maternal gesture of hers. Even when she was five she liked to mother him, and admonish him whenever he worked too late or drank wine or failed to win the London Marathon. She was one of those finger-wagging, imperious little girls. Her daddy belonged to her. Now she rubs and pats other men, at least half a dozen in the past year, if *My Saucy Bark* and its 'Six Short Songs' are a guide. It's the bracing existence of these fellows that helps him control his single tear.

She wears an unbuttoned scuffed leather trenchcoat of dark green. A Russian fur hat dangles from her right hand. Beneath the coat, grey leather boots at knee height, a dark grey woollen skirt, a thick, loose sweater and a grey and white silk scarf. The stab at Parisian chic doesn't extend to her luggage – her old student backpack is on its side at her feet. He's still holding her by the shoulders, trying to place what's changed in six months. An unfamiliar scent, a little heavier perhaps, a little wiser around the eyes, the delicate face set a little more firmly. Most of her life is a mystery to him now. He sometimes wonders if Rosalind knows things about their daughter that he does not.

Under his scrutiny, the pressure of her smile is growing, until she laughs and says, 'Come on, Doctor. You can be straight with me. I've become an old hag.'

'You're looking gorgeous, and way too grown up for my taste.'

'I'm bound to regress while I'm here.' She points behind her at the sitting room and mouths, 'Is Granddad here?'

'Not yet.'

She wriggles clear of his hold, loops her arms around his shoulders and kisses him on the nose. 'I love you and I'm so happy to be back.'

'I love you too.'

Something else is different. She's no longer merely pretty,

she's beautiful, and perhaps also, so her eyes tell him, a little preoccupied. She's in love and can't bear to be parted. He pushes the thought away. Whatever it is, she's likely to tell Rosalind first.

For a few seconds they enter one of those mute, vacuous moments that follow an enthusiastic reunion – too much to be said, and a gentle resettling needed, a resumption of ordinary business. Daisy is gazing about her as she takes off her coat. The movement releases more of her unfamiliar perfume. A gift from her lover. He'll have to try harder to rid himself of this gloomy fixation. She's bound to love a man other than himself. It would be easier for him if her poems weren't so wanton – it isn't only wild sex they celebrate, but restless novelty, the rooms and beds visited once and left at dawn, the walk home down wet Parisian streets whose efficient cleansing by the city authorities is the occasion for various metaphors. The same fresh start purification was in her Newdigate launderette poem. Perowne knows the old arguments about double standards, but don't some liberal-minded women now argue for the power and value of reticence? Is it only fatherly soft-headedness that makes him suspect that a girl who sleeps around too earnestly has an improved chance of ending up with a lower-grade male, an inadequate, a loser? Or is his own peculiarity in this field, his own lack of exploratory vigour, making for another problem of reference?

'My God, this place is even larger than I remember.' She's peering up through the banisters at the chandelier hanging from the remote second-floor ceiling. Without thinking, he takes her coat, laughs and hands it back.

'What am I doing?' he says. 'You live here. You can hang it up yourself.'

She follows him down to the kitchen, and when he turns to offer her a drink, she hugs him again, then strides away with a little stagey skip into the dining room, and beyond, into the conservatory.

'I love it here,' she calls to him. 'Look at this tropical tree! I love this tree. What have I been thinking of, staying away so long?'

'Exactly my question.'

The tree has been there nine years. He's never seen her in this mood. She's walking back towards him, arms outstretched as though on a tightrope, pretending to wobble – it's the sort of thing a character in an American soap might do when she wants important good news wrung from her. Next thing, she'll be turning pirouettes around him and humming show tunes. I feel pretty. He takes two glasses from a cupboard and a bottle of champagne from the fridge and twists the cork off.

'Here,' he says. 'There's no reason to wait for the others.'

'I love you,' she says again, raising her glass.

'Welcome home my darling.'

She drinks and he notices, with some relief, that it isn't deeply. Barely a sip – no change there. He's in watchful mode, trying to figure her out. She can't keep still. She wanders with her glass around the central island.

'Guess where I went on my way from the station,' she says as she comes back towards him.

'Um. Hyde Park?'

'You knew! Daddy, why weren't you there? It was simply amazing.'

'I don't know. Playing squash, visiting Granny, cooking the dinner, lack of certainty. That sort of thing.'

'But it's completely barbaric, what they're about to do. Everyone knows that.'

'It might be. So might doing nothing. I honestly don't know. Tell me how it was in the park.'

'I know that if you'd been there you wouldn't have any doubts.'

He says, wanting to be helpful, 'I watched them set off this morning. All very good natured.'

She grimaces, as though in pain. She's home at last, they

have their champagne, and she can't bear it that he doesn't see it her way. She puts a hand on his arm. Unlike her father's or brother's, it's a tiny hand with tapering fingers, each with a remnant of a childish dimple at the base. While she speaks he's looking at her fingernails, gratified to see them in good condition. Longish, smooth, clean, glazed, not painted. You can tell a lot from a person's nails. When a life starts to unravel, they're among the first to go. He takes her hand and squeezes it.

She's beseeching him. Her head is as crammed with this stuff as his own. The speech she gives is a collation of everything she heard in the park, of everything they've both heard and read a hundred times, the worst-case guesses that become facts through repetition, the sweet raptures of pessimism. He hears again the UN's half-million Iraqi dead through famine and bombing, the three million refugees, the death of the UN, the collapse of the world order if America goes it alone, Baghdad entirely destroyed as it's taken street by street from the Republican Guard, Turks invading from the north, Iranians from the east, Israelis making excursions from the west, the whole region in flames, Saddam backed into a corner unleashing his chemical and biological weapons – if he has them, because no one's really proved it convincingly, and nor have they shown the connection to Al-Qaeda – and when the Americans have invaded, they won't be interested in democracy, they won't spend any money on Iraq, they'll take the oil and build their military bases and run the place like a colony.

While she speaks he gazes at her with warmth and some surprise. They're about to have one of their set-pieces – and so soon. She doesn't usually talk politics, it's not one of her subjects. Is this the source of her agitated happiness? The colour rises from her neck, and every extra reason she gives for not going to war gathers weight from the one before and lifts her towards her triumph. The dark outcomes she believes in are making her euphoric, she's slaying a dragon with every stroke. When she's done she gives a little affectionate push on his forearm, as though to shake him awake. Then she makes a face of mock sorrow. She longs for him to see what's true.

Conscious of taking up a position, girding himself for combat, he says, 'But this is all speculation about the future. Why should I feel any certainty about it? How about a short war, the UN doesn't fall apart, no famine, no refugees or invasions by neighbours, no flattened Baghdad and fewer deaths than Saddam causes his own people in an average year? What if the Americans try to organise a democracy, pump in the billions and leave because the President wants to get himself re-elected next year? I think you'd still be against it, and you haven't told me why.'

She pulls away from him and faces him with a look of anxious surprise. 'Daddy, you're not *for* the war, are you?'

He shrugs. 'No rational person is for war. But in five years we might not regret it. I'd love to see the end of Saddam. You're right, it could be a disaster. But it could be the end of a disaster and the beginning of something better. It's all about outcomes, and no one knows what they'll be. That's why I can't imagine marching in the streets.'

Her surprise has turned to distaste. He raises the bottle and offers to top up her glass but she shakes her head and sets her champagne down and moves further away. She isn't drinking with the enemy.

'You hate Saddam, but he's a creation of the Americans. They backed him, and armed him.'

'Yes, and the French, and Russians and British did too. A big mistake. The Iraqis were betrayed, especially in 1991 when they were encouraged to rise against the Ba'athists who cut them down. This could be a chance to put that right.'

'So you're for the war?'

'Like I said, I'm not for any war. But this one could be the lesser evil. In five years we'll know.'

'That's so typical.'

He smiles uneasily. 'Of what?'

'Of you.'

This isn't quite the reunion he imagined, and as sometimes happens, their dispute is getting personal. He's not used to it, he's lost his touch. He feels a tightness above his heart. Or is it the bruise on his sternum? He's well into his second glass of champagne, she's hardly touched her first. Her dancing impulses have vanished. She leans by the doorway, arms folded squarely, the little elfin face tight with anger. She responds to his raised eyebrows.

'You're saying let the war go ahead, and in five years if it works out you're for it, and if doesn't, you're not responsible. You're an educated person living in what we like to call a mature democracy, and our government's taking us to war. If you think that's a good idea, fine, say so, make the argument, but don't hedge your bets. Are we sending the troops in or not? It's happening now. And making guesses about the future is what you do sometimes when you make a moral choice. It's called thinking through the consequences. I'm against this war because I think terrible things are going to happen. You seem to think good will come of it, but you won't stand by what you believe.'

He considers, and says, 'It's true. I honestly think I could be wrong.'

This admission, and his pliant manner, make her angrier. 'Then why take the risk? Where's the cautionary principle you're always going on about? If you're sending hundreds of thousands of soldiers to the Middle East, you better know what you're doing. And these bullying greedy fools in the White House don't know what they're doing, they've no idea where they're leading us, and I can't believe you're on their side.'

Perowne wonders if they're really talking about something else. Her 'so typical' still bothers him. Perhaps her months in Paris have given her time to discover fresh perspectives on her father, and she doesn't like them. He turns the thought away. It's good, it's healthy to have one of their old head-to-head arguments, it's family life resumed. And the world matters. He eases himself onto one of the high stools by the centre island, and gestures for her to do the same. She ignores him and remains by the door, arms still crossed, face still closed. It doesn't help that he becomes calmer as she grows more agitated, but that's his habit, professionally ingrained.

'Look Daisy, if it was down to me, those troops wouldn't be on the Iraq border. This is hardly the best time for the West to be going to war with an Arab nation. And no plan in sight for the Palestinians. But the war's going to happen, with or without the UN, whatever any government says or any mass demonstrations. The hidden weapons, whether they exist or not, they're irrelevant. The invasion's going to happen, and militarily it's bound to succeed. It'll be the end of Saddam and one of the most odious regimes ever known, and I'll be glad.'

'So ordinary Iraqis get it from Saddam, and now they have to take it from American missiles, but it's all fine because you'll be glad.'

He doesn't recognise the rhetorical sourness, the harshness in her throat. He says, 'Hang on,' but she doesn't hear him.

'Do you think we're going to be any safer at the end of all this? We'll be hated right across the Arab world. All those bored young guys will be queuing up to become terrorists . . .'

'Too late to worry about that,' he says over her. 'A hundred thousand have already passed through the Afghan training camps. At least you must be happy that's come to an end.'

As he says this, he remembers that in fact she was, that she loathed the joyless Taliban, and he wonders why he's interrupting her, arguing with her, rather than eliciting her views and affectionately catching up with her. Why be adversarial? Because he himself is stoked up, there's poison in his blood, despite his soft tone; and fear and anger, constricting his thoughts, making him long to have a row. Let's have this out! They are fighting over armies they will never see, about which they know almost nothing.

'There'll be more fighters,' Daisy says. 'And when the first explosion hits London your pro-war views . . .'

'If you're describing my position as pro-war, then you'd have to accept that yours is effectively pro-Saddam.'

'What fucking nonsense.'

As she swears he feels a sudden surge in his being, driven partly by astonishment that their conversation is moving out of control, and also by a reckless enlivening joy, a release from the brooding that has afflicted him all day. The colour has gone from Daisy's face and the few freckles she has along her cheekbone are suddenly vivid in her share of the basement kitchen's pools of downlighting. Her face, which typically in conversations is at a quizzical angle, confronts him with a level glare of outrage.

Despite his leap of feeling, he looks calm as he takes a drink of champagne and says, 'What I meant is this. The price of removing Saddam is war, the price of no war is leaving him in place.'

It was meant as a conciliatory point, but Daisy doesn't hear it that way. 'It's crude and ugly,' she says, 'when the war lobby calls us pro-Saddam.'

'Well, you're prepared to do the one thing he'd most like you to do, which is to leave him in power. But you'll only postpone the confrontation. He or his horrible sons are going to have to be dealt with one day. Even Clinton knew that.'

'You're saying we're invading Iraq because we haven't got a choice. I'm amazed at the crap you talk, Dad. You know very well these extremists, the Neo-cons, have taken over America. Cheney, Rumsfeld, Wolfovitz. Iraq was always their pet project. Nine eleven was their big chance to talk Bush round. Look at his foreign policy up until then. He was a know-nothing stay-at-home mouse. But there's nothing linking Iraq to nine eleven, or to Al-Qaeda generally, and no really scary evidence of WMD. Didn't you hear Blix yesterday? And doesn't it ever occur to you that in attacking Iraq we're doing the very thing the New York bombers wanted us to do – lash out, make more enemies in Arab countries and radicalise Islam. Not only that, we're getting rid of their old enemy for them, the godless Stalinist tyrant.'

'And I suppose they wanted us to destroy their training camps and drive the Taliban out of Afghanistan, and force Bin Laden on the run, and have their financial networks disrupted and hundreds of their key guys locked up . . .'

She cuts in and her voice is loud. 'Stop twisting my words. No one's against going after Al-Qaeda. We're talking about Iraq. Why is it that the few people I've met who aren't against this crappy war are all over forty? What is it about getting old? Can't get close to death soon enough?'

He feels a sudden sadness, and a longing for the dispute to come to an end. He preferred it ten minutes ago, when she told him she loved him. She's yet to show him the proofs of *My Saucy Bark* and the artwork for the cover.

But he can't stop himself. 'Death's all around,' he agrees. 'Ask Saddam's torturers at Abu Ghraib prison and the twenty thousand inmates. And let me ask you a question. Why is it among those two million idealists today I didn't see one banner, one fist or voice raised against Saddam?'

'He's loathsome,' she says. 'It's a given.'

'No it's not. It's a forgotten. Why else are you all singing and dancing in the park? The genocide and torture, the mass graves, the security apparatus, the criminal totalitarian state – the iPod generation doesn't want to know. Let nothing come between them and their ecstasy clubbing and cheap flights and reality TV. But it will, if we do nothing. You think you're all lovely and gentle and blameless, but the religious nazis loathe you. What do you think the Bali bombing was about? The clubbers clubbed. Radical Islam hates your freedom.'

She mimes being taken aback. 'Dad, I'm sorry you're so sensitive about your age. But Bali was Al-Qaeda, not Saddam. Nothing you've just said justifies invading Iraq.'

Perowne is well into his third glass of champagne. A big mistake. He's not a practised drinker. But he's viciously happy. 'It's not just Iraq. I'm talking about Syria, Iran, Saudi Arabia, a great swathe of repression, corruption and misery. You're about to be a published writer. Why not let it bother you a little, the censorship, and your fellow writers in Arab jails, in the very region where writing was invented? Or is freedom and not being tortured a Western affectation we shouldn't impose on others?'

'Oh for God's sake, not that relativist stuff again. And you keep drifting off the point. No one wants Arab writers in jail. But invading Iraq isn't going to get them out.'

'It might. Here's a chance to turn one country around. Plant a seed. See if it flourishes and spreads.'

'You don't plant seeds with cruise missiles. They're going to hate the invaders. The religious extremists will get stronger. There'll be less freedom, more writers in prison.'

'My fifty pounds says three months after the invasion there'll be a free press in Iraq, and unmonitored Internet access too. The reformers in Iran will be encouraged, those Syrian and Saudi and Libyan potentates will be getting the jitters.'

Daisy says, 'Fine. And my fifty says it'll be a mess and even you will wish it never happened.'

They had various bets after arguments during her teenage years, generally concluded with a mock-formal handshake. Perowne found a way of paying up, even when he won – a form of concealed subsidy. After an exam seemed to go badly for her, seventeen-year-old Daisy angrily put twenty pounds on never getting into Oxford. To cheer her up he raised his side of the deal to five hundred, and when her acceptance came through she spent the money on a trip to Florence with a friend. Is she in the mood for shaking hands now? She comes away from the door, retrieves her champagne and moves to the far side of the kitchen and appears interested in Theo's CDs by the hi-fi. Her back is firmly turned on him. He remains on his stool at the centre island, playing with his glass, no longer drinking. He has a hollow feeling from arguing only a half of what he feels. He's a dove with Jay Strauss, and a hawk with his daughter. What sense is he making? And how luxurious, to work it all out at home in the kitchen, the geopolitical moves and military strategy, and not be held to account, by voters, newspapers, friends, history. When there are no consequences, being wrong is simply an interesting diversion.

She takes a CD from its box and posts it in the player. He waits, knowing he'll get a clue to her mood, or even a message. At the piano intro he smiles. It's a record Theo brought into the house years ago, Chuck Berry's old pianist, Johnnie Johnson, singing 'Tanqueray', a slouching blues of reunion and friendship.

> *It was a long time comin',*
> *But I knew I would see the day*
> *When you and I could sit down,*
> *And have a drink of Tanqueray.*

She turns and comes towards him with a little dance shuffle. When she's at his side he takes her hand.

She says, 'Smells like the old warmonger's made one of his fish stews. Can I be of use?'

'The young appeaser can set the table. And make a salad dressing if you like.'

She's on her way to the plate cupboard when they hear the doorbell, two overlong unsteady rings. They look at each other: it's not promising, that kind of persistence.

He says, 'Before you do that, slice a lemon. The gin's over there, tonic's in the fridge.'

He's amused by her theatrical eye-rolling and deep breath.

'Here goes.'

'Stay cool,' he advises, and goes upstairs to greet his father-in-law, the eminent poet.

Growing up in the suburbs in cosily shared solitude with his mother, Henry Perowne never felt the lack of a father. In the heavily mortgaged households around him, fathers were distant, work-worn figures of little obvious interest. To a child, a domestic existence in Perivale in the mid-sixties was regulated uniquely by a mother, a housewife; visiting a friend's house to play at weekends or holidays, it was her domain you entered, her rules you temporarily lived by. She was the one who gave or withheld permission, or handed out the small change. He had no good reason to envy his friends an extra parent – when fathers weren't absent, they loomed irascibly, preventing rather than enabling the better, riskier elements of life. In his teens, when he scrutinised the few existing photographs of his father, it was less out of longing than narcissism – he hoped to discover in those strong, acne-free features some promise for his own future chances with girls. He wanted the face, but he didn't want the advice, the refusals or the judgments. Perhaps he was bound to regard a father-in-law as an imposition, even if he'd acquired one far less imposing than John Grammaticus.

Right from their first meeting in 1982 when he arrived at the chateau hours after consummating his love for Rosalind on a lower bunk on the Bilbao ferry, Senior House Officer Perowne was determined not to be patronised, not to be treated like a prospective son. He was an adult with specialised skills that could stand alongside those of any poet. Through Rosalind, he knew of 'Mount Fuji', the much anthologised Grammaticus poem, but Henry didn't read poetry and said so without shame at dinner that first night. At that time John was deep into his *No Exequies* – his last extended creative period as it turned out – and what some junior doctor didn't read in his spare time failed to intrigue him. Nor did he seem to care or even notice, later when the Scotch was on the table, the same doctor disagreeing with him on politics – Grammaticus was an early fan of Mrs Thatcher – or music – bebop had betrayed jazz – or the true nature of the French – venal to a man.

Rosalind said the next morning that Henry had tried too hard to get the old man's attention – the opposite of what he intended, and a very irritating remark. But even though he ceased to be argumentative, nothing much changed between them after that first evening, even after marriage, children and the passing of more than two decades. Perowne keeps his distance, and Grammaticus is happy with the arrangement, and looks straight through his son-in-law to his daughter, to his grandchildren. The two men are superficially friendly and at bottom bored by each other. Perowne can't see how poetry – rather occasional work it appears, like grape picking – can occupy a whole working life, or how such an edifice of reputation and self-regard can rest on so little, or why one should believe a drunk poet is different from any other drunk; while Grammaticus – Perowne's guess – regards him as one more tradesman, an uncultured and tedious medic, a class of men and women he distrusts more as his dependency on it grows with age.

There's another matter, naturally never discussed. The house on the square, like the chateau, came to Rosalind's mother Marianne through her parents. When she married Grammaticus, the London house became the family home where Rosalind and her brother grew up. When Marianne died in the road accident, the terms of her will were clear – the London house passed to the children, and John was to have St Felix. Four years after they were married, Rosalind and Henry, living in a tiny flat in Archway, raised a mortgage to buy out her brother who wanted an apartment in New York. It was a joyful day when the Perownes and their two young children moved into the big house. These various transactions were made without ill-will. But Grammaticus tends to behave on his occasional visits as if he's returning home, as if he were an absentee landlord greeting his tenants, asserting his rights. Or perhaps Henry is too sensitive, having no place in his constitution for a father figure. Either way, it irks him; he prefers to see his father-in-law, if at all, in France.

As he goes towards the front door, Perowne reminds himself, against the promptings of the champagne, to keep his feelings well disguised; the purpose of the evening is to reconcile Daisy to her grandfather, three years on from what Theo has named, in honour of various thrillers, 'The Newdigate Rebuff'. She'll want to show him the proofs, and the old man should rightfully claim his part in her success. On that good thought he opens the door to see Grammaticus several feet away, standing in the road, with long belted woollen coat, fedora and cane, head tipped back, his features in profile caught in the cool white light from the lamps in the square. Most likely he was posing for Daisy.

'Ah Henry,' he says – the disappointment is in the downward inflection – 'I was looking at the tower . . .'

Grammaticus doesn't shift position, so Perowne obligingly steps out to join him.

'I was trying to see it', he continues, 'through the eyes of Robert Adam when he was setting out the square, wondering what he would have made of it. What do you think?'

It rises above the plane trees in the central gardens, behind the reconstructed façade on the southern side; set high on the glass-paned stalk, six stacked circular terraces bearing their giant dishes, and above them, a set of fat wheels or sleeves within which is bound the geometry of fluorescent lights. At night, the dancing Mercury is a playful touch. When he was small, Theo liked to ask whether the tower would hit the house if it fell their way, and was always gratified when his father told him it most certainly would. Since

Perowne and Grammaticus have not yet greeted each other or shaken hands, their conversation is disembodied, like a chat-room exchange.

Perowne, the courteous host, joins in the game. 'Well, he might have taken an engineer's view. All that glass, and the unsupported height, would have amazed him. So would the electric light. He might have thought of it more as a machine than a building.'

Grammaticus indicates that this is not the answer at all. 'The truth is, his only analogy at the end of the eighteenth century would have been a cathedral spire. He was bound to think of it as a religious building of some kind – why else build so high? He'd have to assume those dishes were ornamental, or used in rites. A religion of the future.'

'In which case, not far out.'

Grammaticus raises his voice to speak over him. 'For God's sake, man. Look at the proportions of those pillars, the carving on those capitals!' Now he's jabbing his cane towards the façade on the square's east side. 'There's beauty for you. There's self-knowledge. A different world, a different consciousness. Adam would have been stunned by the ugliness of that glass thing. No human scale. Top heavy. No grace, no warmth. It would have put fear in his heart. If that's going to be our religion, he'd've said to himself, then we're truly fucked.'

Their view of the Georgian pillars of the east façade includes in the foreground two figures on a bench about a hundred feet away wearing leather jackets and woollen watch caps. Their backs are turned and they're sitting close together, hunched forward, so that Perowne assumes that a deal is in progress. Why else sit out here so intently on a cold February night? Sudden impatience comes over him; before Grammaticus can continue to damn the civilisation they share, or exult in another well out of their reach, he says, 'Daisy's waiting for you. She's making you a powerful drink.' He takes his father-in-law's elbow and shoves him gently in the direction of the wide, brightly lit open door. John is well into his expansive, relatively benign stage and Daisy shouldn't miss it. Reconciliation won't be a theme of the later phases.

He takes his father-in-law's coat, stick and hat, shows him into the sitting room and goes to call down to Daisy. She's already on her way up with a tray – a new bottle of champagne as well as the old, the gin, ice, lemon, extra glasses for Rosalind and Theo, and macadamia nuts in the painted bowl she brought back from a student trip to Chile. When she gives him a querying look he makes a cheerful face: it's going to be fine. Thinking she and her grandfather are bound to embrace, he takes the tray and follows her in. But Grammaticus, who's standing in the centre of the room, draws himself up rather formally, and Daisy holds back. It could be he's surprised by her beauty, just as Henry himself was; or struck by her familiarity. They go towards each other murmuring respectively, 'Daisy . . . Granddad', shake hands, and then, by a compact enforced by the movement of their bodies which they can't reverse once it's begun, they awkwardly kiss cheeks.

Henry sets down the tray and mixes a gin and tonic. 'Here you are,' he says. 'Let's raise a glass. To poetry.'

The old man's hand, he notices, is shaking as he takes his gin. Lifting their glasses, humming or grunting without quite repeating the words a mere bonesetter has no right to utter, Daisy and her grandfather drink.

Grammaticus says to him, 'She's the image of Marianne when I first met her.'

His eyes, Perowne notes, are not moist like his own were; despite the passion and the mood reversals, there's something controlled and untouchable, even steely about Grammaticus. He has a way of sailing through encounters, of being lofty, even in close company. Long ago, according to Rosalind, in his thirties, he developed the manner of the old and grand, of not caring what anybody thinks.

Daisy says to him, 'You look awfully well.'

He puts his hand on her arm. 'I re-read them all in the hotel this afternoon. Bloody marvellous, Daisy. There's no one like you.' He drinks again, and quotes in a curious singsong.

> My saucy bark, inferior far to his
> On your broad main doth bravely appear.

He's twinkly, and teasing her the way he used to. 'Now. Be honest. Who is the other poet with talent the size of a galleon?'

Grammaticus is fishing for the tribute he believes must be his by right. A little too soon in the evening. He's going too fast. It's quite possible that Daisy has dedicated her book to her grandfather, although Perowne has worries about that. Another reason why he wanted to see the proofs.

Daisy is confused. She goes to speak, changes her mind, and then says through a forced smile, 'You'll just have to wait and see.'

'Of course, Shakespeare didn't really think he was a little sailing boat among the ocean-going competition. He was trying it on, being sardonic. So perhaps you are too, my dear girl.'

She's hesitant, embarrassed, struggling with a decision. She hides behind her raised glass. Then she puts it down on the table and seems to make up her mind.

'Granddad, it's not "doth bravely appear".'

'Of course it is. I taught you that sonnet.'

'I know you did. But how can the line scan with "bravely"? It's "On your broad main doth *wilfully* appear".'

The twinkle in Grammaticus simply vanishes. His rigid gaze rests on his granddaughter, and she glares back, just the way she did at her father in the kitchen. She's spoken up in a spirit of disloyalty, and she's standing her ground. For Henry, the word 'scan' triggers an unwanted memory, a prick of work anxiety about a hundred-and-ninety-thousand-pound shortfall in the funds the Trust has set aside for the purchase of a more powerful MRI scanner. He's written the memo, he's been to all the meetings. Was there something else he should have done? An e-mail to be forwarded perhaps. Of scanning in poetry, he's in no position to say that 'wilfully' is an improvement on 'bravely'.

Grammaticus says, 'Well, there you go. It doesn't scan. How about that? Henry, how are things at the hospital?'

In more than twenty years he's never asked about the hospital, and Henry can't permit his daughter to be brushed aside. At the same time, it's wondrous: three years apart, and these two are falling out within the minute.

He gives a plausible impression of being amused in saying lightly to Grammaticus, 'My own memory plays far worse tricks than that.' Then he turns to Daisy. She's backed off a pace and looks like she might be searching for an excuse to leave the room. He's determined to keep her there.

'Clear this up for me. How is it "wilfully" scans and "bravely" doesn't?'

She's perfectly good-natured, explaining the facts of life to her father, and rubbing it in for Grammaticus.

'"On your broad main doth wilfully appear" is five feet, five iambs. You know, ti-tum, weak strong. There are always five in this kind of line. "Bravely" would leave it a beat short and it wouldn't sound right.'

While she's speaking Grammaticus is lowering himself onto one of the leather sofas with a conspicuous groan that partly obliterates her final words.

He says, 'Don't be too hard on an old man. "It was no dream; I lay broad waking". Plenty of short lines in Shakespeare, dozens of them in the sonnets. If he'd written "bravely", we'd *make* the bugger scan.'

'That's bloody Wyatt,' Daisy murmurs below the old man's hearing.

Perowne glances at her and raises a covert finger. She's won her point and surely knows she should let her grandfather have the last word. Unless she wants to fight on until dinner, and beyond.

'I suppose you're right. We would. More gin, Granddad?' There's no audible edge in her voice.

Grammaticus passes her his glass. 'I'll do the tonic myself.'

When that's done, Daisy lets a few seconds pass for the silence to neutralise, then murmurs to her father, 'I'll go and finish the table.'

Perhaps Henry's too preoccupied, or too impatient, to make a decent job of this reunion. Does it matter? If Daisy has out-grown one more tutor in her life, what's he supposed to do about that? There's a change in her he doesn't understand, a certain agitation that keeps fading into a smoothness of manner, a degree of combativeness that rises and retreats. And he doesn't wish to be left alone drinking with his father-in-law. He longs for Rosalind to arrive home with all her homely skills – the mother's, daughter's, wife's, lawyer's.

He says to Daisy, 'I'd love to see this proof copy.'

'All right.'

Perowne sits on the other sofa, facing Grammaticus across the scarred, polished thakat table and pushes the nuts towards him. They listen to her softly cursing as she rummages in her backpack in the hall. Neither man can be troubled with small talk. Even if they could agree on what's worthwhile talking about, neither would have any interest in the other's opinion. So they remain in contented silence. Sitting down comfortably for the first time since he entered the house, his feet delightfully relieved of his weight, his mood enhanced by wine and three glasses of champagne on an empty stomach, his hearing still faintly impaired by Theo's band, his thighs aching again from the squash, Perowne abandons himself to a gentle swell of dissociation. Nothing matters much. Whatever's been troubling him is benignly resolved. The pilots are harmless Russians, Lily is well cared for, Daisy is home with her book, those two million marchers are good-hearted souls, Theo and Chas have written a fine song,

Rosalind will win her case on Monday and is on her way, it's statistically improbable that terrorists will murder his family tonight, his stew, he suspects, might be one of his best, all the patients on next week's list will come through, Grammaticus means well really, and tomorrow – Sunday – will deliver Henry and Rosalind into a morning of sleep and sensuality. Now is the moment to pour another glass.

He's reaching for the bottle and checking his father-in-law's drink when they hear a loud metallic jiggling from the hall, a scream from Daisy, a baritone shout of 'Yo!' followed by the thunderous slam of the front door which sends concentric ripples through the poet's gin; then a soft thud and grunt of bodies colliding. Theo is home and embracing his sister. Seconds later, entering the sitting room hand in hand, the children present a tableau of their respective obsessions and careers, precious gifts, Henry unjealously concedes, from their grandfather: Daisy holds a copy of her bound proof, her brother grips his guitar in its case by the neck. Of all the family, Theo is by far the most relaxed with Grammaticus. They have their music in common, and there's no competition: Theo plays, his grandfather listens and tends his blues archive – now being transferred to hard disk with the boy's help.

'Granddad, don't get up,' he calls as he leans his guitar against the wall.

But the old man is getting to his feet as Theo comes over, and the two hug without inhibition. Daisy comes and sits beside her father and slides her book into his lap.

Grammaticus has hold of his grandson's arm and is enlivened, rejuvenated by his presence. 'So. You've a new song for me.'

The proof is aquamarine with black lettering. As he stares at the title and its author's name, Perowne slips his arm around his daughter's shoulders and squeezes, and she moves closer to him to see her book through his eyes. He sees it through hers, and tries to imagine the thrill. At her age he was a swotting fifth-year medical student in a universe of Latin names and corporeal facts, far removed from such possibilities. With his free hand he turns to the title page and together they read the three words again, and this time they're bound within a double-edged rectangle, *My Saucy Bark*, Daisy Perowne, and at the foot of the page, the publisher's name followed by London, Boston. Her boat, of whatever size, is launched upon the transatlantic currents. Theo is saying something, and he looks up.

'Dad. Dad! The song. What did you think?'

When the children were tiny, one took care with the even distribution of praise. These high-achieving kids. He should have been discussing the song earlier when he was alone with Grammaticus. But Henry needed his drifting half-minute of positive thinking.

He says, 'I was swept away.' And to everyone's surprise, he tips his chin towards the ceiling and sings with tolerable accuracy, 'Let me take you there, My city square, city square.'

Theo takes from his coat pocket a CD and gives it to his grandfather. 'We made a recording this afternoon. It's not perfect, but you'll get the idea.'

Henry returns his attention to his daughter. 'I like this London, Boston. Very classy.' He traces the tiny block capitals with his finger. Over the page he reads with relief the dedication. *To John Grammaticus.*

In sudden anguish, Daisy is whispering in his ear, 'I don't know if it's right. It should have been to you and Mum. I just didn't know what to do.'

He squeezes her again and murmurs, 'It's exactly right.'

'I don't know if it is. I can still change it.'

'He put you on the path, it makes perfect sense. He's going to be very happy. We all are. You did the right thing.' And then, in case there's any trace of regret in his voice, he adds, 'There'll be other books too. You can work your way round the whole family.'

Only then is he aware, from tremors in her form huddled

up against his own and a flush of body warmth, that she's crying. She pushes her face into his upper arm. Theo and his grandfather are in the other part of the room, by the CD shelves, discussing a boogie pianist.

'Hey, little one,' he says into her ear. 'What is it, my darling?'

She cries harder, soundlessly, and shakes her head, unable to talk.

'Shall we go upstairs to the library?'

She shakes her head again, and he strokes her hair and waits.

Unhappy in love? He tries to resist speculation. There's no particular instance from her childhood he can remember, but it's a vaguely familiar experience from long ago, waiting for her to recover and tell him what's making her cry. She was always eloquent. All those novels she read as a child, especially after her grandfather took her in hand, schooled her in the accurate description of feelings. Henry leans back and patiently, lovingly holds his daughter. She's no longer tearful, but she continues to press her head into his shoulder and her eyes are closed. Her book lies open on his lap, still at the dedication page. Behind him, Theo and his grandfather are discussing recordings and personnel, and like true devotees, they speak in murmurs, making the room feel calm. Grammaticus has another gin in his hand, his third perhaps, but is eerily sober. Perowne feels pins and needles moving along his upper arm where Daisy's head is pressing. He looks down at her fondly, at what little he can see of her face. Not even the first traces of ageing or experience around the corner of her visible eye, only clean taut skin, faintly purple, like the peripheries of a bruise. The outward show, the new toys of sexual development obscure the fact that childhood tails away slowly. Daisy had breasts and periods when her bed was still so stuffed with teddy bears and other soft animals there was barely room for her. Then it was a first bank account, a university degree, a driving licence that concealed the lingering, fading child which only a parent can still recognise in the newly formed adult. But watching her now, he knows that however she cuddles against his side, this is no innocent. It's likely her mind is turning fast, faster than his can, perhaps around a broken mosaic of recent events – raised voices in rooms, flashes of Parisian streets, an open suitcase on an unmade bed, whatever is distressing her. You stare at a head, a lushness of hair, and can only guess.

This second dreamy interlude may have lasted five minutes, perhaps ten. At one point, as the logic of his thoughts begins to disintegrate, he closes his eyes and lets himself drift backwards and down, a pleasant sensation confused with notions of a muddy tidal river, and of untying with clumsy fingers a knotted rope that is also a means of converting currency and changing weekends into workdays. But even as he sinks, he knows he mustn't sleep – there are guests, and other responsibilities he can't immediately identify. At the sound of Rosalind opening the front door he stirs and looks expectantly across his left shoulder. Daisy too half raises her head, and the conversation between Theo and Grammaticus breaks off. There's an unusually long pause before they hear from the hall the sound of the door closing. Perowne thinks his wife might be burdened with shopping or packages, or legal bundles, and is about to get up to help when she comes in. She moves slowly, stiffly, apparently wary of what she is about to find. She's carrying her brown leather briefcase and she's pale, her face is stretched, as though invisible hands are compressing and pulling the skin back towards her ears. Her eyes are wide and dark, desperate to communicate what her lips, parting and closing once, are unable to tell them. They watch as she stops and looks back at the doorway she has come through.

'Mum?' Daisy calls out to her.

Perowne disentangles himself from his daughter and rises to his feet. Even though Rosalind is wearing a winter coat over her business suit, he imagines he can actually see the racing of her pulse – an impression derived from her rapid, shallow breathing. Her family is calling her name and beginning to go towards her, and she's moving away from them, and backing herself against the high living-room wall. She warns them off with her eyes, with a furtive movement of her hand. It isn't only fear they see in her face, but anger too, and perhaps in the tensing of her upper lip, disgust. Through a quarter-inch gap between the hinged side of the door and its frame, Perowne sees in the hall a form, no more than a shadow, hesitate then move away. From Rosalind's reaction they sense a figure coming into the room before they see it. And still, the shape Perowne can see in the hall hangs back: he realises well before the others that there are two intruders in the house, not one.

As the man enters the room, Perowne instantly recognises the clothes; the leather jacket, the woollen watch cap. Those two on the bench were waiting for their chance. A moment before he can recall the name, he recognises the face too, and the peculiarity of gait, the fidgety tremors as he positions himself close, too close, to Rosalind. Rather than shrinking from him, she stands her ground. But she has to turn her head away to find at last the word she has been trying to articulate. She meets her husband's eye.

'Knife,' she says as though to him alone. 'He's got a knife.'

Baxter's right hand is deep in the pocket of his jacket. He surveys the room and the people in it with a tight pout of a smile, like a man bursting to tell a joke. All afternoon he must have dreamed of making this entrance. With infinitesimal tracking movements of the head his gaze switches from Theo and Grammaticus at the far end of the room, to Daisy, and finally to Perowne just in front of her. It is, of course, logical that Baxter is here. For a few seconds, Perowne's only thought is stupidly that: *of course*. It makes sense. Nearly all the elements of his day are assembled; it only needs his mother, and Jay Strauss to appear with his squash racket. Before Baxter speaks, Perowne tries to see the room through his eyes, as if that might help predict the degree of trouble ahead: the two bottles of champagne, the gin and the bowls of lemon and ice, the belittlingly high ceiling and its mouldings, the Bridget Riley prints flanking the Hodgkin, the muted lamps, the cherry wood floor beneath the Persian rugs, the careless piles of serious books, the decades of polish in the thakat table. The scale of retribution could be large. Perowne also sees his family through Baxter: the girl and the old fellow won't be a problem; the boy is strong but doesn't look handy. As for the lanky doctor, that's why he's here. Of course. As Theo said, on the streets there's pride, and here it is, concealing a knife. When anything can happen, everything matters.

Henry is ten feet away from Baxter. When Rosalind warned of the knife, he froze mid-step, in an unstable position. Now, like a child playing grandmother's footsteps, he brings the back foot level with the front, and plants it well apart. With her eyes and a faint shake of her head Rosalind is urging him away. She doesn't know the background; she thinks these are mere burglars, that it is sensible to let them take what they want and hope they will leave. Nor does she know the pathology. All day long, the encounter on University Street has been in his thoughts, like a sustained piano note. But he'd almost forgotten about Baxter, not the fact of his existence, of course, but the agitated physical reality, the sour nicotine tang, the tremulous right hand, the monkeyish air, heightened now by a woollen cap.

With a look, Baxter lets him know that he too has seen his step, but what he says is, 'I want all them phones out of your pockets and on the table.'

When no one moves he says, 'You two kids first.' And he says to Rosalind, 'Go on, tell them.'

'Daisy, Theo. I think it's best to do it.' There's more anger than fear in her voice now, and some rebellion in the understated 'I think'. Daisy's hands are shaking and she's having trouble getting the phone out of the tight pocket of her skirt. She makes exasperated little gasps. Theo puts his phone on the table and comes round to help her, a good move, his father thinks, since it brings him almost to his side. Baxter's right hand is still deep in his jacket. If they can agree on the moment, they're in a good position to rush him.

But Baxter has the same thought. 'Put hers next to yours and go back to where you were. Go on. Right back. Further.'

Somewhere in Henry's study, in a drawer full of junk, is a pepper spray he bought many years ago in Houston. It might still work. Down in the external vaults, in among the camping gear and old toys, is a baseball bat. In the kitchen are any number of cleavers and choppers. But the bruise on his sternum suggests he'd lose a knife fight in seconds.

Baxter turns to Rosalind. 'Now yours.'

She exchanges a look with Henry and puts her hand in the pocket of her coat. She places the phone in Baxter's palm.

'Now you.'

Perowne says, 'It's upstairs charging.'

'Don't make it worse, cunt,' Baxter says. 'I can see it.'

The top of the phone is visible above the curving cut of his jeans' pocket. The shape of the rest is picked out by a bulge in the denim.

'So you can.'

'Put it on the floor and slide it across to me.'

To encourage him, Baxter at last takes the knife from his pocket. As far as Perowne can tell, it's an old-fashioned French kitchen knife, with an orange wooden handle and curved blade with no sheen. Careful to make all his movements unsurprising and slow, he kneels down and pushes his phone towards Baxter. He doesn't pick it up. Instead, he calls out, 'Oi Nige. You can come in now. Pick up them phones.'

The horse-faced lad pauses self-consciously in the doorway. 'Fucking size of this place.' When he sees Perowne he says, 'Aw. Mr Road Rage.'

As his friend is gathering up the phones, Baxter says, 'What about poor granddad over there? Don't tell me they haven't bought you a phone.'

Grammaticus comes away from the shadows and takes a few paces towards him. In his right hand is his empty glass. 'Actually, I don't own one. And if I did, I'd be inviting you to ram it up your cowardly arse.'

Baxter says to Henry, 'Is this your dad?'

It's not the moment for fine distinctions, and he thinks he's making the right answer when he says, 'Yes.'

But he's exactly wrong. Baxter walks unevenly, in his dipping pole-punter's roll, across the room, pausing only to step around Nigel. The knife in his hand is held firmly, point down.

'That wasn't very nice, a posh old gent like you.'

Sensing disaster, Perowne tries to get between Baxter and Grammaticus, but Nigel stands in his way, grinning. There's no time. Perowne calls out quickly, 'You've got no quarrel with him.'

But in that moment Baxter has arrived in front of the old man, and though Theo, immediately guessing what's coming, flings out a protective arm, Baxter's hand flashes in an arc in front of the old man's face. They hear a soft crack of bone, like a green branch breaking. All the Perownes exclaim, an 'oh' or a 'no', but their worst fears are not realised. It wasn't the hand that held the knife that struck Grammaticus. Bare knuckles have simply broken his nose. As his legs give way and he drops, Theo catches him and lowers him so that he's on his knees, and takes the glass from him. Without a sound, without giving his attacker the satisfaction of a groan, Grammaticus covers his face with his hands. Blood trickles from just below his wristwatch.

Until now, Henry suddenly sees, he's been in a fog. Astonished, even cautious, but not properly, usefully frightened. In his usual manner he's been dreaming – of 'rushing' Baxter with Theo, of pepper sprays, clubs, cleavers, all stuff of fantasy. The truth, now demonstrated, is that Baxter is a special case – a man who believes he has no future and is therefore free of consequences. And that's simply the frame. Within it are the unique disturbances, the individual expression of his condition – impulsiveness, poor self-control, paranoia, mood swings, depression balanced by outbursts of temper, some of this, or all of it and more, would have helped him, stirred him, as he reflected on his quarrel with Henry this morning. And it will be driving Baxter on now. There's no obvious intellectual deterioration yet – the emotions go first, along with the physical coordination. Anyone with significantly more than forty CAG repeats in the middle of an obscure gene on chromosome four is obliged to share this fate in their own particular way. *It is written.* No amount of love, drugs, Bible classes or prison sentencing can cure Baxter or shift him from his course. It's spelled out in fragile proteins, but it could be carved in stone, or tempered steel.

Rosalind and Daisy are converging on John Grammaticus where he kneels beside the sofa. Theo helplessly rests a hand on his grandfather's shoulder. Perowne's own path remains blocked by Nigel – there's no way past without physical struggle. Baxter, knife still in his right hand, steps aside and with a fidgety, wavering left hand removes his woollen cap and loosens the zip on his jacket. Awkwardly, he lights a cigarette. As he smokes, he jiggles the zip's tag and looks on at the scene around the man on the floor, shifting his weight lopsidedly between left and right foot. He seems to be waiting to see what he himself will do next.

But for all the reductive arguments, Perowne can't convince himself that molecules and faulty genes alone are terrorising his family and have broken his father-in-law's nose. Perowne himself is also responsible. He humiliated Baxter in the street in front of his sidekicks, and did so when he'd already guessed at his condition. Naturally, Baxter is here to rescue his reputation in front of a witness. He must have talked Nigel round, or bribed him. The lad is a fool to make himself an accessory. Baxter is acting while he still can, for he must know what's in store for him. Over the coming months and years the athetosis, those involuntary, uncontrolled movements, and the chorea – the helpless jitters, the grimacing, the jerky raising of the shoulders and flexing of fingers and toes – will overwhelm him, render him too absurd for the street. His kind of criminality is for the physically sound. At some point he'll find himself writhing and hallucinating on a bed he'll never leave, in a long-term psychiatric ward, probably friendless, certainly unlovable, and there his slow deterioration will be managed, with efficiency if he's in luck. Now, while he can still hold a knife, he has come to assert his dignity, and perhaps even shape the way he'll be remembered. *Yeah, that tall geezer with the Merc made a big fucking mistake when he trashed old Baxter's wing mirror.* The story of Baxter deserted by his men, defeated by a stranger who was able to walk away unscathed, all that will be forgotten.

And what was that stranger thinking of, when he knew about the condition, has seen his colleagues' patients, even corresponded a few years ago with a neurosurgeon in Los Angeles about a new procedure? The idea was to graft stereotactically onto regions of the caudate and putamen a cocktail of foetal stem cells from three different sources, and minced-up nerve tissue from the patient. It never really worked out, and Perowne wasn't tempted by it. Why could he not see that it's dangerous to humble a man as emotionally labile as Baxter? To escape a beating and get to his squash game. He used or misused his authority to avoid one crisis, and his actions have steered him into another, far worse. The responsibility is his; Grammaticus's blood is on the floor because Baxter thinks the old man is Perowne's father. A good start's been made on dishonouring the son.

Rosalind and Daisy are crouching by Grammaticus with paper tissues.

'It's all right,' he's saying in a muffled voice. 'I've broken it before. On some bloody library steps.'

'You know what?' Baxter calls across to Nigel. 'We've been here all this time and no one's offering us a drink.'

This is an opportunity to get clear of Nigel and edge round the low table to where the tray stands. Henry's anxious to draw Baxter into his part of the room, away from the group around Grammaticus. What he fears is an outburst from Rosalind or one of the children when Baxter is close by. Touching one of the champagne bottles with a forefinger, Perowne looks enquiringly at Baxter and waits. Rosalind's arm is round Daisy's shoulders as they tend Grammaticus. Nearby, Theo stands with his gaze fixed on the floor several feet ahead – sensibly avoiding eye contact with Baxter who has managed to pull his fidgeting hand away from the tag of his zip. His knife is back in his pocket.

He says, 'Yeah. Two gins straight up, ice and lemon.'

The boon of reducing further Baxter's physical coordination has to be set against the risk of making his disinhibition even uglier. It's a choice, a calculation Perowne in his terror finds he can make. He bends like an apothecary to the task, and fills two wine glasses to the brim with Tanqueray, and adds a slice of lemon and an ice cube to each. He passes one to Nigel, and holds the other up for Baxter. The table is in the way; to Henry's relief, he comes forward, around the sofa and table to take the drink.

'Look,' Perowne says. 'For the sake of argument, I'm prepared to accept I was in the wrong this morning. If you want your car repaired . . .'

'Been reconsidering, have you?'

The glass is not stable in Baxter's hands, and when he turns to wink at Nigel, a quantity of gin is spilled. Perhaps it's the habit of concealing his condition that causes him to steady the glass against his lips and empty it in four smooth gulps. In that short time, Perowne is thinking about the landlines into the house and whether Baxter took the trouble to

cut them. There's also a monitored panic button by the front
door, and another in the bedroom. Is this fantasy again?
Distress is making him nauseous. With Theo's assistance,
Rosalind and Daisy are helping Grammaticus to his feet.
Even though Perowne attempts with a surreptitious flick of
his hand to wave them further down their end of the room,
they're bringing him by the fire.

'He's cold,' Rosalind says. 'He needs to lie down.'

So much for that plan. Now they are bunched together
again. At least Theo is on hand. But surely, it's already
decided, rushing Baxter is childish dreaming. Nigel will
have a weapon. These two are real fighters. What else then?
Are they to stand around and wait until Baxter uses his knife?
Henry feels himself rocking on his feet in fear and indecision. A strong urge to urinate keeps nudging between his
thoughts. He wants to catch Theo's eye, but he also senses
that Rosalind might know something, or have an idea. The
way she brushed against his side could be significant. She's
right behind him, settling her father on the sofa. Daisy seems
calmer now – looking after her grandfather has helped her.
Theo stands with his arms crossed, still staring tensely into
the ground, possibly calculating. His forearms looks strong.
All this talent in the room, but useless without a plan and
a means to communicate it. Perhaps he should act alone,
wrestle Baxter to the floor and trust the others will pile in.
More fantasising, and with Baxter so volatile, so savagely
carefree, the possibilities for harm multiply. All this beloved
and vulnerable flesh. Henry's self-cancelling thoughts drift
and turn, impossible to marshal. The proper thing would be
to hit Baxter hard in the face with a clenched fist and hope
that Theo will take on Nigel. But when Henry imagines himself about to act, and sees a ghostly warrior version of himself leap out of his body at Baxter, his heart rate accelerates
so swiftly that he feels giddy, weak, unreliable. Never in his
life has he hit someone in the face, even as a child. He's only
ever taken a knife to anaesthetised skin in a controlled and

sterile environment. He simply doesn't know how to be reckless.

'Come on then, landlord.'

Willingly, for this is his only scrap of a strategy, Perowne takes the gin and refills Baxter's outstretched glass and tops up Nigel's. As he does so Henry becomes aware that Baxter is staring past him at Daisy. The fixity of the look, and that same bottled-up little smile, causes an icy contraction across the surface of Henry's scalp. Baxter spills more gin as he raises the glass to his mouth. He doesn't shift his gaze, even as he sets his drink down on the table. Disappointingly, he's taken only a single sip. He hasn't said much since his attack on Grammaticus, and it's likely that he too is without a plan; his visit is an improvised performance. His condition confers a bleak kind of freedom, but he probably doesn't know how far he's prepared to go.

They're all waiting, and Baxter says at last, 'So what's your name then?'

'My God,' Rosalind says quickly. 'You come near her, you'll have to kill me first.'

Baxter puts his right hand in his pocket again. 'All right, all right,' he says querulously. 'I'll kill you first.' Then he brings his gaze back onto Daisy and repeats in exactly the same tone as before, 'So, what's your name then?'

She steps clear of her mother and tells him. Theo unfolds his arms. Nigel stirs and moves a little closer to him. Daisy is staring right at Baxter, but her look is terrified, her voice is breathless and her chest rises and falls rapidly.

'Daisy?' The name sounds improbable on Baxter's lips, a foolish, vulnerable nursery name. 'And what's that short for?'

'Nothing.'

'Little Miss Nothing.' Baxter is moving behind the sofa on which Grammaticus is lying, and beside which Rosalind stands.

Daisy says, 'If you leave now and never come back I give

you my word we won't phone the police. You can take anything you want. Please, please go.'

Even before she's finished, Baxter and Nigel are laughing.
It's a delighted, unironic laughter, and Baxter is still
laughing as he stretches out a hand towards Rosalind's
forearm and pulls so that she falls back onto the sofa in a
sitting position by Grammaticus's feet. Both Perowne and
Theo start towards him. At the sight of the knife, Daisy
gives a short muffled scream. Baxter is holding it in his
right hand which rests lightly on Rosalind's shoulder. She
stares rigidly ahead.

Baxter says to Perowne and Theo, 'You go right back across
the room. Go on. Right back. Go on. See to them, Nige.'

The distance between Baxter's hand and Rosalind's right
common carotid is less than four inches. Nigel is trying to
shove Perowne and Theo into the far corner by the door, but
they manage to back away from him and into separate, diagonally facing corners, ten or twelve feet on either side of
Baxter – Theo by the fireplace, his father towards one of the
three tall windows.

Henry tries to keep not only the panic, but the entreaty
from his voice. He wants to sound like a reasonable man.
He's only partially successful. His heart rate makes his voice
thin and uneven, his lips and tongue feel inflated. 'Listen
Baxter, your only argument is with me. Daisy's right. You
can take what you want. We won't do a thing about it. The
alternative for you is psychiatric prison. And you've got a
lot more time left than you think.'

'Fuck off,' Baxter says without turning his head.

But Perowne goes on. 'Since we talked this morning I've
been in touch with a colleague. There's a new procedure from
the States, coupled with a new drug, not on the market, but
just arriving here for trials. First results from Chicago are
amazing. More than 80 per cent are in remission. They're
starting twenty-five patients on it here next month. I can get
you on the trial.'

'What's he on about?' Nigel says.

Baxter makes no response, but some tension, a sudden stillness along the line of his shoulders suggests he's considering. 'You're lying,' he says at last, but a lack of emphasis encourages Perowne to go on.

'They're using the RNA interference we talked about this morning. The work's come on quicker than anyone thought it could.'

He's tempted, Henry is sure he's tempted. Baxter says, 'It isn't possible. I know it isn't possible.' He says this, and he wants to be convinced.

Henry says quietly, 'Well, I thought so too. But it seems it is. The trial starts on March the twenty-third. I talked to a colleague this afternoon.'

In a sudden surge of agitation, Baxter blocks him out. 'You're lying,' he says again, and then louder, almost shouting, protecting himself against the lure of hope. 'You're lying and you better shut up or watch my hand.' And the hand bearing the knife moves nearer Rosalind's throat.

But Perowne doesn't stop. 'I promise you I'm not. All the data's upstairs in my study. I printed it out this afternoon and you can come up with me and . . .'

He's cut off abruptly by Theo. 'Stop it Dad! Stop talking. Fucking shut up or he'll do it.'

And he's right. Baxter has pushed the blade flat against the side of Rosalind's neck. She sits upright on the sofa, hands clasping her knees, face empty of expression, her gaze still fixed ahead. Only a tremor in her shoulders shows her terror. The room is silent. Grammaticus at the other end of the sofa has at last removed his hands from his face. The blood congealed above his upper lip thickens his look of horror and disbelief. Daisy stands by the armrest that supports her grandfather's head. Something is welling up in her – a shout or a sob – and the effort of suppressing it darkens her complexion. Theo, despite the cautionary shouts, has moved a little closer in. His arms dangle uselessly at his sides.

Like his father, he can look only at Baxter's hand. Perowne watches and tries to convince himself that Baxter's silence suggests he's struggling with the temptation of the drug trials, the new procedure.

From outside comes the sound of a police helicopter, probably monitoring the dispersal of the march. There's also a sudden cheerful racket of voices and footsteps on the pavement outside as a group of excited friends, foreign students perhaps, come round the square and turn towards Charlotte Street where the restaurants and bars will be filling up. Central London is already launched upon another Saturday evening.

'So, anyway. What I was trying to do is have a conversation with this young lady here. Miss Nothing.'

Nigel, who stands leering in the centre of the room, his moist lips and horsy face suddenly animated, says insinuatingly, 'You know what I'm thinking?'

'I do, Nige. And I was thinking the same thing myself.' Then he says to Daisy, 'I want you to watch my hand ...'

'No,' Daisy says quickly. 'Mum. No.'

'Shut up. I haven't finished. You watch my hand and listen. All right? You mess, about, we're lost. You listen carefully. Take your clothes off. Go on. All of them.'

'Oh God,' Grammaticus says quietly.

Theo calls across the room. 'Dad?'

Henry shakes his head. 'No. Stay where you are.'

'That's right,' Baxter says.

Baxter is addressing not Theo but Daisy. She stares at him in disbelief, trembling, shaking her head faintly. Her fear is exciting him, his whole body dips and shudders.

Daisy manages to say in a whisper, 'I can't. Please ... I can't.'

'Yes you can, darling.'

With the tip of his knife, Baxter slices open a foot-long gash in the leather sofa, just above Rosalind's head. They stare at a wound, an ugly welt, swelling along its length as the ancient, yellowish-white stuffing oozes up like subcutaneous fat.

'Fucking get on with it,' Nigel mutters.

Baxter's hand and the knife are back on Rosalind's shoulder. Daisy looks at her father. What should she do? He doesn't know what to tell her. She bends to remove her boots, but she can't free the zip, her fingers are too clumsy. With a cry of frustration she goes down on one knee and tugs at it until it yields. She sits on the floor, like a child undressing, and pulls off her boots. Still sitting, she fumbles with the fastener at the side of her skirt, then she gets to her feet and steps out of it. As she undresses she shrinks abjectly into herself. Rosalind is shaking badly as Baxter leans over her shoulder and steadies his fidgety hand with its blade against her neck. But she doesn't turn away from Daisy, unlike Theo who appears so stricken that he can't bear to look at his sister. He keeps his gaze fixed on the floor. Grammaticus too is looking away. Daisy goes faster now, pulling off her tights with an impatient gasp, almost tearing at them, then throwing them down. She's undressing in a panic, pulling off her black sweater and chucking that down too. She's in her underwear – white, freshly laundered for the journey from Paris – but she doesn't pause. In one unbroken movement she unhitches her bra and hooks off her knickers with her thumb and lets them fall from her hands. Only then does she glance at her mother, but only briefly. It's done. Head bowed, Daisy stands with her hands at her sides, unable to look at anyone.

Perowne hasn't seen his daughter naked in more than twelve years. Despite the changes, he remembers this body from bath times, and even in his fear, or because of it, it is above all the vulnerable child he sees. But he knows that this young woman will be intensely aware of what her parents are discovering at this very moment in the weighted curve and compact swell of her belly and the tightness of her small breasts. How didn't he guess earlier? What perfect sense it makes; her variations of mood, the euphoria, that she should cry over a dedication. She's surely almost beginning her second trimester. But there's no time to think about it. Baxter has not shifted his position. Rosalind has tremors in her knees now. The blade prevents her turning her head towards her husband, but he thinks she's straining to find him with her eyes.

Daisy is before them and Nigel says, 'Jesus. In the club. She's all yours, mate.'

'Shut up,' Baxter says.

Unseen, Perowne has taken half a step towards him.

'Well, well. Look at that!' Baxter says suddenly. He's pointing with his free hand across the table at Daisy's book. He could be concealing his own confusion or unease at the sight of a pregnant woman, or looking for ways to extend the humiliation. These two young men are immature, probably without much sexual experience. Daisy's condition embarrasses them. Perhaps it disgusts them. It's a hope. Baxter has forced matters this far, and he doesn't know what to do. Now he's seen her proof lying on the sofa opposite, and seizes an opportunity.

'Pass me that one, Nige.'

As Nigel moves to retrieve the book, Henry shuffles closer. Theo does the same.

'*My Saucy Bark*. By Saucy Daisy Perowne.' Baxter flips the pages in his left hand. 'You didn't tell me you wrote poems. All your own work, is it?'

'Yes.'

'Very clever you must be.'

He holds the book out towards her. 'Read one. Read out your best poem. Come on. Let's have a poem.'

As she takes the book she implores him. 'I'll do anything you want. Anything. But please move the knife away from her neck.'

'Hear that?' Nigel giggles. 'She says anything. Come on, Saucy Daisy.'

'Nah, sorry,' Baxter says to her, as though he's as disappointed as anyone else. 'Someone might creep up on me.'

And he looks across his shoulder at Perowne and winks.

The book is shaking in her hands as she opens it at random.

She draws breath and is about to start when Nigel says, 'Let's hear your dirtiest one. Something really filthy.'

At this, all her resolution is gone. She closes the book. 'I can't do it,' she wails. 'I can't.'

'You'll do it,' Baxter says. 'Or you'll watch my hand. Do you want that?'

Grammaticus says to her quietly, 'Daisy, listen. Do one you used to say for me.'

Nigel calls out, 'Fucking shut up, Granddad.'

She looked at Grammaticus blankly when he spoke, but now she seems to understand. She opens the book again and turns the pages back, looking for the place, and then, with a glance at her grandfather, she begins to read. Her voice is hoarse and thin, her hand can barely hold the book for shaking, and she brings the other hand up to hold it too.

'Nah,' Baxter says. 'Start again. I didn't hear a word of that. Not a thing.'

So she starts again, barely more audibly. Henry has been through her book a few times, but there are certain poems he's read only once; this one he only half remembers. The lines surprise him – clearly, he hasn't been reading closely enough. They are unusually meditative, mellifluous and wilfully archaic. She's thrown herself back into another century. Now, in his terrified state, he misses or misconstrues much, but as her voice picks up a little and finds the beginnings of a quiet rhythm, he feels himself slipping through the words into the things they describe. He sees Daisy on a terrace overlooking a beach in summer moonlight; the sea is still and at high tide, the air scented, there's a final glow of sunset. She calls to her lover, surely the man who will one day father her child, to come and look, or, rather, listen to the scene. Perowne sees a smooth-skinned young man, naked to the waist, standing at Daisy's side. Together they listen to the surf roaring on the pebbles, and hear in the sound a deep sorrow which stretches right back to ancient times. She thinks there was another time, even further back, when the earth was new and the sea consoling, and nothing came between man and God. But this evening the lovers hear only sadness and loss in the sound of the waves breaking and retreating from the shore. She turns to him, and before they kiss she tells him that they must love each other and be faithful, especially now they're having a child, and when there's no peace or certainty, and when desert armies stand ready to fight.

She looks up. Unable to control the muscular spasms in her knees, Rosalind still gazes at her daughter. Everyone else is watching Baxter, and waiting. He's hunched over, leaning his weight against the back of the sofa. Though his right hand hasn't moved from Rosalind's neck, his grip on the knife looks slacker, and his posture, the peculiar yielding angle of his spine, suggests a possible ebbing of intent. Could it happen, is it within the bounds of the real, that a mere poem of Daisy's could precipitate a mood swing?

At last he raises his head and straightens a little, and then says suddenly, with some petulance, 'Read it again.'

She turns back a page, and with more confidence, attempting the seductive, varied tone of a storyteller entrancing a child, begins again. 'The sea is calm tonight. The tide is full, the moon lies fair upon the straits – on the French coast the light gleams and is gone . . .'

Henry missed first time the mention of the cliffs of England 'glimmering and vast out in the tranquil bay'. Now it appears there's no terrace, but an open window; there's no young man, father of the child. Instead he sees Baxter standing alone, elbows propped against the sill, listening to the waves 'bring the eternal note of sadness in'. It's not all of antiquity, but only Sophocles who associated this sound with the 'turbid ebb and flow of human misery'. Even in his state, Henry balks at the mention of a 'sea of faith' and a glittering paradise of wholeness lost in the distant past. Then once again, it's through Baxter's ears that he hears the sea's 'melancholy, long withdrawing roar, retreating, to the breath of the night wind, down the vast edges drear and naked shingles of the world.' It rings like a musical curse. The plea to be true to one another sounds hopeless in the absence of joy or love or light or peace or 'help for pain'. Even in a world 'where ignorant armies clash by night', Henry discovers on second hearing no mention of a desert. The poem's melodiousness, he decides, is at odds with its pessimism.

It's hard to tell, for his face is never still, but Baxter appears suddenly elated. His right hand has moved away from Rosalind's shoulder and the knife is already back in his pocket. His gaze remains on Daisy. The relief she feels she manages to transform, by a feat of self-control and dissembling, into a look of neutrality, betrayed only by a trembling in her lower lip as she returns the stare. Her arms hang defencelessly at her sides, the book dangles between her fingers. Grammaticus grips Rosalind's hand. The disgust with which Nigel listened to the poem a second time has only just faded from his face. He says to Baxter, 'I'll take the knife while you do the business.'

Henry worries that a prompt from Nigel, a reminder of the purpose of the visit, could effect another mood swing, a reversion.

But Baxter has broken his silence and is saying excitedly, 'You wrote that. You *wrote* that.'

It's a statement, not a question. Daisy stares at him, waiting.

He says again, 'You wrote that.' And then, hurriedly, 'It's beautiful. You know that, don't you. It's beautiful. And you wrote it.'

She dares say nothing.

'It makes me think about where I grew up.'

Henry doesn't remember or care where that was. He wants to get to Daisy to protect her, he wants to get to Rosalind, but he's fearful as long as Baxter remains near her. His state of mind is so delicately poised, easily disturbed. It's important not to surprise or threaten him.

'Oi, Baxter.' Nigel cocks his head at Daisy and smirks.

'Nah. I've changed my mind.'

'What? Don't be a cunt.'

'Why don't you get dressed,' Baxter says to Daisy, as though her nakedness was her own strange idea.

For a moment she doesn't move, and they wait for her.

'I can't believe it,' Nigel says. 'We gone to all this trouble. '

She bends to retrieve her sweater and skirt and begins to pull them on.

Baxter says eagerly, 'How could you have thought of that? I mean, you just wrote it.' And then he says it again, several times over. 'You wrote it!'

She ignores him. Her movements are abrupt as she dresses, there could even be anger in the way she kicks aside the underwear she leaves lying on the floor. She wants to cover herself and get to her mother, nothing else matters to her. Baxter finds nothing extraordinary in the transformation of his role, from lord of terror to amazed admirer. Or excited child. Henry is trying to catch his daughter's eye in the hope of silently warning her of the need to go on humouring Baxter. But now she and her mother are embracing. Daisy is kneeling on the floor, half lying across Rosalind's lap, with her arms around her neck, and they're whispering and nuzzling, oblivious to Baxter hovering behind them, making frenetic little dips with his body. He's becoming manic, he's tripping over his words, and shifting weight rapidly from one foot to the other. Daisy let her book drop on the table when she went to Rosalind. Now Baxter nips forward and seizes it, waves it in the air, as if he could shake meaning from it.

'I'm having this,' he cries. 'You said I could take anything I want. So I'm taking this. OK?' He's addressing himself to the nape of Daisy's neck.

'Shit,' Nigel hisses.

It's of the essence of a degenerating mind, periodically to lose all sense of a continuous self, and therefore any regard for what others think of your lack of continuity. Baxter has forgotten that he forced Daisy to undress, or threatened Rosalind. Powerful feelings have obliterated the memory. In the sudden emotional rush of his mood swing, he inhabits the confining bright spotlight of the present. This is the moment to rush him. Henry looks across at Theo who makes a slow-motion nod of agreement. On the sofa, Grammaticus is sitting up, with his hands on his daughter's and grand-daughter's shoulders. Rosalind and Daisy remain in their embrace – hard to believe they think they're out of danger, or that by ignoring Baxter they're making themselves more secure. It's the pregnancy, Henry decides, the overwhelming fact of it. It's time to act.

Baxter is almost shouting again. 'I'm not taking anything else. You hear? Only this. It's all I want.' He clutches the book like a greedy child fearing the withdrawal of a treat.

Henry glances across at Theo again. He's edged nearer, and he looks tensed, ready to leap. Nigel stands between them, watching – but he's disaffected and there's a chance he'll do nothing. And besides, he, Perowne, is closer to Baxter and will certainly reach him before Nigel can intervene. Again, Perowne feels his pulse knocking in his ears, and sees a dozen ways in which it can go wrong. Henry glances once more at Theo, and decides to count in his mind to three, and then go, no matter what. One . . .

Suddenly Baxter turns. He's licking his lips, his smile is wet and beatific, his eyes are bright. The voice is warm, and trembles with exalted feeling.

'I'm going on that trial. I know all about it. They're trying to keep it quiet, but I see all the stuff. I know what's going on.'

'Fuck this,' Nigel says.

Perowne keeps his tone flat. 'Yes.'

'You're going to show me this stuff.'

'Yes, the American trial. It's upstairs, in my office.'

He had almost forgotten his lie. He looks again at Theo

who now seems to be prompting him with his eyes to go along with this. But he doesn't know that there's no trial. And the price of disappointing Baxter will be high.

He's put the book in his pocket and has taken the knife out and waves it in front of Perowne's face.

'Go on, go on! I'll be right behind you.'

He's so high now, he could stab someone in his joy. He's babbling his words.

'The trial. You show me everything. All of it, all of it . . .'

Henry wants to go to Rosalind, touch her hand, speak to her, kiss her – the smallest exchange would be enough, but Baxter is right in front of him now, with that peculiar metallic odour on his breath. The original idea was to draw him away from the others, and to separate him from Nigel. There's no reason not to carry this through. So, with a final despairing look in Rosalind's direction, Henry turns and walks slowly towards the door.

'You watch them,' Baxter says to Nigel. 'They're all dangerous.'

He follows Perowne across the hall, and they start up the stairs, their steps ringing out in time on the stone. Henry is trying to recall which papers lying around on his desk he can plausibly pass off. He can't remember, and his thoughts are confused by the need to make a plan. There's a paperweight he can throw, and a bulky old stapler. The high-backed orthopaedic office chair will be too heavy to lift. He doesn't even own a paper knife. Baxter is one step behind him, right on his heels. Perhaps a backward kick is the thing.

'I know they're keeping it quiet,' Baxter is saying again. 'They look after their own, don't they?'

They're already halfway up. Even if the trial existed, why would Baxter believe that this doctor would keep his word rather than call in the police? Because he's elated as well as desperate. Because his emotions are wild and his judgment is going. Because of the wasting in his caudate nucleus and putamen, and in his frontal and temporal regions. But none of this is relevant. Perowne needs a plan, and his thoughts are too quick, too profuse – and now he and Baxter are on the broad landing outside the study, dominated by the tall window that looks onto the street, just where it runs into the square.

Henry hesitates for a moment on the threshold, hoping to see something he might use. The desk lamps have heavy bases, but their tangled wires will restrict him. On a bookshelf is a stone figurine he would have to go on tiptoe to reach. Otherwise, the room is like a museum, a shrine, dedicated to another, carefree age – on the couch covered with a Bukhara rug his squash racket lies where he tossed it when he came up to look at Monday's list. On the big table by the wall, the screen saver – those pictures from the Hubble telescope of remote outer space, gas clouds light years across, dying stars and red giants fail to diminish earthly cares. On the old desk by the window, piles of papers, perhaps the only hope.

'Go on then.' Baxter pushes him in the small of his back and they enter the room together. It's a dreamy sensation, of going quietly, numbly, without protest towards destruction. Henry doesn't doubt that Baxter is feeling free enough to kill him.

'Where is it? Show me.'

His eagerness and trust is childlike, but he's waving his knife. For their different reasons, they both long for evidence of a medical trial and an invitation for Baxter to join the privileged cohort. Henry goes towards the desk by the window where two piles of journals and offprints lean side by side. Looking down, he sees an account of a new spinal fusion procedure, and a new technique for opening blocked carotid arteries, and a sceptical piece casting doubt on the surgical lesioning of the globus pallidus in the treatment of Parkinson's Disease. He chooses the last and holds it up. He has no idea what he's doing beyond delaying the moment. His family is downstairs, and he's feeling very lonely.

'This describes the structure,' he starts to say. His voice quavers, as a liar's might, but there's nothing he can do but keep talking. 'The thing is this. The globus pallidus, the pale globe, is a rather beautiful thing, deep in the basal ganglia, one of the oldest parts of the corpus striatum, and uh divided in two segments which . . .'

But Baxter is no longer paying attention – he's turned his head to listen. From downstairs they hear rapid heavy footsteps crossing the hall, then the sound of the front door opening and slamming shut. Has he been deserted for the second time today? He hurries across the study and steps out onto the landing. Henry drops the article and follows. What they see is Theo coming towards them at a run, leaping up the stairs three at a time, his arms pumping, his teeth bared savagely with the effort. He makes an inarticulate shout, which sounds like a command. Henry is already moving. Baxter draws back the knife. Henry seizes his wrist with both hands, pinning the arm in place. Contact at last. A moment later, Theo lunges forwards from two steps down and takes Baxter by the lapels of his leather jacket, and with a twisting, whip-like movement of his body pulls him off balance. At the same time, Perowne, still gripping the arm, heaves with his shoulder, and together they fling him down the stairs.

He falls backwards, with arms outstretched, still holding the knife in his right hand. There's a moment, which seems to unfold and luxuriously expand, when all goes silent and still, when Baxter is entirely airborne, suspended in time, looking directly at Henry with an expression, not so much of terror, as dismay. And Henry thinks he sees in the wide brown eyes a sorrowful accusation of betrayal. He, Henry Perowne, possesses so much – the work, money, status, the home, above all, the family – the handsome healthy son with the strong guitarist's hands come to rescue him, the beautiful poet for a daughter, unattainable even in her nakedness, the famous father-in-law, the gifted, loving wife; and he has done nothing, given nothing to Baxter who has so little that is not wrecked by his defective gene, and who is soon to have even less.

The run of stairs before the turn is long, the steps are hard stone. With a rippling, bell-like sound, Baxter's left foot glances along a row of iron banister posts, just before his head hits the floor of the half-landing and collides with the wall, inches above the skirting board.

They are in various forms of shock, and remain so for hours after the police have left and the paramedics have taken Baxter away in their ambulance. Sudden bursts of urgent, sometimes tearful recall are broken by numb silences. No one wants to be alone, so they remain in the sitting room together, trapped in a waiting room, a no man's land separating their ordeal from the resumption of their lives. With the resilience of the young, Theo and Daisy go downstairs to the kitchen and return with bottles of red wine, mineral water and a bowl of salted cashews, as well as ice and a cloth to make a compress for their grandfather's nose.

But alcohol, tasty as it is, barely penetrates. And Henry finds that he prefers to drink water. What meets their needs is touch – they sit close, hold hands, embrace. The parting words of the night-duty CID officer were that his colleagues would be coming in the morning to take formal statements from them individually. They were therefore not to discuss or compare their evidence. It's a hopeless prescription, and it doesn't even occur to them to follow it. There's nothing to do but talk, fall silent, then talk again. They have the impression of conducting a careful analysis of the evening's horrible events. But it's a simpler, more vital re-enactment. All they do is describe: when they came in the room, when he turned, when the tall horsy one just walked out of the house . . . They want to have it all again, from another's point of view, and know that it's all true what they've been through, and feel in these precise comparisons of feeling and observation that they're being delivered from private nightmare, and returned to the web of kindly social and familial relations, without which they're nothing. They were overrun and dominated by intruders because they weren't able to communicate and act together; now at last they can.

Perowne attends to his father-in-law's nose. John refuses to go to casualty that night, and no one tries to persuade him. The swelling already makes a diagnosis difficult, but his nose hasn't shifted from the midline position, and Perowne's guess is a hairline fracture to the maxillary processes – better that than ruptured cartilage. For much of this stretch of the evening Henry sits close to Rosalind. She shows them a red patch and a small cut on her neck, and describes a moment when she ceased to be terrified and became indifferent to her fate.

'I felt myself floating away,' she says. 'It was as if I was watching all of us, myself included, from a corner of the room right up by the ceiling. And I thought, if it's going to happen, I won't feel a thing, I won't care.'

'Well, *we* might have,' Theo says, and they laugh loudly, too loudly.

Daisy talks with brittle gaiety about undressing in front of Baxter. 'I tried to pretend that I was ten years old, at school, getting changed for hockey. I disliked the games mistress and hated taking my clothes off when she was there. But remembering her helped me. Then I tried to imagine that I was in the garden at the chateau, reciting to Granddad.'

The unspoken matter is Daisy's pregnancy. But it's too soon, Henry supposes, because she doesn't refer to it, and nor does Rosalind.

Grammaticus says from behind his compress, 'You know, it sounds completely mad, but there came a point after Daisy recited Arnold for the second time when I actually began to feel sorry for that fellow. I think, my dear, you made him fall in love with you.'

'Arnold who?' Henry says, and makes Daisy and her grandfather laugh. Henry adds, but she doesn't seem to hear, 'You know, I didn't think it was one of your best.'

He knows what Grammaticus means, and he could begin to tell them all about Baxter's condition, but Henry himself is undergoing a shift in sympathies; the sight of the abrasion on Rosalind's neck hardens him. What weakness, what delusional folly, to permit yourself sympathy towards a man, sick or not, who invades your house like this. As he sits listening to the others, his anger grows, until he almost begins to regret the care he routinely gave Baxter after his fall. He could have left him to die of hypoxia, pleading incapacity through shock. Instead, he went straight down with Theo and, finding Baxter semi-conscious, opened his airway with a jaw thrust; assuming spinal damage, he showed Theo how to hold Baxter's head while he improvised a collar out of towels from the half-landing bathroom. Downstairs, Rosalind was calling an ambulance – the landlines were not cut. With Theo still holding Baxter's head, Perowne rolled him into a recovery position, and looked at the other vital signs. They weren't too good. The breathing was noisy, the pulse slow and weak, the pupils slightly unequal. By this time, Baxter was murmuring to himself as he lay there with eyes closed. He was able to respond to his name and to a command to clench his fist – Perowne put his Glasgow Coma Score at thirteen. He went to his study and phoned ahead to casualty, spoke to the registrar and told him what to expect, and to be ready to order a CT scan and alert the neurosurgeon on duty. Then there was nothing to do but wait out the last minutes. During that time they managed to ease Daisy's book from Baxter's pocket. Theo continued to support his head until two lads from the hospital in green jump suits arrived, put in a line and under Perowne's instruction administered colloid fluid intravenously.

Two police constables arrived in support of the ambulance, and a few minutes later, the CID man turned up. After he'd met the family, and heard Perowne's account, he told them it was too late, and everyone was too upset now to be giving statements. He took from Henry the licence plate number of the red BMW and made a note of the Spearmint Rhino. He examined the gash in the sofa, then he went back upstairs, knelt by Baxter, prised the knife out of his hand and dropped it in a sterile plastic bag. He took a swab of dried blood from the knuckles of Baxter's left hand – it was likely to be blood from Grammaticus's nose.

The detective laughed out loud when Theo asked him whether he and his father had committed any crime in throwing Baxter down the stairs.

He touched Baxter with the tip of his shoe. 'I doubt if he'll be making a complaint. And we certainly won't be.'

The detective phoned his station to arrange for two constables to be sent to the hospital to stand guard over Baxter through the night. When he was conscious, he'd be arrested. Formal charges would follow later. After the warning about sharing evidence, the three policemen left. The paramedics chocked and blocked Baxter on a spinal board and carried him away.

Rosalind appears to make an impressive recovery. Perhaps it's only half an hour after the police and ambulance men have left, when she suggests that it might do everybody good to come and eat. No one has an appetite, but they follow her down to the kitchen. While Perowne reheats his stock and takes from the fridge the clams, mussels, prawns and monkfish, the children lay the table, Rosalind slices a loaf of bread and makes a dressing for the salad, and Grammaticus puts down his icepack to open another bottle of wine. This communal activity is pleasurable, and twenty minutes later the meal is ready, and they are hungry at last. It's even faintly reassuring that Grammaticus is on his way to getting drunk, though he remains at a benign stage. It's about this time, as they're sitting down, that Henry learns the name of the poet, Matthew Arnold, and that his poem that Daisy recited, 'Dover

231

Beach', is in all the anthologies and used to be taught in every school.

'Like your "Mount Fuji",' Henry says, a remark that pleases Grammaticus immensely and prompts him to stand to propose a toast. John's in his twinkly mode, an effect heightened by his clownishly swollen nose. The evening has the appearance of being back on course, for in his hand is the proof copy of *My Saucy Bark*.

'Forget everything else that's happened. We're raising our glasses to Daisy,' he says. 'Her poems mark a brilliant beginning to a career and I'm a very proud grandfather and dedicatee. Who would have thought that learning poems by heart for pocket money would turn out to be so useful. After tonight I think I must owe her another five pounds. To Daisy.'

'To Daisy,' they reply, and as they lift their glasses she kisses him, and he hugs her in return – the reconciliation is made, the Newdigate Rebuff is forgotten.

Henry touches the wine to his lips, but finds he's lost his taste for alcohol. Just as Daisy and her grandfather sit down, the phone rings and since he's nearest, Henry goes across the kitchen to take the call. In his unusual state, he doesn't immediately recognise the American voice.

'Henry? Is that you, Henry?'

'Oh, Jay. Yes.'

'Listen. We got an extradural, male, mid twenties, fell down the stairs. Sally Madden went home with the flu an hour ago, so I've got Rodney. The kid's keen and he's good and he doesn't want you in here. But Henry, we have a depressed fracture right over the sinus.'

Perowne clears his throat. 'Boggy swelling?'

'Right on the spot. That's why I'm stepping in. I've seen inexperienced surgeons tear the sinus lifting the bone, and four litres of blood on the floor. I want someone senior in here and you're the nearest. Plus you're the best.'

From across the kitchen comes loud, unnatural laughter, exaggerated like before, almost harsh; they're not really pretending to have forgotten their fear – they're simply wanting to survive it. There are other surgeons Jay can call on, and as a general rule, Perowne avoids operating on people he knows. But this is different. And despite various shifts in his attitude to Baxter, some clarity, even some resolve, is beginning to form. He thinks he knows what it is he wants to do.

'Henry? Are you there?'

'I'm on my way.'

Five

The family is used to Perowne's occasional departures from dinner – and in this case there may even be some reassurance, a suggestion of a world returning to the everyday, in his announcement that he's been called to the hospital.

He leans by Daisy's chair and says into her ear, 'We've a lot to talk about.'

Without turning, she takes his hand and squeezes. He's about to say to Theo, perhaps for the third time that evening, You saved my life, but instead he half smiles at his son and mouths, 'See you later.' Theo has never seemed so handsome, so beautiful as now. His bare lean arms lie across the table; the solemn, clear brown eyes and their curling lashes, the blind perfection of hair, skin, teeth, the unbent, untroubled spine – he gleams in the half-light of the kitchen. He raises his glass – mineral water – and says, 'You sure you're up to this, Dad?'

Grammaticus says, 'He's right, you know. It's been a long night. You could kill some poor bugger.' With his swept-back silver hair and nose compress he resembles a patched-up lion in a children's book.

'I'm fine.'

There's been talk of Theo fetching down an acoustic guitar to accompany his grandfather in 'St James Infirmary', for

Grammaticus is in the mood for a Doc Watson imitation. Rosalind and Daisy want to hear the recording of Theo's new song, 'City Square'. There's an air of unnatural festivity around the table, of wild release which reminds Henry of a family outing to the theatre the previous year – an evening of bloody and startling atrocities at the Royal Court. At dinner afterwards they passed the evening in hilarious reminiscence of summer holidays, and drinking too much.

When he's said his farewells and is leaving, Grammaticus calls after him, 'We'll still be here when you get back.'

Perowne knows this is unlikely, but he nods cheerfully. Only Rosalind senses the deeper alteration in his mood. She rises and follows him up the stairs and watches him as he puts on his overcoat and finds his wallet and keys.

'Henry, why did you say yes?'

'It's him.'

'So why did you agree?'

They are standing by the front door with its triple locks and the keypad's comforting glow. He kisses her, then she draws him towards her by his lapels and they kiss again, longer and deeper. It's a reminder, a resumption of their morning lovemaking, and also a promise; this is surely how they must end such a day. She tastes salty, which arouses him. Far below his desire, lying like a granite block on the sea floor, is his exhaustion. But at times like this, on his way to the theatre, he's professionally adept at resisting all needs.

As they pull away he says, 'I had a scrape in the car with him this morning.'

'I gathered that.'

'And a stupid showdown on the pavement.'

'So? Why are you going in?' She licks her forefinger – he likes this glimpse of her tongue – and straightens his eyebrows for him. Thickening, with unruly tendrils of ginger, grey and unblemished white tending to the vertical, evidence of the clotted testosterone that can also cause ear and nostril hair to grow like winter sedge. More evidence of decline.

He says, 'I have to see this through. I'm responsible.' In reply to her querying look he adds, 'He's very sick. Probably Huntington's.'

'He's obviously nuts as well as nasty. But Henry. Weren't you drinking earlier? Can you really operate?'

'It was a while ago. I think the adrenaline's rather cleared my head.'

She's fingering the lapel of his coat, keeping him close. She doesn't want him to leave. He watches her tenderly, and with some amazement, for her ordeal is only two or three hours behind her and now here she is, pretending to be entirely herself again and, as always, keen to know the components of an unusual decision, and loving him in her precise, exacting way, a lawyer to the core. He forces his gaze from settling on the abrasion on her throat.

'Are you going to be all right?'

She's lowered her eyes as she orders her thoughts. When she lifts them he sees himself, by some trick of light, suspended in miniature against the black arena of her pupils, embraced by a tiny field of mid-green iris.

She says, 'I think so. Look, I'm worried about you going in.'

'Meaning?'

'You're not thinking about doing something, about some kind of revenge are you? I want you to tell me.'

'Of course not.'

He pulls her towards him and they kiss again, and this time their tongues touch and slide by each other – in their private lexicon a kind of promise. Revenge. He suddenly doubts he's ever heard the word on her lips before. In Rosalind's slightly breathless utterance, it sounds erotic, the very word. And what is he doing, leaving the house? Even as he frames the question, he knows he's going; superficially, it's simple momentum – Jay Strauss and the team will already be in the anaesthetist's room, starting work on his patient. Henry has an image of his own right hand

239

pushing open the swing doors to the scrub room. In a sense, he's already left, though he's still kissing Rosalind. He ought to hurry.

He murmurs, 'If I'd handled things better this morning, perhaps none of this would've happened. Now Jay's asked me in, I feel I ought to go. And I want to go.'

She looks at him wryly, still trying to gauge his intentions, his precise state of mind, the strength of the bond between them at this particular moment.

Because he's genuinely curious to know the story, but also to deflect her, he then says, 'So we're going to be grandparents.'

There's sadness in her smile. 'She's thirteen weeks and she says she's in love. Giulio is twenty-two, from Rome, studying archaeology in Paris. His parents have given them enough money to buy a little flat.'

Henry contends with fatherly thoughts, with nascent outrage at this unknown Italian's assault on the family's peace and cohesion, at his impertinently depositing his seed without first making himself available for inspection, evaluation – where was he now, for example? And irritation that this boy's own family should know before Daisy's, that arrangements are already in hand. A little flat. Thirteen weeks. Perowne leans his hand on the door lock's ancient brassy knob. At last Daisy's pregnancy – the evening's buried subject – rises before him in clear light, a calamity and an insult and a waste, a subject too huge to confront or lament now, when he is waited for up the road.

'Oh God. What a mess. Why didn't she tell us? Did she think about a termination?'

'Out of the question, apparently. Darling, don't start boiling over when you're about to operate.'

'How are they going to live?'

'The way we did.'

In a bliss of sex and graduate poverty, taking turns with baby Daisy as together they sleeplessly raced through a law degree and first law job, and the early years of neurosurgery. He remembers himself after a thirty-hour shift, carrying his bicycle four floors up a cement stairwell towards the insomniac wail of a teething infant. And in that one-bedroom flat in Archway, folding the ironing board away in order to fuck late at night on the living-room floor by the gas fire. Rosalind may have intended such recollections to mollify him. He appreciates the attempt, but he's troubled. What's to become of Daisy Perowne, the poet? He and Rosalind meshed their timetables and worked hard at sharing the domestic load. Italian men, on the other hand, are *pueri aeterni*, who expect their wives to replace their mothers, and iron their shirts and fret about their underwear. This feckless Giulio could destroy his daughter's hopes.

Henry discovers he's clenching a fist. He relaxes it and says untruthfully, 'I can't think about it now.'

'That's right. None of us can.'

'I better go.'

They kiss again, unerotically this time, with all the restraint of a farewell.

As he opens the door she says, 'I'm still worried about you going in like this. I mean, in this mood. Promise me, nothing foolish.'

He touches her arm. 'I promise.'

As the door closes behind him and he steps away from the house, he feels a clarifying pleasure in the cold, wet night air, in his purposeful stride and, he can admit it, in being briefly alone. If only the hospital were further away. Irresponsibly, he prolongs his walk by half a minute by going across the square, rather than down Warren Street. The few fine snowflakes he saw earlier have vanished, and during the evening it has rained; the square's paving stones and cobbled gutters shine cleanly in the white street light. Low smoky cloud grazes the top of the Post Office Tower. The square is deserted, which also pleases him. As he hurries along the eastern side, near the high railings of the gardens, under the bare plane trees stirring and creaking, the empty square is reduced to its vastness and the simplicity of architectural lines and solemn white forms.

He's trying not to think about Giulio. He thinks instead about Rome, where he attended a neurosurgery symposium two years ago, in rooms overlooking the Campo dei Fiori. It was the mayor himself, Walter Veltroni, a quiet, civilised man with a passion for jazz, who opened the proceedings. The following day, in honour of the guests, Nero's palace, the Domus Aurea, much of it still closed to the public, was made available, and Veltroni along with various curators gave the surgeons a private tour. Perowne, knowing nothing about Roman antiquity, was disappointed that the site appeared to be underground, entered by a gated hole in a hillside. This was not what he understood by a palace. They were led down a tunnel smelling of earth and lit by bare bulbs. Off to the sides were dim chambers where restoration work was in progress on fragments of wall tiles. A curator explained – three hundred rooms of white marble, frescos, intricately patterned mosaic, pools, fountains and ivory finish, but no kitchens, bathrooms or lavatories. At last the surgeons entered a scene of wonders – painted corridors of birds and flowers and complicated repeating designs. They saw rooms where frescos were just appearing from under a sludge of grime and fungus. The palace lay undiscovered for five hundred years under rubble until the early Renaissance. For the past twenty years it had been closed for restoration, and its partial opening had been part of Rome's millennial celebration. A curator pointed out a jagged hole far above them in an immense domed ceiling. This was where fifteenth-century robbers dug through to steal gold leaf. Later Raphael and Michelangelo had themselves lowered down on ropes; marvelling, they copied the designs and paintings their smoking torches revealed. Their own work was profoundly influenced by these incursions. Through his translator, Signor Veltroni offered an image he thought might appeal to his guests; the artists had drilled through this skull of brick to discover the mind of ancient Rome.

Perowne leaves the square and heads east, crosses the Tottenham Court Road and walks towards Gower Street. If only the mayor was right, that penetrating the skull brings into view not the brain but the mind. Then within the hour he, Perowne, might understand a lot more about Baxter; and after a lifetime's routine procedures would be among the wisest men on earth. Wise enough to understand Daisy? He's not able to avoid the subject. Henry refuses to accept that she might have chosen to be pregnant. But for her sake he needs to be positive and generous. This Roman Giulio may be just like the admirable boiler-suited types he saw in the gloomy chambers of the Domus Aurea, dabbing away at mosaic tiles with their toothbrushes – archaeology is an honourable profession. It's his duty, Henry supposes, to try to like the father of his grandchild. The despoiler of his daughter. When he condescends at last to visit, young Giulio will need to exert much native charm.

On Gower Street the sanitary teams are still at work, cleaning up after the demonstration. Perhaps they've only just begun. From noisy trucks, generator-powered arc lights illuminate mounds of food, plastic wrappings and discarded placards which men in yellow and orange jackets are pushing forward with wide brooms. Others are shovelling the piles onto the lorries. The state's embrace is ample, ready for war, ready to clean up behind the dissenters. And the debris has a certain archaeological interest – a Not in My Name with a broken stalk lies among polystyrene cups and abandoned hamburgers and pristine fliers for the British Association of Muslims. On a pile he steps round are a slab of pizza with pineapple slices, beer cans in a tartan motif, a denim jacket, empty milk cartons and three unopened tins of sweetcorn. The details are oppressive to him, objects look too bright-edged and tight, ready to burst from the packaging. He must be in a lingering state of shock. He recognises one of the sweepers as the man he saw this morning cleaning the pavements in Warren Street: a whole day behind the broom, and now, courtesy of untidy world events, some serious overtime.

Around the hospital's front entrance there's the usual latenight Saturday gathering, and two security guards standing between the double sets of doors. Typically, people emerge, though not completely, from a drunken dream and remember they last saw a friend being lifted into the back of an ambulance. They find the hospital, often the wrong one, and emphatically demand to see this friend. The guards' job is to keep out the troublemakers, the abusive or incapable, the ones likely to throw up on the waiting-room floor, or take a swing at authority, at a light-boned Filipino nurse or some tired junior doctor in the final hours of her shift. They're also obliged to keep out the rough sleepers who want a bench or piece of floor in the institutional warmth. The sample of the public that makes it to a hospital late on a weekend night is not always polite, kind or appreciative. As Henry recalls, working in Accident and Emergency is a lesson in misanthropy. They used to be tolerated, the assaults as well as the dossers, who even had their own little corner in A and E. But these last few years what's now called the culture has changed. The medical staff have had enough. They want protection. The drunks and loudmouths are thrown out onto the pavement by men who've worked as bouncers and know their business. It's another American import, and not a bad one – zero tolerance. But there's always a danger of chucking out a genuine patient; head injuries, as well as cases of sepsis or hypoglycaemia can present as drunkenness.

Perowne pushes a way through the small knot of people. When he reaches the first door the guards, Mitch and Tony, both West Indian, recognise him and let him through.

'How's it going?'

Tony, whose wife died of breast cancer last year and who's thinking of training as a paramedic, says, 'Quiet, you know, relative like.'

'Yeah,' Mitch says. 'We just got the quiet riot tonight.'

Both men chuckle and Mitch adds, 'Now Mr Perowne, all the wise surgeons got the flu.'

'I'm truly unwise,' Henry says. 'There's an extradural.'

'We seen him.'

'Yeah. You better get up there, Mr Perowne.'

But instead of going straight ahead to the main lifts, he makes a quick detour through the waiting area towards the treatment rooms, just in case Jay or Rodney while waiting has come down for another case. The public benches are quiet, but the long room has a battered, exhausted look, as though at the end of a successful party. The air is humid and sweet. There are drinks cans on the floor, and someone's sock among the chocolate bar wrappers from the vending machines. A girl has an arm round her boyfriend who's slumped forward, head between his knees. An old lady wearing a fixed, faint smile waits patiently with her crutches resting on her lap. There are one or two others staring at the floor, and someone stretched out full length, asleep on a bench, head covered by a coat. Perowne walks past the treatment cubicles to the crash room where a team is working on a man who's bleeding heavily from his neck. Outside, in the majors' area, by the staff base, he sees Fares, the on-duty A and E registrar whom he spoke to on the phone.

As Perowne approaches, Fares says, 'Oh right. That friend you phoned about. We've cleared cervical-spine. The CT scan showed a bilateral extradural with a probable depressed fracture. He dropped a couple of points so we called in a crash induction. They took him upstairs half an hour ago.'

An X-ray of the neck – the first investigative measure – suggests there'll be no complications with Baxter's breathing. His level of consciousness as measured by the Glasgow Coma Score has fallen – not a good sign. An anaesthetist – probably

Jay's registrar – was called down to prepare him for emergency surgery which will have involved, among other things, emptying Baxter's stomach.

'What's his score now?'

'Eleven down from thirteen when he came in.'

Someone calls Fares's name from the crash room, and by way of excusing himself he says as he leaves, 'Bottle fight in a bus queue. And oh yeah. Mr Perowne. Two policemen went up with your friend.'

Perowne takes the lift up to the third floor. As soon as he steps out into the broad area that gives onto the double doors of the neurosurgical suite, he feels better. Home from home. Though things sometimes go wrong, he can control outcomes here, he has resources, controlled conditions. The doors are locked. Peering through the glass he can see no one about. Rather than ring the bell, he takes a long route down a corridor that will bring him through intensive care. He likes it here late at night – the muted light, the expansive, vigilant silence, the solemn calm of the few night staff. He goes down the wide space between the beds, among winking lights and the steady bleeps of the monitors. None of these patients is his. Now that Andrea Chapman has been moved out, all the people on yesterday's list are back in their wards. That's satisfying. In the marshalling area outside the ICU, the space looks unnaturally empty. The usual clutter of trolleys has been removed – tomorrow they'll be back, and all the bustle, the constantly ringing phones, the minor irritation with the porters. Rather than call Rodney or Jay out of the theatre, and to save time, he goes straight to the changing room.

He taps a code in the number lock, and steps into a cramped and homely squalor, a particularly masculine kind of pigsty suggestive of several dozen delinquent boys far from home. He uses a key to open his locker and starts to undress hurriedly. Lily Perowne would have been horrified – scattered across the floor are discarded scrubs, some clean, some used, along with the plastic bags they came in, and trainers, a towel, an old sweater, a pair of jeans; on the tops of the lockers, empty Coke cans, an ancient tennis-racket press, two unrelated sections of a fly-fishing rod that have been lying there for months. On the wall a peevish computer-printed notice asks, Is it possible to discard towels and greens in the appropriate manner? Some wag has written 'no' underneath. Another more official sign advises, Don't take risks with your valuables. There used to be a sign on the lavatory door saying, Please Raise the Seat. Now there's one saying, in resignation, To complain about the state of the lavatory dial extension 4040. A prospective surgical patient would not feel reassured by the racks of white clogs, stained with yellow, red and brown, with dried hard little friezes of gore, and the faded, clumsily inscribed Biro names or initials. It can be vexing, to be in a hurry and not find a matching pair. Henry keeps his own in his locker. He takes his scrubs, tops and bottoms, from the 'large' pile and pulls them on, and makes a point of binning the plastic bag. Despite the chaos around him, these actions calm him, like mental exercises before a chess game. At the door he takes a disposable surgical cap from a pile and secures it behind his head as he goes along the empty corridor.

He enters the theatre by way of the anaesthetic room. Waiting for him, sitting by their machine, are Jay Strauss and his registrar, Gita Syal. Round the table are Emily, the scrub nurse, Joan, the runner, and Rodney – looking like a man about to be tortured. Perowne knows from experience how wretched a registrar feels when his consultant has to come out, even when it's an obvious necessity. In this case it hasn't even been Rodney's decision. Jay Strauss has pulled rank. Rodney's bound to feel that Jay has grassed him up. On the table, obscured by surgical drapes, is Baxter, lying face down. All that's visible of him is the wide area of his head shaved to the rear of the vertex, the crown. Once a patient is draped up, the sense of a personality, an individual in the theatre, disappears. Such is the power of the visual sense. All that remains is the little patch of head, the field of operation.

There's an air in the room of boredom, of small talk exhausted. Or perhaps Jay has been holding forth on the necessity of the coming war. Rodney will have been reluctant to voice his pacifist views for fear of being taken apart.

Jay says, 'Twenty-five minutes. That's pretty good, chief.'

Henry raises a hand in greeting, then gestures at the young registrar to accompany him to the light box where Baxter's scans are on display. On one sheet, sixteen images, sixteen bacon slices through Baxter's brain. The clot, trapped between the skull and its tough membranous inner lining, the dura, sits across the midline, the division between the two hemispheres of the brain. It's two inches or so below the vertex and is large, almost perfectly round, and shows pure white on the scan, with telltale precise margins. The fracture is clearly visible too, seven inches long, running at right angles to the midline. In its centre, sitting right on that midline, is shattered bone, where the skull has partially caved in. Right below that depressed fracture, vulnerable to the sharp edges of displaced bone tilted like tectonic plates, runs a major blood vessel, the superior sagittal sinus. It extends along the fold – the falx – where the two hemispheres meet, and it's the major vein draining blood away from the brain. It sits snugly in the groove formed where the dura wraps separately round each hemisphere. Several hundred millilitres per minute flow through the sinus and it's possible for a surgeon to tear it while lifting the broken bone. So much blood escapes, you can't see to make a repair. This is when a year-two registrar can panic. And this is why Jay Strauss has called Henry.

While he's looking at the scans, Perowne says to Rodney, 'Tell me about the patient.'

Rodney clears his throat. His tongue sounds thick and heavy. 'Male, in his twenties, fell downstairs about three hours ago. He was drowsy in casualty, with a Glasgow Coma Score of thirteen dropping to eleven. Skull lacerations, no other injury recorded. Normal C-spine X-ray. They did a scan, ordered a crash induction and sent him straight up.'

Perowne glances over his shoulder at the monitors on the anaesthetic machine. Baxter's pulse shows eighty-five and blood pressure one hundred and thirty over ninety-four.

'And the scan?'

Rodney hesitates, perhaps wondering if there's a catch, something he didn't notice that could compound his humiliation. He's a big lad, occasionally and touchingly homesick for Guyana where he has ambitions to set up a head injury unit one day. He once had hopes of playing rugby for a serious team until medicine and neurosurgery took him over. He has a friendly, intelligent face, and the word is that women adore him and he puts himself about. Perowne suspects he'll turn out well.

'It's a midline depressed fracture, both extradural and –' Rodney points to an image higher up the sheet and a small white mass shaped like a comma – 'subdural too.'

He's seen the only slightly unusual feature, a clot below the dura as well as the larger one above it.

'Good,' Perowne murmurs, and with that one word Rodney's evening is rescued. There is, however, a third abnormality the registrar will not have noticed. As medicine progresses, certain diagnostic tricks fall into disuse among the younger doctors. In a frame further up the sheet, Baxter's caudate on both sides of the brain lacks the usual convexity, the normal healthy bulge into the anterior horn of the lateral ventricles. Before DNA testing, this shrinking was a useful confirmation of Huntington's Disease. Henry never doubted he was right, but the physical evidence confers its own bleak satisfaction.

Henry says to Jay, 'Is there blood around?'

Gita Syal answers, 'Plenty in the fridge.'

'Is the patient haemodynamically stable?'

'Blood pressure and pulse are OK. And pre-op bloods are fine, airway pressure's fine,' Jay says. 'We're ready to roll, boss.'

Perowne takes a look at Baxter's head to make sure Rodney has shaved him in exactly the right place. The laceration is straight and clean – a wall, a skirting board, a stone-floor landing rather than the grit and filth you see in wounds after a road traffic accident – and has been sewn up by A and E. Even without touching, he can see that the top of his patient's head has an area of boggy swelling – blood is collecting between the bone and the scalp.

Satisfied with the registrar's work, he says to him as he leaves, 'Take the sutures out while I scrub up.' Henry pauses in the corner to choose some piano music. He decides on the 'Goldberg' Variations. He has four recordings here, and selects not the showy unorthodoxies of Glenn Gould, but Angela Hewitt's wise and silky playing which includes all the repeats.

Less than five minutes later, in long disposable gown, gloves and mask, he's back at the table. He nods at Gita to start the CD player. From the stainless-steel trolley Emily has positioned at his side, he takes a sponge on a clamp and dips it in a bowl of Betadine solution. The tender, wistful Aria begins to unfold and spread, hesitantly it seems at first, and makes the theatre seem even more spacious. At the very first stroke of sunflower yellow on pale skin, a familiar content-edness settles on Henry; it's the pleasure of knowing pre-cisely what he's doing, of seeing the instruments arrayed on the trolley, of being with his firm in the muffled quiet of the theatre, the murmur of the air filtration, the sharper hiss of oxygen passing into the mask taped to Baxter's face out of sight under the drapes, the clarity of the overhead lights. It's a reminder from childhood of the closed fascination of a board game.

He sets down the brush and says quietly, 'Local.'

Emily passes him the hypodermic she has prepared. Quickly he injects in several places under skin, along the line of the laceration and beyond. It's not strictly necessary, but the adrenaline in the lignocaine helps reduce the bleeding. At each location the scalp immediately swells into bumps. He sets down the hypodermic and opens his hand. He doesn't have to ask – Emily places within his grasp the nicely weighted skin knife. With it he extends the laceration by several inches, and deepens it. Rodney is close at his side with the bipolar cauteriser, closing off the bleeding points in two or three places. At each contact there is a bleep, and a thin trail of greyish smoke rises with a sharp odour of singed flesh. Despite his bulk, Rodney cleverly avoids crowding his consultant's space and applies the small blue Raney clips that pinch tightly on the parted skin and close off the blood supply.

Perowne asks for the first of the big self-retaining retractors and sets it in place. He lets Rodney attach the second – and now the long incision is stretched apart like a wide-open mouth to reveal the skull and all the damage.

The fracture runs fairly straight. Blood, altered blood, is rising up through it. Once Rodney has washed out the area with saline and wiped it, they can see the crack in the bone is about two millimetres wide – it looks like an earthquake fissure seen from the air, or a crack in a dry riverbed. The depressed fracture in the centre has two segments of bone at a tilt with three other finer cracks radiating from them. There'll be no need to drill a burr hole. Perowne will be able to slip the cutting saw into the larger fissure.

Emily presents the craniotome, but he doesn't like the look of the footpiece – it seems a little skewed. Joan hurries into the prep room and comes back with another. It's satisfactory, and while she unpacks it from the sterile wrapping and fits it, he says to Rodney, 'We'll turn a free flap around the depressed fracture so that we've got full control of the sinus.'

It's said that no one opens up faster than Henry Perowne. Now he goes even more quickly than usual because there's no danger of damaging the dura – the clot is pressing down on it, pushing it away from the skull. Although Rodney leans in with a Dakin's syringe to douse the cutting edge with saline solution, the smell of singed bone fills the theatre. It's a smell Henry sometimes finds clinging to the folds of his clothes when he undresses at the end of a long day. It's impossible to speak over the high-pitched whine of the craniotome. With his eyes he indicates to Rodney that he should observe closely. Exceptional care is needed now as he guides the saw across the midline. He slows, and tilts the footpiece of the drill upwards – otherwise there's a danger that it will catch and tear the sinus. It's a wonder brains come to any harm at all outside an operating theatre when they're encased so thickly in bone. At last Perowne has cut round a complete oval shape behind the crown of Baxter's head. Before he lifts the flap he examines the fragments of the depressed fracture. He asks for a Watson Cheyne dissector and levers them gently up. They come away easily and he puts them into the kidney bowl of Betadine that Emily offers.

Now, using the same dissector, he lifts the whole free flap away from the skull, a large piece of bone like a segment of coconut, and lays it in the bowl with the other bits. The clot is in full view, red of such darkness it is almost black, and of the consistency of recently set jam. Or, as Perowne sometimes thinks, like a placenta. But round the edges of the clot, blood is flowing freely now that the pressure of the bone flap has been relieved. It pours from the back of Baxter's head, over the surgical drapes and onto the floor.

'Elevate the head of the table. Give me as much as you can,' Henry calls to Jay. If the bleed is higher than the heart, the blood will flow less copiously. The table rises, and Henry and Rodney step back in quickly through the blood at their feet and, working together, use a sucker and an Adson elevator to remove the clot. They irrigate the area with saline and at last get a glimpse of the tear, about a quarter of an inch long, in the sinus. The bone flap was well placed – the damage is right in the centre of the exposure. The welling blood immediately obscures their view again. An edge of bone from the depressed fragment must have pierced the vessel. While Rodney holds the sucker in place, Perowne takes a strip of Surgicel and lays it over the tear, places a swab on top and indicates to Rodney to press down with his finger.

Henry asks Jay, 'How much blood have we lost?'

He hears Jay ask Joan how much irrigation has been used. Together they make the calculation.

'Two point five litres,' the anaesthetist says quietly.

Perowne is about to ask for the periostal elevator, but Emily is already placing it in his hands. He finds an area of exposed but undamaged skull, and with the elevator – a kind of scraper – harvests two long pieces of pericranium, the fibrous membrane that covers the bone. Rodney lifts the swab, and is about to lift also the Surgicel from the tear, but Perowne shakes his head. A clot might be already forming and he doesn't want to disturb it. He gently lays the strip of pericranium over the Surgicel, and adds a second layer of Surgicel and the second strip of pericranium, and places a new swab on top. Then Rodney's finger. Perowne rinses out the area again with saline and waits. The opaque milky bluish dura remains clear. The bleeding has stopped.

But they can't begin to close up yet. Perowne takes a scalpel and makes a small incision in the dura, parts it a little and peers inside. The surface of Baxter's brain is indeed covered with a clot, much smaller than the first. He extends the incision and Rodney tucks back the dura with stay sutures. Perowne is pleased with the speed of his junior registrar's work. Rodney uses the Adson to lift out the congealed blood. They wash out with saline, sucker the mix away and wait to see if the bleeding continues – Perowne suspects that one of the nearby arachnoid granulations could be a source. There's nothing, but he doesn't close up just yet. He prefers to wait a few minutes, just to be sure.

In this lull, Rodney goes over to a table by the prep room door and sits down to drink a bottle of water. Emily is busy with the instrument tray, Joan is dealing with the wide pool of blood on the floor.

Jay breaks off a murmured conversation with his registrar to say to Perowne, 'We're fine over here.'

Henry remains at the head of the table. Though he's been conscious of the music, only now does he give it his full attention again. Well over an hour has passed, and Hewitt is already at the final Variation, the Quodlibet – uproarious and jokey, raunchy even, with its echoes of peasant songs of food and sex. The last exultant chords fade away, a few seconds' silence, then the Aria returns, identical on the page, but changed by all the variations that have come before, still tender, but resigned too, and sadder, the piano notes floating in from a distance, as though from another world, and only slowly swelling. He's looking down at a portion of Baxter's brain. He can easily convince himself that it's familiar territory, a kind of homeland, with its low hills and enfolded valleys of the sulci, each with a name and imputed function, as known to him as his own house. Just to the left of the midline, running laterally away out of sight under the bone, is the motor strip. Behind it, running parallel, is the sensory strip. So easy to damage, with such terrible, lifelong consequences. How much time he has spent making routes to avoid these areas, like bad neighbourhoods in an American city. And this familiarity numbs him daily to the extent of his ignorance, and of the general ignorance. For all the recent advances, it's still not known how this well-protected one kilogram or so of cells actually encodes information, how it holds experiences, memories, dreams and intentions. He doesn't doubt that in years to come, the coding mechanism will be known, though it might not be in his lifetime. Just like the digital codes of replicating life held within DNA, the brain's fundamental secret will be laid open one day. But even when it has, the wonder will remain, that mere wet stuff can make this bright inward cinema of thought, of sight and sound and touch bound into a vivid illusion of an instantaneous present, with a self, another brightly wrought illusion, hovering like a ghost at its centre. Could it ever be explained, how matter becomes conscious? He can't begin to imagine a satisfactory account, but he knows it will come, the secret will be revealed – over decades, as long as the scientists and the institutions remain in place, the explanations will refine themselves into an irrefutable truth about consciousness. It's already happening, the work is being done in laboratories not far from this theatre, and the journey will be completed, Henry's certain of it. That's the only kind of faith he has. There's grandeur in this view of life.

No one else in the theatre knows the hopeless condition of this particular brain. The motor strip he's looking at now is already compromised by disease, most likely by deterioration in the caudate and putamen, deep in the centre of the brain. Henry places his finger on the surface of Baxter's cortex. He sometimes touches a brain at the beginning of a tumour operation, testing the consistency. What a wonderful fairy tale, how understandable and human it was, the dream of the healing touch. If it could simply be achieved with the caress of a forefinger, he'd do it now. But the limits of the art, of neurosurgery as it stands today, are plain enough: faced with these unknown codes, this dense and brilliant circuitry, he and his colleagues offer only brilliant plumbing.

Baxter's unmendable brain, exposed under the bright theatre lights, has remained stainless for several minutes – there's no sign of any bleeding from the arachnoid granulation.

Perowne nods at Rodney. 'It's looking fine. You can close up.'

Because he's pleased with him, and wants him to feel better about the evening, Perowne lets his registrar take the lead. Rodney sews up the dura with purple thread – 3-o Vicryl – and inserts the extradural drain. He replaces the bone flap, along with the two broken pieces from the depressed fracture. Then he drills the skull to screw in place the titanium plates that hold the bone secure. This part of Baxter's skull now resembles crazy paving, or a broken china doll's head clumsily repaired. Rodney inserts the subgaleal drain and then sets about sewing the skin of the scalp with 2-o Vicryl and punching in the skin staples. Perowne gets Gita to put on Barber's 'Adagio for Strings'. It's been played to death on the radio these past years, but Henry sometimes likes it in the final stages of an operation. This languorous, meditative music suggests a long labour coming to an end at last.

Rodney puts chlorhexadine on and around the wound and applies a small dressing. It's at this point that Henry takes over – he prefers to do the head dressing himself. He releases one by one the pins of the head clamp. He takes three opened-out large gauze swabs and places them flat on Baxter's head. Around the head he lays two gauze swabs left long. Holding the five swabs in place with his left hand, he begins to wind a long crêpe bandage around Baxter's head while supporting it against his waist. It's technically and physically difficult, avoiding the two drains and preventing the head from dropping down. When at last the head bandage is in place and secured, everyone in the theatre, the whole firm, converges on Baxter – this is the stage at which the patient's identity is restored, when a small area of violently revealed brain is returned to the possession of the entire person. This unwrapping of the patient marks a return to life, and if he hadn't seen it many hundred times before, Henry feels he could almost mistake it for tenderness. While Emily and Joan are carefully pulling away the surgical drapes from around Baxter's chest and legs, Rodney makes sure the tubes, leads and drains are not dislodged. Gita is removing the pads taped over the patient's eyes. Jay is detaching the inflatable warming blanket from around Baxter's legs. Henry stands at the end of the table, cradling the head in his hands. The helpless body is revealed in a hospital gown and looks small on the table. The meditative, falling line of the orchestral strings seems to be addressed to Baxter alone. Joan pulls a cover over him. Taking care not to tangle the extradural and subgaleal drains, they turn Baxter onto his back. Rodney slots a padded horse-shoe into the end of the table and Henry rests Baxter's head on it.

Jay says, 'You want me to keep him sedated overnight?'

'No,' Henry says. 'Let's wake him up now.'

The anaesthetist will ease Baxter – simply by the with-drawal of drugs – into taking over his own breathing from the ventilator. To monitor the transition, Strauss holds in the palm of his hand a little black sac, the reservoir bag, through which Baxter's breathing will pass. Jay prefers to trust to his sense of touch rather than the electronic array on the anaes-thetic machine. Perowne pulls off his latex gloves and ritu-ally pings them across the room towards the bin. They go in – always a good sign.

He takes off his gown and stuffs that into the bin too, then, still in his hat, goes down the corridor to find a form to do his op note on. At the desk, he finds the two policemen waiting, and tells them that Baxter will be transferred within ten minutes to the intensive care unit. By the time he gets back, there's a different atmosphere in the theatre. Country and Western music – Jay's taste – has replaced Samuel Barber. Emmylou Harris is singing 'Boulder to Birmingham'. Emily and Joan are discussing a friend's wedding as they clean up the theatre – on the night shift this dull task falls to the scrub nurses. The two anaesthetists and Rodney Browne are talking about offset mortgages and interest rates as they make the final preparations for the patient to be transferred to inten-sive care. Baxter lies peacefully on his back showing no signs of consciousness yet. Henry grabs a chair and starts his notes. In the name space he writes 'known as Baxter', and in the date of birth, 'est. age plus/minus 25'. All the other personal details he has to leave blank.

'You've got to shop around,' Jay is telling Gita and Rodney. 'You're in a buyer's market.'

'It's a spray-on tan,' Joan says to Emily. 'She's not allowed in the sun because she gets basal cell carcinomas. Now she's gone bright orange, face, hands, everything, and the wedding's on Saturday.'

The chatter is soothing to Henry as he quickly writes, 'ext/subdural, sup sag sinus repair, pt prone, head elevated & in pins, wound extended/retracted, free bone flap turned . . .'

For the past two hours he's been in a dream of absorption that has dissolved all sense of time, and all awareness of the other parts of his life. Even his awareness of his own existence has vanished. He's been delivered into a pure present, free of the weight of the past or any anxieties about the future. In retrospect, though never at the time, it feels like profound happiness. It's a little like sex, in that he feels himself in another medium, but it's less obviously pleasurable, and clearly not sensual. This state of mind brings a contentment he never finds with any passive form of entertainment. Books, cinema, even music can't bring him to this. Working with others is one part of it, but it's not all. This benevolent dissociation seems to require difficulty, prolonged demands on concentration and skills, pressure, problems to be solved, even danger. He feels calm, and spacious, fully qualified to exist. It's a feeling of clarified emptiness, of deep, muted joy. Back at work and, lovemaking and Theo's song aside, he's happier than at any other point on his day off, his valuable Saturday. There must, he concludes as he stands to leave the theatre, be something wrong with him.

He takes the lift one floor down and goes along a polished, dim corridor to the neurological ward where he makes himself known to the nurse on duty. Then he walks in, and pauses outside a four-bed room to look through the glass. Seeing a reading light on above the nearest bed, he opens the door quietly and goes in. She's sitting up writing in a notebook with a pink plastic cover. As Henry sits down by her bed and before she has time to close her book, he notices that she's drawn for the dot of each 'i' a meticulous heart.

She gives him a sleepy welcoming smile. His voice is barely above a whisper.

'Can't sleep?'

'They gave me a pill, but I can't stop my mind.'

'I get that too. In fact, I had it last night. I was passing by, so – a good time to tell you myself. The operation went really well.'

With her fine dark skin, her round and lovely face, and the thick crêpe bandage that he wound round her head yesterday afternoon, she has a dignified, sepulchral look. An African queen. She wriggles down the bed and pulls the covers round her shoulders, like a child preparing to hear a familiar bedtime story. She hugs her notebook to her chest.

'Did you get it all out like you said?'

'It came out like a dream. It rolled out. Every last bit.'

'What's that word you said before, about how it's going to go?'

He's intrigued. Her change in manner, her communicative warmth, the abandonment of the hard street talk, can't simply be down to her medication, or tiredness. The area he was operating in, the vermis, has no bearing on emotional function.

'Prognosis,' he tells her.

'Right. So doctor, what's the prognosis?'

'Excellent. Your chances of a total recovery are 100 per cent.'

She shrugs herself deeper into the bed covers. 'I love hearing you say that. Do it again.'

He obliges, making his voice as sonorous and authoritative as he can. He's decided that whatever's changed in Andrea Chapman's life is written down in her notebook. He taps its cover with a finger.

'What do you like to write about?'

'It's a secret,' she says quickly. But her eyes are bright, and her lips part as if she's about to speak. Then she changes her mind and clamps them shut and with a mischievous look stares past him at the ceiling. She's dying to tell.

He says, 'I'm very good at secrets. You have to be when you're a doctor.'

'You tell no one, right?'

'Right.'

'You solemnly promise on the Bible?'

'I promise to tell no one.'

'It's this. Right? I've decided. I'm going to be a doctor.'

'Brilliant.'

'A surgeon. A brain surgeon.'

'Even better. But get used to calling yourself a neuro-surgeon.'

'Right. A neurosurgeon. Everybody, stand back! I'm going to be a neurosurgeon.'

No one will ever know how many real or imagined medical careers are launched in childhood during a post-operative daze. Over the years, a few kids have divulged such an ambition to Henry Perowne on his rounds, but no one has quite burned with it the way Andrea Chapman does now. She's too excited to lie covered up. She struggles up the bed, plants her elbow on the mattress, and as best she can with her drain still in place, rests her head on her hand. Her gaze is lowered, and she's thinking carefully before asking her question.

'Have you just been doing an operation?'

'Yes. A man fell down stairs and whacked his head.'

But it's not the patient she's interested in. 'Was Dr Browne there?'

'Yes, he was.'

Finally. She looks up at Henry with an expression of pleading honesty. They are at the heart of her secret.

'Isn't he just a wonderful doctor?'

'Oh, he's very good. The best. You like him, do you?'

Unable to speak, she nods, and he waits a good while.

'You're in love with him.'

At the utterance of the sacred words she flinches, then quickly checks his face for mockery. She finds him impenetrably grave.

He says delicately, 'You don't think he's a little old for you?'

'I'm *fourteen*,' she protests. 'Rodney's only thirty-one. And the thing is this . . .'

She's sitting up now, still pressing her pink book to her chest, joyous to be addressing at last the only true subject.

'. . . he comes and sits where you are, and says to me about how if I want to be a doctor I need to get serious about studying and that, and stop clubbing and that, and he doesn't even know what's happening between us. It's happening without him. He's got no idea! I mean, he's older than me, he's this important surgeon and everything, but he's so *innocent*!'

She outlines her plans. As soon as she's qualified as a consultant – in twenty-five years' time, by Henry's private calculation – she'll be joining Rodney in Guyana to help him run his clinic. After a further five minutes of Rodney, Perowne rises to leave. When he reaches the door she says, 'Do you remember you said like you'd make a video of my operation?'

'Yes.'

'Can I see it?'

'I suppose so. But are you really sure you want to?'

'Oh my God. I'm going to be a neurosurgeon, remember? I really need to watch it. I want to see right inside my head. Then I'm going to have to show it to Rodney.'

On his way out, Perowne lets the nurse know that Andrea is awake and lively, then he takes the lift up to the third floor again and walks back down the long corridor that runs behind the neurosurgery suite and brings him by the main entrance to intensive care. In soothing gloom he goes along the broad avenue of beds with their watchful machines and winking coloured lights. He's reminded of neon signs in a deserted street – the big room has the ephemeral tranquillity of a city just before dawn. At the desk he finds the nurse in charge, Brian Reid, a Geordie, busy filling out forms, and learns that all Baxter's signs are good, that he's come round and is dozing. Reid nods significantly towards the two policemen sitting in the shadows near Baxter's bed. Perowne was intending to walk home as soon as he was satisfied his patient was stable, but as he comes away from the desk, he finds himself going across. At his approach the constables, bored or half asleep, get to their feet and politely explain that they'll wait outside in the corridor.

Baxter is lying on his back, arms straight at his sides, hooked up to all the systems, breathing easily though his nose. There's no tremor in the hands, Perowne notices. Sleep is the only reprieve. Sleep and death. The head bandage doesn't ennoble Baxter the way it did Andrea. With his heavy stubble and dark swelling under the eyes he looks like a fighter laid out by a killer punch, or an exhausted chef, kipping in the storeroom between shifts. Sleep has relaxed his jaw and softened the simian effect of a muzzle. The forehead has loosened its habitual frown against the outrageous injustice of his condition, and gained him some clarity in repose.

Perowne brings a chair over and sits down. A patient at the far end of the room calls out, perhaps in her sleep, a sharp cry of astonishment repeated three times. Without turning, he's aware of the nurse going towards her. Perowne looks at his watch. Three thirty. He knows he should be going, that he must not fall asleep in the chair. But now he's here, almost by accident, he has to stay a while, and he won't doze off because he's feeling too many things, he's alive to too many contradictory impulses. His thoughts have assumed a sinuous, snaking quality, driven by the same undulating power that's making the space in the long room ripple, as well as the floor beneath his chair. Feelings have become in this respect like light itself – wavelike, as they used to say in his physics class. He needs to stay here and, in his usual manner, break them down into their components, the quanta, and find all the distal and proximal causes; only then will he know what to do, what's right. He slips his hand around Baxter's wrist and feels for his pulse. It's quite unnecessary because the monitor's showing a reading in bright blue numerals – sixty-five beats per minute. He does it because he wants to. It was one of the first things he learned to do as a student. Simple, a matter of primal contact, reassuring to the patient – so long as it's done with unfaltering authority. Count the beats, those soft footfalls, over fifteen seconds, then multiply by four. The nurse is still up at the far end of the ward. The constables in the corridor are just visible through a window in the unit's swing doors. Far more than a quarter of a minute passes. In effect, he's holding Baxter's hand while he attempts to sift and order his thoughts and decide precisely what should be done.

Rosalind has left a lamp on in the bedroom, by the sofa, under the mirror; the dimmer switch is turned low and the bulb gives less light than a candle. She's lying curled on her side, with the covers bunched against her stomach, and the pillows discarded on the floor – sure signs of troubled sleep. He watches her from the foot of the bed for a minute or so, waiting to see if he disturbed her as he came in. She looks young – her hair has fallen forwards across her face, giving her a carefree, dissolute air. He goes to the bathroom and undresses in semi-darkness because he doesn't want to see himself in the mirror – the sight of his haggard face could set him off on a meditation about ageing, which would poison his sleep. He takes a shower to wash away the sweat of concentration and all traces of the hospital – he imagines fine bone dust from Baxter's skull lodged in the pores of his forehead – and soaps himself vigorously. As he's drying he notices that even in poor light, the bruise on his chest is visible and appears to have spread, like a stain in a cloth. It hurts less though when he touches it. It feels like a distant memory now, months ago, when he took that blow and felt the sharp ridge of a shock wave run through his body. More insult than pain. Perhaps he should turn the light on after all and examine it.

But he goes into the bedroom, still with his towel, and switches off the lamp. One shutter stands ajar by an inch, casting a blurred rod of soft white light across the floor and up the facing wall. He doesn't trouble himself with closing the shutter – total darkness, sense deprivation, might activate his thoughts. Better to stare at something, and hope to feel his eyelids grow heavy. Already, his tiredness seems fragile, or unreliable, like a pain that comes and goes. He needs to nurture it, and avoid thoughts at all costs. Standing on his side of the bed, he hesitates; there's enough light to see that Rosalind has taken all the covers, and has knotted them under her and against her chest. Pulling them free is bound to wake her, but it's too cold to sleep without them. He fetches from the bathroom two heavy towelling dressing gowns to use as blankets. She's sure to roll over soon, and then he'll take his share.

But as he's getting into bed, she puts her hand on his arm and whispers, 'I kept dreaming it was you. Now it really is.'

She lifts the covers and lets him enter the tent of her warmth. Her skin is hot, his is cool. They lie on their sides, face to face. He can barely see her, but her eyes show two points of light, gathered from the tip of the white bar rising on the wall behind him. He puts his arms around her and as she moves closer into him, he kisses her head.

She says, 'You smell good.'

He grunts, vaguely in gratitude. Then there's silence, as they try out the possibility that they can treat this like any other disturbed night and fall asleep in each other's arms. Or perhaps they're only waiting to begin.

After a little while Henry says quietly, 'Tell me what you're feeling.' As he says this, he puts his hand in the small of her back.

She breathes out sharply. He's asked her a difficult question. 'Angry,' she tells him at last. Because she says it in a whisper, it sounds unconvincing. She adds, 'And terrified still, of them.'

As he's starting to reassure her they'll never come back, she speaks over him. 'No, no. I mean, I feel they're in the room. They're still here. I'm still frightened.'

He feels her legs begin to shake and he draws her closer to him and kisses her face. 'Darling,' he murmurs.

'Sorry. I had this shaking earlier, when I came to bed. Then it calmed down. Oh God. I want it to stop.'

He reaches down and places his hands on her legs – the shivering appears to emanate from her knees in tight, dry spasms, as though her bones were grating in their joints.

'You're in shock,' he says as he massages her legs.

'Oh God,' she keeps saying, but nothing else.

Several minutes pass before the trembling subsides, during which he holds her, and rocks her, and tells her he loves her.

When she's calm at last she says in her usual, level voice, 'I'm angry too. I can't help it, but I want him punished. I mean, I hate him, I want him to die. You asked me what I felt, not what I think. That vicious, loathsome man, what he did to John, and forcing Daisy like that, and holding the knife against me, and using it to make you go upstairs. I thought I might never see you again alive . . .'

She stops, and he waits. When she speaks again her tone is more deliberate. They're lying face to face again, he's holding her hand, caressing her fingers with his thumb.

'When I talked to you at the front door, about revenge I mean, it was my own feelings I was afraid of. I thought that in your position I'd do something really terrible to him. I was worried that you were having the same ideas, that you'd get in serious trouble.'

There's so much he wants to tell her, discuss with her, but this is not the time. He knows he won't get from her the kind of response he wants. He'll do it tomorrow, when she's less upset, before the police come.

With her fingertips she finds his lips and kisses them. 'What happened in the operation?'

'It was fine. Pretty much routine. He lost a lot of blood,

we patched him up. Rodney was good, but he might have had trouble dealing with it alone.'

'So this person, Baxter, will live to face charges.'

Henry doesn't reply to this beyond an uncommitted nasal hum of near-assent. It's useful to consider the moment he'll broach the subject; Sunday morning, coffee in large white cups, the conservatory in brilliant winter sunshine, the newspapers they deplore but always read, and as he reaches forwards to touch her hand she looks up and he sees in her face that calm intelligence, focused, ready to forgive. He opens his eyes into darkness, and discovers he's been asleep, perhaps for only a few seconds.

Rosalind is saying, 'He got terribly drunk, maudlin, the usual stuff. It was hard to take after everything else. But the kids were fantastic. They took him back in a taxi and a hotel doctor came out and looked at his nose.'

Henry has a passing sensation of travelling through the night. He and Rosalind once took a sleeper train from Marseilles to Paris and squeezed into the top bunk together where they lay on their fronts to watch sleeping France go by and talk until dawn. Tonight, the conversation is the journey.

In his comfortable, drifting state he feels only warmth towards his father-in-law. He says, 'He was magnificent though. They couldn't intimidate him. And he told Daisy what to do.'

'He was brave all right,' she agrees. 'But you were amazing. Right from the beginning I could see you planning and calculating. I saw you look across at Theo.'

He takes her hand and kisses her fingers. 'None of us went through what you did. You were fantastic.'

'Daisy held me steady. She had such strength then . . .'

'And Theo too, when he came flying up those stairs . . .'

For some minutes the events of the evening are transformed into a colourful adventure, a drama of strong wills, inner resources, new qualities of character revealed under pressure.

They used to talk this way after family ascents of mountains in the West Highlands of Scotland – things always went wrong, but interestingly, funnily. Now, suddenly animated, they exult in praise, and because it's familiar, and less absurd than eulogising each other, they celebrate the children. These past two decades Henry and Rosalind have spent many hours doing just this – alone together, they like to gossip about their children. These latest exploits shine in the dark – when Theo grabbed his lapels, when Daisy looked him right in the eye. What lovely children these are, such loving natures, what luck to be their parents. But the excited conversation can't last, their words begin to sound hollow and unreal in their ears, and they begin to subside. They can't avoid for much longer the figure of Baxter at the centre of their ordeal – cruel, weak, meaningless, demanding to be confronted. Also, they're talking about Daisy and not addressing the pregnancy. They're not quite ready, though they're close.

After a pause, Henry says, 'The thing is this, surely. His mind is going, and he thought he was coming to settle a score. Who knows what spooky uncontrollable emotions were driving him.' He then describes to her in detail the encounter in University Street, and includes everything he thinks might be relevant – the policeman waving him on, the demonstrators in Gower Street and the funereal drumbeats, his own competitive instincts before the confrontation. While he's talking, her hand is resting on his cheek. They could turn on the lights, but it comforts them, this intimate trusting darkness, the sexless, childlike huddling and talking into the night. Daisy and Theo used to do it, on the top floor with their sleepover friends – little voices still murmuring at 3.00 a.m., faltering against sleep and bravely picking up again. When Henry was ten, a cousin a year younger came to stay for a month while her mother was in hospital. Since he had a double bed in his room and there was nowhere else, his mother put her in with him. Henry and his cousin ignored each other during the day – Mona was plump, with thick lenses in her specs and a missing finger, and above all she was a girl – but on the first night, a disembodied whispering voice from a warm mound on the other side of the bed wove the epic of the school sweet factory visit, and the chocolates cascading down a chute, of the machinery that turned so fast it was invisible, then the swift, painless dismemberment, the spray of blood 'like a feather duster' that coloured the teacher's jacket, of the fainting friends, and the foreman on his hands and knees beneath the machine, hunting for the missing 'part'. Stirred, Henry could answer with no more than a lanced boil, but Mona was sportingly appreciative, and so they were launched in their time capsule, their short lives and some inventiveness sufficient to keep them in horrible anecdotes through the night until the summer dawn, and with different themes through other nights too.

When he's finished his account of the confrontation, Rosalind says, 'Of course it wasn't an abuse of authority. They could have killed you.'

This is not the conclusion he wanted her to reach – he arranged the details to prompt her in another direction. He's about to try again, but she starts a story of her own. This is the nature of these night journeys – the steps, the sequences are not logical.

'While I was waiting for you tonight, before I fell asleep, I was trying to work out just how long it was he held that knife to me. In my memory, it's no time at all – and I don't mean that it seems brief. It's no time, not in time, not a minute or an hour. Just a fact . . .'

As she recalls it, the tremors return, but fainter, then fade away. He holds her hand tightly.

'I wondered if it was because I felt only one thing – sheer terror, no changes, no sense of passing time. But that's not it. I did feel other things.'

Her pause is long. Unable to read her expression, he hesitates to prompt her.

Finally he says, 'What other things?'

Her voice is reflective rather than distressed. 'You. There was you. The only other time I've felt so terrified and helpless was before my operation, when I still thought I was going to go blind. When you came down with me to wait. You were so gawky and earnest. The sleeves of your white coat hardly came past your elbows. I've always said that's when I fell for you. I suppose that's right. Sometimes I think I made that up, and it was later. Then tonight, an even greater terror, and there you were again, trying to talk to me with your eyes. Still there. After all the years. That's what I hung on to. You.'

He feels her fingers graze across his face, then she kisses him. No longer so childlike, their tongues touch.

'But it was Daisy who delivered you. She swung his mood with that poem. Arnold someone?'

'Matthew Arnold.'

He's remembering her body, its pallor, the compact bump containing his grandchild, already with a heart, a self-organising nervous system, a swelling pinhead of a brain – here's what unattended matter can get up to in the total darkness of a womb.

Reading the meaning of his silence, Rosalind says, 'I talked to her again. She's in love, she's excited, she's having this baby. Henry, we have to be on her side.'

'I am,' he says. 'We are.'

His eyes are closed and he's listening intently to Rosalind. This baby's life is taking shape – a year in Paris with its enraptured parents, and then to London where its father has been offered a good position in an important dig – a Roman villa to the east of the City. They might all move in here for a while and live on the square. Henry murmurs his assent, he's glad – the house is big, seven thousand square feet, and needs the sound of a child's voice again. He feels his body, the size of a continent, stretching away from him down the bed – he's a king, he's vast, accommodating, immune, he'll say yes to any plan that has kindness and warmth at its heart. Let the baby take its first steps and speak its first sentence here, in this palace. Daisy wants her baby, then let it happen in the best possible way. If she was ever going to be a poet, she'll make her poetry out of this – as good a subject as a string of lovers. He can't move his head, he can barely move his hand to stroke Rosalind's as she unfolds the future for him, the domestic arrangements – he's following closely, attending to the pleasure in her voice. The first shock is over. She's coming through. And Theo has been talking of his plans too, which will take him away for fifteen months to New York with New Blue Rider as resident band in an East Village club. It has to be, Theo's music needs it and they'll make it work, help him find a place, visit him there. The king rumbles his assent.

Across the square, the wail of an ambulance racing south-wards down Charlotte Street rouses him a little. He pulls himself onto an elbow, and moves closer so that his face is over hers.

'We should sleep.'

'Yes. The police say they're coming at ten.'

But when they've finished kissing he says, 'Touch me.'

As the sweet sensation spreads through him he hears her say, 'Tell me that you're mine.'

'I'm yours. Entirely yours.'

'Touch my breasts. With your tongue.'

'Rosalind. I want you.'

This is where he marks the end of his day. The moment is sharper, more piercing than Saturday's lazy, affectionate beginning – their movements are quick and greedy, urgent rather than joyous – it's as if they've returned from exile, emerged from a hard prison spell to gorge at a feast. Their appetites are noisy, their manners are rough. They can't quite trust their luck, they want all they can get in a short time. They also know that at the end, after they've reclaimed each other, is the promise of oblivion.

At one point she whispers to him, 'My darling one. We could have been killed and we're alive.'

They are alive for love, but only briefly. The end comes in a sudden fall, so concentrated in its pleasure that it's excruciating to endure, unbearably intrusive, like nerve ends being peeled and stripped clean. Afterwards they don't immediately move apart. They lie still in the dark, feeling their heartbeats slow. Henry experiences his exhaustion and the sudden clarity of sexual release merge into a single fact, dry and flat as a desert. He must begin to cross it now, alone, and he doesn't mind. At last they say goodnight by means of a single squeeze of hands – they feel too raw for kisses – then Rosalind turns on her side, and within seconds is breathing deeply.

Oblivion doesn't come to Henry Perowne quite yet – he may have reached the point at which tiredness itself prevents sleep. He lies on his back, patiently waiting, head turned towards the bar of white light on the wall, aware of an inconvenient pressure growing in his bladder. After several minutes he takes one of the dressing gowns from the floor and goes into the bathroom. The marble floor is icy underfoot, the open curtains on the tall north-facing windows show a few stars in a sky of broken, orange-tinted cloud. It's five fifteen, and already there's a rustle of traffic on the Euston Road. When he's relieved himself, he bends over the washbasin to drink deeply from the cold-water tap. Back in the bedroom he hears a distant rumble of an airplane, the first of the morning rush hour into Heathrow, he supposes and, drawn by the sound, goes to the window he stood at before and opens the shutters. He prefers to stand here a few minutes looking out than to lie still in bed, forcing sleep. Quietly he raises the window. The air is warmer than last time, but still he shivers. The light is softer too, the features of the square, especially the branches of the plane trees in the garden, are not so etched, and seem to merge with each other. What can it be about low temperatures that sharpens the edges of objects?

The benches have lost their expectant air, the litter bins have been emptied, the paving has been swept clean. The energetic team in yellow jackets must have been through during the evening. Henry tries to find reassurance in this orderliness, and in remembering the square at its best – weekday lunchtimes, in warm weather, when the office crowds from the local production, advertising and design companies bring their sandwiches and boxed salads, and the gates of the gardens are opened up. They loll on the grass in quiet groups, men and women of various races, mostly in their twenties and thirties, confident, cheerful, unoppressed, fit from private gym workouts, at home in their city. So much divides them from the various broken figures that haunt the benches. Work is one outward sign. It can't just be class or opportunities – the drunks and junkies come from all kinds of backgrounds, as do the office people. Some of the worst wrecks have been privately educated. Perowne, the professional reductionist, can't help thinking it's down to invisible folds and kinks of character, written in code, at the level of molecules. It's a dim fate, to be the sort of person who can't earn a living, or resist another drink, or remember today what he resolved to do yesterday. No amount of social justice will cure or disperse this enfeebled army haunting the public places of every town. So, what then? Henry draws his dressing gown more closely around him. You have to recognise bad luck when you see it, you have to look out for these people. Some you can prise from their addictions, others – all you can do is make them comfortable somehow, minimise their miseries.

Somehow! He's no social theorist and, of course, he's thinking of Baxter, that unpickable knot of affliction. It may be the thought of him that makes Henry feel shaky, or the physical effects of tiredness – he has to put his hand on the sill to steady himself. He feels himself turning on a giant wheel, like the Eye on the south bank of the Thames, just about to arrive at the highest point – he's poised on a hinge of perception, before the drop, and he can see ahead calmly. Or it's the eastward turn of the earth he imagines, delivering him towards the dawn at a stately one thousand miles an hour. If he counts on sleep rather than the clock to divide the days, then this is still his Saturday, dropping far below him, as deep as a lifetime. And from here, from the top of his day, he can see far ahead, before the descent begins. Sunday doesn't ring with the same promise and vigour as the day before. The square below him, deserted and still, gives no clues to the future. But from where he stands up here there are things he can see that he knows must happen. Soon it will be his mother's time, the message will come from the home, or they'll send for him, and he and his family will be sitting by her bed, in her tiny room, with her ornaments, drinking the thick brown tea, watching the last of her, the husk of the old swimmer, shrink into the pillows. At the thought, he feels nothing now, but he knows the sorrow will surprise him, because it's happened once before.

There came a time in her decline when at last he had to move her out of her house, the old family home where he grew up, and into care. The disease was obliterating the housewifely routines she had once kept faith with. She left the oven on all night with the butter dish inside, she hid the front-door key from herself down cracks in the floorboards, she confused shampoo and bleach. All these, and moments of existential bewilderment at finding herself in a street, or in a shop, or someone's house, with no knowledge of where she had come from, who these people were, where she lived, and what she was supposed to do next. A year later she had forgotten her life as well as her old house. But arranging to sell it felt like a betrayal, and Henry made no move. He and Rosalind checked on it, his childhood home, from time to time and he mowed the lawn in summer. Everything remained in its place, waiting – the yellow rubber gloves hanging from their wooden clothes peg, the drawer of ironed dusters and tea towels, the glazed pottery donkey bearing a pannier of toothpicks. A vegetable odour of neglect began to gather, a shabbiness invaded her possessions that had nothing to do with dust. Even from the road the house had a defeated look, and when kids put a stone through the living-room window one afternoon in November, he knew he must act.

Rosalind and the children came with him to clear the place one weekend. They all chose a memento – it seemed disrespectful not to. Daisy had a brass plate from Egypt, Theo a carriage clock, Rosalind, a plain china fruit bowl. Henry took a shoebox of photographs. Other pieces went to nephews and nieces. Lily's bed, her sideboard, two wardrobes and the carpets and the chests of drawers were waiting for a house-clearing firm. The family packed up clothes and kitchenware and unwanted ornaments for the charity shops – Henry never realised before how these places lived off the dead. Everything else they stuffed into bin liners and put out for the rubbish collection. They worked in silence, like looters – having the radio on wasn't appropriate. It took a day to dismantle Lily's existence.

They were striking the set of a play, a humble, one-handed domestic drama, without permission from the cast. They started in what she called her sewing room – his old room. She was never coming back, she no longer knew what knitting was, but wrapping up her scores of needles, her thousand patterns, a baby's half-finished yellow shawl, to give them all away to strangers was to banish her from the living. They worked quickly, almost in a frenzy. She's not dead, Henry kept telling himself. But her life, all lives, seemed tenuous when he saw how quickly, with what ease, all the trappings, all the fine details of a lifetime could be packed and scattered, or junked. Objects became junk as soon as they were separated from their owner and their pasts – without her, her old tea cosy was repellent, with its faded farmhouse motif and pale brown stains on cheap fabric, and stuffing that was pathetically thin. As the shelves and drawers emptied, and the boxes and bags filled, he saw that no one owned anything really. It's all rented, or borrowed. Our possessions will outlast us, we'll desert them in the end. They worked all day, and put out twenty-three bags for the dustmen.

He feels skinny and frail in his dressing gown, facing the morning that's still dark, still part of yesterday. Yes, that will happen, and he'll make the arrangements. She walked him once to a cemetery near her house to show him the rows of small metal lockers set into a wall where she wanted her ashes put. All that's bound to happen, and they'll stand with bowed heads, listening to the Burial of the Dead. Or will they have it for cremations? Man that is born of woman hath but a short time to live . . . He's heard it often over the years, but remembers only fragments. He fleeth as it were a shadow . . . cut down like a flower. Yes, and then it will be the turn of John Grammaticus, one of those transfiguring illnesses that come to a drinking man, or a terminal stab to heart or brain. They'll all take that hard in their different ways, though Henry less than the others. The old poet was brave tonight, pretending not to suffer with his nose, giving Daisy just the right prompt. And when it comes, then there'll be the crisis of the chateau if Teresa marries John and stakes her claim, and Rosalind, formidable in law, pursues her rights to the place her mother made, the place where Daisy, Theo and Rosalind herself spent their childhood summers. And Henry's role? Wise and implacable loyalty.

What else, beyond the dying? Theo will make his first move from home – there'll be no postcards or letters or e-mails, only phone calls. There'll be trips to New York to listen to him and his band bring their blues to the Americans – they might not like it – and a chance to see old friends from Bellevue Hospital days. And Daisy will publish her poems, and produce a baby and bring Giulio – Henry still sees the dark-skinned, bare-chested lover from the poem he misheard. A baby and its huge array of *matériel* to enliven the household, and someone else, not him, not Rosalind, getting up in the night. And not Giulio, unless he's an unusual Italian. All this is rich. And then, he, Henry, will turn fifty and give up squash and marathons, the house will empty when Daisy and Giulio find a place, and Theo gets one too, and Henry and Rosalind will collapse in on each other, cling tighter, their business of raising children, launching young adults, over. That restlessness, that hunger he's had lately for another kind of life will fade. The time will come when he does less operating, and more administration – there's another kind of life – and Rosalind will leave the paper to write her book, and a time will come when they find they no longer have the strength for the square, the junkies and the traffic din and dust. Perhaps a bomb in the cause of jihad will drive them out with all the other faint-hearts into the suburbs, or deeper into the country, or to the chateau – their Saturday will become a Sunday.

Behind him, as though agitated by his thoughts, Rosalind flinches, moans, and moves again before she falls silent and he turns back to the window. London, his small part of it, lies wide open, impossible to defend, waiting for its bomb, like a hundred other cities. Rush hour will be a convenient time. It might resemble the Paddington crash – twisted rails, buckled, upraised commuter coaches, stretchers handed out through broken windows, the hospital's Emergency Plan in action. Berlin, Paris, Lisbon. The authorities agree, an attack's inevitable. He lives in different times – because the newspapers say so doesn't mean it isn't true. But from the top of his day, this is a future that's harder to read, a horizon indistinct with possibilities. A hundred years ago, a middle-aged doctor standing at this window in his silk dressing gown, less than two hours before a winter's dawn, might have pondered the new century's future. February 1903. You might envy this Edwardian gent all he didn't yet know. If he had young boys, he could lose them within a dozen years, at the Somme. And what was their body count, Hitler, Stalin, Mao? Fifty million, a hundred? If you described the hell that lay ahead, if you warned him, the good doctor – an affable product of prosperity and decades of peace – would not believe you. Beware the utopianists, zealous men certain of the path to the ideal social order. Here they are again, totalitarians in different form, still scattered and weak, but growing, and angry, and thirsty for another mass killing. A hundred years to resolve. But this may be an indulgence, an idle, overblown fantasy, a night-thought about a passing disturbance that time and good sense will settle and rearrange.

The nearer ground, the nearest promontory, is easier to read – as sure as his mother's death, he'll be dining with Professor Taleb in an Iraqi restaurant near Hoxton. The war will start next month – the precise date must already have been fixed, as though for any big outdoor sporting event. Any later in the season will be too hot for killing or liberation. Baghdad is waiting for its bombs. Where's Henry's appetite for removing a tyrant now? At the end of this day, this particular evening, he's timid, vulnerable, he keeps drawing his dressing gown more tightly around him. Another plane moves left to right across his view, descending in its humdrum way along the line of the Thames towards Heathrow. Harder now to recall, or to inhabit, the vigour of his row with Daisy – the certainties have dissolved into debating points; that the world the professor described is intolerable, that however murky American motives, some lasting good and fewer deaths might come from dismantling it. Might, he hears Daisy tell him, is not good enough, and you've let one man's story turn your head. A woman bearing a child has her own authority. Will he revive his hopes for firm action in the morning? All he feels now is fear. He's weak and ignorant, scared of the way consequences of an action leap away from your control and breed new events, new consequences, until you're led to a place you never dreamed of and would never choose – a knife at the throat. One floor down from where Andrea Chapman dreams of being carried away by the improbable love of a young doctor, and of becoming one herself, lies Baxter in his private darkness, watched over by the constables. But one small fixed point of conviction holds

Henry steady. It began to take form at dinner, before Jay rang, and was finally settled when he sat in intensive care, feeling Baxter's pulse. He must persuade Rosalind, then the rest of the family, then the police, not to pursue charges. The matter must be dropped. Let them go after the other man. Baxter has a diminishing slice of life worth living, before his descent into nightmare hallucination begins. Henry can get a colleague or two, specialists in the field, to convince the Crown Prosecution Service that by the time it comes round, Baxter will not be fit to stand trial. This may or may not be true. Then the system, the right hospital, must draw him in securely before he does more harm. Henry can make these arrangements, do what he can to make the patient comfortable, somehow. Is this forgiveness? Probably not, he doesn't know, and he's not the one to be granting it anyway. Or is he the one seeking forgiveness? He's responsible, after all; twenty hours ago he drove across a road officially closed to traffic, and set in train a sequence of events. Or it could be weakness – after a certain age, when the remaining years first take on their finite aspect, and you begin to feel for yourself the first chill, you watch a dying man with a closer, more brotherly interest. But he prefers to believe that it's realism: they'll all be diminished by whipping a man on his way to hell. By saving his life in the operating theatre, Henry also committed Baxter to his torture. Revenge enough. And here is one area where Henry can exercise authority and shape events. He knows how the system works – the difference between good and bad care is near-infinite.

Daisy recited a poem that cast a spell on one man. Perhaps any poem would have done the trick, and thrown the switch on a sudden mood change. Still, Baxter fell for the magic, he was transfixed by it, and he was reminded how much he wanted to live. No one can forgive him the use of the knife. But Baxter heard what Henry never has, and probably never will, despite all Daisy's attempts to educate him. Some nineteenth-century poet – Henry has yet to find out whether this Arnold is famous or obscure – touched off in Baxter a yearning he could barely begin to define. That hunger is his claim on life, on a mental existence, and because it won't last much longer, because the door of his consciousness is beginning to close, he shouldn't pursue his claim from a cell, waiting for the absurdity of his trial to begin. This is his dim, fixed fate, to have one tiny slip, an error of repetition in the codes of his being, in his genotype, the modern variant of a soul, and he must unravel – another certainty Henry sees before him.

Quietly, he lowers the window. The morning is still dark, and it's the coldest time now. The dawn won't come until after seven. Three nurses are walking across the square, talking cheerfully, heading in the direction of his hospital to start their morning shift. He closes the shutters on them, then goes towards the bed and lets the dressing gown fall to his feet as he gets in. Rosalind lies facing away from him with her knees crooked. He closes his eyes. This time there'll be no trouble falling towards oblivion, there's nothing can stop him now. Sleep's no longer a concept, it's a material thing, an ancient means of transport, a softly moving belt, conveying him into Sunday. He fits himself around her, her silk pyjamas, her scent, her warmth, her beloved form, and draws closer to her. Blindly, he kisses her nape. There's always this, is one of his remaining thoughts. And then: there's only this. And at last, faintly, falling: this day's over.

DOVER BEACH

The sea is calm tonight.
The tide is full, the moon lies fair
Upon the straits; on the French coast the light
Gleams and is gone; the cliffs of England stand,
Glimmering and vast, out in the tranquil bay.
Come to the window, sweet is the night-air!
Only, from the long line of spray
Where the sea meets the moon-blanched land,
Listen! you hear the grating roar
Of pebbles which the waves draw back, and fling,
At their return, up the high strand,
Begin, and cease, and then again begin,
With tremulous cadence slow, and bring
The eternal note of sadness in.

Sophocles long ago
Heard it on the Aegean, and it brought
Into his mind the turbid ebb and flow
Of human misery; we
Find also in the sound a thought,
Hearing it by this distant northern sea.

The Sea of Faith
Was once, too, at the full, and round earth's shore
Lay like the folds of a bright girdle furled.
But now I only hear
Its melancholy, long withdrawing roar,
Retreating, to the breath
Of the night-wind, down the vast edges drear
And naked shingles of the world.

Ah, love, let us be true
To one another! for the world, which seems
To lie before us like a land of dreams,
So various, so beautiful, so new,
Hath really neither joy, nor love, nor light,
Nor certitude, nor peace, nor help for pain;
And we are here as on a darkling plain
Swept with confused alarms of struggle and flight,
Where ignorant armies clash by night.

Matthew Arnold (1867)

Acknowledgements

I am enormously grateful to Neil Kitchen MD FRCS (SN), Consultant Neurosurgeon and Associate Clinical Director, The National Hospital for Neurology and Neurosurgery, Queen Square, London. It was a privilege to watch this gifted surgeon at work in the theatre over a period of two years, and I thank him for his kindness and patience in taking time out of a demanding schedule to explain to me the intricacies of his profession, and the brain, with its countless pathologies. I am also grateful to Sally Wilson, FRCA, Consultant Neuro-anaesthetist at the same hospital, and to Anne McGuinness, Consultant, Accident and Emergency, University College Hospital, and to Chief Inspector Amon McAfee. For an account of a transsphenoidal hypophysectomy, I am indebted to Frank T. Vertosick, Jr., MD and his excellent book, *When the Air Hits your Brain: Tales of Neurosurgery*, Norton, New York, 1996. Ray Dolan, that most literary of scientists, read the typescript of *Saturday* and made incisive neurological suggestions. Tim Garton Ash and Craig Raine also read this novel at an early stage and were very helpful in their comments. I am grateful to Craig Raine for generously allowing me to attribute to Daisy Perowne the words, 'excited watering can' and 'peculiar rose' from his poem, 'Sexual Couplets', and 'how each\rose grows on a shark infested stem' from 'Reading Her Old Letter about a Wedding', *Collected Poems 1978-1999*, Picador, London 2000. My wife, Annalena McAfee, read numerous stages of draft, and I am the lucky beneficiary of her wise editorial comments and loving encouragement.

IM
London 2004

www.randomhouse.co.uk/vintage